Highland Destiny
by Kathryn Hockett

KATHRYN HOCKETT

Historical Romance

HIGHLAND DESTINY

For my brother, Richard Hockett and the
Scottish heritage that we share. Thanks for
believing in me………

KATHRYN HOCKETT

AUTHOR'S NOTE

An aura of adventure and romance clings to the distinctive way of life of the Highland clans. It was said that out of the Celtic myths and mists the Irish Celts came to settle in the highlands and islands of Scotland, bringing with them a powerful perception of their racial kinship and blood-ties.

Clans were first known by the badges worn on their bonnets and in later years by the tartans they wore. The clans lived by the sword and perished by the sword in their struggle for territory and supremacy.. Loyalty to the clan chieftain was absolute. They took fierce pride in the stories of brave deeds and fateful liaisons of love that were related by the Seanachaidh around the hearth fires.

Though Christian, the Scots were a people of mystics and dreamers who believed in the second sight, a gift of prophecy by visions. The "fey" it was called. From their Celtic forebears came a fabric of superstition, mystery and tradition that is as colorful as any tartan.

Such a mystery surrounds the MacLeods of Dunvegan on the Isle of Skye who trace their ancestry back to King Harald. Their most treasured heirloom is a tattered silk banner called the "fairy flag", said to have been given to a MacLeod husband by his wife before she returned to fairyland after twenty years of marriage. Their parting place near Dunvegan is still known as "Fairy Bridge".

There is a tradition that if the MacLeods are in desperate peril they will become invincible by unfurling this flag during battle. It was used at Glendale in 1490 when they were fighting for their lives against the MacDonalds. The flag was unfurled and soon after the tide of battle turned. In 1520 at Waternish, when once again the enemy was the MacDonalds, the MacLeods were victorious after the flag was unfurled. Though the MacLeods were outnumbered, the MacDonalds imagined a vast army of MacLeods marching down on them.

The fairy flag is said to be the most precious treasure of the MacLeods - "Bratach Sith" is what it is known as and is now kept in the drawing room of Dunvegan Castle - a faded tan silk, carefully darned in red. Legend has it that the MacLeods are waiting until it is necessary to use the flag for the third and last time.

HIGHLAND DESTINY tells the story of two lovers drawn together by the power of the fairy flag. Refusing to be parted they find a passion far stronger than any earthly law, a love as timeless as eternity.

KATHRYN HOCKETT

Prologue: 1520

It was quiet. Too quiet. As Colin MacLeod stood watch atop Dunvegan Castle's tower he squinted his eyes, trying to peer through the fog. Something was just not as it should be. He felt uneasy. Danger seemed to hang in the air, weaving in and out amidst the eerie Highland mist that veiled the lochs and glens like an unearthly shroud.

"Och....." for just a moment he held his breath, not daring to exhale as he listened. What was the nearly unperceivable sound that he heard? Alas, it seemed but a slight stirring that all too quickly vanished into quietness again. Still there had been something. He knew he had not been imagining it.

Leaning over the tower wall, Colin stared down at the bank. It looked down thirty feet or more to the ocean below. From either of the two towers, east or west, perched high over the cliff, the eye of anyone watching could see an enemy approaching. Unless there was fog. Damn the mists!

"I canna see...." Yet for one long shuddering moment he seemed to be gifted with a second sight. He knew they were there, whether he could see them or not. "Intruders.....!" His cry was punctuated by the drone of one note, an eerie though faraway sound that roused Colin MacLeod to action. He must warn the others.

Meanwhile, a menacing shadow moved across the land in the distance. In a raging swarm, the MacDonalds climbed the hills, moving quickly across Duirinish. A faint glint of moonlight was the only light to escape the fog, shining now on the many shields and swords of the clansmen who moved in an unrelenting tide. They had only one purpose in mind. To engage their enem--the MacLeod--in a fierce battle of supremacy for the Isle of Skye.

Malcolm MacDonald marched at the head of the column, his dark thick unsmiling features only partially obscured by a hard leather helmet, his leather jacket, leggings and dirt-stained boots smeared with the grime of travel. Behind him walked his armed clansmen, dour and stolid. Marching two abreast, they formed a dark ribbon over the rocky land as they moved like giant ants towards the rival castle.

The silence of the night was shattered by a droning, pounding, fearsome sound as the din of pipes and drums announced what was to come. Warfare. Violence. Fighting. Death.

"To Dunvegan!" came the cry. The MacLeod stronghold across the loch, the square-towered stone castle isolated by a deep and wide ditch on the land side—this was their destination.

"*Fraoch Eilean.....!*"

The castle was situated on a rock overhanging the sea. Completely surrounded by a moat, its entrances were accessible only by boat, but this did not daunt the MacDonalds. They had come prepared. A fleet of small fishing boats was at their disposal, which was put to good use now as they sailed towards the MacLeod stronghold.

"Now. Gi' them a sound to strike fear in their hearts......" A bloodcurdling war cry echoed through the mists, piercing Dunvegan's walls.

From the castle battlements scrutinizing eyes stared through the fog at the threatening horde. "The

MacDonalds, Colin. Ye are right, they're coming this way."

"The MacDonalds....!"

Cautiously the tall lithe, red-haired man surveyed the scene. There appeared to be about fifty of them. The foe of his clan was coming in a growling, mumbling wave of ferocity that chilled him to the bone, for his own clan was outnumbered two to one.

"We canna win! The odds are against us."

The castle had been constructed with thick walls and was protected by a moat and heavy oak doors, but even so, it would not be impenetrable when there were so many of the MacDonalds.

"Well, they willna win this day. Our clan has enchantment on our side. We are protected."

The MacLeods had a magical flag, that when unfurled, brought triumph to the possessor. The silk banner of tattered brown silk with red embroidery was their most treasured heirloom, believed to make them invincible. It had been handed down to the MacLeods of Dunvegan since the days of the Norse King Harald Hardrada. Or so it was said.

"Fly the fairy flag....."

"Ye heard Colin. The flag, mon. The flag...." Immediately that treasure was snatched from its resting place to fly unencumbered from the parapet. Like a good luck charm, it emboldened the men who left the security of the castle walls to greet the enemy that dared invade the sanctity of their stronghold.

As the pale ghost moon struggled for ascendancy through the swirling fog, the two clans battled. The MacDonalds came in a noisesome, floating tide, pushing across the ditch, breaking down the thick wooden doors, scaling the tower walls with rope ladders. They were met, however, by men equally determined.

Swords slashed. Axes swung. Shields clanked. Dirks struck out. Blood spilled forth in an angry carnage of destruction. Moving In a solid body, the MacLeods engaged the enemy in brutal hand to hand combat, meeting the challenge of the aggressors with a bravery spurred on by the belief that the enchanted flag would give them aid.

"They willna gi' up," several of the MadDonalds gasped in unison. The fighting exploded as rival clansmen spilled inside the tower.

"They fight like demons!"

"Because of the flag! Malcolm spat on the ground before his eyes gave a silent command-- to get that cursed emblem of the MacLeods! With that thought in mind, the fighting exploded. Rival clansmen spilled inside the tower, moving toward the silk banner.

"The flag. Guard the flag!" Colin MacLeod cried.

He leaped about in a frenzy, his weapon darting this way and that in defense of the precious brown silk. His swordsmanship sent more than just a few MacDonalds crashing to the ramparts below. With a cry of victory, Colin pushed his way to the tower, looking toward the flag. The blessed flag.

"Colin!"

The child's voice, though soft, startled him. Undoubtedly the fearsome noise had instigated curiosity.

"Go to yer bed! Now, bairn! Ye canna kin the danger."

"Colin!" the high-pitched greeting erupted into a shrill scream. A warning that came too late.

With a cry of surprise, Colin felt the tip of a MacDonald sword gouge at his flesh, striking him from *behind*. From behind. A coward's blow.

"Blessed God......" A hot gush of blood stained his breacan. His sword clattered to the floor, but somehow he managed to stay on his feet determined that no MacDonald hand would touch the flag or the child. "Flee, wee one!"

Colin's eyes darted to the face of his attacker, then to the small form of the child, then back again.

"Run!"

Frightened into frozen silence at first, the child stood motionless as the danger moved closer, then with a shake her head she at last obeyed. With relief, Colin watched as the little one ran to safety, locking the door behind her.

"Ye willna touch either o' the MacLeod's treasures," he hissed.

The battle was ferocious, but in the end the MacLeod's had won. Limping away, stepping over the bodies of the dead, the MacDonalds retreated.

"The flag. The blessed flag." There was not a man present who did not give the magical dun-colored silk its due. But Colin MacLeod paid a tragic price for his valantry in keeping the fairy flag from enemy hands. Crumpling at last to the floor in a heap, he lay on the cold stones in agony.

It was a time when the MacLeods should have been joyous, for they had won a stout victory over their adversaries, the MacDonalds. But instead, the leader of the clan was stooped and grieved as he looked down upon the writhing form of his son.

"Colin! Colin!" The voice was husky, a deep rumbling thunder that gave full vent to his anger as well as his sorrow. It was an awesome man who spoke, a red-haired, and bearded Scots warrior of immense strength and girth, leader of the MacLeods, whose skill in fighting was legendary. His courage, strength and daring were the reason for the MacLeod victory, his men insisted. That and the blessed possession of the fairy flag

"We hae won, father." Colin MacLeod tried to hide his misery, but he knew well that he was dying.

"Aye, we won." Bending down, the man exhibited a rare gesture of gentleness as he touched his son's face. At that moment he wished he could take his son's suffering upon himself. "But at a terrible price."

"My wound Is mortal. I know...."

"Nae!" He wouldn't admit the truth. "We'll send for someone skilled In healing to tend ye."

"'Tis much too late for that." A shiver of pain convulsed Colin's body.

"Ye talk foolishness, lad. 'Tis not too late." Ah, but he saw the blood seeping from the wound he knew that it was. Already the face of his beloved, robust son was turning as pale as a ghost.

"It is. But we...we won, father." Reaching out Colin clutched his father's hand. "I...I can take heart in..in that. I kept them from the flag and from Cai....."

"Aye, ye guarded it admirably. 'Tis proud of ye I am. Very, very proud."

It was rumored that the first MacLeod had been given the banner as a gift from his wife before she returned to her father in the mythical land that existed in the mists.   A magical flag, Ian thought now.   Very valuable to the clan, but surely not worth his son's life!

"Damn the MacDonalds." They had taken his son from behind, wounding him in the back. The vile cowards. "Oh, Colin!"

"I will be avenged, Father. On my honor I so swear. I will haunt them. I swear that I will. I curse the mon who did this to me. Upon his head I will be avenged. Ye will see."

"And I will make the MacDonalds wish they had never heard the name MacLeod. That is the pledge I make to you now." It was a vow that burned all the brighter in Ian MacLeod's breast as the life of his son ebbed out. For a long time he stared down at the lifeless face of the young man who had been his whole world.

"Sir.....?   What should we do wi' the flag?"   A young beardless boy approached his chieftain shyly, hating to interrupt this moment of grief.

"What?" Ian MacLeod blinked back unmanly tears. "The flag." Oh, that it could bring life back into the body of his son, but that was not in its power. Colin MacLeod was dead and there was nothing that could bring him back from the dead. Nothing to keep him tied to the earth. Or was there?

From that moment on there were those who insisted they had seen the young man pacing back and forth in the tower room. That the castle was haunted was a legend that came to be believed by the villagers in the glen. Colin MacLeod was said to stalk the tower, guarding it as stealthfully in death as he had In life. Waiting for that moment when he could bring his wrath crashing down upon his murderer's head.

HIGHLAND DESTINY

PART ONE: A Fateful Meeting
1538

The Isle of Skye

"But to see her was to love her,

Love but her, and love forever."

Robert Burns: **Ae Fon Kiss**

HIGHLAND DESTINY

Chapter One

The early morning sun danced down upon the land caressing the lush, sweeping green heaths and fields with a brilliant warmth, stroking the rolling hills and craggy gray mountains, teasing the buds to full flower. Gently laughing brooks babbled their way to quiet pools. A breeze stirred faintly, whispering as it swept through the forest glades. In the woods, once skeletal trees, oak, pine, ash and poplar, now proudly wore a thick leafy covering. Birds twittered melodious tunes as they flew from tree to tree.

The fog that often covered the land like a low-flying cloud had faded, leaving the sky clear and blue. Winter had blended into spring with a gentle fury of rain that had left the earth a dazzling shade of green. Flowers covered the highland meadows of Skye, filling the air with their fragrance.

Perched silently atop a ledge of Dunvegan Castle's tower window, Caitlin MacLeod formed a stunning silhouette as she looked down at the vast domain of her clan.   This land that she could see in the distance had been inhabited by the MacLeod Clan for more years than she could even contemplate.

"Like a paradise this morning........" she whispered, though she knew it to be a deceptive calm that made it seem that way.   Unfortunately there were also times when the Isle of Skye could be more tempestuous

For several years the MacLeods had shared this island of Skye with two other clans. To the southwest the MacKinnons held Strath and at times assisted the MacDonalds of Sleat in their skirmishes against the

MacLeods. To the east across Loch Snizort were the lands of the hated MacDonalds themselves, they who marauded the countryside with their savage bands. MacLeods and MacDonalds had been at odds over land possession and other things for as long as Caitlin could remember.

"Och! The MacDonalds!" she said aloud, cursing them with upraised fist.

It had begun two hundred years ago, or so her father said, when the first chief of the Clan MacLeod had challenged the supremacy of the MacDonalds on Skye. Since then there had been a number of bloody feuds and cruelties perpetrated each on the other, represented by the stark patches of charred lands between the green fields and the desolate, blackened remains of what had once been cottages.

These incidents had been a constant source of trouble for her father, for surely it seemed the MacDonalds instigated one argument after another. As leader, ceann-cinnidh, of the MacLeods he led the fighting, causing Caitlin to worry lest something happen to him. To be truthful Ian MacLeod was getting a bit too old for the great responsibility heaped upon his now-stooping shoulders.

Under the ancient Patriarchal system the land belonged to the clan and they worked together and fought together, giving allegiance in time of peace as well as war to the laird. Sometimes a sept or a branch of another clan, too small to protect itself against surrounding clans, entered into a treaty with a neighboring clan for protection, thus there was always fighting.

Warfare. Violence. Like a tireless wind the perpetual feuding swept across the green and rocky land.

There was hardly a family that hadn't lost a loved one. Hardly a clansman who hadn't shed a tear. And still the old hatreds goaded the men into turning their plowshares into swords. Would peace never come to the Highlands? Caitlin thought not, for surely men seemed stubborn in their pride and driven to fighting. Like mischievous, grumbling boys, they seemed anxious to give seed to the ballads that sprang from the misery and the grief of the turmoil.

Caitlin shivered, remembering the night that she too had been caught up in the tragedy of the battling. She had been just three years, frightened, huddling against the stone wall, watching as her elder brother had been struck down. A memory that still haunted her.

"Colin......"

He had given his life to save the beloved fairy flag from being taken by the MacDonalds. A costly price, she thought, even to protect such a treasure. But she wouldn't think about it now and stir up old sadness. It was so peaceful today. The awakening terrain was dotted with grazing sheep, goats and cattle. Contented animals all.

If only I could feel as contented. But in truth she did not. Though spring had always been a time that she welcomed most heartily, this year she could only feel a wariness at its coming. Her father had adamantly insisted that this year she would be old enough to wed, an entanglement she viewed with disdain.

"I dinna want to get married."

Bondage, she called it. Being a young woman of strong will, an independent, resourceful lassie, she valued her freedom. Men were much too bothersome. Thinking of warfare and bickering all the time. That is, when they weren't of the mind to pinch, pat and to fondle.

A soft whispering breeze caressed her face, blowing Caitlin's flaming hair into her eyes. No, she thought stubbornly, she most definitely did not want to marry. Jamie, Adhamh, Alasdair and Seumas were fun to tease, to pester, but it ended there. A wee bit of sparring, a battle of wits, perhaps even a kiss, but only on the cheek. She had learned to keep an arms length away from men. When they were in their cups they too often set their hands to wandering. As for marriage, she had a whimsical view on that. Marriage was but a settlement to impoverish the lassie's father and make of the groom a wealthy man. It was little more than servitude that gave a man an unwilling partner for his nightly gropings.

Caitlin wanted to be in control of any matter. And she had been. She had been the pampered, over-indulged, perhaps even spoiled daughter of the MacLeod chieftain who could come and go as she pleased. She could swim, fish, wrestle, even fight with a sword were she of a mind to. But the moment she took on a husband all that would change. She would be a cook, a bedmate, a mother for her husband's bairns. She would have to answer to someone else, someone perhaps not as manageable as her father. Her freedom would be lost.

"Nae! Not without a fight," she whispered to herself.

Unlike the other women of the MacLeod line, she would not go meekly to her bridal bed like a lamb to slaughter. If Caitlin MacLeod took a husband, it would be a man of her choice. She had no need for a man's arms, or a husband to share her pallet beneath the soft down quilts. Love was just a word the seanachaidh had invented. She had no need of such foolishness. If and when she gave her heart it would be when she was ready to so bind herself. And that would not be for a long, long time, she vowed, ignoring the strange stirring in the pit of her stomach whenever she pondered the matter.

Caitlin tossed her head, sending her dark red hair flying wildly about her shoulders. Oh, if only she had been born a son and not a girl child life might have been so much simpler. She would have been free to fulfill her longing for adventure and her father would have had his precious tanist.

"But I'm not a male and I dinna want a husband."

Somehow she must make her father understand. But oh, it would be a most upsetting matter. After the death of Colin her father had tried to sire another heir, only to know disappointment at the birth of daughter after daughter, Shona, Lorna, Mairi and Ailsa. A devastating blow to her father's manly pride. That she was her father's eldest daughter and the others still little more than children made matters all the more difficult.

"Ye must carry on the MacLeod line", her father had insisted. "Ye must find a mon to take on our proud clan name." Caitlin had heard the story of her clans founding from her father. The clan MacLeod was descended from Leod, son of Olave the Black, who lived two centuries before. Leod's two sons, Tormod and Torquil were founders of the two main branches of the clan. From Tormod came the MacLeods of Dunvegan, Caitlin's kin. And upon her head would come the burden of passing on the MacLeod blood.

"Och," she swore again. If only her brother hadn't died. But he had and it was said that his ghost stalked the tower, still staunchly guarding the fairy flag. "Colin's ghost....."

Caitlin wondered if such whisperings were true or just fantasy, for although others had attested to seeing her brother's wispy presence she had never seen his long-departed spirit. Though not for want of trying. Ever since childhood she had frequented the tower late at night more times than she could even count, hoping for a conversation with her brother; but she had never seen Colin MacLeod no matter how hard she tried. Was it any wonder then that Caitlin had nearly stopped believing.

"There ye are!" Coming up behind her Ian MacLeod was as silent as if he too were a ghost. "Hidin' away up here like some wee fairy, just like when ye were little more than a bairn."

Turning, Caitlin pridefully looked at this big boned giant of a man with red hair and brown eyes the exact shade of her own. Despite his sixty-two years he was still ruggedly handsome, in an older-man sort of way, with a well-defined bone-structure that was striking. Her father was clean-shaven, unlike some of the others of the clan who preferred a beard. The only imperfection in his face was the once perfectly-formed nose that had been slightly flattened in hand-to-hand combat.

"Aye, it's hidin' that I am...." she confessed.

He winked. "Keepin' out o' sight of yer mother and the others to avoid woman's work again I would suppose."

They laughed together.

"Aye. Weavin' and spinnin' hae ne'er been to my liking." It seemed she was rarely in a mood to join the others for the daily tasks. Weaving, spinning, sewing, washing and cooking were tedious at best.   That she found a dozen reasons for avoiding such work any time she could was no secret between father and daughter. But that wasn't the reason she was hiding today. The truth was, she was hiding from him, but didn't tell him that.

"Ah, but how can I scold when I would be of the same mind were I in yer shoes?" He grinned as he reached out to stroke the thick, smooth threads of her hair. "I willna let yer mother know I caught ye up here."

"And in return I'll go back to the hall just in time to measure out for you the biggest portion of porridge."

"Such bribery will insure that I keep this hiding place a secret from your mother......" Ian MacLeod laughed again, but his fondness for her shone in his eyes. "Ah, ye bonny little imp, ye hae always known ye rule my heart."

Ian looked at his daughter with an appraising eye. She was pretty...perhaps even beautiful. With a chiseled nose, high cheekbones and enormous dark-fringed brown eyes. Her mouth was sculpted with full lips that were a deep pink; her cheeks were now flushed most prettily His daughter's slender waist and long legs were no doubt the envy of all the women, her well-formed breasts and slim hips would inspire the songs of many a bard.

Caitlin was dressed in a forest green arasaid, a long garment that reached from the head or neck, to the ankles, fastened at the breast with a large brooch and at the waist by a belt. Beneath this colorful length of material she wore a gown of thin beige wool which clung to her gentle curves. She made him very proud, this daughter of his. She was a fit mate for the boldest warrior. Nae, even a chieftain.

"Do I rule yer heart, Father?" His saying so calmed her fears. Surely he would not be of a mind then to see her leave his hearth just yet. She gazed upon her father's face trying to discern his thoughts.

"That ye do!" Which made the subject he felt he had to bring up now all the more difficult to express. The matter of his daughter's marriage. They had talked about the matter before and Caitlin had persuaded him to let her have her way in the matter, but this time there could be no waiting. If he was going to have an heir soon he must insist. He wanted a grandchild.

"Then ye canna send me away." She felt triumphant.

"Caity!" Taking a deep breath he blurted out, "It's time I must, despite my wish that I could keep ye here forever. I hae decided its time to choose a husband."

"Nae!" At last the subject she had feared was put forth. Still she tried to keep her poise.

"Aye! We canna wait." Ian MacLeod seemed inordinately pleased with the suggestion he put forth. "I hae decided that a MacKinnon would be a perfect choice. Ronald the chieftain's son...."

Caitlin sniffed her disdain as she crossed her arms stubbornly. "Not only is he is bowed of leg and long of nose, but he is much too tall. I wouldna marry him."

Not to be deterred, Ian MacLeod had a second choice. "His cousin Dugald it will be then!"

Caitlin sighed, disturbed with the matter. The MacKinnons lived too far away. "He is too young, Father. A mere boy with but a hint of a beard. I've heard that he chatters all the time."

Ian's good humor was quickly fading. "Ronald's uncle then. Uisdean MacKinnon. He is recently widowed."

She shook her head. "He is much too old." Though the man was rumored to be handsome, Caitlin had no liking for being a man's second wife, nor a stepmother to his many children. "And...and ye can tell him that."

"By God, lassie, ye try my patience." Only by the greatest of selfcontrol was Ian able to control his temper. "I canna tell him such a thing."

"Then don't tell him anything at all," she shot back haughtily, determined to stand firm. "But know this and know this well. I willna marry. Not this year." Not ever, she thought, but did not say.

"Ye will if I say so!"

Caitlin tried to make him understand, her outburst sputtering to just a spark. "There is no reason why I shouldna be happy." Caitlin had always had her father firmly wrapped around her little finger, thus she was certain that he would eventually comply with her wishes.

"Is there not?" Ian thundered. He reached out, not to strike her but to take her by the hand, drawing her down to sit beside him on a large slab of the tower stone. "It is your duty to marry a mon who can carry on as leader of the clan when I am gone. Ye know that, lassie."

"I know." Even so, a stubborn streak deep within kept her from giving in. "And I will marry. But not this spring. Another year......"

"Another year and then another and another!" Ian was tired of giving in to his daughter. Her mother was right then. He had spoiled the girl. "Nae, ye willna get yer way this time. It will be as *I* say."

"As you say," she repeated dutifully, hiding her fierce feelings of rebellion, at least for the moment.

Clenching his jaw he put forth another possible suitors name. "If ye dinna want to marry into the clan MacKinnon I'll send ye farther away then. To Mull. A MacQuarie it will be for yer husband. Hugh MacQuarrie, that chieftain's son."

She shook her head fiercely. "Nae. I willna leave the Island of Skye!"

"Ye willna!" Ian swallowed his angry retort, somehow maintaining his calm. "And just what makes ye think ye have a say?"

Seeing that he was dangerously close to loosing his temper, Caitlin backed down a bit. "I suppose I dunna. But I thought that ye loved me."

"I do." He took her hand, trying to come to terms with the problem. He had a pensive look on his face as he paused to think. "Perhaps..... Aye. Among our own there are several possible choices." He rattled off six names, ending with, "Seumas and Jamie." All young men who had displayed their valor.

"Seumas and Jamie?" Caitlin was horrified. Of all her clansmen they were the ones most deeply guilty of being womanizers.

"A wise choice for I hae little liking for sending you to another clan, dearie." His smile showed how pleased he was with himself. "I'll soon be rocking the next generation of MacLeods on my knee, taking them up to their beds when they fall asleep before the warm fire. Come to think of it, lass. Choosing one of our own does please me."

She was aghast. For all his pretense of affection all he seemed to be thinking about now was his precious heir. She meant nothing to him at all. Having wee ones tied a woman down. Caitlin wasn't certain she was ready just yet. "And that's all I'm to be, a breeder for your grandsons and granddaughters? I hae no say in the matter of who shares my bed?"

"Nae!"

"We'll see." Despite the precarious position she found herself in, she could not help but exhibit her own anger, tilting her chin up in the proud manner her father had always admired. Her show of defiance now, however, only added fuel to his already hostile mood.

"Ye will marry the mon that I proclaim!"

"Nae!"

"I am the MacLeod. Must you be reminded of that fact? My word is law." He bristled with the audacity of her refusal. "Were I to chose him, you would marry the very devil himself at my command."

"Would I?" Caitlin seethed with an anger to match her father's own. "I think not. I will not marry at all." Her temper had always been her greatest fault and now it poured forth full force. "Ye will hae to bring me kicking and screaming to the altar. It will be an embarrassing moment for the great MacLeod chief if ye dare push me into this. Think upon that, Father."

He could nearly imagine such a scene. "Is that so? Ye would so defy me!" His own anger was so great that for a moment he thought to strike her, but the look in her eyes stilled his hand. She was so like him that it was like looking into a mirror. With a growl he clenched his fists.

"To keep my freedom, aye that I would." Boldly she stood up, facing him squarely.

Folding his arms across his chest he gave proof that he would brook no defiance. "If ye dare refuse I....I will hae ye exiled. I mean that!"

Caitlin gasped. The clan was perhaps the most important thing in all their lives. A man's very being, his identity, was permanently bound to the clan. To be driven out, to face exile was to lose all sense of self-worth. "Ye wouldna!"

"Ah, but I would." It was time he taught her respect.

"Nae! Nae!" Covering her face with her hands she wept frustrated, angry tears.

Usually swayed by a display of a woman's emotions, Ian forced himself not to bring Caitlin any comfort. The lassie needed to be taught a lesson, needed to be tamed.

"I will, I so swear it if ye dunna change yer ways, lass." He softened a bit. "Ah, Caitlin, why must ye make it so hard? Why can't ye be like most men's daughters?"

She lifted her face. "Because I am *me*."

"Aye, ye are." He thought a moment. "Ah, lass ye canna see that I want what is best for ye but I do. And because of that I am agreed to give ye one more chance. I'll invite all the eligible laddies here to the hall, I will, and give ye yer pick." It was an idea that made him puff out his chest with pride to be oh so clever.

HIGHLAND DESTINY

Chapter Two

Flames in the vast hearth danced about illuminating the Macleod banner, a triple-towered castle floating on an azure background. It hung proudly for all to see alongside the shields, swords, dirks and claymores which told of the MacLeod bravery. Tables bulged with platters and bowls that were brimming with food: smoked haddock, roast grouse with sprigs of heather, roast venison, pickled herring, boiled goose eggs, beet root salad, curds, wild carrots, honey cakes, and wild raspberries. Barley broth bubbled noisily in a cauldron over the fire, its stream giving off an appetizing aroma.

The great hall rang with raucous laughter, yet the revelry had not yet reached its peak. The MacLeod and his guests had not had the chance to drink themselves into a stupor, Caitlin thought dryly. For the moment at least it was somewhat tranquil in the hall. Ah, but she doubted that it would stay that way. After dinner the men would again partake of their favorite pastime. Drinking.

She turned to her sister. "Look at them, Shona!" she said, the disdain clear in her tone. "They sound much like a herd o' bleating goats, no doubt boasting to each other about their prowess. Well, I will hae none o' them."

"None?" Shona gasped as she accidentally nicked her thumb with a knife while chopping at a turnip. "Ah, but Father has gathered them here together so that ye can choose. Ye mustna say that ye willna pick one, for ye know well what Father has threatened."

"That he will exile me if I dunna obey." Caitlin smiled impishly. "Ah, but I know him. He wouldna. He is all bluff and bluster."

Shona wasn't so certain. "Mayhap, but ye canna take a chance surely."

"Och, so ye think I should blindly do as I am told and bind myself to just any ambitious laddie?" Stubbornly she shook her head. "I willna, father or no father."

At first she had actually believed her father's threat of exile, but she knew him well. When it came right down to it, he wouldn't have the heart to hurt her in such a vile way. No, he would give in this time just as he had all the others. One more year. She would make him see that he must agree. She was determined, for she would have none of the vain men assembled in the hall.

"Let Father parade them up and down as he chooses, I mean what I say. I am determined to remain a maiden."

"Och, Caity!" Shona wore a look of worry, a look her sister quickly teased into a smile.

"Dunna fash yerself. All will be fine, and then perhaps ye can marry yon laddie." Caitlin nodded her head in the direction where a grinning Geordie Beaton stood. He was a tall, lithe youth with unruly curly dark hair that framed a face that was handsomely chiseled.

"Marry....Me.....?" Following her sister's gaze, Shona blushed as her eyes met the hazel-eyed young man's. Hastily she looked away, but not before she had witnessed the wink he freely gave her. "Ach, it is my fondest wish that when I get a wee bit older Father will let me marry him."

Caitlin had an ulterior motive. If Shona was promised then perhaps their father would stop pestering her to choose a husband. "Ye favor him, 'tis plain to see," Caitlin whispered. "By the looks that pass between ye, it seems Father would be wise to waste no time in joining ye together."

"Caity!" Again Shona blushed, though she was not so embarrassed that she did not cast the young man another longing glance. "Do ye think he feels the same?"

Caitlin nodded. "I do." Despite her protestations about love, she felt just a wee bit of longing to have a man look at her that way, a longing she quickly brushed away as she tersely took her place beside her father. She was the only female seated on the raised dais of stone that ran the full length of the hall across from the fireplace. Though it was an honor, Caitlin had little cause to feel pleased, considering the reason.

"Smile, lass. 'Tis a happy occasion I gather these laddies together for, not a funeral." He made a sweeping gesture with his hand. "Many a fine mon these are, Daughter. Look them over."

She did, critically, deciding at once that not a one of them was for her. It was, however, an opinion she kept to herself, at least for the moment. She was hungry and wanted to appease her appetite before she set herself to quarreling. With that thought in mind, she eagerly plucked up one of the fruit-decorated bannocks that were being passed around. She nearly choked on the round, flat oatcake, however, as her father stood up and made his announcement.

"Welcome one and all to this most joyous occasion, that being the choosing of my soon-to-be son-in-law and the sire of my grandsons." Taking Caitlin's hand, he pulled her to her feet. "Before this night is over, one of ye will be most lucky, most lucky indeed if ye catch my daughter's eye."

Ian MacLeod gestured with his hand, signaling the start of a small procession. Tall, short, fat, thin, full-bearded, clean-shaven, long-haired and even balding, one by one all the eligible men in the room passed by where Caitlin stood. It was the most humiliating moment of her life.

"Ach, Daughter, see how that fine mon looks at ye...."

"Like he's a rat and I a piece of cheese," Caitlin countered quickly with a toss of her head.

"Look, Donnie MacKinnon is trying to get yer eye. He's such a fine, fine strong laddie who would no doot be most capable of getting ye wi' child."

"Were I to let him in my bed, which I assure ye I would no'!" folding her arms across her chest, Caitlin cast a scowl in that young man's direction.

"Kenneth McQuar..."

"Nae! On a battlefield his girth might be an advantage but no' wi' me."

"Dougal Mc...."

"Nae! He is much too sure of himself."

"Ewan Ca..."

"Nae,! He is too shy."

One by one her father pointed to each man with the same results. Stubbornly Caitlin either gestured scornfully with thumbs down or shook her head "no."

"Too fat. Too thin. Too short. Too tall. Nae. Nae. Nae."

"I swear to ye, Daughter, ye would try the patience of a saint. But hear me well. Before this night is over ye *will* choose!" With that determined thought in mind the MacLeod proposed a toast. "To the lucky mon, whoever that might be."

"Look no further," called out a husky voice. "Ian MacLeod, ye seek a husband for yer daughter. That mon should be me."

Looking up, Caitlin saw a tall, lithe, blond gentleman. He was an attractive man with wide blue eyes, long eyelashes, and a cleft in his chin. Instinctively she knew the man to be Rory Gordon. As vain a man as ever there was. Oh, he was good to look upon, perhaps, but not the kind of man a girl should want to marry. Quickly she started to state that opinion, but her father's hand across her lips silenced her.

"Sit down beside us," Ian MacLeod invited.

"Father!" Her protestation was useless, and thus she was forced to suffer the man's presence as they ate.

"I should hae waited until a later hour to make proper introductions, but I was of a curiosity," Rory Gordon stated. "I was anxious to see yer daughter up close." His eyes raked over Caitlin with a stare that struck her with coldness all the way to the bone. Perhaps because there was no friendliness in his eyes. Instead, it seemed that his mind was ticking away as he thought of all the advantages of being married to the MacLeod's daughter.

"As I told you, my daughter is bonny!" Ian said boastfully. "And she is as sweet of temper as a lamb," he lied.

"Aye!" Rory Gordon's eyes continued their traveling, running from the curve of her neck, to her shoulders, then lower in much the same manner as if he were buying a cow, Caitlin thought indignantly. "She is as you say, very bonny. She'll do."

His manner sorely wounded Caitlin's pride. Do? Instantly she bristled. She was the one choosing, not he.

"Aye." He patted Ian on the back. "Seek no farther. Ye hae found yer son-in-law."

"Ah, is that so…." Caitlin was just about to tell him just what she thought of that declaration, but, sensing her intentions, Ian MacLeod tried to rescue the moment. He maneuvered it so that Rory Gordon could sit beside his daughter. Those whom he pushed aside glowered their anger, but he ignored them as he cunningly arranged it so that Caitlin and Rory shared a trencher. Winking mischievously in her direction, he patted the Gordon on the shoulder, giving hint that Rory was his favorite.

Caitlin was grim. "Ye hae come from far away. 'Tis anxious ye must be to find a wife."

He mumbled in answer, concentrating on a piece of beef as if he were a man half starved.

"But then as cold as it is here on Sky, ye will need a warm body to lie beside ye at night."

He raised his brows. "Aye."

Caitlin smiled as she said, under her breath. "Our fine shaggy-haired cows make wonderful companions." And a cow was all he would find as a bed mate, on that point she was determined. She was just about to tell Rory Gordon so when four pipers appeared. A skirl of bagpipes announced the music as the room was cleared for dancing. Before she had time to protest Caitlin found herself swept into Robbie MacKinnon's arms.

He was tall, much more so than she, making her feel feminine and somehow fragile. His chin just touched the top of her head. At first he simply held her as the music began weaving a spell, then slowly his strength moved her across the dance floor. Despite herself, Caitlin found herself enjoying him as a dancing partner.

"So, hae ye picked yer fine laddie yet?"

Caitlin answered quickly. "Nae, nor will I, for I hae it in my mind to be alone."

"As hae I." Robbie quickly explained that he was being prodded by his father into marrying. "I hae it in my mind to keep my freedom, but were I to be looking for a wife 'tis you I would pick, Caitlin nic Ian."

Despite herself, she smiled at the compliment. Suddenly the music changed to a livelier pace. Caitlin's partner changed , too. Rory Gordon had reclaimed her and led her in a twisting and whirling display of intricate steps. Soon they were out of breath and dizzy. Taking her hands in his when the dance was over, he kissed them, letting his lips brush her fingers as lightly as the wings of a butterfly.

Startled, Caitlin pulled away. "Do ye think me so easily won? A dance and a kiss in exchange for the MacLeod name and power?"

"Aye, for of all men assembled I am best."

"The best! Ha!" Well , she would soon let him know where his quick wooing had taken him. For that matter she would let them all know exactly where they stood, she thought as she not5ed the smug look upon all the men's faces. It was time.

Holding up her hand, Caitlin silenced the musicians." I hae made my choice," she said as all eyes turned her way.

"Ye hae chosen." Ian MacLeod raised his eyes to the ceiling as if to give praise to God.

"Aye."

The room was silent as everyone stared. Caitlin could even hear the sounds of breathing. For just a moment her bravado faltered. Did she dare?

"Och, speak, Daughter. Dunna leave us in suspense." MacLeod was all smiles.

"I choose....." Caitlin made a sweeping gesture with her arm, then let her arm fall to her side. Softly she said, "None of ye!"

"What?" Ian MacLeod cocked his head, certain that he must have heard her wrong.

Once again Caitlin's courage wavered until she forced herself to imagine what it would be like to be tied in bondage with any of the louts assembled within the room. This time her voice was loud and strong.

"I do not want any of these men as husband, Father. In truth, there is nary a one that pleases me."

"By the blessed saints!"

Like a thundercloud, Ian MacLeod stormed across the room, grabbing his daughter roughly by her arm. It was at that moment Caitlin was forced to see the error of her ways. Her father was angry, so much so that he was nearly blinded by his fury. Instinctively, Caitlin pulled back.

"Father!"

"Ye hae shamed me. Before all."

Foolish girl, what had she done? No doubt her father would lock her in her room for creating a scandal. Or would her punishment be worse? Caitlin trembled as she remembered her father's threat of exile.

"Father....please....I didna want....."

"But ye will. Aye that ye will." Trembling with rage, Ian MacLeod made his own proclamation, a vow that tumbled from his lips before he could even think. "Ye will hae a husband all right, Daughter. The next stranger who comes to the Macleod stronghold, be he warrior, bard, or even a fishermon, 'tis he who will be yer husband."

"Ye canna mean…" Caitlin was stunned.

"I do!" It was a startling proposal, but by the expression on his face and the look in his eyes it was obvious that the MacLeod meant to keep his word. "Aye, the first mon who crosses the MacLeod threshold will be the one that ye shall wed." With an air of finality he stalked away, leaving her to face her punishment alone.

Chapter Three

Far to the south of the MacLeod stronghold, four miles from Armadale on a headland near Teangue in Sleat, stood another castle. Castle Camus by name, the MacDonald seat of power. There it was dark and stormy. The kind of night when ghosts, witches and sea beasts stirred. The wind came like a roar, driving inland from the sea. Rain lashed wickedly at the shuttered windows, the wind skirled and whined through the many cracks and crevices of the castle, causing the torches in the wall sconces to flicker.

In the inner bailey it was a noisy jumble of milling men and horses as the clansmen of Castle Camus sought shelter from the storm. Even the rain, however, did not daunt the mock fight going on. The sputtering torchlights reflected upon the slashing swords and upraised shields of the two young men engaging themselves in a "practice" battle. And as the bold, brash clansmen thrust and parried those of more experience took great delight in shouting out criticisms.

"Gregor, ye move as slowly as if ye were an old mon. And your thrust is from the right side all the time. Makes ye an easy target."

"Niall, vary yer aim."

"Bold move. Now ye've got him......"

"Good, Niall. Good. Ye dodged him just in time."

The sound of sword on sword rent the air as the two cousins fought a furious game to show who was the better man. It was just the sort of test of strength and skill which both men thrived on. A grueling exhibition. Like two dancers, they moved back and forth, swaying in time to some unheard rhythm, circling one another. And all the while their swords slashed gracefully through the air, weaving dazzling patterns as the steel blades caught the light from the torch's flames.

"The finest swordsmen on all o' Skye."

"Ach! The best in the Highlands."

Both fighters were of equal height, well-muscled with bodies that bespoke of men used to constant exercise, but that is where the similarity ended. Gregor MacDonald's hair and beard were dark brown, his eyes as black as twin coals. Niall MacDonald on the other hand was swarthy of complexion but as fair of hair as his cousin was dark. His thick tawny hair had just a hint of a curl and was worn long so that it brushed his shoulders. His strong chin and jaw were visible for he was too vain to hide his face behind a beard.

"Och! Ye fight like a bairn," Gregor was taunting now, trying to goad Niall into making a mistake.

"Fight like a bairn do I?" With a deep throaty laugh, he lashed out, striking his cousin with the flattened breadth of his sword to avoid drawing blood. "That is a strike!"

"Oh, it is, is it? Then here is one in answer!" This time it was Gregor who was successful, making it a point to draw blood, a thin trickle but a real wound none-the-less. "Ach, excuse me, cousin!"

A cry of pain was his answer as Niall lunged. This time his blow was parried, as was Gregor's try at another purposeful slashing.

"I'll prove to all who are watching that *I* should be my uncle's tanist." It was a prize the dark-haired man fiercely desired. The "tanist" was the person next in succession to the Chief, according to the Scottish laws of tanistry or succession by the laws of cousinry. As nephews of Malcolm both men had an equal right to the honor. Niall's mother had been a MacKinnon, his father a MacDonald, Malcolm's brother. Gregor's claim to the tanistry was from his mother's side for she had been Malcolm's oldest sister.

"Or ye will prove yerself a fool!" Niall's eyes were hazel, twinkling as if with suppressed merriment. He'd win this match with his dolt of a cousin or not be worthy of his clan's name. "Which will it be, Cousin?"

"Fool ye call me?" Gregor's facial contours were boldly chiseled, his mouth slanted downward so that he appeared as if he were always frowning. Certainly he never exhibited a sense of humor. "And just what are ye?"

"I'll be the village simpleton if I let such as ye win the day." Niall MacDonald was of a more jovial countenance. A man who was not afraid to laugh at himself.

The two men were a study of contrasts in temperament, as different as the night is from the day. Gregor was easily fueled to anger, Niall needed to be goaded into losing his temper. At the moment he was successful in keeping his head, while his cousin was already hopelessly provoked.

"Ye willna win!"

"I will."

"Willna."

"Will!"

Gregor was deadly with a sword, but Niall's lightning-quick agility was more than his match. Again and again Gregor lunged, his anger making him careless. Niall blocked each thrust. With a last concentrated effort he sent his cousin's sword tumbling to the ground.

"Niall wins this one!" The others in the clan gave full vent to their praise. It was apparent that of the two they favored Niall. Perhaps because he had gone out of his way to foster camaraderie. Or because he had the self-assurance of a man who was willing to take risks and likewise willing to accept the consequences of his decisions. A brave man. A canny man. The kind of man who was a born leader.

"We'll meet again at this time tomorrow, Gregor. 'Twill be yer turn to be victor." Niall stuck out his hand amiably, but his cousin ignored the gesture. So, it was to be hard feelings again was it?

Bending down Niall cross-laced his curans which had come undone in the fracas. He did not see Gregor pick up his sword, raising it up with intent to do mischief. Only a shouted warning kept Niall from serious injury.

"Gregor. Ye son of a dog!" Niall spat his cousin's name with scorn as he ducked. With a grumbled oath he lashed out with his fist, striking Gregor full on the chin. A sobering blow that seemed to quell any further attempts at retaliation.

Disdainfully he eyed the other man. His dislike of his surly, scowling cousin was intense and all for good reason. From the moment Niall had set foot in the hall, Gregor had made it obvious that he was to be an enemy. He had babbled vicious rumors, cheated whenever they sparred at mock combat so as to win at any price, and tried his best to humiliate Niall at every turn. And all the while he showed a far different face to their uncle, pretending to be Niall's advocate. Only by his wits and a measure of good luck had Niall managed to counteract such duplicity.

"Why?" It was a question that was deeply troubling, but a matter he had little time to contemplate further for one of his younger cousins came with a summons. "Malcolm is asking to see the both of ye," he announced, pointing first at Niall then at Gregor. "On a matter of great importance."

The two men picked up their discarded breacons, wrapping them round their waists, draping them over their shoulders. As always Gregor was off in a run, anxious to please the uncle who held such power. Niall's gait, however, was more leisurely. The two men approached the thick wooden door to the chamber, Gregor elbowing himself into the position of entering first.

Inside a great fire roared, its flames dancing orange and blue light. A welcome respite from the dampness of the bailey. Malcolm MacDonald lounged drunkenly in his high-backed wooden chair by the roaring hearth, taking long gulps of his ale as he amusedly watched his two nephews. Little did they know that he purposefully stirred up the sense of competition between them. It did the young pups good to have to fight for the honor he would bestow on one of them. Whoever became his tanist would have to earn the title.

"You sent for us..." Niall's deep voice and Gregor's higher pitched utterance blended in unison.

"Aye. That I did." Slowly Malcolm looked from one to the other, keeping them in suspense. "The time has come to make my choice....."

He leaned towards Gregor in his preference because the young man was of a kindred spirit to his own.

Daring. Sly. Of brute strength with little conscience to get in the way. Merciless when necessary. That one had a robustness that was almost overpowering. And yet a voice inside his head whispered that it was Niall who was the better man. Since he had first come from the MacKinnon side of the isle, after his fosterage there, he had become an integral part of the MacDonald clan. He drew men to him with a fierce show of loyalty that was seldom equaled. Certainly he was the most intelligent of the two. And his distinction on the battlefield had done the MacDonalds proud.

"My Tanist will be......" But why should I choose, he thought. He would leave it to fate. A test of wit and skill between them. It would be interesting. "The Tanist will be....." Purposefully he teased them, pausing overlong before he said, "the one who earns it."

"What?" Niall and Gregor were both stunned.

Malcolm grinned. "He who thinks of a way to prove himself to be the ablest leader."

"Proves himself....?" Gregor looked questioningly at his uncle.

"Some deed of valor for the good of the clan. Something that will secure once and for all our dominance on the isle."

Gregor shrugged in confusion. "What must I do?"

Malcolm offered his nephews a wry smile. "That is but another part of the test. It is up to *you* to think of what must be done."

Niall threw the end of his breacan feille over his shoulders with a jaunty air. He knew at once just what *he* was going to do. There was but one answer really. He would boldly sneak into the MacLeod's stronghold of Dunvegan castle and steal the "fairy flag." Without it the MacLeods would have lost their magic. When the MacDonalds engaged in battle a third time, *they* would be victorious. What greater act of daring, cunning and courage could he do. His uncle would surely be so impressed that he would name him as tanist immediately thereafter.

"Tanist." The lofty honor sounded good upon his tongue. An honor he deserved. An honor his daring deed would insure.

After the hearth fires had burned down to ash and he had returned to his room, Niall still pondered the matter, liking the scheme more and more the longer he thought about it. What's more his friend Ogg, a tall giant of a man, liked it too.

"Imagine. Stealing it right out from underneath the very noses of those cursed MacLeods. I canna think of a finer jest," he offered.

"Nor an act that could ever be as stunning a blow."

The flag was rumored to have three magical properties. Flown on the battlefield it ensured a MacLeod victory, as had been seen in the past. Spread on his marriage-bed it endowed the MacLeod chief with children. Ian MacLeod had not taken the promise seriously, had laughingly said he would depend on his own prowess and he was now without a male heir. Unfurled at Dunvegan it was said to charm herring into the loch. It would be a great loss to the MacLeods were they to find it stolen from its hiding place.

Throwing a log on the fire, Niall watched as it flared up, illuminating his face. "I hae heard that the flag is kept in the tower. The tower where Colin MacLeod was struck down. 'Tis there I will go first."

"Ooooooooooooo!" Ogg made a high-pitched, eerie sound, spreading his arms wide. "And get nabbed by the ghostie who lives there."

"Ghost. Ha!" Niall scoffed at that story. "I dunna believe in such spirits."

Ogg shivered. "I do. I hae seen them wi' me own eyes. Fearsome spectacles."

Niall laughed, mockingly. "I would be more fearful o' the MacLeod's daughter. From what I hear she's a hellion that would make any ghost worth his salt cower."

"Aye, a shrew, or so it's whispered. One so bold, so willful that she has openly scorned all wi' whom her father would hae her wed." Ogg revealed the latest gossip being whispered around the hearth fires. That the MacLeod had sworn to marry his daughter to the first eligible male who entered the clan's castle.

"So Ian is trying to pawn the headstrong lassie off, is he now?" Niall clucked his tongue. "Sure and she must be as plain of face as a cow, but obviously not as docile."

"Nae. T'is said that she is bonny. Verrrry, verrrry bonny."

Niall did not have a reply to this, he simply stared at Ogg, his face a mask. He seemed to be deep in thought about the matter, but when he spoke it was about the MacLeod's flag and not his daughter. "I will get it, Ogg. Somehow. Some way!"

With Ogg he carefully formulated a plan. He would go by boat, traveling the waters like a fisherman. At the first wisp of dawn on the morrow he would set out on his daring mission. Within three days time the fairy flag would be in Malcolm's possession and Niall would be tanist.

KATHRYN HOCKETT

Chapter Four

A thick enveloping mist swirled like grasping fingers inland, clinging to the dewy ground of Armadale Bay. The stench of the decaying fish, discarded on the sand and rocks, drifted through the air. A reminder that the people of the nearby village made their living by fishing.

Niall MacDonald waited, watching as the ocean slapped the murky waves against the shore. Waiting for the boat that would take him up the coastline to Waternish. He had had no trouble in persuading one of the fisherman to loan him a tiny vessel, a small curach constructed with wicker frame and covered with hides. With a steadfast bribe he was also able to convince that fisherman to be his guide and to keep this journey a secret so that Gregor would not hear of Niall's daring deed.

Folding his arms across his chest Niall thought again about what he was planning. Was it possible? Dunvegan Castle's assets were the moat that surrounded it and the walls which were said to be ten feet thick in places. But Niall was not to be discouraged. The MacLeods were much too sure of themselves. It was true that the castle was guarded against feuding and marauding armies but against one man? Surely he could take them unaware, climb to the tower, find the flag and carry it away.

"A clever and resourceful mon can get past any fortifications," he said aloud. He would take a boat within the boat, something hardly bigger than a man to cross the moat. As to the walls, he would scale them much the way he had his favorite mountains when he was a boy. By hook and rope.

I can do it. I will do it. He wasn't afraid of the MacLeods. The thought of the dungeon and its cruelties was the only thing that sobered his enthusiasm. He would have to be cautious lest he end up rotting there like those poor dead fish that tormented his nostrils when the breeze blew in from the sea. Above all he must not admit to being a MacDonald or his doom was sealed, he thought impatiently scanning the horizon.

At last he saw it, a dark shadow against the rocky shoreline. The small fishing boat skimmed through the waters, pulling inland when it reached the agreed-upon meeting place. The water whipped and churned around the currach as he settled himself within. He was greeted with a wide smile as the rotund, ruddy-faced fisherman introduced himself.

"Peadar is my name."

"Niall. Nephew to Malcolm." His relation to the great clan leader though acknowledged did not keep him from having to help row the boat. Gripping the handles tightly, Niall pushed and pulled with all his might. The sooner he got to the MacLeod stronghold the sooner he would be back. Besides, this promised to be quite exciting, at least so he thought.

Alas, as the wind buffeted the currach, the sea voyage proved to be far from the enticing adventure he had supposed. As the familiar shores of Sleat vanished into the mists he felt an unnerving sense of wariness. The violently churning ocean turned his insides upside down. The waves threatened to capsize the boat. More than once or twice he was tempted to turn back.

"Dinna fash yerself. It will be a long, tedious journey but I'll get ye to Loch Dunvegan all in one piece," the fisherman said, sensing Niall's thoughts.

The jagged coastline seemed to extend for miles, nonetheless, true to his word Pedar steered the tiny boat with the greatest skill past the Point of Sleat, heading for Tarskavaig Bay and beyond. Niall had heard tales of mermaids and sea people and he could not help but wonder if these creatures were waiting even now to snatch the boat as it bounced on the water.

"Hae ye ever seen a mermaid, Peadar?" he asked, staring at the churning waters.

"Once. A bonny, bonny dark-haired lassie with silver tail and fins. She blew me a kiss."

"Did she now!" Niall fully hoped that he would see one too but he was disappointed. He reasoned that perhaps the water was just too turbulent.

Up and down, back and forth, the boat rocked unendingly. Niall and Peadar traveled until a dusting of powdery stars dotted the skyline and yet they had only come half way. Niall looked up at the familiar constellations, contenting himself by counting stars. Then it was his turn to sleep. Closing his eyes he was lulled by the soft rhythm of Peadar's oars, soothed by the rise and dip of the blades as they slapped the waves.

A cold spray of ocean mist splashed into his eyes. Niall awoke just the first beams of light tugged at the morning sky to see the breathtaking grandeur of Duirinish's rock formations, solidified lava from a long extinct volcano, silhouetting the horizon, peeking up through the clouds. Taking up the oars again, Niall aided the fisherman in moving the boat through the waves.

"The Norsemen called this Skuyo, Isle of Clouds," he said, "because of the mist." All his life he had heard that story, yet only now did he realize the full depth of the haunting beauty.

"It looks like fairyland...." Peadar responded, pausing in his rowing to gape. Then with a shrug he started up again.

They traveled all day in a seeminly unending, up and down churning. Peadar kept Niall amused with stories of his fishing journeys—which Niall thought might come in handy. Niall told of battles he had won. Forced camaraderie soon blossomed into something akin to friendship in the two men as they guided the boat through the sea. At last when Niall was beginning to think they would never reach Dunvegan Peadar announced, "Dunvegan Head just around the curve. We're nearly there."

Both men quieted as they concentrated on guiding the boat toward Loch Dunvegan. In the narrowest part of the inlet Niall ordered Peadar to row the boat to shore. He disembarked on the white sand-strewn beach near a fjord like inlet. It was there that the fisherman beached the skiff.

"Now remember. Wait for me here, Peadar." It wouldn't take long.

On the shore, shells, driftwood, logs and seaweed littered the rock-strewn sand. Niall made his way through the tangled seaweed, carrying the man-size currach on his back like some enormous shield. The journey to Dunvegan Castle would be a long and exhausting one he knew, complicated by the fact that he didn't know exactly where it was. Traveling in the fading light of dusk made visibility all the more trying

Huffing and puffing Niall proceeded, missing Peadar's company all the more with each step. The long hours seemed even longer without the fisherman's chatter, but he knew it much wiser to go alone. There was less chance of a mistake that way and besides, he wouldn't have wanted the young fisherman to get himself into any trouble. The MacLeods were said to show little mercy to any trespassing to cause mischief.

Guided only by the fires that glowed in the dark, the smoke pouring from the crofters' cottages, he moved along. Being in another clan's territory made him very vulnerable. As he pushed his way through the foliage Niall attuned his ears to any alarming sound, but paused only once, that being when a flock of night birds made their presence heard.

Onward, he walked, until his arms ached from the burden of the tiny boat and his legs were so sore he could hardly move them. Then, just when Niall was about to give up ever seeing Dunvegan, the roughly-hewn stronghold came into view. Like some multi-eyed monster its windows glowed through the darkness.

Quickening his pace, Niall hurried towards the castle. Slipping the tiny boat into the water he skimmed across the waters without any difficulty. Why, this was going to be as easy as taking honey from a slumbering bear, he thought, his ego stroked with his success. By the time he reached the western wall he was feeling cocky. True, it was a perilous climb but he could manage it.

A long length of rope was tied around Niall's waist, acting as a belt; but he unwrapped it now. After tying the rope to the hook that he carried in his hand, he swung it around and around his head, flinging it upward. It struck a soft piece of the stone, the sharp points embedding in the wall. Slowly he climbed up, hand over hand. Up. Up. Up. Until his fingers were raw and bleeding. Taking a deep breath, loathing the thought of falling into the slimy and evil-smelling waters of the moat he looked down. The drop looked awesome and he held his breath as he continued climbing.

Suddenly he lost his footing. Like a spider handing from its fragile thread he swung to and fro. There was a loud splash as his frantic kicking sent a rock flying into the moat. For just a moment Niall was certain that this crazy scheme would send him hurling to his death, but he somehow managed to regain his balance. Moving steadily up the rope he reached the nearest window and climbed inside.

It was dark and quiet. Not even one taper was lit. A good omen for a man stealthfully invading another's territory, yet unnerving too. Niall was cautious as he lowered himself down, but not careful enough. He gasped as he found himself engulfed in a powdery substance.

"By Saint Michael!" As if he were swimming he fought to free himself. "What the.....?" He was in a large barrel. It was easy enough to escape from once he had made that discovery, however. Pulling himself out he had to laugh as he struck his tinderbox and fumbled around for a candle. "A flour barrel." He had fallen unceremoniously into the castle's supply of flour. It covered him from head to toe.

Niall might have taken time to brush himself clean had it not been for a squeaking sound. Blowing out the candle he hid behind the barrel just as a paunchy man entered to gather a few supplies. Niall quickly assessed that it must be the cook! Fearing detection, he darted in an out of the shadows as he fled to the stairway, running up two whole flights, his heart racing. He had little doubt but that his life would be forfeit if he were found now. It was all too obvious that he was an intruder.

He raced recklessly through the darkness, barely seeing where he was going. Finally he found himself before a wooden door. Though he pulled frantically at the iron handle, it was locked. Swearing beneath his breath he went on to the next door and the next. He hesitated, listening for the sound of footfalls.

Carefully ascertaining that no guards were about he continued on his way, then hearing footsteps again, he quickly opened the door to the nearest room and stepped inside. Again he struck his tinderbox, lighting just one wall sconce. He found himself in a tower room. A room cluttered with all sorts of weapons and other relics. Cobwebs decorated the ceiling, a coat of dust layered the furniture. In curiosity he explored. Was the fairy flag within?

"We'll soon see," he whispered with bravado. Still, he couldn't help feeling more than a bit apprehensive about the whole thing. He had to be very careful lest he be caught red-handed by anyone wandering about. "Hopefully the Macleods will all be snuggled in their beds and I will be long gone wi' the flag before they arise." Closing his eyes for just a moment he tried to imagine the MacLeod hall. The fires would have burned to ashes. The *seanachaidh* would have stopped chattering his tales. The great hall would be empty. Quiet.

"Aye, I'll be safe." With that thought in mind, Niall started rummaging through all the objects in the tower room.

Down below in the great hall, the hearth fire had burned down to ash. It was silent. The *seanachaidh* had ceased his stories. All the clansmen and women had sought their beds, save a few, including Caitlin who still prowled about. The argument she had had with her father was on her mind. In but a moment, with only a few words, her whole future had been put in jeopardy because of her stubbornness and her father's great pride.

He can't mean it. He wouldn't really force me to marry the next man who comes to the castle. It was but a threat said in anger to curb my temper and frighten me into submission. Or was it? The possibility that her father might well have been deadly serious, that she might be forced to go far away from her homeland, played on Caitlin's mind.

Her eyes flitted about the room as if to brand a permanent image in her mind for the days ahead when she might be far away from here. Memories. So many memories. Down the center of the hall was a long hearth over which big pots from the evening's meal were still placed. How many stories of fairies, water beasts, witches and ghosts had she listened to in front of the evening fire? Though her family was Christian they knew that their lives would always be ruled by older beliefs too, knew that other beings occupied Skye as surely as did those of flesh and blood. As a child she had listened in awe to such stories and tales of long ago.

Before this same hearth she had blissfully enjoyed the music from fiddle, harp and pipes, riotous songs or soothing songs of reverie that had at last lulled her to sleep. Somehow she had always awakened to find herself in her bed, thinking perhaps the fairies had bewitched her and brought her to her room. Now in her adult years she knew it had been her father who had carried her off to bed, holding her tenderly and lovingly within the strength of his arms. Now he was pushing her into the arms of a man who might well be a stranger. A husband. How strange that sounded. Just a few days ago she had laughingly talked with one of her sisters about such a thing, had viewed her adamant opposition to any suggestion of marriage. How quickly one's fate could change.

A loom and several spindle whorls for spinning of wool stood against the farthest wall and Caitlin curled her mouth in a bittersweet smile as she recalled how often she had rebelled at joining the women for their daily chores. Cooking, weaving, and sewing bored her. Washing with the harsh lye soap seemed a thankless task. Waulking, or hand shrinking woolen cloth was a long and laborious process which she had no fondness for. In truth, she had scorned woman's work, finding a dozen reasons for avoiding tasks any time she could. But now, oh, what she wouldn't give to be able to stay among these women instead of women she did not even know.

"I wish... that I could stay here forever........" she thought, but knew it was unlikely, at least now. All she could hope was that there would be no newcomers to the castle, at least until her father had time to let his temper cool a wee bit. She would talk with him then and somehow make him understand her feelings.

"Well, well, well, the bride to be......"

Caitlin didn't even bother to turn. She knew who the voice belonged to. Jamie. "Not if I can help it."

"Lassie, 'tis whispered that ye hae no say." He threw a log onto the hearth, relighting the fire with a torch ignited by one of the wall sconces, then laughed "The proud and haughty Caitlin MacLeod will be given to the first mon who crosses the threshold. Well, it serves ye right, lass, considering that ye could hae had me."

"Ha!" She pointed her nose towards the high, beamed ceiling.

"But ye said nae." There was disappointment in his tone. "Why?"

She answered honestly. "Because I couldna trust ye where other lassies are concerned, Jamie. I want a mon I know will be true for ever more."

A muscle tightened in his jaw, his eyes squinted. He opened his mouth to speak but in the end couldn't say the lie. "Ye hae been reading too many fairy tales, Caitlin. Forever after just doesna happen. But I would give ye honor and respect and be true to ye in my own way."

Which means that he expects to be able to wander, albeit discretely, she thought, feeling her cheeks grow hot at the very thought. Slowly she turned around to face him. "It isna good enough."

His face turned into a mask of anger. "Then go straight to the devil, Caitlin MacLeod." He strode quickly to the door, but turned around before he pushed it open. "And we will see just what kind of a mon ye end up wi' as yer honored husband." His tone insinuated that he hoped whoever it was turned out to be totally unsuitable, someone who would make her deeply sorry she had scorned him.

"Aye, we will see." She held his gaze steadily. In the end it was Jamie who looked away. Caitlin stared after him as he left the hall, slamming the door behind him.

Only after Jamie had left did Caitlin allow her composure to slip. Her hands were trembling. He was right. Maybe she would end up with someone who would make her regret that she had told Jamie no. Maybe she wouldn't be able to talk her father out of his decision this time. Maybe....

"Maybe, maybe, maybe," she breathed. Well, she wouldn't let anyone or anything get her down. Not even her father. She might be female but she was a MacLeod through and through. Just as brave in her way as Colin. "My dearest elder brother...."

Without even realizing it, Caitlin's steps took her towards the tower where the air was chilly and damp. Lighting a torch she took a step up the stairs, then another and another. If Colin's ghost really did roam about she was determined to find out tonight, for if ever she needed to engage in conversation with his restless spirit it was now.

Oh, please be there! Please materialize if only for a few moments. I need you so.....

Closing her eyes, Caitlin said a silent prayer, then touched her fingers to the door handle. Slowly, quietly she pulled it down, pushing it open ever so slightly, optimistic that somehow her brother would have sensed her desperate need.

"Please exist, Colin. Please........" Taking a deep breath, at that moment she really did believe. Even so, she was not fully prepared for the apparition that met her eyes. A ghostly white form who could be none other than *him!* "Oh!"

Niall was too entranced to hear the door open but he heard the gasp. Turning around he saw the most beautiful woman he had ever beheld standing there. A woman with hair the color of fire whose mouth was agape as she stared in disbelief.

"Colin!" she breathed. "Colin! Blessed Saints, it *is* you!"

HIGHLAND DESTINY

Chapter Five

A lone torch flickered and sparked, casting unearthly shadows on the wall, faintly illuminating the masculine form that stood in the tower room. It was difficult to see details, but from what she could make out, Caitlin was convinced that this eerie white figure was an unearthly being. It was a ghost! And not just any ghost.

"Colin...." She said again, her eyes widening, her voice trembling just a little as she tried to still her quivering jaw.

Though she had hoped beyond hope to at last see him, a chill swept over Caitlin at the very sight. She drew her arasaid more closely about her. Spirits of the dead were frightening to behold, she thought, even if it was the spirit of her brother. Still, she fought to maintain her calm. She didn't want to act cowardly or panic and frighten Colin away. And yet.....

Caitlin's hands shook as a myriad of memories flitted through her mind. She was a child again, tiptoeing to the tower to investigate the loud noises that had awakened her from her slumber, little knowing the horror she would witness.

That man is going to hurt him! He's going to hurt my brother! Colin, watch out! Colin, beware! She remembered a sword descending with lightning speed, remembered the blood, heard once again in her mind her terrified scream.

"Oh, no! Colin." Hurriedly she closed her eyes, hoping to shut out the frightening images of warfare and death.

At the sound of the name, Niall stiffened, then when there was no reprisal, he relaxed. The lass didn't seem to pose a threat, and thus he answered, "Aye, lass, I'm here." Having prepared himself for flight or a fight if his presence was discovered, Niall was surprised at this turn of events. Pleasantly so. Hopefully this case of mistaken identity would be beneficial.

"For so many hears I hae been coming here, hoping ye would come...." She said softly, clenching her hands together so tightly that the fingernails bit into her palms.

The young woman had been hoping to see him? Niall smiled for just a moment as he realized that she had mistaken him for someone else. But who? Not a MacDonald surely, for he had purposefully dressed in the plain garb of a fisherman so that his clothing would not give him away.

"Ye wished, did ye?"

"Aye, I wished and now at last ye hae appeared," Caitlin continued. "As if somehow ye sensed how much I wanted to see ye again."

Cocking his head, Niall leisurely assessed the young woman who had come upon him. "Well, lass, ye didna wish any harder than I." Whoever this young woman was, whoever she had been expecting to see, she bewitched him.

Look at that hair! Like a fire, a raging flame that whipped about her shoulders. Catching the glow of the torch, her hair blazed with magenta highlights. Niall moved closer, his gaze caressing the mounds of the woman's breasts, moving to the narrow waist which he knew he could span with his hands. The gentle swell of her hips and long legs were outlined by her gown, completing the enchanting image.

"I hae watched for ye and waited so long I had begun to think that ye didna exist." Caitlin lifted her head, staring at the presence before her. *Strange how piercing those hazel eyes are,* Caitlin thought, shivering under his stare. She had not thought a ghost's eyes would be so fiery, so filled with life, and yet they were.

"Well, I do exist!" And by all the saints so did she, a vision that completely enthralled him. Niall had known a hundred women who were by all measures beautiful, and yet when he looked into those brown eyes he was lost, caught up in a fascination more potent than a witch's spell. It was totally unusual for him to feel such a sudden, compelling explosive physical attraction, and yet he did.

"Surprising how strong ye seem. Are ye as solid as ye appear?" A frown creased Caitlin's brow as she took a step toward him. She was deeply curious, and thus she blurted out, "Tell me. If I touch ye, what will it be like? Will it be like touching air? If I touch ye, will ye up and disappear?"

"Disappear?" He was taken aback by her question. For a moment he feared she must be daft. Perhaps one of those cast off from the others and left to roam the upper rooms because they were not right in the head. So thinking he took a step back.

"No, Colin, dunna shrink from me." For a moment she felt foolish, and thus she explained. "I've never seen a ghost before ye see."

Ghost? As the realization of what she meant swept over him, Niall was first stunned then amused. She thought he was a ghost! She had called him Colin. No doubt she meant Colin MacLeod, the brave laddie who had been killed in this very tower protecting the very treasure he had come to steal. This lovely lassie believed him to be that long-deceased personage. And her so believing might very well save his life.

"Ah, lass, ghosts are really no different from mortals."

"No different?" Caitlin reached out.

"Except that ye canna touch me," he hastened to reply.

She raised her brow. "Why?"

He explained quickly. "Yer hand will pass right through me, hinny, no matter how it might appear. Spirits such as I hae no flesh or blood."

Niall thrust out his arms, affecting what he thought to be his most "haunting" pose.

"That's why I can walk through walls as if they were no' even there. Saves me the bother of having to open doors when I am mulling about up here guarding the wee flag."

"Really? Ye can walk through doors and walls."

"Aye."

Caitlin regarded him thoughtfully, trying to imagine just what that must be like and imagined that despite the advantages it must be lonely. "Is...is it terrible being dead?" A blunt question.

"Sometimes yes, sometimes no." This time he couldn't resist a grin as his voice lowered to a mere whisper. "For ye see, lass, we ghosts still hae the same desires we had in the flesh." Looking at the young woman, Niall felt his blood stir. "Only we canna do anythin' about them."

"Oh......." Caitlin knew well that he meant more than just the longing for eating and drinking. Was it any wonder then that she blushed.

"But dunna fash yerself. Over the years I hae trained myself to be content." He winked. "But I would be far happier if I could be haunting some of those roguish MacDonalds instead of languishing up here."

"The MacDonalds!" Caitlin spoke the name like a curse. "I will n'er forgi' them for killing ye, Colin dear."

"Ach, nae! Scurvy rascals though they be." Seeing a chance to use his mistaken identity as a ghost to his advantage, Niall turned the conversation to the fairy flag. "They havena a chance against us, though, lass, as long as we hae the flag. Which is why I hover here in the tower so diligently, guarding it wi' such zest."

"Aye guarding it as loyally in death as ye did in life, Colin dear." Without realizing it, Caitlin looked towards an old wooden chest, revealing the flag's hiding place to Niall without even saying a word.

Ah, so there it is. Keeping his eye on the red-haired girl, Niall inched toward the chest, hardly daring to believe his luck. *Careful, Niall, don't be too hasty*, he instructed himself. *Move slowly. Slowly.* As he moved, he tried to keep her distracted with talk. "Such a lovely lass as yerself shouldna frown. Dunna keep anger inside ye because of what happened a long time ago."

"'Tis not just that." She sighed. "'Tis Father."

"Father?" Positioning himself so that the chest was behind him, he fumbled with the lid.

Caitlin was relieved to be able to come right to the point. "Father is going to gi' me away, Colin, and I do no' wish to marry." Her eyes were imploring. "What can I do?"

"Do?" Keeping his head up, his eyes level with hers, Niall slowly lifted the creaky wooden lid. "Why, tell him ye willna do it."

"I did."

"And?" Reaching inside, he cautiously felt around for the slick, cool silken flag.

"He threatens to gi' me to the first mon who walks across the threshold."

"He does?" Niall's eyes widened in surprise. It couldn't be, could it? This lovely red-haired girl couldn't be the daughter of that sour-faced old MacLeod. Was this then the infamous Caitlin?

"And I do believe he means it."

"Nae." Niall's jaw tensed. *Of course. He should have known it to be Caitlin MacLeod. Her chin was too strong, clearly showing her to be a lass that would not be easily managed. Even the fiery hair gave proof to that.*

"Ache, but I fear he meant every word. 'Tis married I will soon be and not a mon of my choosing."

"He doesna mean it."

"Ah, but he does and I dunna know what I can do except run away."

She looked so lovely, so forlorn, that for a moment Niall was distracted from his mission. "And go where?" he found himself thinking the most foolish thoughts.

"I dunna know, Colin. I just dunna know."

"Och, lass!" He found himself longing to reach out to her, to comfort her, but the feel of the flag touching his fingers brought him back to reality. No! Lovely or not, he must not dally here. Caitlin MacLeod meant trouble. He had best get the flag and leave this place as soon as he could. So thinking, he made a grab for the flag as soon as she lowered her head. Hastily he drew it out and stuffed it in his shirt.

"Colin?" Unfortunately his act did not go unseen. "What are ye doing?"

"Keeping the flag safe, lass. Just keeping it safe." For just a moment he turned his back on her as he moved toward the window, wondering just how quickly he could scramble down the rope. When he turned around again he was astonished to see that she had picked up an old sword and was actually brandishing it at him. "Lass?"

"Ye are no' ghost." In the act of retrieving the flag from the chest, the intruder's fingers had brushed against the wood, wiping off the white substance covering them. Now as Caitlin looked at him, she saw that his was no ghostly appendage but a hand like any other man's.

Her threatening stance, the way she held the sword gave Niall reason to fear. It was no wonder he hurried to assure her. "Ah, but I am a ghost, *sister* dearie."

"And I am a banshee." She didn't know the why or wherefore he had tried to deceive her, but whatever the reason she knew him to be a thief who now held possession of something not only she but her entire clan held precious. "A banshee whose wail will be proclaiming yer death if ye don't return that flag ye just stole to its rightful place."

"Flag?" Niall feigned innocence.

"Which ye hae hidden beneath yer shirt, *brother* dear." She took a step toward him. "Put it back!"

For just a moment he was motionless as he thought the matter out carefully. He didn't want to put it back. He had come too far to fail now. Yet neither did he want to be skewered by some slip of a girl no matter how pretty.

"Ye heard me. Put it back!"

"Nae!"

Lasing out with her sword, she slashed his fingers, drawing blood. "Ah, ye see. Ghosts do no' bleed. At least so I hae heard." Her hostility made her eyes glow like amber.

"Who are ye?"

He didn't answer.

"Cat got yer tongue?" Just to make certain he knew she was deadly serious, she exclaimed, "I'm just as skilled wi' this as any mon."

"I wouldna doubt it." Something about her seemed to foretell that she would be skilled at anything she did. Even so, he could not part with the flag, and thus, instead of backing down, Niall moved hurriedly toward the window.

Caitlin moved with all the agility of a streak of lightning and blocked his way. The very air crackled with tension. And danger. "Take one more step and ye *will* be a ghost."

"And that would be such a pity." Niall's smile was roguish. His eyes caressed her with a boldness few had dared, held her gaze, forced her to acknowledge that there was a mutual attraction between them. "For it would mean that I could ne'er make love to ye, lassie." As he spoke, his eyes swept over her suggestively.

"Ach!" Caitlin was attracted to him, but she would have rather jumped from the tower window than admit it to herself. Perhaps that was why she was doubly hostile as she poked the point of her sword into his ribs. "Sweet talk and compliments will do ye no good. Start walking."

"Walking? Where?" For just a moment he looked bemused with the situation, then as he felt the sharp point stick him through his shirt, he slowly took a step forward. Only a fool would anger a woman, particularly one who was armed. "Where are ye taking me?"

"To my father." He wouldn't be so smug and arrogant facing the mighty Ian MacLeod. Her father had made even the bravest man cower when faced with his anger."

"To yer father." He startled her with another smile. "Good. Good."

"Good?" Of all things he might have said, she certainly wasn't expecting this answer.

"Aye, ye see, lass, *I* am the first mon to cross the MacLeod threshold." Was he imagining it or had she gone quite pale?

"Ye canna be....be…"

"Ah, but I am."

Niall had fitfully thought of a way out of his predicament and had come up with the perfect scheme. He would concoct the story of being a fisherman come to claim the hand of the MacLeod daughter. It would buy him some time until he could think of a way to escape.

Chapter Six

The stairs leading to the lower floors of the castle were drafty but that was not the reason that Caitlin felt chilled. It was because of the quandary she found herself in. A real "carfuffle" to be sure. She had caught a stranger in the tower, a man who had made an attempt to steal the Fairy Flag, for which he should be punished. At the same time, however, that man had cunningly reminded her of her father's promise, to marry her off to the first stranger who set foot inside the castle. That man, as her captive had pointed out, was him.

"Shall we go?" Niall's voice was low, a husky rumble that seductively teased her as he spoke.

Caitlin was hesitant for just a moment as she pondered what to do. Her father was a man who always adhered to his vows but surely under the circumstances he wouldn't even consider this tawny-haired rogue as a suitor. Or would he? Certainly the broad-shouldered, muscular man looked well able to wield a sword. And he had proven himself to be bold. And clever. And strong. All were attributes her father admired in a man.

Ah, but the flag. Her father's pride and joy. This man had blatantly tried to make off with it. Being a thief would surely spell the doom of this arrogant intruder. Moreover he was still in possession of the flag, clear admission of his guilt. That thought gave her assurance as she pressed the sword against her captive's back, gesturing for him to walk down the stairs.

"Aye, let us go." Now it was Caitlin who grinned self-assuredly. "Ye think ye be glib of tongue, laddie, but Ian MacLeod will soon hae ye speechless with fear."

Niall didn't give her any back talk. Though he walked with a swagger he couldn't fool himself. He was apprehensive about meeting the MacLeod, *ceann tigh* of his enemies. Warily moving down the stairs he could only hope that he would get out of this nightmare with a whole skin. She had called him glib of tongue but he knew it would take a seanachaidh's skill to talk his way out of this one.

He darted a quick look sideways, thinking about escape, only to find that her eyes were steadily trained upon him. Lovely brown eyes that they were, they showed not even a trace of compassion. Were he to try to run away would she stab him? He wasn't certain, but didn't want to take a chance. Caitlin nic Ian was as strong minded a lass as he had ever crossed paths with. And she was angry. Far better to take his chances with her father, he decided, viewing each step with trepidation.

Down, down, down. The distance to the MacLeod's chamber seemed nearly as great a distance as it had been to the MacLeod castle, Niall thought sourly. Then all of a sudden the ominous destination loomed all too clearly in his path. An awesome portcullis, which at the moment was as worrisome as that behind which the devil himself waited. Worse yet were the growling russet-hued wolfhounds that guarded the door. Bristling and baring their teeth, they gave warning of what they would do if he made a wrong move.

"They dunna seem to like ye," Caitlin pointed out, taking note of the largest dog's snarl.

"That's because they dunna know me yet," Niall shot back, hoping the dogs wouldn't bite. "Easy. Easy." He moved slowly, carefully past the two animals, hoping that they had been fed. Nervously he brushed the flour off his garments.

"Or because they *do*," Caitlin retorted with mock sweetness, raising her hand to knock loudly upon the door.

A bellowed "Who is it?" thundered from the other side. "Who disturbs a mon's sleep?"

"Caitlin, Father. I hae trapped a ghost."

"What?" The door was yanked open and Niall found himself face to face with his fiercest enemy. A giant of a man who now looked him up and down assessingly. "Ach, he is no ghost."

"Nae, but he masqueraded as one," Caitlin answered, giving Niall a look that warned that he would soon be in dire trouble.

"Masquaraded?" The MacLeod's eyebrows shot up warningly.

"Aye, to get his hands on this." Reaching into Niall's shirt she withdrew the Fairy Flag. Incriminating evidence.

"Och!" Ian MacLeod yanked it from Caitlin's hand. His brows furled in barely suppressed rage, then blistering Niall with his gaze he asked, "Why?"

In that moment Niall could picture himself hanging in chains from the MacLeod's dungeon wall until he was little more than bones. Still, he somehow kept his poise, despite the wolfhounds growling. "For the sake of love," he blithly answered.

"Love?" Ian MacLeod's eyes narrowed to slits, taking on a look of stark coldness, his jaw stiffened. His expression warned of danger if Niall did not respond quickly.

"The love I bear yer daughter, who I hae looked upon from afar for a long, long time." Taking Caitlin's hand, he squeezed her cold fingers so hard that she winced. "I thought to daringly remove the flag from its hiding place and give it into yer hands. I wanted to prove my bravery before asking for yer daughter's hand."

"Wha....?" Caitlin tried to speak but her words came out in a strangled gasp as she pulled her hand away. The liar!

Ian swore beneath his breath, then his words exploded the silence. "To lay hands on the Fairy Flag is the gravest misdeed a mon can do the clan."

"If so, then I am sorry. Niall answered, bowing humbly before the man he knew had his life in his hands. "But I meant no harm."

"Meant no harm, ye say. I tell ye it doesna matter. Ye transgressed." Reaching down, Ian MacLeod scratched each dog behind the ears, then returned his attention to Niall.

Man to man they stared at one another, each making their judgment. Niall could tell at once that Ian MacLeod was a harsh man, a fighting man, yet at the same time a man who would exhibit fairness if he thought him deserving.

"If I did, then I beg yer mercy," he said, looking Ian MacLeod directly in the eye, remembering that Ian MacLeod had spilled an ocean of MacDonald blood. Was his to be next?

"Mercy. Ha!" Having recovered her voice, Caitlin was scathing. "Ye planned to take away the very emblem of the MacLeod's strength and soul. The gravest ill ye could do to us, as my father says."

"I didna leave the castle wi' it," Niall insisted. That at least might save him.

"Because I wouldna let ye," she challenged, standing toe to toe and nose to nose with him.

"Ah, lass, had I wanted to flee wi' the flag I would hae done it. I didna want to." His voice was impassioned. "I repeat again, I didna take it from these walls. I but wanted to prove that I was cunning, and brave. A daring, though foolish act but one that I dunna regret since it gave me a chance to get close to ye, lass."

"Close? Ha!" With a toss of her head she exhibited her scorn. "I got close enough to you to know that ye smell of fish." She wrinkled her nose.

"Because I am a fisherman," he retorted, angry at her scorn. "An honest calling that insures that those, living comfortably within the castle, eat well." Balling his hands into fists he fought to control his temper. The lass had a viper's tongue and a stubbornness that clearly needed taming. Too bad he wouldn't be around long enough to get the chance.

"A fishermon?" Circling Niall several times, Ian MacLeod clucked his tongue. "Ye dunna look it." For a moment he seemed to be suspicious. "Ye seem to hae a fighting mon's strength."

Niall thought quickly. "I keep my arms strong by rowing and casting out lines. And by fighting wi' staffs wi' my brothers. Any mon has to be prepared."

"Ye dinna say." Ian MacLeod looked at Niall with a measure of respect. "And would ye then think yerself strong enough to fight a battle to prove yer innocence or guilt."

Niall answered quickly. "I would." There was a long pause as he gathered up his courage. "And would ye think yerself noble enough to keep the vow ye made?" he countered.

"Vow?"

"According to yer own words yer bonny daughter should be given to me as my wife, no matter if I am the winner or loser of this battle ye plan." Turning to Caitlin he smiled, thinking all the while that her old scar-faced war horse of a father wouldn't dare kill his son-in-law. "Unless I hae miscalculated, I am the first mon to enter the castle since ye made yer vow. Am I not?"

Ian MacLeod nodded grimly. "Ye are."

"Nae!" Caitlin wrestled with the dilemma of her fate, feeling a fiercesome pressure pushing at her chest as her worst fear came true. For a moment she feared she couldn't breath. "Father, ye wouldna. He is just a fishermon."

"Ah, but I would." Ian MacLeod's eyes glittered in the torchlight. "I warned ye, Caity. I put forth mon after mon of noble heritage, but ye goaded me into this, lass. Just remember." For the moment Niall's guilt was forgotten as the MacLeod seemed intent on proving a point to his daughter.

"I dunna care. I willna marry him if he wins a hundred combats." Folding her arms across her chest she looked like defiance personified. "A fishermon is a fishermon and n'er the mon for me. I refuse to marry him."

"Then ye would shame me, daughter." The MacLeod slammed his fist into the palm of his hand to vent his annoyance. "As this mon has pointed out, I made a vow."

"But......"

"Hush. The MacLeod has spoken." Taking Niall by surprise he plucked a sword from its resting place on the wall and threw it at him. If he was stunned by Niall's quick reflex action in catching it by the handle, he didn't show it. "So, tomorrow at the first light of day, ye will hae a chance to prove yerself to me, laddie. By combat it will be proven if ye are guilty or innocent of any misdeed."

A nerve in Niall's jaw ticked angrily. "If I am proven innocent I will hae for myself a bride, but if I lose?"

"So much the worse for ye," Caitlin replied with a toss of her head. "Mayhap ye should hae stuck to yer fish and not hae dallied where ye had no business."

"Aye, and mayhap I would hae done just that had I known the MacLeod's daughter was such a foul-tempered witch. After today I find I prefer the company of mackerel to ye lass."

"Ahhhhhh!" Caitlin looked at her father, thinking that he would come to her aid verbally, but Ian MacLeod was smiling not angry.

Niall continued, whispering angrily. "I dunna want to marry ye, Caitlin MacLeod, any more than ye be wanting marriage with me." Was there another way out? Again he asked, "What is to be my fate if I lose?"

"Either way ye are considered betrothed to my daughter so that I can keep my vow. But if ye are guilty...." The verdict didn't need to be spoken aloud. Niall understood only too well. "I willna lose." He dare not!

"Father!" Caitlin wanted to rage at him, plead with him, get down on her knees if it would do any good.

The stubborn jaw of her father was held so rigidly set, however, that she knew he would not go back on his word.

And so I am to be the wife of a simple fisherman. It was the gravest insult, not to be born. Even so, Caitlin knew she had no say. Men. They didn't understand one wit about a woman, she thought unhappily. All they knew was fighting and war. And because women didn't fight and kill they had no voice in their own lives. No power at all. It was a sobering admission, yet the way of things.

"Aye, because I hae declared it so." Again, the MacLeod had spoken.

"As ye wish." Caitlin hung her head, then quickly raised it again. She turned the full venom of her anger on Niall. "But know this, fishermon. All the while I am watching this combat my father has commanded, I will be cheering on yer opponent." That said she turned her back and leaving Niall in the care of her father, stalked back up the stairs.

The loud thud of the door slamming awoke Shona from a peaceful sleep. Opening her eyes, she stared into the darkness. "Caitlin?" she propped herself up on one elbow, calling out again, "Caitlin?"

"Aye, 'tis me." The tone of her voice gave the gravity of her mood away.

"What's wrong, hinny?"

"F..F..Father!" She gasped the story between sobs. "I thought he was a ghost, but then I caught him trying to steal the flag and…."

"Steal the flag? Father?"

"Nae! Nae, the fishermon."

"Fishermon? What fishermon?" Thrusting aside the covers, Shona stood up. Walking over to Caitlin, she put her arm around her in the manner Cailin always did to her when she was upset. "Come, sit down on the bed and tell me, hinny. Slowly. Calmly."

Caitlin moved quickly across the room, plopping down on the thick mattress. "I came upon a stranger in the tower. I thought him to be Colin."

"Thought him to be a ghost?"

Caitlin nodded. "He was covered from head to toe with flour. It was dark and I a foolish ninny."

"Foolish? Never." Shona sat beside her.

"Aye, I was, and he a rogue if ever there be one." It angered her as she thought about it all. How he must have been laughing at her all the while as she had prattled on and on about his being a ghost. All the while he had been planning on stealing the MacLeod's greatest treasure. "But he was nae a ghost. He was a thief."

"The flag!" Shona clutched at her sister's arm.

"....Is safe, though I fear I cannot say the same for me." She took a deep breath. "Oh, Shona, Father has given me away." In as calm a manner as she could manage, Caitlin told the whole story.

"The stubborn old goat." Shona drew her legs up on the bed, hugging them tight as she asked, "Ach, but is he handsome?"

"The fishermon?" Though she hated to admit it even to herself, Caitlin found herself telling the truth. "Aye! Extremely. But I dunna care, Shona. I hae no liking for what is going on."

"Aye, but I think it sounds grand. A mon fighting for ye, Caity. What more could any woman want/"

She answered in one word. "Love." Leaning back on the pillows, she crossed her arms behind her head and gave the matter considerable thought. "I want a mon who loves me for myself, not because I'm the Macleod's eldest daughter. Caitlin closed her eyes. Oh, if only the stranger were not just a fisherman looking to better himself by an advantageous marriage, she might have felt so differently. As it was, his intrusion into the castle and into her life promised to cause nothing but calamity.

Chapter Seven

The combat was to be held in the same field where games were often played. It was a level stretch of hard ground covered with a dusting of wild grass and surrounded by rocks upon which the spectators sat. Caitlin's heart was in her throat as she watched the two men file onto the field. The fisherman didn't have a chance, did he?

No. I am safe. The stranger who had pretended to be a ghost didn't have a chance, for he was to have a fiercesome opponent. Angus, a brawny young man that was well known for his prowess. Looking at him, Caitlin could see that he was bigger and more ominous in his appearance than the fisherman. It was only a matter of time until he had the intruder, who only knew nets and oars, begging for mercy on his knees.

Nor was Caitlin the only one of that opinion. She heard wagering going on, men in the crowd deciding a winner and placing bets on the outcome. Few chose the fisherman.

"It will be a slaughter," one man said loudly, an opinion shared by several of the others. Still, it didn't seem to daunt the intruder to the castle.

"For ye, lass!" Raising his sword he saluted her in acknowledgement that she was his lady and there to fight for her. An action that she promptly snubbed.

"Ye dinna hae a chance," she taunted, wondering why he didn't seem to realize that. Sauntering onto the field he had a boldness she was certain would soon be cowered. And oh, how she relished the sight of the arrogant interloper being brought to his knees. Marry her indeed!

Voices rose in a cheer as Niall and Angus took their places, Angus removing his plaid; Niall his garments and throwing them to the ground. Just as the warriors in battle did, they would fight nearly naked—with just a loincloth--and Caitlin blushed at the sight of the fisherman's tall, well-muscled body. She remembered what the women had whispered around the cooking fires, that the newcomer looked to be well endowed. Now that he was devoid of his garments their chatter had proven to be true. Not that Caitlin would admit that, however.

I won't even look at him, she thought stubbornly, only to go back on her word in the blink of an eye. Though she tried to look the other way, her eyes were drawn again and again to the fisherman. His skin was golden where it had been exposed to the sun and she could only suppose that when he was out on his boat he rode the waves without his clothes. A strange thing to do, considering that it was often cold.

"He is a fine looking mon," a young cousin sitting next to her cooed. "Look at those shoulders. At that chest. Those legs. And his......" Foolishly the girl twittered, but her chatter had drawn Caitlin's attention to the part of him that marked the fisherman a male. The loincloth left little to the imagination.

"Just looking at him is strangely exciting. Stirring," another cousin said with a sigh.

"Ha!" Caitlin pretended to disagree, but the harm was already done. She felt a stirring in her blood, a languid heat, that brought forth a longing that shamed her. A maiden shouldn't think such thoughts, especially about such a man.

"That dark blond hair. I hae ne'er seen a lion, but I hae heard aboot them and would think he would resemble such a magnificent....."

"Oh hush!" Poking her cousin in the ribs, Caitlin gave vent to her annoyance with it all. Well, all the silly swooning would soon be over when he proved himself a coward, handsome or not.

The eerie drone of the bagpipes silenced all talk as the two adversaries advanced, swords leveled. Like a grotesque dance they bent and swayed. The air rang with the sound of blade on blade. It was a brutal fight. Grueling. Dangerous. Even so, Caitlin was surprised to see that the fisherman was making a good showing for himself. Certainly he was giving as good as he was getting. Though she wouldn't have admitted it, he was slowly earning her respect.

Well perhaps I dinna wish him to lose too miserably after all........ But lose he must, she told herself, grimacing as he narrowly ducked out of the way of his opponent's sword. For if he didn't she would soon find herself wed. *And being a wife to such a man would be terrible. Wouldn't it?* Nodding her head she gave herself reassurance that it would. And all the while the battle raging on the field grew fiercer and fiercer.

The sun beat down full force as the two men lashed out at each other again and again. Sweat ran into Niall's eyes blinding him for an instant. Caitlin could nearly feel his pain as the tip of Angus blade tore the flesh of his arm. Covering her mouth with her hand she stifled her cry.

"So, Caitlin. It seems ye dunna dislike him so much after all," her cousin was quick to point out.

"I just dinna want him to be killed," she responded stiffly. "A long stay in the dungeon for him is all I desire." Or so she told herself. Then why was she gripping her hands so tightly together? Why did she gasp as Angus missed the fisherman's head by little more than a finger's length?

Niall's arm blazed with pain. Despite his torment, however, he used his wits. He pressed in, driving his brawny opponent back as he tried to maneuver him onto the rough ground and over the rocks. Niall plied him on the right side, then on the left, moving with the grace of a mountain cat.

"Look at him. He moves like some ancient god," Caitlin's cousin proclaimed. It as obvious how much she was smitten.

"Luck. Sheer luck. That is all that it is....." Even so, Caitlin was impressed, but suspicious as well. How was it possible for a man who made his living with a net to be able to counter Angus' attacks so skillfully? It was a matter she was determined to find out, she thought as she watched the combat proceed.

Niall pulled himself from the ground, keeping his eyes on his adversary's sword, feeling his head grow light as the blade whistled before him. He could feel his breath hammering inside his chest and knew that he was winded. His arm felt so heavy that it took great effort to lift it.

"Ye willna escape me so easily this time." Disappointed that his weapon had not drawn blood, Niall's foe threw himself upon him. Locked together in combat the two men rolled upon the ground as the clansmen rumbled their excitement.

"By God! I had no idea the mon could fight. He's a natural born swordsman." Ian's eyes held a new respect.

Freeing himself from the large man's grip, Niall stood up. This time it was he who initiated the assault, diving for Angus's legs. With a sudden burst of strength he tore the sword from his adversary's hand and hurled it away. Was the crashing in his ears from the onlookers or from his heart? He fought to catch his breath, certain that his lungs were so cramped there would be no room for any air.

Angus scrambled to retrieve his weapon. The sound of sword on sword rent the air as the two men renewed their furious battle, a test of strength, courage and fortitude. Niall's aching eyes seemed to imagine three men at one time hurtling toward him, lunging, striking. Shaking his head, he sought to clear his vision as Angus poked out with the tip of his blade. Pain pierced Niall's shoulder. The warmth of his own blood seeped from the fresh wound in his arm, mingling with the first to run in a rivulet down his arm.

Angus was trying to maneuver him to the slope of the ground to gain advantage of footing but Niall would have none of that. Over and over again he remembered the tales of prowess and how the heroes of old had won their battles and he mimicked their daring.

"Perhaps this willna be a rout after all," a young boy shouted out.

"Look. Angus is getting angry. And when he does he sometimes loses his head."

Caitlin looked up, dismayed to see that it was true. Angus was brawny and strong, it was true but what he had in strength he lacked in brains. Now it was clear to see that the fisherman was easily out-thinking him, goading him into foolish moves.

Come on. Come on," Niall taunted, baiting his combatant as one might a bear. He had to win! He would win. For the sake of the MacDonald honor. For the sake of his own.

"Hmmmph." Again and again the large man lunged, his anger at being so easily thwarted making him careless. His senses honed by danger, his sword arm swinging forward, Niall blocked each thrust until with a sudden burst of strength he knocked his enemy's sword from his hand again.

Caitlin blinked her eyes and in just that short span of time Niall had Angus on the ground the blade of the sword pressed against his neck. The clansmen roared their excitement.

"Nae!" She couldn't believe it. Somehow she felt betrayed. By Angus. By her father. By all the ghosts and spirits of the MacLeod who had allowed this atrocity to occur. She wanted to rebel, to shout out, but all she could do was to sit there, stunned as she listened to her father's proclamation.

"As has been promised, the fisherman is declared innocent of any evil doing concerning the Fairy Flag."

His announcement was met with shouts and cheers for there was none among them who did not place value on a winner.

"And.....and......." Ian MacLeod cleared his throat. "He has won himself a very dear prize. The hand of my daughter, Caitlin." The words were spoken. Cailtlin's fate was sealed.

A soft whispering breeze caressed Caitlin's face as she stood atop the castle battlement wall-walk. She was going to be married. Her father had publically made the declaration. To the victor came the reward. Still, she couldn't quite believe it. Belonging to someone else for the rest of your life was an unnerving thought. To be married, to a man she hardly even knew seemed so strange. Bothersome. Odd. And yet that was the way of things. A woman's fate was never in her own hands but in the hands of those she loved and trusted.

Father, how could ye? To him it was all so simple, just like playing a chess game. He wasn't being hardhearted about the matter, to the contrary he had told her a hundred times or more that he wasn't at all happy about what he had to do. It was just that he needed a successor to take over as clan leader when he grew old and senile. If that made her feel a bit like a human sacrifice, like little more than a womb to breed the future MacLeod, well again, that was the way of clan life.

To tell the truth, despite her irritation at the situation, Caitlin knew she could have fared worse. There were those women who had been forced to marry weak men, old men, ugly men and fools. At least her future bridegroom was none of these.

Will I be happy? Can I learn to be content? Will I grow to love my husband?

Love. Did it really exist or was it just a pleasant story warbled by the bards? Was it just a dream that women succumbed to despite its impossibility? Or was it all a lie?

Caitlin's mother was impossible to talk with on the matter. She was always bitter on the subject. Angry. Defiant. It was not all kisses and embraces, she had insisted. She had said that there were things a wife had to do that were less than enjoyable, but necessary if there were to be children.

"Men lust, women love," she had said over and over again. But was it true? Caitlin blushed as she remembered the vibrant stirrings she had felt deep within her at the sight of the fisherman's body. Stirrings she had not been able to control no matter how hard she tried. Even now, remembering, she felt her body come to life with a strange tormented longing.

Oh, but he was a man who held the eye, she had to give him that. Strange that though he wore the same saffron dyed shirt as the other men, a similarly draped breacan sported, however, with a rakish air, he looked infinitely more dashing than the others. She thought him handsome, had to grudgingly admit that he was brave. But marry him?

Caitlin drew in a deep breath of fresh air, then let it out in a sigh. Just what did she think of her bridegroom to be? Her emotions were hard to define and were certainly confusing. She disliked the man, thought him a strutting rooster did she not? No. If she were totally honest with herself she would have to admit that he kindled a host of sensations she'd never thought she would feel. Desire?

From what Caitlin had heard the women chatter about she knew it to be so. Some talked of their husbands with awe, some in rapture and there were others who spoke of hating the "duties" they were called upon to enact. Men could be tender it seemed or brutes. What would the tall, muscular tawny-haired fisherman be like?

"Caitlin." The voice was low, a husky familiar rumble.

"So, 'tis ye," she whispered without even turning around. "Did ye come here to gloat?"

"Gloat?" He laughed softly. "No. Just to appreciate the beauty you offer, soothing and stimulating to a man's eyes. And to talk."

"Talk?" Reaching up she brushed her flaming red hair out of her eyes. "What could we possibly hae to talk about?"

"I can think of many things." He wanted to see her smile, hear her laugh. Instead, however, he contented himself with looking at her. She reminded him of a beautiful bird and he had no wish for her to elude him. If he moved closer would she fly away?

"Such as our wedding?"At last Caitlin turned to him.

"Aye." Slowly he moved forward, longing to gather her into his arms. Under different circumstances Niall suspected they might really have had a chance of being happy. "Caitlin."

Her hands stretched out as if to push him away were he to come too close. "Ye want to talk. We'll talk." Her face was as expressionless as a mask.

"I only wanted to say that It wasna my intent to make ye unhappy."

"It doesna matter. *I* do no' matter. Not to you, not to the MacLeod."

"Oh, but you do." He wanted to quickly heal the rift between them. It would make things so much easier.

"Then why do ye no' leave me alone?"

"Because......." He slowly moved towards her.

Her eyes blazed fire. "Ach, no! I willna believe yer lies. Ye came to steal the flag, laddie, no' to marry up wi' me. I caught ye and so ye concocted yer story." She paused, then added, "at least let's hae truth between us."

"Truth. Aye, I'll tell it plainly. I find ye very, very bonnie, Caitlin. On that I dunna hae to lie." His eyes were bold as he assessed what soon would belong to him, at least until he left the MacLeod stronghold. "I look forward to our marriage and....."

"I dunna want to consumate our marriage." There, she had said it.

There was a long moment of silence as Niall thought the matter out, then he said gently, "if, as happens with maidens such as yerself, ye are afraid of what happens between a woman and a mon, I will make it a most pleasant encounter. I......"

"I am no' afraid. I just refuse to accept any mon against my will."

"I see." Her words were a devastating blow to his pride. "I'm no ogre, lass."

"Nae, ye are not. But neither am I some prize." She spoke honestly. "A woman wants to be wooed, not won in combat."

"Wooed?" There was something enticing about her wide, sensuous mouth. For just a moment all he could think about was kissing her. Would her lips be as soft as they looked?

"Wooed." The way he was gazing at her made her shiver. Hastily she turned her head. "Besides, I dunna even know yer name."

"My name is Niall." That much he could reveal.

"Niall." She liked the name. Somehow it seemed to suit him.

"Don't shut yer heart to me, lass.." The way she kept looking away was annoying. Gently grasping her by the shoulders, he turned her around. For one timeless moment they stared at each, both wondering how just a look could be so exciting.

Without a word Niall caught a fistful of her long silken hair and wrapped it around his hand, drawing her closer. With the tips of his fingers he traced the line of her cheekbones, the shape of her mouth, the line of her brows.

"Give it a chance, Caitlin......." His face hovered only inches from her own. "Give me a chance." His appraising gaze seemed to cherish her, his words mesmerized her and though Caitlin knew all the reasons she should pull away, she somehow did not. Then all at once it was too late.

At first he simply held her, his hands exerting a gentle pressure to draw her into the warmth of his embrace. Then before Caitlin could make a sound his mouth claimed hers in a gentle kiss, one completely devastating to her senses. She was engulfed in a whirlpool of sensations. Breathless, her head whirling she allowed herself to be drawn up into the mists of the spell. New sensations clamored within her. All she could think about was that her fantasies were right. A kiss could be most enjoyable.

Leaning against him, Caitlin savored the feel of his strength, dreamily she gave herself up to the fierce sweetness of his mouth, her lips opening under his as exciting new sensations flooded through her. She was aware of her body as she had never been before, relished the emotions churning within her.

Niall's lips parted the soft yielding flesh beneath his, searching out the honey of her mouth. With a low moan he thrust his fingers within the soft, silken waterfall of her hair, drawing her ever closer. Desire choked him, all the hungry promptings of his fantasies warring with his reason. His lips grew demanding, changing from gentleness to passion as his hands moved down her shoulders and began to roam at will with increasing familiarity. More than anything in the world he wanted to make love to this young woman. If there was to be a wedding between them, he wouldn't agree to keeping their union celibate. Only the village simpleton would strike such a bargain.

"If it's wooing that ye want, then I agree," he whispered. "And I promise to hae ye cooing like a dove in no time."

"Cooing?" Caitlin stiffened, remembering that she was the MacLeod's daughter. Not some village wench to tumble. "Let me go...." she commanded.

"Let you go?" He did. with a sudden step backward that nearly made her stumble.

Caitlin was angry, thus she threw the first insult that she could think of at his head. "Fishermon! I wilna let ye e'er touch me!"

"Because ye think yerself so high and mighty?" Niall bit his lip against the words he longed to say, that his lineage was every bit as good as hers, perhaps better since he was a MacDonald. Instead he said simply, "Well, there will come a time when ye will hae to step down from yer pedestal and walk among the common folk."

Oh, how she riled him. There were hundreds of pretty young women in the Highlands, yet somehow at this moment she was the only one he wanted. Because she was playing hard to get? Perhaps. Niall was used to women throwing themselves into his arms. Well, he would have this lass begging for his kisses too. Soon.

"And become a fishermon's wife, weaving nets?" Caitlin affected a haughty air. "I think not."

"And *I* think......."

Niall was interrupted before he was able to give her the scolding she deserved. A young man had come upon them, informing him that the MacLeod desired an audience with him.

"Dunna leave just yet." Caitlin followed after him as he descended the stairs, knowing full well what her father wanted to talk about. The wedding. She wanted to hear, wanted to know what was going to come but knew that she would not be consulted in any way. It was as if she were invisible. Inconsequential. That did not mean that she could not eavesdrop as soon as the door behind her father and her future husband was closed, however. Putting her ear to the keyhole, she listened.

"There is much I like about you. I hae need of such in my clan," she heard her father say. *"All my daughters are bonnie lassies. But women after all. Being my son-in-law will gi' ye a measure of importance."*

Ha, Caitlin thought. Importance that will soon go to his head. Having been just a fisherman she doubted that this Niall would be able to handle being a man of influence. Well, she would keep him in line.

"My only hope of carrying out my line is through grandsons so I am hoping that ye will be quick about......." There was the sound of ribald laughter.

"Father!" she breathed, blushing to the roots of her hair. Men. They were all alike, thinking of nothing but what went on under the covers.

"I'll put it to ye bluntly. One of the terms of the marriage contract is that ye gi' me grandsons right away. If ye be unable......."

"Ye hae it on my word that I will most gladly gi' ye a grandchild right way."

"Ach!" Caitlin covered the gasp with her hand. How could he? How could her father be so crude. As if what he was negotiating was little more than the usual kind of business. He was talking about the use of her body as if talking about the use of his lands. How could she ever forgive him?

The usual haggling followed and the cleric sent in to draw up the contract. It specified the bride's dowry, several rich acres of pastureland between the two strongholds. Land made fertile with the blood of the clan in their fight against the MacDonalds. Ian in turn asked for the use of Niall's fleet of fishing boats, insisted on being given one out of every five fish that were caught, and requested that Niall lend a fighting hand whenever there was need.

"All is agreed." Caitlin heard her "bridegroom" say.

"Then the banns will be posted on the next three successive Sundays. In the meantime there will be a celebration. Feasting. Dancing. Drinking."

"To celebrate my servitude," Caitlin said aloud. Well, let them think that all was said and done. They would soon find out that things were not always as easy as they at first appeared.

Chapter Eight

The MacLeod clan had gone all out for the festivities that evening. The large hall was bathed in firelight and candle glow, from the planked floor to the high lofty ceiling. Flames in the vast hearth danced about spewing tongues of red and yellow, illuminating the clan banner hanging proudly for all to see. Rushes and herbs - basil, balm, chamomile, costmary, and cowslip had been freshly strewn on the floor for the occasion. The walls of the castle were ornamented with hanging objects and artifacts - shields, swords, dirks and clay'mors--which told of the MacLeod bravery.

Tables covered with platters and bowls were nearly sagging under the weight of the food piled high - wild duck with wine sauce, smoked haddock, roast grouse with sprigs of heather, roast venison, pickled herring, boiled goose eggs, beet root salad, curds, wild carrots, honey cakes and wild raspberries. Barley broth bubbled noisily in a cauldron over the fire, its steam giving off an aroma which heightened appetites. The aroma of roasting meat permeated the air. Platters were artfully arrayed with fruits and vegetables in great variety. Red heather and ropes of laurel hung from wall and ceiling alike and combined their fragrance with the tantalizing aroma of the betrothal feast. A celebration Ian had promised and indeed that's what it was.

HIGHLAND DESTINY

A raised dias of stone ran the full length of the hall, across from the fireplace upon which many of the guests sat. Ian MacLeod sat in one of the massive chairs at a table placed across from the others. Raised at a lofty heighth by means of a platform he looked awesome as he peered down at the assemblage. Extra trestle tables and several benches had been assembled to accommodate the overflow of clansmen. Niall sat to the left of the MacLeod and the vacant chair to his right was unquestionably for the bride to be. A bride that was still conspicuous by her absense.

Where is she? Why isn't she here? Niall was impatient. He watched as Ian MacLeod was served the heroes portion, the first cut of meat, a gesture to show him to be the bravest of the clansmen and to assure that his status was noted by all present. As Niall drank and supped he looked at the door from time to time, but his staring didn't bring his bride-to-be into the room any sooner.

She wouldn't dare be conspicuous by her absence. Or would she. The longer he sat staring at the door the more he drank and the more he drank the more certain he became that he was about to be snubbed.

"Oh no! I willna let her" Bolting up from his chair, he made his way to the door. He would find her. Even if he had to search the entire castle. Find her and bring her here. If he had to carry her into the hall kicking and screaming, he would make certain she obeyed.

Caitlin was at the moment taking plenty of time in readying herself for the night's celebrating. And why not? She was in no hurry to go to a celebration that in her heart emphasized her doom.

Caitlin plundered her large wooden trunk and pulled several items of clothing from the pegs on the wall, determining to find just the right garments to wear tonight. Indeed she would clothe herself with as much care as if she were going into battle. Perhaps in a way she was, she mused.

"My old threadbare undertunic" she decided aloud and a dun-colored arasaid, the one Shona had woven for her a long time ago on the large loom in the ladies' hall. Plain garments. If her father was going to marry her to a fisherman she would look like a fisherman's wife.

She was expert in draping the saffron and blue striped arisaid around her slim body, tucking it around her hips, fitting it snugly around her waist with a brown leather belt. Yards and yards of cloth fell in graceful folds just below her ankles, then lopped up to cover her shoulders like a shawl. She secured it with a broach, a hand worked gold circle with intricate scrollwork.

Observing herself in a long steel mirror she smiled as she stared back at her reflection with a certain amount of gratification. If she had decided to look like a fisherman's wife, however, she did not want to smell like one. Picking up a small packet of flowers and herbs that Shona always used in her bath, she made the decision to be frivolous on this occasion.

Since it was the third day of the week it would be the women's turn to bathe. And since everyone would be at the celebration she would have the room all to herself. In truth, perhaps she would feel much better once she had the warm cocoon of water surrounding her. It would relax her and give her time to think things out, to get used to the idea of having a husband. So thinking, she grabbed an old woolen tartan and made her way to the bath house.

Pushing open the thick wooden portal, Caitlin was grateful to see that all of the six large wooden tubs that studded the rush strewn floor were empty. She would have the seldom granted opportunity of privacy. A well for washing or drinking water was available at the central drawing point thus she busied herself with procuring a plentiful supply, filling the buckets and heating the water in the large iron pots that were perched over an open fire.

Struggling under the heavy burden of the large cauldrons she nonetheless managed to carry them to one of the tubs, completing the job of filling her bath. Turning around, lifting the skirts of her under tunic up to her knees in preparation of disrobing she heard the door creak. The sudden unwelcome feeling that someone was staring at her crept over her. Whirling around she was startled to find herself face to face with the fisherman again.

"So here you are," he said tonelessly, shutting the door behind him.

"Here I am indeed," she snapped, holding the tartan protectively up to her bosom to hide the outline of her breasts beneath the thin linen. "Tell me, are ye here to "haunt" the bath house?" she asked making reference to his masquerade as a ghost, or to try and steal the flag again?"

The soft orange-yellow glow of flickering torchlight illuminated the room and gave her a clear view of his manly form. Hardly the body of a ghost. Her eyes took in his broad shoulders and muscled arms.

"I came looking for ye!"

"Oh?" She pretended not to know how late the hour was or that she was remiss in being absent from the hall. Well as ye can see I was about to take a bath."

"A bath. Now?"

"Now!"

So that was the game she was playing. Well, Niall thought, two could play at the same game. "Then so will I." That said, he deliberately began to strip off his garments. Soon he was naked to the waist, wearing only a breacan, revealing his manly torso and the thick wisp of dark golden hair covering his chest. For a long moment all Caitlin could do was stare.

"We are all alone…" She said, feeling a measure of apprehension.

"And formally betrothed." He took a step forward.

She backed away and looked towards the door. "That doesna give ye any liberties, at least yet." The only way out was to go past him and this she did not want to do. She wanted to maintain as great a distance as possible between them.

"Nae, not yet." But just wait a while, his hot, burning eyes seemed to say.

"Not ever," Caitlin taunted. "I will marry ye because I must but I am not a brood mare." She tossed her head, sending her fiery hair flying about her shoulders.

"Ye must want children, lassie." The idea of a MacLeod bearing his child made him smile. What magnificent irony. Almost as good as bringing back the Fairy Flag.

"Someday......."

In the silence that pervaded the room each one was conscious of the other, the subject of babies reminding each of them of how the seed was planted.

"I want to make love to ye, Caitlin. I want ye to want that too."

She was aware of him in every nerve, pore and bone in her body. "So that ye can easily fulfill the terms of the marriage contract?"

"Nae. Because ye are like a living dream. So very desirable."

He could not keep his eyes from the cleft between her breasts that showed just slightly when she bent over, nor could he keep from watching the sway of her hips as she moved. In a flickering glance he took in everything about her.

By all the saints, he unnerved her most definitely, confused her with contradicting emotions. In the end it was fear that won out, however. Caitlin started to turn away but just at that moment he reached out and captured her hand. Bending low over it, he pressed his warm mouth into the palm in a gesture he'd heard was used at the Scottish court.

In a gesture of defiance, she pulled her hand away. "Don't....." It made her feel too fluttery. Too vulnerable to the feelings he stirred within her. She found herself remembering the pressure of those warm knowing lips against hers.

The soft material of her tunic tightened across her firm breasts. Niall fought against the urge to force her in his arms. It would only goad her resentment. Instead he chose to a more gentle kind of persuasion. "I'm a fishermon not a bard. I know not any flowery words that will make ye fall in love with me. All I can do is speak the truth and hope yer heart will listen. Don't turn yer back on me, lass. Gi' me a chance." An impassioned plea. Then he slipped his garments back on and disappeared through the door.

Oh, but he was the canny one, she thought. Even so, the wall she had built around her heart crumbled just a little. Strange but she hummed to herself as she quickly bathed then as soon as she was dressed, she slipped through the doorway and down the circular staircase that led to the second floor.

Boisterous laughter and mumbled voices stilled as the crowd caught sight of her. When Caitlin entered everyone turned their head. The whispered gasps sounded like the rustling wind, but she ignored them, making her way to the table.

"Daughter, were ye already married I would gi yer husband my approval to beat ye," Ian grumbled beneath his breath. "Ye shame him and ye shame me by looking poverty stricken."

"And ye shame me by this mockery of a marriage," she retorted. Even so, she felt a small twinge of guilt. Perhaps the fisherman was right. Perhaps she should give him a chance, albeit a small one.

Caitlin was quiet as cups were filled to the brim with fiery whiskey. Tankards were passed among the revelers again and again. Dogs snapped at the table scraps tossed to them, fighting now and again over a tasty morsel.

The aroma of fruit decorated bannocks, baked specially for the occasion wafted in the air as they were passed around, but Niall had lost his appetite. He wished the evening would end, that he could take her by the hand and lead her away from this melee. There were many questions he wanted to ask, many things to be said, he to her and she to him.

"Aren't ye hungry?" Caitlin's tone was gentle, showing an unusual caring as she turned to Niall.

"I've already eaten too much." The truth that he was starved for much more than food. She was so lovely in the candlelight. He wanted to touch her again as he had in the bathhouse and was afforded that opportunity when she picked up a scone and handed it him. He took her small gift, their fingers brushing in a gentle caress, one that sparked a flame deep within him .

Caitlin's sparkling eyes met his over the rim of her cup as she sipped her wine. She stared into his eyes, eyes that regarded her so intently. She wished she could read his mind. The unhappy look upon his face nearly made her feel sorry for him. Nervously she tugged at her broach wondering if he had changed his mind about marrying her. She had given him quite a time. And after all, at least he was handsome. She could have done worse. Glancing at him out of the corner of her eye she began to see her betrothed in a whole different light.

Amidst the candle glow and firelight, the bard stood and began strumming the strings of his harp. He sang a droning, seemingly endless account of the MacLeod ancestry and a lavish praise of the clan, which usually held Caitlin in rapt attention, but now caused her to be anxious for its end. She had other things on her mind. Like getting to know her bridegroom for one thing. It suddenly struck her that she knew nothing about him at all.

The wine she sipped relaxed her but when she looked in her groom's direction she felt a mild anxiety. What did she really know about this man who was to become he husband? As if sensing her searching eyes, he looked again in her direction and she could tell that he was troubled too. Was he wondering the same things she was wondering.

What will it be like to share my life with this man? Would she enjoy his lovemaking and moan with pleasure at his touch? What would she experience in the years that lay ahead? With a sigh she turned her attention back to the bard, closing her eyes, her mind gently drifting with thoughts of what was to come. At last the song ended and the men clapped and roared their approval.

Grudgingly Niall joined in, remembering all the while that with each MacLeod victory had come a MacDonald defeat and MacDonald death. How then could he even pretend to agree to this farce of a wedding? Because the woman was beautiful and he lusted for her? Though he knew this to be partly so, he denied it to his conscious mind. It was to get his hands on the flag and only that.

"Caitlin MacLeod is a shrew. I will be well quit of her when I leave this castle", he said to himself. Yet at the same time he felt a conflicting emotion. A strange sense of loss for what might have been had they each been other than they were.

The room became silent as Ian MacLeod stood up. "As ye know, we're gathered tonight to make celebration." He took Caitlin's hand, gently pulling her to her feet. "My daughter will gi' her hand in marriage to Niall, the fishermon. A fine and brave lad as ye hae all seen."

Caitlin looked at the tawny-haired man expecting him to smile at her. She was met by a cold stare and could only wonder why. Was he then marrying her only for the sense of power being the MacLeod's son-in-law brought? Were his tender words in the bath house nothing but words then. Empty words? For the first time in her life her confidence slipped. Though always sure of herself, she was not so sure of herself now. Sweet Jesu, what had she gotten herself into with her stubbornness?

Goblets, tankards and platters were cleared away. Benches were pushed back, the trestle tables folded and placed against the wall in preparation for dancing. The pipes began their keening, a familiar tune Caitlin recognized at once. First the men danced alone, a rousing dance of high kicking feet, then the women joined in, chosing partners for a spirited reel which set every foot tapping.

The Great Hall was a din of laughing, talking, accompanied by the drone of skirling pipes and the thumping feet of dancers. But Caitlin had no heart for the revelry. For the first time in her life she sincerely wished she could make herself invisible - flee the hall and the man who put her emotions into such violent turmoil.

Chapter Nine

Darkness was gathering under the high lofty ceiling. Shadows hovered in the corners and behind the massive pillars of the room like eerie spirits waiting to pounce. The flames engulfing the huge logs in the hearth sputtered and burned low. One by one the smoking candles and torches that had once brightened the hall flickered, hissed, and then died out.

The hour was growing even late. The women had retired with the small children leaving the men alone at their drinking. Very few guests lingered at the trestle tables. Watching and waiting, Niall thought to himself that if he were patient, if he lingered in the hall, eventually the opportunity would arise when he could once again get his hands on the Fairy Flag.

"Just a little longer....." he murmured, then raising a mug of whiskey to his lips he tried to relax as he waited it out, tried to remove Caitlin MacLeod from his mind.

One slim, haughty red-haired lass was not going to get the best of him. He'd prove to her just how little he cared. He'd avoid that often-frowning miss, pretend she was as invisible as a ghost whenever he was forced to be in her company. Aye, that he would. He'd bite his tongue before he gave her one kind word. He would be damned before he'd look her way. He'd hurry and be done with this business of the fairy flag and return to the MacDonald Hall without another thought about her..

"So, the happy bridegroom."

Niall was startled as one of the men came up behind him, a tall dark-haired youth with the look of a fighter about him. "Aye, the happy bridegroom," he answered, trying to sound enthusiastic. All the while he was envisioning his "betrothed" in his mind as if she still sat beside him, her nose at that lofty angle, her flaming hair tumbling down her back in thick waves. He had always told himself that women were as plentiful as waves in the sea. But no one was like Caitlin MacLeod. Niall leaned his elbows on the table, wanting to be alone.

Solitude was not to be his. "Jamie is my name." The young man plopped down on the chair that Caitlin had vacated.

"Niall."

"I know." There was a sparkle in Jamie's eye. "And I know just what ye are contemplating."

"Oh?" For a moment Niall was worried. There were some who were said to have the fey. Hopefully this man wasn't among them.

"Ye think to gain power on Skye by mating wi' the MacLeod's daughter. But it willna work." The expression on Jamie's face was smug.

"Ye dunna say." At that moment Niall thoroughly disliked the other man. He knew his type. A man with an inflated sense of himself. "And just why would that be?" He tried to make the question sound casual, tried to hide his aversion to the clansman.

"Ye willna be accepted. Not really." He sniffed disdainfully. "Once a fishermon, always a fishermon." Without even noticing Niall's look of anger he rattled on. "So ye see, ye hae tied yerself to that hellion for naught."

"That hellion, as ye call her, will soon be my wife." Niall's eyes glittered a warning. "I would caution ye to hold yer tongue."

"Well, I'll be......" Jamie threw back his head and laughed. "Ye must be daft, laddie. Ye are taken wi' the stubborn lass."

Taken with her? Niall shook his head, denying the truth, but heaven help him it was true.

"Because she doesna want to be yours. The forbidden fruit is always sweeter."

A muscle tightened in Niall's jaw. His eyes were cold. "And the grapes a man canna claim are always sour." He took another gulp of his whiskey, suddenly putting two and two together. "She didna want ye, did she."

The barb struck home. "Caitlin MacLeod is a fool."

"Or as wise as the Brieve who gives out the laws." Now it was Niall's turn to chuckle.

Jamie pursed his lips in anger. Raising his fist he looked as if he might lash out, but with a smirk he merely said, "The laugh will be on ye, fishermon, for getting far, far more than ye bargained for." That said he left in a huff.

More than I bargained for? Niall imagined for a moment Caitlin MacLeod lying naked in her bridal bed. Strange how he'd never even contemplated marrying before, had always thought marriage a curse. He must be bewitched. "Aye much more......" For just a moment he nearly forget just why he had come to the MacLeod stronghold. Forgot the anger between his clan and hers. Then all too quickly reality pushed away his lustful fantasies.

Rising to his feet, he strode up and down the hall like a prowling wolf, waiting and watching as one by one the men departed for their chambers. Lingering behind, Niall watched stealthfully as the lights were extinguished, leaving the castle in near darkness. Brushing his long hair over his shoulder, he moved toward the door with all the furtiveness of his desperation.

He'd get himself in the tower room as quickly as possible. How he hoped that the flag had been put back in the same place. If Caitlin had hidden it somewhere else he would just have to tear the castle apart until he found it. Looking from side to side, Niall cautiously made his way up the stairs, little realizing that he was being watched.

"Just as I thought......" She had hoped that she was wrong but as Caitlin watched Niall's assent to the tower room his own actions fiercely condemned him. "The villain!"

She was stung with a mixture of anger and sadness. For just a moment she had actually thought that there was hope for them in this travesty of a marriage. Now she knew that she was wrong. He only wanted one thing from the MacLeod stronghold and that something wasn't her.

"He is a thief!" And what else? What prompted him to this deceitful action? She could only wonder as she watched in outraged silence, then stealthfully followed him.

Fumbling around in the dark, Niall cursed as he anxiously searched the tower room for the flag. If he were caught he had little doubt but that this time it would mean his life. A man could only talk themselves out of trouble once. There would be no second battle to redeem himself. Ian MacLeod would have his hide. He would......

Niall heard a noise behind him, but not soon enough to move aside before he was jumped upon from behind. For just a moment he was held immobile by his assailant, then in a burst of strength he got the upper hand.

"Aha. Ye had me but now I hae ye!"

Caitlin opened her mouth to curse him, but words would not come. She was winded. Her heart beat painfully in her breast, she couldn't breathe. Nevertheless she struggled fiercely.

"Stop yer fighting or by God I will......" In that moment Niall grabbed hold of his attacker's wrists. Small wrists. Fine boned. Though it was dark he knew. "Caitlin."

She somehow forced herself to answer. "Aye, it's me."

"Following me like a shadow."

"Because I knew ye couldna be trusted." There was a tone of disappointment in her voice. "Oh, how could ye? And after Father gave ye a second chance."

Her criticism stung him, as did the sudden slap to his cheek as he freed her arms. Wordlessly Niall rubbed at his face. "I hae my reasons, Caitlin." Oh, damn the lass. He was incensed that she had once again so thoroughly hindered his plans.

"Reasons? Well, they will be interesting to hear, do ye ken?"

He did understand. All too well. It made Caitlin MacLeod very dangerous to his wellbeing at the moment. All she had to do now was call out and bring the house down upon his head and he would find himself food for the gulls. But there was a way to insure that he would be safe. All he had to do was put his hands around her throat and squeeze.

Silence her. Silence her forever. She is the only person blocking your victory and escape.

Slowly he brought his hands up, then quickly let them fall to his side. No, he couldn't kill her.

She is my enemy. A MacLeod. Her father has given orders that have sent dozens of MacDonalds to their death. And yet that didn't matter. All he knew was that he couldn't harm a hair upon her lovely head. Even so, that didn't keep him from threatening.

"I should strangle ye!"

Caitlin jumped back. "Do and my father and the others will hunt ye down like a dog."

"No doubt they would. But it wouldna bring ye back to life." He shook his head. "Ah, Caitlin, lass. Do wi' me what ye will. I am not a murderer." Oh, but she smelled so good. Like spices mixed tantalizingly with flowers.

"Ye didna want to marry me." Stange how that stung her pride despite her protestations about matrimony herself. "Did ye?"

Wisely Niall didn't answer.

"Yer fine story to my father was naught but a foul lie, just as I knew all along. Well, it will soon be told to all and then ye will be punished just as ye should be."

"Nae!" Once again Niall raised his hands, the realization that he must silence her foremost on his mind. As his eyes held and locked with Caitlin's, however, he knew the futility of even contemplating the act. "Do wi' me what ye will, I canna harm ye."

For just a moment she was shaken. There had been something in his eyes when he had looked at her. A gentleness, a look of caring. Could it be? She told herself that it could not. The fisherman was nothing but an opportunist whose presence here was disruptive and dangerous. Still, she said, "It seems that ye cannot." At least she could give him that. "And I will remind Father of that when he decides upon yer punishment." Which she knew well would be to languish in the oubliette, a dungeon within a dungeon where the unfortunate prisoner had just sufficient room to lie in complete darkness. A custom the Scots had learned from the French long ago. There he would slowly die of starvation with no hope of rescue. A gruesome end.

"Ah, ye will speak to yer father on my behalf. Then most sincerely I thank ye." Niall mockingly bowed, all the while masking his apprehension. Oh, but she would stir up a bee's nest down below. The entire castle would be up in arms when she sounded the alarm. Unless he silenced her. Why then was he merely standing by like a suicidal fool? Why didn't he at least tie her up. Gag her. Insure her silence. Why didn't he.......

As the door burst open it was quickly out of his hands. "What is going on up here?" Ian MacLeod burst through the door, a torch held aloft in his hands. Suspiciously he looked first at Caitlin then at Niall. Niall realized in that moment that it was possible the MacLeod had been testing his loyalty. Blindly he might have walked into a trap. "Well, Daughter?"

Tell him. Tell him that the man he so heartlessly betrothed me to is obviously a danger to the clan. Tell him that you found him with the flag. Tell him. A myriad of emotions coursed through Caitlin's body as she looked her father right in the eye. She opened her mouth to tattle, nearly choking as she said instead, "He...he...." A cry rose in her soul and she started to condemn Niall but ended up whispering, "We were.....were doing a bit of kissing, Father."

"Kissing?" His thick brows shot up in surprise.

"That is what those who are betrothed to be married do, isn't it?" For the life of her, Caitlin would never understand why she had lied for the fisherman, but she had. And in so doing had sealed her own fate lest she be found out to be a deceiver.

Ian was pleased. "Aye. Aye."

Wordlessly Niall played along with the charade, putting his arm around Caitlin and drawing her close.

"Ach, they say that a threesome is a bother, especially when one is the father," Ian said with a wink. Hurriedly he headed for the door, talking more to himself than to them. "I knew it would happen if ye but allowed yerself. I knew it, Caity." He was decidedly jovial as he bounded from the room.

"Why?" It was the only word that escaped from Niall's lips as the door closed behind the MacLeod.

Why had she shielded him? He had been caught trying once again to steal the flag, and although he hadn't actually pilfered it, she knew. She knew. Then why? "Ye lied for me, lass. Tell me why."

"I dunna know," she whispered. And she didn't. Surely it didn't make any sense.

"Is it possible that ye care for me then at least a little?" Niall asked, his ego bolstered by the act.

"Nae!" And just to prove it she reminded him that his fate was still in her hands. Were she to change her mind he might still find himself languishing in the dungeon. "And I will tell if you e'er try to take the flag again." She pointed toward the door. "Go, and remember I will be watching ye."

Niall lay in bed staring up at the ceiling as he mulled over a dozen things in his mind, foremost the MacLeod's daughter's last words to him. "Go, and remember I will be watching ye."

Watching! The very idea of being spied upon like a naughty boy angered him. He was one of the mighty MacDonalds, the most powerful, widespread, and ancient of all the Highland clans. The Macdonalds had ruled the Highlands as Lords of the Isles for nearly four centuries. How then could he allow some slip of a lassie to threaten him? And yet......

His annoyance at the situation quickly cooled as he remembered that she could have so easily betrayed him to her father. Just one word, one hint, and he would have found himself trussed up like a goose ripe for plucking. Instead, she had covered for him and told her father that the two of them had more amorous things in mind. Did he?

Yes. He was taken with the MacLeod woman. She was bold, beguiling, and beautiful. Unfortunately she was also a distraction to his purposes. He must ignore her, thrust her into a part of his brain where he would not be tempted. He had to be aware of his purpose here at all times and keep an arm's length away from the girl.

Alas, it was an easy vow to whisper but a difficult one to keep. The moment he closed his eyes her image danced about in his brain teasing him like an aphrodisiac. He remembered the way her breasts had felt as she had brushed against his chest, the way her fiery hair tumbled around her shoulders, the way her eyes glittered when she was angry. He remembered the way----

Niall sat up in bed with a start. What was happening to him? When had it happened. Worse yet, how was he going to control it? What exactly was he going to do? Was he going to ignore the lass or take advantage of being betrothed?

Usually Niall tried to avoid searching his soul, fearing an inward look at what drove him on. Now, however, he thought it wise to take time to think. Really think.

What are you to do about Caitlin MacLeod?

Slowly his thoughts gained coherence as he sorted out his emotions. He had come to the MacLeod stronghold with but one thought in mind, to steal the fairy flag so that he could increase his esteem and usefulness to his clan. How was he ever to suspect that such a simple mission could be so complicated by his feelings. Feelings he was not quite sure he could really identify.

Again Niall asked himself, *what am I to do about Caitlin MacLeod?*

The creaking of the door put aside the question for the moment as Niall realized he was no longer alone. Staring through the darkness, he sought a glimpse of the intruder. Who was it? Someone who posed a danger? Just in case, Niall reached for the sword he had sheathed beside the bed.

"Who is there?"

Had he expected an answer it wasn't forthcoming. Instead, he heard a rustle of cloth and the soft tread of steps as the "visitor" sped away. The escape was not hasty enough, however.

"Caitlin!" Like an enchanting ghost she had come to his room, and although Niall could only assume that she had come there to spy, her late-night visit nonetheless left him even more confused about his feelings.

HIGHLAND DESTINY

Chapter Ten

Clouds and sunlight competed over the green valley. Niall MacLeod had two full days of festivities awaiting the clan as part of the betrothal ceremony. Games. Hunting. It appeared, however, that nature might not be entirely cooperative.

"Oh, who cares. Mayhap 't'is a sign."

Opening the shutter of her small bedchamber window, Caitlin peered out through the slits, gazing at the sky, thinking how the day matched the bleakness of her mood. Last night to save the fisherman's life she had lied. A sorry thing to do to her own clan no matter the reason.

"May they all forgive me!"

Her eyes touched upon her clansmen and women as they went about their morning chores. The inner courtyard rang with the sound of women's laughter and the chatter of the men as they went about the preparations for the days events. They were happy. Content. Looking forward to the marriage that would likely bring forth the new chieftain for the clan. But how happy would they be if they knew what Caitlin knew?

"Och!"

Surely it was a calamity, one which had haunted her all through the night. She hadn't slept a wink. Acutely conscious of the fact that Niall was situated just down the hall from her own chamber, she had listened to each and every sound outside in the hall, fearful that he might try to steal the flag again. At last, returning to the tower, she had taken the flag from its hiding place and brought it down to her chamber where it would be safe. Tucking it amongst her belongings she had returned to her bed only to toss and turn. She'd made so much noise in fact that she was certain poor Shona's slumber had been disturbed.

"Get a hold on yerself, lassie," she scolded silently, still caught up in her guilt. "Stop wondering what might happen." It would only bring her more frustration. What was done was done. The lie was told. It was over and done with. All she could do was to keep her eye on the fisherman and make certain that no further mischief was done.

And go on with the wedding? How could a woman be married to a man she did not trust when trust was so important? In anger she stripped off her sleeping tunic and flung it across the room. A comb and the pillow followed. Oh, how could she have been such a fool as to lie to her father, especially for the fisherman?

"Fie, sister, What has gotten in to ye?" Shona's voice held a tone of scolding as she bounced from the bed to retrieve Caitlin's things.

"I'm sorry....."

"Och, so he's gotten under yer skin more than I realized. I should hae known." Shona clucked her tongue in sympathy.

Caitlin sighed, turning her back on her sister as she dressed in a long saffron-hued shirt and a loin cloth. "I dunna ken what ye mean," she said defensively.

" Aye, ye do. I know what's wrong, Caity."

"Ye canna." Caitlin kept her eyes averted from her sister. Somehow the honey-haired girl seemed always to be able to see into her sister's heart and mind. Caitlin could not afford that now.

"I do. Yer disappointed that he's not some noble tanist or chieftain." Gently touching her shoulder, Shona turned Caitlin around to face her, looking deeply into her eyes. "But oh, e'en if he were ye could not hae married a man who could equal him for looks."

"Nae, it was the mattress, that's all. It's lumpy and needs to be restuffed and I...I didna get a wink of sleep all night."

"I dunna imagine ye did." Playfully she tugged at Caitlin's hair in rebuke, stifling a giggle.

"Shona! Dunna think that......I...that I...." Caitlin sighed, hurriedly nodding. "Aye, I was thinking about my betrothed all right." It was not really an untruth. Tossing her flaming red hair, she returned to the window trying to make light of the subject. Looking at the crags and hills she tried to focus her thoughts on other things but Niall McDonald hovered in the room like a ghost.

"Has he kissed ye, Caity?" Shona's eyes sparkled with romantic-tinged curiosity.

Caitlin blushed. "Aye."

"And.....?"

"And what?" Why did her voice sound so shaky?

"Was it....was it wonderful?" Her closed eyes, the hand at her throat made it obvious Shona was experiencing the kiss vicariously.

"We willna talk it."

Wrapping a plaid similar to the kind the men wore, about her waist and shoulders, braiding her hair, Caitlin quickly left the room, hurrying to the hall down below.

The drone of bagpipes, trill of harps and the sound of happy chatter filled the air. A dozen or more smiling faces greeted Caitlin as she walked through the door. Though she was not in a particularly good mood everyone else was, and the gaiety was infectious, soon wiping away her frown. Everyone was busily working at some task or other, thus Caitlin took her place beside the women preparing the food. Breakfast was to be simple--porridge and fruit and fish, for the men were eager to be about the day's activities. Filling a cauldron with water from a wooden bucket, Caitlin was anxious for her chore to be done so that she could hurry out to the field. Perhaps the games would take her mind off her troubles.

She brought the water to a boil and let the oatmeal trickle into it. From the corner of her eye she scanned the room as the men filed in. And there he was. Fisherman or chieftain, he stood out like a bull amidst rams. He wore a white shirt instead of the more usual saffron and a colored breacan of bright green and black plaid, striped through with yellow and red. The long ends were draped over his left shoulder and pinned in place with a brooch. A leather sporran hanging from a belt covered his maleness. Even in the crowded room she was aware of him and he was equally aware of her. Over and over again she could feel his eyes staring.

With a chill she remembered last night, thought about the danger she had been in. He could have murdered her. Could have stolen the flag then silenced her accusation forever. Why hadn't he? Stirring the pot constantly with a spurtle--a wooden sitck about a foot long, she glanced his way, but hastily averted his gaze the moment he glanced back.

What is he thinking? Is he wondering if he is still in danger? Does he fear that I will tell on him after all? Or does he sense that I am more drawn to him emotionally than I will admit? Does he think that I am weak for not decrying his attempted thievery? Or does he feel smug and secure? Is he sorry that he did not strangle me or throw me from the tower? Or is he grateful for my silence?

She let the porridge cook steadily for a half hour as she mused about the matter, stirring to watch for lumps. But though she was determined not to scorch the porridge, she nearly did. And all because of him. That only emphasized to her what trouble he could be and already was.

Breakfast was eaten standing. Caitlin ate her oatmeal with fresh milk and salt, choosing wild berries and curds to appease her voracious appetite. When Shona teased her about it she retorted that she needed her strength for what was planned for the day. Her brow puckered in concentration. Today there would be further celebrating. Games. Horse racing. Such competition would surely make her forget what had happened last night and help sooth her conscience. Wouldn't it? So hoping she merged with the crowd as they left the great hall.

Banners flew, bagpipes played on, tents were placed haphazardly about. There was the same enthusiasm and joviality as when appreciating a fair. A field just outside the castle's walls was used for the popular game of shinnie, a simple game using curved sticks and a ball. It was a dangerous sport, one said to be the fastest ball game in the world. To play it a man needed to possess extraordinary athletic abilities--a quick eye, ready hand and a strong arm and be an excellent runner and wrestler as well.

Niall was quick and strong, ran with easy grace cutting back and forth across the pasture with his stick. Fighting the others for the ball with a reckless ferocity, he strove to impress all those who scorned his supposed occupation with boats and nets.

The field had the appearance of a battle scene. Cailtlin watched, thinking that the fiserman would make a poor showing, but he threw herself into the fracas, seemingly pleased when he caught sight of a look of surprise merged with admiration on her face.

Grudgingly, Caitlin had to admire him. He was more than a match for Erskin, Malcolm and even Jamie. This fisherman swung his stick as powerfully as her father wielded his sword. One more reason to make her suspect that he was not who or what he said he was. But then who was he?

"Ye fight as furiously as the MacLeod's during a battle," she said when the game was over, stunned that he could have learned the game so quickly. How was that possible. Or had he played the game before? "Let's see how ye measure up with a bow."

Niall moved towards a group of clansmen who were arming themselves for the hunt.   Caitlin   took time to choose a bow for herself, running her hands over the wood, testing the tension of the cord.

"Hunting with a bow? What other skills do ye have?" Niall asked.

Suspicion crowded into her thoughts. Why was Niall curious about her skill with arms? Was he assessing her as one might an enemy?

"My father has taught all his daughters to shoot and shoot well." Again, her words held a warning. "I've been hunting since I was no higher than my father's knee."

"There isn't anything ye canna do well it seems," he answered, reaching out to touch her on the shoulder.

Caitlin shrugged off his hand. "Aye. Remember that lest ye forget." A knot squeezed in the pit of her stomach as she noted that he was taking a dirk with him as well as a bow. She would have to be careful not to be alone with him lest her danger still not be over. Perhaps his interest in the hunt was because he envisioned a hunting accident.

"Forget?" His eyes stared straight into hers. "There is nothing I would ever allow myself to forget about ye, Caitlin. Nothing." *She is a MacLeod. Remember that lest ye forget.*

The hunters made their way through the forest amid a tangle of horsemen, Ian MacLeod's huge russet Wolf hounds leading the way, hot on the scent. Their voices mingled in an eager racket of barking which echoed through the lonely forest as they sighted their prey across a large burn.

It was a Predominantly oak forest Niall noticed. Some pine and birch. Much of the ground was high with a lot of bare rock and scrub, difficult to travel through. On such ground there was no animal better adapted than the red deer. Trees of many kinds grew well in the sheltered parts on this base-rich soil from the volcanic rock. There were green, even terraces with occasional gullies. Truly it was a beautiful landscape, Niall thought as he walked along. But MacLeod territory. He must remember that as well, he thought, breaking into a run. He was determined to catch up with Caitlin

MacLeod at the top of the hill. He had to talk with her. Had to know what she planned.

"Caitlin, wait!"

Hearing the frantic shout of her name only made Caitlin run faster. Only when she had caught up with her father did she allow herself to feel safe.

"We got one, daughter," she heard her father call out.

Bows were raised as the clan chieftain gave the signal. A whir of arrows stung the air, bringing down the quarry of a large red deer.

"On target!" Ian MacLeod's triumphant cry was accompanied by the sound of trampling feet and a splash as the hunters forded the water. Niall, however, did not follow. He was interested in more important things than feeling a deer. His quarry was Caitlin. In a flash of yellow and black she ran by him. She seemed to be intent upon filling her eyes with the beauty of the woodland, but Niall kept his eyes upon her. Wearing that short garment similar to a man's, her shapely, long legs were plainly visible beneath the hem of the plaid, drawing his stare again and again.

For the moment Caitlin had forgotten all about her fear of Niall as she took off in search of a bird that had disappeared into the forest. Following, she was careful to duck her head to avoid being struck in the face by the low-hanging branches. Pausing only for a moment by the bank of a small pool she looked down and it was only in that moment that she realized he was beside her

"Dinna touch me!"

"I was merely....."

Run, she thought. Get away from him. Do not tempt fate! But as she turned away he sought to stop her. He didn't want her to leave. They had to talk about last night.

"Caitlin." Having snagged and entangled his breacon in a low hanging branch, he hurriedly took out his dirk with the intent to free himself, little realizing the panic it would inspire.

"No!" Catching sight of the weapon, Caitlin's worst fears were unleashed. So, when all was said and done he was a murderer and wanted to kill her away from the castle.

"Caitlin!"

Ignoring his cry, she bolted around him, fearful of what he might say or do. She had to reach her father, had to tell him the truth before they were all ruined.

"Caitlin!"

Running so hard that she could hardly catch her breath, Caitlin looked over her shoulder. He was catching up with her. She had to move faster. She had to.......

Usually as familiar with this landscape as she was with her own hand, Caitlin forgot in her panic the way the terrain suddenly dropped down into nothing, descending sharply into the valley below. Taking a step forward she stumbled. Then she was falling. Plummeting down, down, down.

"Caitlin!" Niall shouted. His voice echoed in her ears, then she felt a fierce jolt slam through her body. She struck her head, crying out against the pain, then escaped into blessed oblivion. The sound of the fisherman calling out her name was the last thing she heard.

Chapter Eleven

Niall ran frantically towards the edge of the hill, looking down at the crumpled figure lying on the ground. "Caitlin!" Her eyes were closed. She looked frighteningly still. Scrambling down the hillside he bent over her unconscious form, whispering a fervent prayer. Please let her be alive! Seemingly his plea was answered for as he put his head to her breast he could hear her heartbeat.

"Caitlin!"

Her breathing was even though her face looked ashen. Apparently she'd struck her head when she had fallen. The cut on her forehead attested to that. Niall gently wiped the blood away with his fingertips. Cautiously he examined her, probing her arms and legs to determine if there were any broken bones. There did not seem to be, but still he was careful. He'd seen men suffer such tumbles in battle, knew it could be dangerous to move someone if they were hurt internally or had injured their spine. Even so, he could not just leave her here on the hard ground all alone. She needed help. She needed him.

Looking hastily about him Niall tried to get his bearings. He seemed to recall passing a small crofter's cottage a few yards back. At the time he'd only glanced at it, his thoughts intent on Caitlin and catching up with her so that they could talk. Now, carefully lifting her up in his arms, cradling her head against his chest, he headed that way.

"Ye are going to be just fine, lassie. Just fine."

But was she? Looking down, mesmerized by how vulnerable she appeared, he could only hope that she wasn't more gravely injured than he suspected.

"I'll take care of ye!" An all-consuming sense of protectiveness surged through him, an emotion he'd never felt for a woman before. He felt the urge to safeguard her, to shield her, and to love her as he made his way back towards the cottage. He would find someone to watch after her while he went back to find her father. Or would he?

It is a perfect opportunity to steal the flag, he thought. The MacLeods were all out hunting and Caitlin was out cold! He could hurry back to the castle, find the flag, and be away from the MacLeod stronghold before the others knew what had happened. He had to do it!

But he could not! He couldn't leave her. Kicking open the door of the cottage, Niall looked all around him, taking note of the cobwebs. The walls of the cottage were cracked in several places. It had been left in a ruinous state. Broken pottery, pieces of wood and straw littered the earthen floor. The interior was covered with a thick coating of dust which caused Niall to cough as he pushed his way inside. As he scanned the small one-roomed dwelling he caught sight of a straw-mattress in the corner. Gently he placed Caitlin upon it.

"Caitlin!" Oh, how he longed for her to open her eyes, to speak to him, even if her tone was scolding. "Oh, why did ye run from me lass? Why?" What had he done to so frighten her?

Standing over her, Niall loosened her clothing to make her more comfortable, then he studied her intently. His breath was trapped somewhere in the area of his heart as he stared at the loveliness presented to him. She looked so fragile, so pretty, so desirable.

What would the MacLeod's do if I carried her off to the MacDonald stronghold? He wondered. *Would they follow? Would they start another war? Undoubtedly.* And so, the feelings that stirred in his heart for her were hopeless. But though he tried to ignore the desire that stirred within him at the sight of her tiny waist, firm breasts and long perfectly shaped legs, it was impossible. She was even more beautiful than he had supposed. Ach, how he wished he really was just a simple fisherman. It could have been so easy then. As it was he had been caught in the web of his own deception.

Niall brushed her fiery hair aside to examine her head, wincing at the sight of the large lump. In empathy he felt her pain. "Poor lassie." It was no wonder she was still deeply asleep, he thought. He'd had experience tending the wounded, knew a cold damp cloth would bring some relief. Tearing off a strip of his breacan, he dipped it in a rain barrel outside the door, laid it on Caitlin's forehead and sat back to wait.

"Caitlin! Bending down beside her, he called her name over and over again, his pulse quickening as he saw her eyelids flutter. "Caitlin."

She was so lovely, he mused, from the tip of her toes to the top of her red-haired head. He let his eyes move tenderly over her in a caress, lingering on the rise and fall of her breasts. For just a moment he gave in to temptation and kissed her soft warm mouth. A parting kiss, he thought. A sad tribute to what might have been. With a regretful sigh he moved away from her, keeping an arms length away, to return to his vigil. She was the kind of woman he had been searching for but the one woman he could never hope to obtain. Malcolm MacDonald would never welcome a MacLeod into the clan, nor would Ian MacLeod welcome him were he to find out who he really was. The longing that he felt would forever remain unfulfilled. And yet at the moment that didn't matter. All he wanted was for her to open her eyes.

Niall sat unflinchingly by Caitlin's bedside leaving only to change the cold cloth on her head. He stared at her, entranced by the way the sunlight from the tiny window played across the curves of her body beneath the coverlet, creating tantalizing shadows and reminding him of her beautiful body. The thoughts rambling through his head were dangerous and he shook his head furiously to clear such musings.

You have one purpose here and one purpose only, he reminded himself silently. *The flag. Remember.*

"Ohhhhh!"

"Caitlin?"

She was moaning, moving her head from side to side. It was the first hopeful sign she'd given of returning to consciousness. Reaching out he touched her face, relishing the softness of her skin.

"Wake up, lass." Seeing her eyelashes flutter again he took her hand, willing her to open her eyes.

As if subconsciously hearing him she stirred, putting her hand to her temple. "Mmmmm. My head," she moaned. Instinctively she reached out feeling disoriented, clinging to him, needing stability in a turbulent, whirling world. The closeness of her soft curves was nearly his undoing. The brush of their bodies wove a cocoon of warm intimacy that he relished, yet his passion was tempered with a more tender feeling.

Light flickered before Caitlin's eyelids as she struggled to open her eyes. Where was she? She was confused. "What happened?" she asked softly.

"Ye fell, lass." Pushing her fiery-hued hair aside, he examined her injury yet again. His fingers were strokes of softness as he touched her, making her feel warm and tingly inside. She nestled closer, her face buried against his chest.

"Ohhhhh.""

"And hit yer head on a rock."

Suddenly recognizing his voice, Caitlin's eyes flew open to find him sitting on the edge of the mattress, his fingers entwined in her hair. His face illuminated by sunlight was the first thing her eyes focused on. She'd know that profile anywhere. "Niall!" She remembered now that she had dreamed that he had kissed her. Had he? Her thoughts were hazy, her head throbbed painfully as she sat up.

"Aye. 'Tis me. I brought ye here," he murmured huskily, remembering their brief embrace.

"Brought me where?"

"A crofter's cottage near the spot where you fell."

"Oh......"

They stared at each other, two silent, shadowy figures in the dimly lit cottage, each achingly aware of the other. The very air pulsated with expectancy. Caitlin could not help but wonder what he was going to say, what he was going to do. Sitting like a stone figure, her eyes never once left him as he moved forward.

"Ah, Lassie. When I saw you fall I thought.....I feared!" He pulled her roughly against him. "By the Saints I never realized until that moment how very special you are to me." The tone of sincerity in his voice deeply touched her.

"Special?"

"Aye, that you are."

Slowly Niall bent his head, kissing her with a fierce, single-minded passion. A kiss that sent her head spinning. Was it any wonder then that she clung to him to keep from falling?

"Ah, lass...." he murmured against her mouth, pulling her closer. Her lips parted in an invitation for him to drink more deeply of her mouth. He did, igniting a warmth that engulfed them both from head to toe.

His hand slid over the curve of her hip and downward to the place where her thigh was bare. Her flesh burned where he touched her.

"I hae lain awake at night imagining this," he breathed, "and this." His fingers dipped inside her clothing, touching the peaks of her breasts.

Caitlin felt as if she had stepped into another realm, some place where there were no thoughts, only feelings. Breathlessly she returned his kisses, tingling with pleasure when he began to hungrily probe the inner warmth. Following his lead she returned his kiss, tentatively at first then passionately, tangling her fingers in the thick golden bristle of his hair.

"Caitlin!"

All he could think about was the pounding of his heart as he relished the warmth of her body. She'd haunted his dreams no matter how fiercely he'd tried to put her from his mind. And now she was here. His betrothed, a voice inside his head shouted out. Why not take advantage of that fact. Here and now. They might have only this moment.....

Capturing her slender shoulders he pulled her up against him as his mouth moved hungrily against hers. Her head was thrown back, the masses of her fiery hair tumbling in a thick cascade over his arm, tickling his neck. "Ah, lassie. Lassie!"

Caitlin was aware of her body as she had never been before. Her breasts tingled with a new sensation. Fighting against her own desire was more difficult than she could ever have anticipated. How could she push him away? How could she ignore the heated insistence in her blood. There was a weakening readiness at his kiss, a longing she couldn't explain but which prompted her to push closer to him, relishing the warmth of his hands as he outlined the swell of her breasts.

Caitlin didn't understand this all-consuming need to be near him, she only knew that Niall alone aroused an urgent need within her, a longing to embrace him. She craved his kisses, his touch and wanted to be in his arms forever. Dear God, she was helpless against this powerful tide that raised gooseflesh up and down her arms and legs.

"Niall." She moaned his name into his hair as his lips left her mouth. Soft sobs of pleasure echoed through the cottage's silence and she was surprised to find that they came from her own throat. Her senses were filled with a languid heat that made her head spin. She closed her eyes, giving herself up to the dream of his nearness.

Gently he traced a path from her jaw, to her ear to the slim line of her throat until his lips found her breasts, tracing the rosy peak. Dear God, she tasted so sweet. He was mesmerized by her, by how right it felt to hold her in his arms, his hip touching her stomach, his chest cradling the softness of her breasts. The longing to make furious love to her overpowered him. Kissing was not enough to satisfy the blazing hunger that raged through him. She was too tempting and the delicious fact that she was responding to him made him cast all caution aside. Compulsively his fingers savored the softness of her breasts as he bent his mouth to kiss her again, gently lowering her onto her back.

She stared up at him, watching as he studied her and the look of desire she saw branded on his face alarmed her. Her woman's body craved the maleness of him but her logical mind rebelled. Through the haze of her pleasure she suddenly remembered. She had fallen because she had been running away from *him.*

"Take yer hands away," she commanded.

"What?" Reluctantly he moved away, though he didn't want to.

"I said get yer hands off me, fisherman!" Glaring defiantly at him, she ignored the clamor in her own body and blamed what had happened entirely on him.

"Fishermon." He rolled away from her, coming to his feet, standing with his legs sprawled apart, his arms crossed over his chest. His breathing was deep as he struggled to get control of himself, his emotions. He swore a violent oath as he raised his hands, palms towards her. "There, my hands are gone from ye. Are ye satisfied?"

"No!" Cautiously she looked around for the dirk, only allowing herself to relax when she realized he was not armed. Even so, she was wary. "I willna be satisfied until ye are far, far away." Her flashing eyes made accusations.

"Why ye ungrateful....!" He seethed inwardly. I should have left you lying there Caitlin MacLeod!" A muscle in his jaw ticked warningly.

"Aye, that ye should hae, I be thinking. And ye might hae, except ye wanted to make certain of....."

"Of what?" Just what was she hinting. "Say it! I canna guess, I hae not the sight."

She took a deep breath, then made the accusation. "I saw ye come after me with yer knife. That's why I ran."

"Saw me......!" It was too ridiculous for words.

"But when ye saw me fall ye thought ye wouldna hae to do yer gruesome deed." Her breath hissed out as she continued. "Ye thought yer secret would be safe. That I was dead. But ye were wrong."

Niall exploded with rage. "If ye were not a woman I would make ye eat those words." He practically shouted at her. "If I was trying to kill ye why would I hae carried ye here, woman? Answer that if ye can!"

"Oh, I dunna ken....." She felt confused. Addled. *Oh, if only I could read yer mind and know for sure.*

Rejection and unfulfilled passion merged in a potent rage within his veins. "Well, ye can know this. I am a mon of honor. I would ne'er harm a hair on yer head, no matter what ye may believe. God strike me down, I tell ye true."

Instantly she regretted her volatile temper and her cursed quick tongue. She had ranted, she had raved because she had been afraid. She had the feeling that he would long remember her careless words.

"What's going on in here?" Jamie became an unwelcome guest as he burst through the door.

"She fell!" Niall didn't even make pretense of being polite. He just wasn't in the mood.

"Fell?" Jamie's concern proved that he had some kind of feelings for his clanswoman.

"She tumbled over the hill."

"Tumbled?" Jamie's look challenged Niall.

"Fell." Niall's eyes blazed as he looked first at Jamie, then at Caitlin. "I gi' my word I didna push her."

Jamie shrugged. "I wasna thinking that ye did, only that ye should hae taken better care of her. I would hae." He pushed his way past Niall and knelt by the bed. "How are ye feeling, hinny?"

"My head hurts a bit, but that is all. I hit my…my head." As a reminder, her head began to pound violently and she put her hand to her temple as she sat up. "Niall came to my aid and brought me here."

"I'll bet he did." The smirk on his face made no secret of Jamie's meaning.

"I did."

"To hae a sampling before the wedding?" His hands reached out to Caitlin, but Niall, grabbing him by the wrist, pulled them away.

"Nae." Only narrowly did Niall hold his temper in chick. "Unlike ye, I can keep my hands to myself."

For a moment it appeared that there might be a fight. And there might have been had Caitlin not hurried to act as mediator.

"Leave Niall be! He has done nothing to censor." She tried to get to her feet but felt dizzy so she sat back down. "'Twas my own fault I fell. If not for yon laddie I might hae fared worse." Once again she came to his defense, though she had made far worse accusations.

"Then ye believe me?" Niall raised one eyebrow in question.

"Aye." Still, she didn't completely trust him. How could she? "For the moment I declare a truce. And ye?"

Niall didn't answer; he merely shrugged, glowering as Jamie rose to his feet and stepped in between.

"Come, Cait!" his lips curled up slightly. "The women folk hae been busy preparing another feast while we've been gone. I'm hungry." He boasted of the number of animals killed, as if he had been the one to kill them all. "Six rabbits, four red deer, a roe buck, and several birds. The MacLeod's keisan will be filled to the brim with gave. And yer father felled a buck at a hundred and seventy yards."

"For *our* betrothal feast!" Niall felt possessive and hastened to remind the dark-haired young man of his claim. "Caitlin's and mine." That said, he bent down, sweeping her up in his arms.

"What are ye going to do?" She felt a strange surge of excitement, feeling his arms clamped so tightly around her.

"Carry ye all the way back to the hall if need be."

She could have told him then and there that she was strong enough to walk, yet Caitlin remained silent, enjoying the moment. There was no use denying it, she liked being in his arms.

Chapter Twelve

The great hall was warmly lit, the roaring fire inviting. Having dressed in a kirtle of plain beige wool and a brightly colored arisaid of yellow and green, Caitlin looked feminine and lovely. Entering the hall with her head held high, she took the honorary seat beside her father on the left, which would be hers throughout the period of preparation for her wedding. Her mother would be seated on the right.

The hall fluttered with frenzied activity as large kegs of whiskey and ale were tapped and venison was prepared for cooking. The Highlanders would boil a quarter of flesh, whether mutton, veal, goat or deer in the paunch of the beast. The animal's skin was turned inside out, cleaned and fixed to hang on a hoop over the fire. Now the meat sizzled and gave off a tantalizing aroma. Caitlin could not argue her hunger.

"Something for your appetite, Caity." Caitlin's mother smile as she offered her daughter an oatcake from a large wooden tray. Caitlin dipped it in honey, cherishing its sweetness. As the future bride she was to have the honor of taking the first bite of all the delicacies tonight.

"It...it seems so strange that I will be a bride."

"I know." The blue eyes of Caitlin's mother shimmered with suppressed tears.

"Och, this is a time for merriment, not for cryin'!" Ian's voice was gruff but Caitlin thought she detected a mist of moisture in his own eyes. "A daughter is born to be a mother some day. And yet......"

"It is always hard to hand them over to another," Caitlin whispered. Indeed, Ian's youngest daughter had been the first to go, fostered out to the MacKinnon's to strengthen friendship between the clans when she was but five years old. In turn the MacKinnon's small son was growing up at the MacLeod hearth.

The custom of fosterage did much to bind members of clans together, or so Ian insisted. Fosterage consisted in the mutual exchange of the infant members of families, the children of the Chief being included. Since Ailsa was little more than a babe it had seemed significantly appropriate for her to be the one chosen for fosterage.

"Kindred to forty degrees, fosterage to a hundred, as they say." The custom had the advantage of enabling one half of the clan world to know the other half and how they lived.

She'd never forget how he'd cried when his youngest daughter had been bundled off by the leader of the MacKinnon clan. And now in a way he was losing Caitlin too. Handing her over to belong to another man, no more to be his little girl. That the fisherman had agreed to live at the castle and to take on the MacLeod name did not make it any easier.

The hall rang with raucous laughter, a babble of voices and the underlying accompaniment of music. A parade of trays and bowls passed Caitlin's way. Strangely enough though she had thought herself to be famished she only nibbled at the fare, trying to quiet the unusual feelings stirring in the pit of her stomach. Certainly her head ached. As if a wee brownie was inside, pounding with a hammer. Ignoring the pain that throbbed in her head she looked in Niall's direction, fantasizing about being carried back to the castle in his arms. The look that passed between them had the potency of a kiss, then looking hastily away Caitlin joined in the revelry that rioted in the room.

Get hold of yourself, Caitlin Nic Ian! she scolded silently but it was no use. Caitlin knew she could deny it no longer. She was drawn to the fisherman devastatingly, beyond thought, beyond reason. Indeed, she did not have to look his way to know where he stood, how he moved. She sensed it. Every time he turned his heated gaze her way the hair at the back of her neck prickled in anticipation. It was a feeling that unnerved her, she who had always had complete control over her emotions before.

A vision flashed before her eyes of a man pressed close against her body beneath the quilts, lulling her to blissful sleep by the steady rhythm of his heartbeat. Closing her eyes she allowed herself the luxury of dreaming until her father's elbow nudged her in the ribs.

"The dancing, daughter, the dancing. It's up to you to lead it."

Ian MacLeod rose from the table and signaled for the dancing to begin. Within a matter of moments the room was transformed, tables pushed back, chairs and benches pushed against the wall. Caitlin chose her father as her first partner as the clansman hooted their approval.

"Let's see Caitlin dance. It's her betrothal we're celebrating," cried out Jaimie.

"Aye, let's see her kick her feet." Angus boldly winked.

"Every body must dance."

Three pipers appeared accompanied by the bard on his lute, and a small boy on a tambor. Ian MacLeod danced with the agility of a young lad, laughing all the while.

"Ye remind me of yer mother, lassie. It's as if the years hae been wiped away. We danced together she and I at our own marriage feast. And now our wee bonnie daughter has grown up. Where hae all the years gone, hinny?"

"Perhaps the witches hae stole them." One of the powers with which witches were accredited was that of the Evil Eye. By merely looking at something they could destroy, corrupt or acquire it. That was why Caitlin always wore a potent talisman around her neck to guard against them.

"Perhaps..." He reflected on that notion. "Certainly it seems that only the dark powers could be so cruel as to bring old age upon us so quickly."

Laughing young women chose partners and one by one other pairs of dancers took to the floor as Caitlin and her father returned to their seats. Stepping gracefully, quickly, toes pointed with precision, hands thrown upwards in exuberation or warmly extended to smiling partners the revelers frolicked. The couples met and parted moving their feet in spirited abandonment. Her father told her that long ago this type of dancing was part of a magic ritual and surely there was a primitive aura about it , she thought.

Patterns of dancers formed, then just as quickly dissolved to form new patterns. Breacons swayed jauntily, skirts rippled as the tunes from the fiddler and bagpipes filled the great hall.

"Let's see Caitlin dance wi' the fishermon!"

"Aye, let's see how the fishermon can dance."

"Is he as skilled at that as with a sword?"

"Let's take a wager on it."

"Come on!"

Caitlin was unable to ignore the round of shouts which echoed all around the hall and in truth perhaps she didn't really want to. Drawing in a deep breath she watched as Niall walked with lion-like grace across the wooden floor, then she was in his arms, surprised by how at home she felt there.

"Ye hae been ordered to dance with me."

"Aye, so ye hae..."

"Come." He whispered, "I want them all to know that ye belong to me."

Caitlin's breath stilled at the touch of his warm hand. Her blood quickened as his arms encircled her waist. There was a glow in his eyes and she reveled in the knowledge that in spite of their many quarrels he still wanted her. It was as heady a feeling as drinking too much ale.

The pipes began keening, and she moved her feet dreamily as smoke from the hearth fires swirled about the hall. It was like a dream and she was caught up in the spell. All around them her clansmen were clapping and cheering, stamping their feet in time to the music, watching as a member of a rival clan swirled her around the room.

Caitlin had never felt so passionately alive! Her whole being was filled with conflicting emotions. He was swinging her around on his arm, whirling her about to a jaunty tune. Her bright red hair flew about her shoulders in a fiery web as laughter bubbled from her throat. She felt immensely happy, danced with complete abandon. Kicking up her heels, bending her slim waist, her eyes fused with his as for just a moment their faces were mere inches apart, close enough for a kiss. They were too breathless to speak but their expressions conveyed a mutual attraction to each other.

"Let me show you a dance we do in my village," he said at last, longing to fit her soft curves against him. He explained, hurriedly showing the others how to do the steps. It was a different kind of dance one in which the women executed the intricate steps of a dance as they moved in a circle, men on the outside women on the inside.

"Ye're as graceful as a bird. Is there nothing ye can't do?" The sound of Niall's low, husky voice teased her ears. His hard muscular body seemed to press against her own and burn where it touched. His gaze seemed to strip her naked and with a blush she remembered his caress.

She made no effort to pull away as he grasped her by the waist and lifted her high in the air as the pipes keened on. Indeed she sought the firm, strength of his arms. Their hearts pounded in unison. For a moment it was as if the two of them were all alone in the vast room. Och, if only he were not so handsome and yet it was much more than that. He had revealed strength, a determination today on the field that she could not help but admire. He was in every way a most masculine man. And soon he would belong to her.

Even long after the fires dimmed, as she had settled in her bed, Caitlin's mind danced with memories of the time she'd shared with Niall in the forest and in his arms tonight. Once again she couldn't sleep but this time it was because of happy thoughts, not recriminations.

"I hae to see him." Bolting up in bed the necessity to be held in his arms goaded her into leaving the small chamber. Haunting the halls like a ghost she made her way towards his room. Suddenly an arm slipped around her shoulders and she gasped. "Who.....?"

"Me!" Niall's voice enveloped her like a welcome cloak.

"Niall." She would never have wanted to let him know how glad she was that it was him yet her voice betrayed her. "What are ye doing here? I didna even hear ye."

"I was on my way to yer room. I....I just wanted to be close to ye." A rare confession from such a proud man. "And what about ye?"

"The same."

"Oh!" He slipped his arm around her shoulders as he steered her around a sharp corner and down a short flight of steps. There was a crazy leap in her pulse as she felt the firm pressure of his hand. "Be careful. Watch the stairs. They're steep and slippery."

At last they came to a spot that was dark and private. Cupping her face in his hand he tipped her chin up. "So, give me a kiss, hinny. It's what we both want."

"A kiss?" She played it coy. "And just why should I be giving one to ye?"

"Because....because I canna live without it."

Caitlin felt his arms around her as he crushed her tight against him and her blood screamed with delight. Somehow it seemed that it was with him that she belonged.

"Niall....." Compulsively she reached out to him, closing her fingers against his as he took her hand.

"Ah....lassie, what ye do to me." His breath was warm against her face, his voice husky. With a soft groan he bent his head, captured her shoulders and brought her closer as he crushed his mouth demandingly against hers. So much for good intentions, he thought. Compulsively his hand closed over her breast, his thumb moving back and forth over the peak as he slid his mouth down her throat. Oh why was it this particular lassie that stirred him so? Desire alone or much, much more?

Niall kissed her over and over but kisses alone did not quell the blazing hunger that raged through him. His hand trembled as he pushed her away as suddenly as he had sought the embrace. She was too tempting, too soft and yielding in his arms. A moment longer and he would do something he could never forgive himself for. Take her before the wedding. So thinking he pulled away.

"Niall?" Caitlin was totally confused. He was as unfathomable as the tide, pursuing her one moment, pushing her away the next. "What is wrong?"

"I canna kiss ye without wanting more." There he had said it. "But we must wait."

"Wait....?" At that moment she didn't want to. Her head whirled in a dizzying awareness of him. The length of his hard, muscular body felt hot against her own. She felt desire spread languidly through her body, working its way up from her knees to the top of her head. A warm, tingling feeling. "Mayhap I dunna want to, Niall." She touched his arm.

"Oh, God. Caitlin, my Caity....." This time his kiss went far beyond a mere touching of lips. His tongue searched the contours of her mouth in a sensuous, exploring caress that intensified her newly found passion. With an increasing measure of boldness, she mimicked the gentle exploration of his lips and tongue, helpless against the powerful tide that consumed her, a quivering sensation that shot through her body like a fist. Then she felt his hand slide down to cup her breast and she was lost. She wanted him here and now. Oh, but she was such a brazen hussy.

As for Niall, the heat of his body was steadily climbing. His breath was coming quickly between his parted lips. He was totally ruled by his emotions, having the devil's own time resisting the temptation she presented. Taking her hand he pulled her slowly downward.

"I want to take off yer clothes, to touch you, learn every secret of yer body. I want to caress yer breasts, feel the warmth of yer hands touching me as I am touching ye." He pulled her up against him, showing her what male arousal felt like. He felt her shiver. "I want to be so deeply sheathed in yer softness that we are like one being. That's what I want at this moment."

"And I....I want that too." Putting her arms around him, she felt as if she were flying. Desire was like a fever and she reveled in the sensations flooding her body.

"Caity, my sweet, sweet, Caity......" Dropping his head, he kissed the valley between her breasts, then caressed each soft mound with his lips and tongue, teasing the peaks until she gasped aloud.

"Ah, Niall, I love ye so. How glad I am that I am to be yer wife."

"Wife."

The word hovered in the air like a ghost, bringing him back down to earth. He swore beneath his breath softly. What he was about to take didn't belong to him.

MacLeod or no, Caitlin deserved better treatment than to be tumbled like some trollop. Thus, without saying another word he gripped her shoulders and in a seemingly determined mood propelled her up to the stairs.

"Niall, where are ye taking me?"

"Back to your chamber, lass." He pushed her ahead of him, up the narrow steps. Bad enough to steal the MacLeod's flag without stealing his daughter's virginity as well.

"Why?" She felt bereft and lonely without his arms around her.

"A matter of virtue and honor."

She scoffed. "I dunna care about them. I dunna care at all. I want....."

He stifled her protests with his kiss, then pulled away, walking her to her door. "I do care." Though often known to whisper words of love that he did not mean, Niall meant them now. "I love ye, Caitlin MacLeod. I do." He felt suddenly lonely and very, very sad. "Just remember that."

"Remember?" She laughed, cuddling up against him. "Why should I when I'll hae ye with me?"

"Just do." Kissing her lightly on the lips he bid her a sad goodnight, regretting that it would soon be goodbye.

HIGHLAND DESTINY

Chapter Thirteen

Caitlin shivered but not because it was cold in the room. She was nervous, mentally ticking off the time until she would be married. "So soon." Too soon. She wasn't ready. Despite her newfound feelings for the fisherman, despite the wild primitive feelings he had unleashed, she hadn't gotten used to the idea. Perhaps in truth she never would.

Soon I will no longer be a maiden. Despite her attraction for Niall, the thought brought a small stab of fear. Would he be gentle? Would she feel the same surging desire for him on her wedding night that she had last night? Closing her large brown eyes she gave herself up to dreams and visions of her coming marriage. There would be walks in the moonlight, kisses in the shadows, late nights and early morning snuggled together beneath the quilts. She wanted to believe in love and she might have had she not also heard some of the women complain about marriage.

Love is not all hugs and kisses. There are moments of the greatest embarrassment. Times when there is pain.

Cursing the fisherman beneath her breath for complicating her life, she rested her needlework in her lap and pulled her chair closer to the fire. Caitlin looked down at the sewing she held in her hands and tried her best to concentrate once again upon her stitches. Breathing out a sigh, she struck her needle into the coarse cloth, gasping out in pain as she stuck her finger.

"Damn!" she swore, forgetting herself for a moment as she uttered one of Niall the fisherman's favorite oaths.

"Caitlin! Such an expression does not become ye," Caitlin's mother, Fiona, frowned as she chided her daughter. "Ye are to be a married woman soon. I willna hae ye swear like some...some Englishmon!"

Stubbornly Caitlin refused to apologize, but she did glance at her mother out of the corner of her eye. Oh, how she wished that she and her mother had the kind of relationship other young women had with their mothers. Caitlin's father had always taken her side, and thus a wall had arisen up between Caitlin and Fiona.

"Caitlin, did ye hear me?"

This time Caitlin nodded. Rising from her seat, she picked up a large log and threw it on the fire, basking in the warmth and glow it gave as the fires consumed it.

It was silent in the room, as all the women were engrossed in their stitchery. There was always mending to be done as well as sewing new garments. It was work Caitlin abhorred and avoided every time she could, but it was work she knew she must now get used to. As her mother had often reminded her, married women had to make themselves useful to their husbands, in more ways than one.

Useful...It sounded so hollow, so cold.

"Caitlin, stop daydreaming. Come, try on this gown." Caitlin felt the cool linen as her mother slipped it over her head. "I want everything to be perfect—your hair, the garments that you wear, the wedding feast. Everything. It is only right that the eldest daughter of Ian MacLeod be given the best," Fiona exclaimed.

It seemed as if the mother who had always ignored her had suddenly become obsessed with the most minute details of the wedding preparations. Fiona had spent hours sewing Caitlin's matrimonial wardrobe, had diligently taken a hand in the food preparations.

"The best…" Caitlin breathed, staring down at the hem of her gown.

"Are ye afraid, Caitlin?"

"Nae!" Caitlin answered too quickly but she couldn't hide the shadow that flitted across her face.

"Ye are!"

"I'm no….!" There was no use lying. "perhaps a little. After all, 'tis ye who are always preaching that it is hard being married."

"Because men rarely consider a woman's feelings. They can be selfish, Caitlin, and marriage is much more than kisses."

"So I have heard." Mockingly Caitlin put her hands beneath the gown making it look like she was with child. "'Tis a means for bringing Ian MacLeod's grandchildren into this world."

"A noble duty!" her mother admonished. She studied her daughter for a long time, then smiled. "Ah, Caitlin, you'll soon learn the ways of men. But a word of caution. Your husband-to-be doesna seem as easy a mon to wind round yer finger as yer father has been."

"Nevertheless, I will tame him," Caitlin insisted, "somehow, some way." Caitoin could feel the blood rising in her cheeks.

"Or he will tame ye." For just a moment Fiona was lost in her own private world but she quickly recovered.

"Never!" Reaching up, Caitlin tugged off the gown, then tilting her head to one side, she asked of the other woman, "Has Father tamed ye?"

"In some ways."

Caitlin couldn't keep herself from blurting out, "Do ye love Father?"

Fiona gasped at the blunt question but did not answer. Her silence bothered Caitlin, for she imagined the silence to be an answer in the negative. *Something is wrong. Something Mother has not told me.*

It was Fiona's turn to ask the question. "Do ye love the bonny young man yer father has betrothed ye to?"

"I don't think so, but I do hae certain feelings when he touches me." Caitlin hugged herself tight as she thought about it, then realizing her mother was looking at her, she put her hands back down at her sides. "Besides, he's better than Uisdean MacKinnon or any of the other fine men Father thought to gi' me to."

"Aye, his only fault is that he has spent his life keeping company with fish." Her mother sniffed her disdain. "But then at least I dunna hae to worry about my daughter going hungry."

"What's that ye say, woman?" Though he usually avoided the women's quarters, Ian MacLeod strode boldly in, like a rooster entering a hen house.

"I was just saying that I most highly approve o' yer choice for our grandchildren's father, even if he is a humble mon."

"Humble?" Ian laughed. "In truth, Wife, I would call him anything but that." Playfully he tugged at Caitlin's hair. "He'll be a good mate for my overbold lassie here. A mon wi' whom she can grow old."

"Old!" Leaning against the familiar strength of her father's chest, Caitlin tried to imagine what Niall would look like when he reached her father's age.

"Aye, he will be a boon to the MacLeod clan. I felt it the first time I saw him."

"Is that why ye didna throw him in the dungeon?" Caitlin questioned.

"It is." He looked inordinately proud of himself. "I gambled, Daughter, and I won."

She tickled him under the chin. "Oh, did ye now? We will see."

Ian MacLeod might not have made such a statement had he been able to see Niall through the stone walls. Last night he had made his decision to leave as soon as possible, and thus Niall was busy gathering together the few belongings he had brought with him and those he had been given as wedding presents. He put the smaller items in the sporran hanging from the belt at his waist; a larger satchel was to be saved for a possession he longed to be his. The flag!

I have to go! He declared silently. *As soon as possible. I canna let this all drag out and thus hurt the lassie all the more.* And himself.

Looking toward the door, Niall shrugged his shoulders, hoping that it would be as easy to cast off his unhappiness.

"Oh, Caity!" He remembered the way her lips had felt beneath his when he had kissed her. He thought of how right she had felt in his arms. Why? Why did she have to be a MacLeod?

She's beginning to care for you, but you cannot let that keep you from what you must be doing. You came here to steal the flag, Niall MacDonald, and that's exactly what you have to do.

"The ultimate betrayal." One for which she would never be able to forgive him. Even so, it had to be done.

Chapter Fourteen

Darkness gathered under the high, vaulted roof. The flickering torches hissed and sputtered as if in warning. The smoke from the waning fire looked like a ghost. Large shadows danced on the wall, tall and menacing. It was the hour when the spirits roamed.

"The night before my wedding," Caitlin whispered, taking her place beside her father in the small, circular tower chamber.

In Gaelic tradition Ian MacLeod had summoned the "seer" to look into the future and tell what was in store for his daughter and her husband-to-be. Not only did the MacLeod clan hold the distinction of having the best bagpipers in the Highlands—the skirl of their pipes would stir any Scots blood—but also they had Elspeth, the most famous seer throughout the Highlands.

She was a direct descendant of the Celtic Druid seers. Many of the neighboring clans and those of the islands used her services, but Skye was her homeland. She was a MacLeod through and through, born in Durinish on the west side of Skye. Not only did she see but also *heard* voices. No one doubted her ability, for what she foretold would eventually happen.

Elspeth was yet in her middle years. She would often see the fairy folk and a person's dopfelgager, or "other self." If this other self was seen, then the person's death was believed to be imminent.

With trepidation, Caitlin eyed the dark-haired, long-nosed woman, feeling a shiver along her spine. Elspeth had skin that was ghostly pale, an angular face, narrow lips, eyebrows that were dark and bushy. Not comely at all, yet the woman had a regal pride. She wouldn't bow to anyone. Not even the MacLeod. Was the woman secretly a witch as some had claimed? Truly, as the woman turned and stared at her with her piercing dark eyes, it seemed so.

"Ah, the lovely bride," she said in a voice that was strangely soothing despite her appearance.

"The treasure and the hope of the MacLeod," Ian declared, "as are ye, Elspeth." He had always had complete faith in her ability, but even more so since she had told of his son's coming death. Many years ago before the battle that robbed him of Colin, Elspeth had been walking the glen near the cemetery. It was a midnight that was dark and grave. Elspeth had gone into a trance in which she saw the graves open and the occupants leaving to make room for one more body, that of Colin Macleod, the chief's son.

Though the story was told to Ian weeks before the battle that took Colin's life, he had shrugged it off as being naught but an illusion. He had tried desperately to put what she had said out of his mind but she had foreseen that there would be a violent battle in which Colin's life would end. After the MacDonald's attack on the stronghold, however, as he had cradled his dead son's body in his arms, he had remembered. Then a week after Colin had been killed, Elspeth had once again had a vision where she saw the same ghosts returning to their graves.

Some Highlanders thought Elspeth was not only a seer but a white witch, able to cure all manner of illnesses. Others thought of her only as a seer able to see future events whether for good or for evil. All knew that she had the "gift of sight," because she was famous among all the Highlanders for seeing events and objects others could not see, her dictates often passed for law. Although she was a very influential person, she charged no fee for her services.

There was no doubt that Elspeth's prophetic powers made a deep and lasting impression on the minds of all who came in contact with her. Elspeth insisted that she could seek no aid for herself from her visions which often came upon her at random and against her will. Tonight, however, she was calling upon her gift of the sight at the request of the MacLeod.

"Begin," the MacLeod said now.

Caitlin watched nervously as Elspeth spread her hands in an arch over her head, raised her chin and began chanting in an ancient tongue. If the woman had the fey, and obviously she had proven that she did, then wasn't it probably that there were things that had happened, or were going to happen that were better not to be revealed? What had happened in the tower, for instance.

Oh, if only I could take her aside, ask her all the question I have about Niall, she lamented. As it was, Caitlin's future was to be exposed before her father's favored men who were gathered together in a circle around her. Ian MacLeod exhibited a moment of distinct pride as he watched the woman before him wrap herself in a bull hide and enter into a trancelike state. There was something eerie about her eyes as she looked toward the ceiling. It was as if she could see through the wood and the stone to the very heavens themselves.

"What does she see?" Caitlin's whisper was sternly silenced by her father's elbow in her rib.

"Aaaiiieee!" Elspeth wailed. She drew a circle, stepped into it, crossed her arms and chanted in a low voice. "Speak to me," she murmured.

"Who? Who does she want to speak?" Again, Caitlin was silenced.

It was an inopportune time to speak, for at that very moment Elspeth's eyes flew open and she stared directly into Caitlin's eyes as if she could see into her soul. She shuddered, mumbling all the while, then seemed to be in silent conversation with someone. Her voice was deep, mesmerizing.

"I see a stranger. One who has come by water….."

"Niall," Caitlin breathed.

"A golden lion. From his loins will spring forth the strongest of the Macleods. Strong sons and daughters."

"Aha. I knew it!" Now it was Ian Macleod who spoke out. "I knew at once that he was the one for my Caity. A voice told me so."

"But beware…" Elspeth grabbed at her chest. "Danger. Deceit. Death. They await like thorns. Catching us unaware." Sinking to her knees, the seeress cradled her arms around herself, rocking back and forth, listening to a voice no one else could hear. Quiet filled the darkened room. Only shadows flickered against the stone walls. The floor creaked. It was so still Caitlin could hear the sound of breathing.

"Father, make her tell us what she hears….."

Elspeth shuddered. Her eyes narrowed, her voice grew thick. Lifting her head, she looked towards the ceiling again. "I see blood and fire. Enough to cover the glens of Skye."

"We are going to be at war?" a cold sweat broke out upon Ian's brow. "Because of Caitlin marrying a fishermon?" His tone seemed to say that if that was the way it would be he would break his vow.

"Not because of him but because of another. A dark man whose soul is as black as his hair. 'Twas he who killed yer son."

Ian bolted to his feet. "Who is he? I will run him through. I will….." He suddenly remembered himself. Sinking back down, he did not interrupt again, though he drummed his fingers on the arms of his chair so roughly that he practically wore holes in the arms.

"Some MacDonald or other. Death to them all," one of the clansmen threatened.

"Aye, death to any MacDonald who would dare cross our threshold," the other voices echoed. Pandemonium broke out as the men discussed amongst themselves the possibility that one of the MacDonalds might try to force his way into the wedding ceremony.

"We'll cut any MacDonald to pieces who dares come anywhere near."

"Spawns of the devil!"

"Bringers of death."

It took Ian's shout of order to get the men quiet again, but all semblance of tranquility was shattered. Suspicion reigned, and danger seemed to lurk in the darkness. There was now a stain on the future and on Caitlin's marriage.

Chapter Fifteen

Night-flying birds, Ghosts, witches and a frightening assortment of evil-looking spirits haunted Caitlin's dreams. An eerie distortion of voices and pictures disturbed her sleep. Moaning she tossed and turned reliving that moment when the seer had shrieked out her portent of misfortune. "Danger, deceit, death," she had warned, brought on by a dark man whose soul was as black as his hair. The man who was Colin's murderer.

"No!"

Flinging herself onto her stomach, Caitlin was besieged with terrifying visions that wove in and out of her dreams. She remembered having tiptoed to the tower, remembered bits and pieces of that moment when her beloved elder brother had been struck down. A face danced before her eyes. A frightening face.

"Colin.....!"

He was going to kill her brother, murder him, but there was nothing she could do. She tried to move but it was as if her feet were stuck to the floor, she wanted to cry out, but her voice was frozen in an eternal, soundless scream. Hands were grabbing her, shaking her, so hard that she could nearly feel her teeth rattle.

"Caity, wake up....."

"No....!" Caitlin's eyes flew open to see Shona standing over her. Remembering her nightmare she covered her mouth with her hand.

"Caity, what ails ye? Ye were talking in yer sleep something fitful?"

"Ails me?" Caitlin's heart was beating so wildly that it took a long moment for her to steady its tempo. "No..nothing ails me. Wedding nerves, that is all."

"Excitement." Shona winked. "Well just let me be saying that I hae heard the lassies talk an ye are the envy of more than quite a few, fishermon or no'."

Caitlin didn't really hear her sister. Bolting from the bed she was in too much of a hurry to find a talisman. Something to guard against the evil that had been foretold.

Shrugging into her gown and arasaid, she searched for and found her cross made out of rowan wood. The rowan, called by some the mountain ash was said to give protection from witchcraft and evil. Slipping it over her head, she felt relieved, that is until she saw a Wheatear perched outside her window. The little bird was said to be a bringer of bad luck and deeply feared in Orkney and Skye. A bad omen for a wedding day, Caitlin thought, her face paling and her hands growing cold.

"It's growing late. Ye slept over long. There are so many things to be done." A Highland wedding was an elaborate and lengthy affair with much ritual attached to it.

Gently tugging at her hand, Shona led her to the bath house where a tub of steaming water awaited. A pile of thick woolen towels were spread on an airer to warm before the fire. In a daze Caitlin stood still as several of the women stripped her of her gown.

"Oh, how I envy ye," one of the younger girls breathed, making no secret of her attraction to Caitlin's bridegroom.

"He is as bonnie a mon as was ever seen on Skye."

"A mon who looks like some Viking lord of old."

Stepping into the water, Caitlin sighed with pleasure as the pleasantly warm water surrounded her. She lay back as the women soaped her hair but though she tried to relax it was impossible. Even the soothing cocoon of water could not slow the pounding of her heart or make her forget the coil that was forming in her stomach. Soon her life would change forever. No longer would she be a maiden but a wife. No more would she sleep all alone. Her life would be forever entwined with the life of another. A heady thought.

"Oh, the men. What devils they are." Rinsing her sister's hair, Shona related that already there was wagering going on as to how soon she would find herself with child.

"Most of the men are betting on a son. They say the fishermon looks virile," Caitlin's sister Lorna confided, handing Caitlin a towel.

"It had better be a male child or Father will hae the fishermon's head," Shona retorted.

The chatter ceased as two of the older women arrived carrying Caitlin's dress the pale yellow material of which was finely woven and artfully done. It was was artfully decorated with embroidery. She could nearly imagine in her mind's eye a woman's form bent to the task, sitting before the hearth fire. A white tonnage pinned with an elaborately worked broach of gold, a belt of leather and several pieces of brass intermixed giving the semblance of a chain, emphasized the trimness of her waist and completed her attire. As was the custom she was barefoot.

"T'will be a sunny day, a perfect day to be wed."

"And ye have perfect laddie."

The young women chattered and laughed with as much exuberance as if they were to be the brides. They combed and brushed her hair until it shone with a red fire. Unmarried lassies bound their hair and wore a snood but married women left their hair to hang free. As a symbol of her newly-wedded state, therefore, Caitlin's side hair was braided, her back hair left to flow down her back.

"Ye look bonnie, Caity!"

"Like some regal queen."

Caitlin stood before the large polished steel mirror, studying her reflection. Her father would say "stand tall and proud, ye are a MacLeod! A bonnie one at that." Was she? Would Niall think her to be pretty? Though seldom conscious of her looks, she was critical now, pinching her cheeks to make them pink, licking her lips to make them shine. Then she walked down the stairs to make her grand entrance before all.

"Ach, daughter, ye truly are a wondrous sight." Standing beside Niall, Ian MacLeod was all smiles. Taking a large cup from the hands of a young male servant he held it forth to Caitlin. "Drink!"

The cup was adorned with a sprig of rosemary and colored ribbons and looked like some pagan offering. As she took a sip of the spiced wine, Caitlin could not help but wonder if some ancient Celtic tribal bride had held such an object in her hand. Handing the cup to Niall she smiled, forgetting for the moment the trauma of last night. She told him that the cup had been handed down for generations, all the way from the first chieftain of the MacLeod Clan.

"And I will gi' it to my son when he weds," Niall exclaimed, to be rewarded by a hearty slap on the back from Ian. With a nod of his head, Ian signaled it was time for the merry-making. Rising to his feet he flung back his chair, lept upon it and raised aloft the bridal cup as a whirling, high-stepping jubilant, laughing group of revelers gave vent to their joy.

It was Highland custom for bride and groom to ride pillion on the back of a strong gelding thus Caitlin walked beside Niall to the stables, mounting behind him on a long-haired Highland horse for the short ride to the castle chapel on the other side of the courtyard. On the back of the horse, in a leather pouch was placed the marriage money, guarded by two strong Highlanders who walked on each side of the animal. A musical accompaniment of musicians playing harp flute and bagpipes proceeded.

Niall's hands were gentle as he helped Caitlin dismount. "I'll be good te ye, I promise I will," he said softly. And he would. For the brief span of time they were together he would try to make her happy. And perhaps he could convince her to go with him when he left.

Caitlin's smile was sincere. "I know ye will!" Entering the chapel she stood tall and proud as she took the lighted candle the priest held forth. The holy man asked the standard questions as a matter of formality; if she was of age, if she swore that she and he betrothed were not within the forbidden degree of consanguinity, if her parents consented to the marriage, if the banns had been posted and finally and most importantly of all if she and her groom both gave free consent to the match.

"Then come forth daughter, to be joined in this holiest of vows."

Caitlin walked down the aisle, looking neither right nor left. She was fearful of the wedding night, why not admit it? She who thought nothing of wrestling and fighting with swords was afraid of being physically claimed by so obviously masculine a man. Even so, she somehow made it to that spot where the priest awaited. There she knelt at her future husband's feet in a gesture of submission.

"Rise!"

Together they faced the priest and repeated their solemn vows. The priest sprinkled her with holy water and recited an intricate mass. The ceremony unfolded so quickly that Caitlin hardly remembered what she had said. It was just babbled words in a foreign tongue. And all the while as she remembered the seer's warning she clutched tightly to her rowan cross.

The joining of right hands concluded the transfer of a gift, Caitlin's virginity for Niall's protection and loyalty. Niall then slipped onto three of his new wife's fingers, one after another, the blessed ring that signified marriage, a blessed circle of gold that would protect her from assault by demons.

"With this ring I thee wed, with this gold I thee honor, and with this dowry I thee endow."

"A token of love and fidelity," the priest intoned.

Love and fidelity. Would he grow to love her. Would she grow to love him. Indeed, did she already?

The final phase of the ceremony was enacted. The groom was the recipient of the priest's kiss of peace, then bent to transmit that kiss to his bride. And all the while Caitlin felt as if she were in a trance, watching all of this take place to another young woman. It was a dream. Just a dream.

Returning to the hall, bride and groom presided over the wedding feast that consisted of cold mutton and fowl and all the usual dairy produce, scones, cheese, oatcakes. Whiskey was drunk and the couple toasted by all.

After the feast, a riotous dance ensued, the bridal couple taking the lead in the "wedding reel". The whirling, high-stepping jubilant, laughing throng of revelers gave vent to their joy. Brightly lit torches illuminated the steps of the dark winding staircase that led to the bridal chamber. A chattering drunken throng accompanied the newly married couple up the winding stairs and to their room.

The key element to the wedding was the blessing of the bedchamber and the bed to dispel any curse that might have compromised the couple's fertility and to wipe away any taint of female adultery. So many times Niall had wanted to make Caitlin his. Now the moment was at hand as bride and groom took their places in bed under the watchful eyes of a circle of close relations.

"Ah, in this very bed there will the seed be sown that will mend my heartache." Ian looked on, waiting expectantly. And then Niall's wildest dream came true as the fairy flag was hung over the nuptial bed to ensure a fertile wedding night.

Once witnessed together in bed, the couple was to be left alone to consummate the marriage. The nuptial bed, which was a crucial element in marriage, symbolized what was at stake; power in and over private life. The Highland belief was that honor, marriage and a person's very being was for the sake of the clan. The betterment of all.

The priest talked of death or annulment prior to the nuptial, the surviving party to the espousal was not free to remarry a brother, sister or other relative of the other party. Relations by affinity were taboo to the fourth canonical degree and relations of consanguinity were taboo to the seventh degree. Then he intoned, "Have joy of each other....."

One by one the guests started to leave, to give the newly couple time to be alone. The festivities would continue for most of the night and for several days but for Niall and Caitlin their time would be spent in a far different manner. The very thought made her tremble, while at the same time she tingled with anticipation as she heard his husky voice.

"Bonnie, Bonnie Caitlin....."

Cradling her against his chest, Niall lay silent for a long, long time as he savored her presence beside him. Then, with the greatest of tenderness he slowly, leisurely began the love play that would culminate in the satisfaction of his greatest desire.

Murmuring Caitlin's name Niall buried his face in the silky strands of her hair, inhaling the delicate fragrance of flowers in the luxurious softness. His lips traveling slowly down the soft flesh of her throat, tasting the sweetness of her skin. Then with impatient hands he quickly loosened her garments, laughing softly as he realized how clumsy his fingers were.

"I am skilled at untangling fishing nets but all thumbs with lassie's garments, I fear," he exclaimed softly, his fingers parting the fabric of her gown to cup one firm, budding breast.

It seemed his hands were everywhere, touching her, setting her body afire with a pulsating flame of desire. At first frightened, Caitlin gave in to the passion he inspired, writhing beneath him, giving herself up to the glorious sensations he was igniting within her. When at last she was naked, her long flaming hair streaming down her back, he looked at her for a long while, his face flushed with passion, his breath a deep-throated rasp. She was beautiful, more so than he could have ever dreamed.

"Bonnie, so very, very bonnie." His hands moved along her back sending forth shivers of pleasure, he in the touching and she in being touched. Her waist was small, her breasts perfection, her legs long and shapely. As she stood bathed in candlelight he let his eyes roam over her body.

"Am I?" Caitlin made no effort to hide her curves from his piercing gaze. As he touched her she gloried in the thought that her body pleased him, her pulse quickening at the passion which burned in his eyes. Gone was her maidenly modesty. This was her fate, her destiny to belong to this man. She felt that in every bone, every muscle, every sinew of her body. Fee on the seer's portent of evil. It couldn't be true. Something ill could not come from something that felt suddenly so right.

"Caitlin...." He spoke her name softly, caressingly. Their kisses were tender at first but the burning spark of their desire burst into flames. Desire flooded his mind, obliterating all reason. Wrapped in each other's arms, they kissed, his mouth moving upon hers, pressing her lips apart, hers responding, exploring gently to the sweet firmness of his. Shifting her weight she rolled closer into his embrace. How could she deny what was in her heart? Deep inside her was the inborn need to belong to him. Strange, when she had once so feared belonging to any man.

Oh, blessed Christ, Niall thought. How could he have ever realized the full effect her nearness would kindle? She fit against him so perfectly, her gentle curves melting against his own hard body. It was as though Caitlin had been made for him.

"Our bodies are filled with magic," he whispered against her mouth. He kissed the corners of her lips, tracing the outline with his tongue. He parted her lips seeking the sweetness he knew to be there. His hands moved on her body, stroking her lightly - her throat, her breasts, her belly, her thighs. With reverence he positioned his hands to touch her breasts. Gently. Slowly. Until they swelled in his hands. He wanted to be gentle but it took all his self-control to keep his passion in check. He wanted to make it beautiful for her, wanted to be the perfect lover.

His exploration was like a hundred feathers, everywhere upon her skin arousing a deep, aching longing. Caitlin closed her eyes to the rapture. Without even looking at him she could see his strong body, amber eyes and tawny hair and thought again what a handsome man he was. Yet it was something far stronger that drew her, the gentleness that had merged with his strength. She touched him, one hand sliding down over the muscles of his chest, sensuously stroking the warmth of his flesh in exploration. She heard the audible intake of his breath and that gave he the courage to continue in her quest.

"Caitlin.....!"

He held her face in his hands, kissing her eyelids, the curve of her cheekbones, her mouth. "Caitlin. Caitlin," He repeated her name over and over again as if to taste of it on his lips.

"I am glad that I please you, for you please me too, so very much." Her fingertips roamed over his shoulders and neck and plunged into his thick, dark blond hair as he kissed her once again, a fierce joining of mouths that spoke of his passion. Then after a long pleasurable moment he drew away, drawing the shirt over his head, stripping off his breacan. When he was completely naked, he rolled over on his side and drew her down again alongside him.

"I like the feel of your skin against me," he breathed.

The candlelight flickered and sparked, illuminating the smooth skin on his chest. He was a muscular man, more so than she had supposed. Although he was thin around the waist and hips, his chest was expansive. The thick, chest hair was soft as she reached out to him. Her hands caressed his chest, her brown blue eyes beckoning him, enticing him to enter the world of love she sensed was awaiting them both.

Caitlin was shattered by the all consuming pleasure of lying naked beside him. A heat arose within her as she arched against him in sensual pleasure. Her breath became heavier and a hunger for him that was like a pleasant pain went from her breasts down to her loins. A pulsing, tingling sensation that increased as his hand ran down the smoothness of her belly to feel the softness nestled between her thighs.

Caitlin gave way to wild abandon, moaning intimately, joyously as her fingers likewise moved over his body. She felt a strange sensation flood over her and could not deny that before he left, she wanted their spirits to be joined together. She wanted his erect manhood to fill her with excitement and pleasure. His strong arms were around her, his mouth covering her own. She shivered at the feelings that swept over her.

The light of the three candles illuminated their bodies, hers as smooth as cream, his muscular form of a darker hue. He knelt down beside her and kissed her breasts, running his tongue over their tips until she shuddered with delight. Whispering words of love he slid his hands between her thighs to explore the soft inner flesh. At his touch she felt a slow quivering deep inside that became a fierce fire as he moved his fingers against her.

Supporting himself on his forearms he moved between her legs. Slowly he caressed his pelvis against her thigh, letting her get accustomed to the hardness of his maleness. Caitlin had no fear now that the moment had come. All thought of the doom that had been foretold was wiped away by Niall's tenderness.

"Love me, Niall," she breathed. Arching up, she was eager to drink fully of that which she had only briefly experienced.

"Aye. Oh, I will my sweet, sweet love." Taking her mouth in a hard, deep kiss he entered her softness with a slow but strong thrust, burying his length within the sheath of her softness, allowing her to adjust to his sudden invasion. She was so warm, so tight around him that he closed his eyes with agonized pleasure. He knew at that moment that love was the true meaning of life, the only thing on earth that was truly worth obtaining. Closing his eyes he wondered how he could ever have thought that anything was important as this. Ambition. At the moment the only thing he wanted was to bring her pleasure, give her his devotion.

As they came together spasms of feeling wove through Caitlin like the threads of a tapestry. She had never realized how incomplete she had felt until this moment. Now joined with him she was a whole being. Feverishly she clung to him, her breasts pressed against his chest. Their hearts beat in matching rhythm even as their mouths met, their tongues entwined, their bodies embraced in the slow sensuous dance of love. She was consumed by his warmth, his hardness and tightened her thighs around his waist as she arched up to him, moving in time to his rhythm.

"Niall...!" It was as if he had touched the very core of her being. There was an explosion of rapture as their bodies blended into one. It was an ecstasy too beautiful for words. Love, such a simple word and yet in truth it meant so much.

Languidly they came back to reality, lying together in the aftermath of passion, their hearts gradually resuming a normal rate of rhythm. Niall gazed down upon her face, gently brushing back the tangled red hair from her eyes.

"Sleep now...." he whispered, still holding her close. With a sigh she snuggled up against him, burying her face in the warmth of his chest. He caressed her, tracing his fingers along her spine until she drifted off.

Chapter Sixteen

Niall's arm lay heavy across Caitlin's stomach, the heat of his body warming hers as they lay entwined. The sound of his breathing brought a flush of color to her cheeks as she remembered the way she had moved against him. Her senses had responded to Niall the moment he had touched her. Beneath his hands and mouth her body had come alive and she had been lost in a heat of desire she had never believed possible. For a moment in time she had acted like someone wild, someone crazed. She had whispered to him the boldest things, asking him, no begging him to do things she would never have even thought of before.

"Ye hae bewitched me, fishermon." Surely that was what he had done. But if that was so then the bewitchment hadn't yet ended nor had her yearning to do everything all over again.

Whispering his name, Caitlin stroked the expanse of Niall's shoulders and chest remembering the heated passion they had shared. His skin was warm and smooth roughened by a thatch of hair on his chest. Against her breasts it had been more pleasurable than she might have ever have imagined.

"Caitlin?" Niall cherished the blessing of finding her cradled in his arms, her mane of bright red hair spread like a cloak over her shoulders. He felt an aching tenderness and drew her closer. "There now, lassie, that wasn't so bad was it?"

"Not too bad," she answered, too stubborn to tell him how deeply stirring their lovemaking had been. She snuggled into his arms, laying her head on his shoulder, curling into his hard, strong body. If she wasn't yet in love with her handsome husband, well then she was perilously close.

His hand moved lightly over her hip and down her leg as he spoke. Weeks of frustration and worry just seemed to have melted away. She was his! At last he had come to know the glorious sweetness of her body. Oh but her genuine outpouring of passion had been such a precious gift.

"I'd like to wake up every morning and find ye next to me," he confided, nibbling at her earlobe playfully. But that was not what destiny had in store for him. No matter what vows had been spoken, his union with her could not be forever, no matter how much he wished that it could be. "Caitlin......"

"Ye will........" He was her husband. She belonged to him. A truth that far from upsetting her now made her feel happy and content. Niall was everything a woman could wish for. The other lassies were right to be eaten up with jealousy. Determinedly she shoved aside any misgivings and clung to her optimistic feelings. At this moment she wanted with all her heart to make this union a successful marriage. Though her fierce pride had at first rebelled at being given in marriage to fisherman, she knew now that there was not a better man in all of Skye.

"Caitlin.....I......" He remembered her eyes bright with desire as he had kissed her. Eyes that would blaze anger once she realized what he had done.

I don't want to hurt you. That was never my intent. But dear God it was inevitable. He was a MacDonald. His loyalty belonged to his clan. That loyalty meant putting the good of his clansmen above all else.

"Caitlin....." he whispered again, but though there were many things he wished to say he ended up not saying a word. Instead, he reached for her, a primal growl in his throat as he kissed her hard. He caught her lips, nibbling with his teeth.

Slowly he began the caressing motions that had so deeply stirred her the first time they had made love. He touched her from the curve of her neck to the soft flesh behind her knees and up again, caressing the flat plain of her belly. Moving to her breast he cupped the soft flesh, squeezing gently. Her breast filled his palm as his fingers stroked and fondled. Lowering his head he buried his face between the soft mounds.

"So smooth. 'Tis said there is nothing like a woman's softness."

"Nor a man's strength." She was not content to be only the recipient of pleasure but felt a need to give pleasure as well. With that desire in mind she moved her palms over the muscles and tight flesh of his body.

"Caitlin.....!" A long shuddering sigh wracked through him. "Oh, how I love your hands upon me."

Caitlin was instilled with a new-found confidence, knowing she could so deeply stir him. She continued her exploration as if to learn every inch of him. In response she felt his hard body tremble against hers.

"Ahhhh..." The sound came from deep in his throat.

Stretching her arms up she entwined them around his neck, pulling his head down. Her mouth played seductively on his, proving to him how quickly she could learn such passionate skills. Then they were rolling over and over in the bed, sinking into the warmth and softness. Caitlin sighed in delight at the feel of his hard, lithe body atop hers. Her entire body quivered with the intoxicating sensations. She would never get tired of feeling Niall's hands on her skin, of tasting his kisses.

Before when they had made love, Caitlin had been just a bit shy, holding a small bit of herself back from her pleasure. Now she held nothing back. Reaching out she boldly explored Niall's body as he had done to hers - his hard-muscled chest and arms, his stomach. His flesh was warm to her touch, pulsating with the strength of his maleness. As her fingers closed around him, Niall groaned.

"Caitlin!" Desire raged like an inferno, pounding hotly in his veins. His whole body throbbed with the fierce compulsion to plunge himself into her sweet softness and yet he held himself back, caressing her once more, teasing the petals of her womanhood until he could tell that she was fully prepared for his entry.

"Oh, lassie....."

His tongue touched hers, gently opening her mouth to allow him entrance. his tongue thrusting into her mouth at the same moment his maleness entered the softness nestled between her thighs. She felt his hardness entering her, moving slowly inside her until she gasped with the pleasure. Her body arched up to his, searing him with the heat of her passion. Warm, damp and inviting she welcomed him.

Writhing in pleasure she was silken fire beneath him, rising and falling with him as he moved with the relentless rhythm of their love. They were spiraling together into the ultimate passion. Climbing together. Soaring. Sweet, hot desire fused their bodies together, yet there was an aching sweetness mingling with the fury and the fire. They spoke with their hearts and hands and bodies words they had never uttered before in the final outpouring of their desire.

Afterwards she cuddled happily in his arms, her head against his chest, her legs entwined with his. Noticing that he was tense, she gazed into his face, disconcerted to see a frown there. How could he be even remotely unhappy after what they had just shared? "Niall, what are ye thinking?"

He was thinking of the Fairy Flag, wondering if in truth it was really worth the price he was going to have to pay. "About nothing really. Except....."

"Except?"

"That there are often things beyond a mon's control. Times when other men and circumstances control his destiny."

The Fairy Flag. He could not allow himself to leave without it, though leaving was the very last thing on his mind right now.

"Just as my father controlled my destiny." She lay soft and warm against him, her breasts tightly pressed to his chest. Her long hair tickled his chest as it flowed between them. "But though I rebelled against ye at first, I want ye to know that being yer wife makes me happy now, Niall."

A wave of tenderness washed over him as he reached out to stroke the soft red tresses, brushing it out of her eyes. "And being here with ye makes me the happiest of men." It was the truth and no lie. He was happy. As if to give proof, he held her tightly against him as if he would never let her go.

It was the truth. He was happy. So happy that it made what he had to do now all the more tragic. Oh, that he really were a fisherman. At that moment were he able to trade places with Peadar he would have done so without blinking an eye. But such things just weren't possible. He was a MacDonald, a cousin in line to be tanist. He could not allow himself to turn against his clan for the sake of his own happiness.

"Oh, Caitlin...." His eyes were moist as he lay gently stroking her hair.

Only after she had fallen asleep, when the soft sound of her breathing seemed to assure that she would not easily awaken did he pull away from her. The moment he had been waiting for had regrettably come.

"Goodbye, lassie," he whispered, feeling remorse clutch at his heart. "Ye'll ne'er know how much this pains me." Far more than it would her, or so it seemed right now.

Oh, how she will hate me when she awakens and finds out what I have done. Even so, Niall didn't even hesitate. Reaching overhead where the flag had been unfurled above them, he tugged the fairy flag down with one hard yank, then without allowing himself to have any second thoughts, he picked up his garments that were lying on the floor and quickly put them on.

"Caitlin...." He choked.

Niall knew he should hurry away, but for just a moment in time it was as if his feet were glued to the floor. All he could do was to look down at the lovely face of the young woman who had given him such love and joy. He would remember. For the rest of his life this night would be branded in his heart, in his mind.

"Caitlin," he whispered again.

Bending down, he couldn't resist the temptation to kiss her, his lips lightly brushing her forehead, lingering. Then he was off, moving toward the door with incredible haste, yet with one backward glance, then another and another. Reaching the door, he grabbed the latch, twisted it, pushed open the door. Like the ghost he had once professed himself to be, he disappeared from the room.

HIGHLAND DESTINY

Chapter Seventeen

The flames from the wall sconces flickered, casting eerie shadows against the walls as Niall moved about the castle. Clinging to the shadows, alert to every sound, he stealthfully crept up the stairs. He wore the fairy flag beneath his breacan and he could only hope that it would not bode him ill. If it was good luck for the Macleods, would it bring bad luck to a MacDonald? He would soon see.

"Careful. Careful," he cautioned to himself as he came around a corner. He paused, looking first left then right. If he were caught leaving the castle there would be no way he could account for his actions. A man just did not leave his bride alone on the night of their wedding. If he were apprehended, only by a miracle would he get off with his life. There would be no way he could talk his way out of trouble this time.

Strange. It seems much too easy. Ridiculously so. There were hardly any guards in the stairwells or corridors. No one to stop Niall or even try to block his way. This seemed much too easy.

"A trap?" Or was it just that the men were preoccupied with their ale-guzzling and were too besotted to give much of anything else a thought? He could only wonder as he made his way to the wall just outside the tower. Niall's nerves were on edge. Cautiously he took a rope from his hiding place. He had to make his way down to the ground far below, for he was unarmed, helpless were he to be set upon by any of the MacLeod's men. He would be a target for swords while he was here atop the wall, a target for arrows once he was dangling over the edge. Nevertheless he had to take the chance or plan on staying in the MacLeod stronghold permanently. There would be no better opportunity for escape than tonight.

Securing the rope, Niall scanned the area, taking one final look at the interior of Dunvegan Castle, then he climbed over the edge of the wall. It was his misfortune that as he did, a large stone came loose to clatter loudly against the turret as it crashed downward.

"What was that?" Niall heard a voice shout out. "Who goes there?" Niall could see the top of the clansman's head as he moved toward the wall. Frantically he catapulted downward. He had to reach the ground before he was either pierced thru with an arrow or the rope was cut and he crashed to his death. Already the clansman was slicing through the rope as he shouted out at the top of his lungs for help.

"God help me!" Niall breathed, fearful that he was about to meet a gruesome end. As it was, the fairy flag or God or both seemed to bring him good fortune. The rope was stronger than one might have supposed. Strong enough to allow Niall to reach a spot just a few feet above the rocks before it gave way. He fell and was winded, but as he pushed himself up he could tell there were no broken bones.

That did not mean he was safe, however. The skirl of bagpipes, the beating of drums, the blare of trumpets told him an alarm had been sounded. It would only be a short time before the entire castle was roused. Once that happened he would be the object of a relentless hunt. Well, he was determined that he wouldn't get caught.

Dodging in and out among the rocks, Niall knew that vow to be more bravado than reality. The ocean was at hight tide, crashing against the rocks with a ferocity that was terrifying even to a fighting man. Even had Peadar been waiting for him, which he knew he wouldn't be after all this time, the sea was no way to journey tonight. He would have to go the long and hard way over the rocky land, on foot.

The moon was shrouded by dark clouds, his only guide the light of the fading stars. Nevertheless, he plucked up his courage. He would get back to Sleat and be welcomed as a hero once he handed over the fairy flag. He would be made tanist, a worthy reward. Enough to make any man happy.

Happy? For just an instant Caitlin's face flashed before his eyes. But then perhaps happiness was only a dream after all…..

Caitlin stirred, stretching her arms and legs in slow, easy motions as she came awake. She smiled as she remembered her wedding night. She had never known such happiness existed, but she had found it in the arms of a fisherman. Marriage, at least this part of it, was infinitely pleasing.

Love. It was a wonderful word. It warmed her, made her feel safe. In short it was a blessed emotion.

I will be a good wife, she vowed silently. Even if that meant giving in to woman's work and the discipline marriage brought, Caitlin was willing to try. Niall made her happy. How then could she have worried so about the outcome of what was obviously meant to be.

"Niall….?" Wanting to renew the sensation of lying in Niall's arms she turned over on her side, searching for him with her hands and eyes. "Niall…..?"

He was gone.

Just like a man. No doubt he had slipped away to join with the revelers who were celebrating their wedding. A Highland wedding was a lengthy affair and theirs had just begun. Well, she would soon remind him that there were more enjoyable things that could be done in the quiet of the night. With that thought in mind, she rose from the bed, hurriedly slipped on a tunic and went in search of him.

The stones were cold to her bare feet as Caitlin climbed up and down the stairs, seeking her groom. "Niall?"

So preoccupied was she that at first she didn't even notice the frantic cries of the sentry, but at last they penetrated through her pleasant daydreams.

"Someone has gone over the wall! Someone has left the castle in a manner that bodes no good."

Someone? The longer and harder Caitlin searched for Niall the more she came to realize just who that someone might be. Even so, she refused to listen to the voice in her head that whispered he had left her. No. No. He would never do that, not after what they had shared last night. He was simply cloistered away somewhere. He would reappear. She was certain of it.

Certain? Why then did she find herself drawn to that spot where she had watched her father put the fairy flag? Why were her fingers trembling as she fumbled about in search of it?

"Gone!"

No. Her father must have come in to retrieve it and chosen another hiding place. Niall would never....

Ah, but he had. The heartbreaking evidence was clear. Oh, yes, he had stolen the flag in the dead of night and then disappeared.

Tears streamed down her cheeks but she dashed them away. A MacLeod must never cry. Not over a man, even if he was a husband. Despite that vow, however, the knowledge that she had been betrayed threatened to destroy her.

PART TWO: A Woman Scorned

"Heaven has no rage like love to hatred turned,

Nor hell a fury like a woman scorned."

William Congreve: **The Mourning Bride, Act II, sc,**
8

Chapter Eighteen

Smoke from the cooking fires stung Caitlin's eyes as she worked diligently at the loom, or at least she blamed the moisture in her eyes on the smoke. Her anger and heartache merged together, threatening to choke her. How could he? How could he have done such a loathsome thing? How could he have mouthed words that would bind them together, make love to her not once but twice and then just up and go?

"Ohhhhhhh!" The very question filled her with an anger that threatened to destroy her. She had been used then callously cast aside without even a second thought. The fisherman had wanted to get his hands on the fairy flag and now thanks to her he had, though what purpose he had for it the clan still could not fathom. Unless it was to increase the fish in the lochs where he fished.

The fairy flag had threefold magical powers that included making fighters invincible in battle, promising fertility in a marriage and lastly if put over the loch it brought the herring shoals. So it seemed that Caitlin's virginity had been bartered for the sake of a school of fish.

"How could he?" This time the tears that stung her eyes flowed freely down her cheeks.

Caitlin remembered all too vividly that moment when she had awakened to find the place beside her in bed empty. Rising she had gone in search of Niall only to be swept up in the tumult created when the alarm was sounded. The entire castle had been alerted that someone had scaled the castle wall. That someone she had all too soon realized had been her loving groom. Worse yet she had discovered that he had gone and not gone alone. The fairy flag was conspicuous by its absence. It was missing, stolen. That reality had been Caitlin's final blow.

"Fisherman, och, how I hate thee." And she did, at least for the moment. Hated him with an intensity, a burning rage, that nearly poisoned her. "He left me behind without even so much as a word......"

Worse yet she couldn't forget him. He filled her thoughts by day and her dreams by night, haunting her like a ghost. "Being here with ye makes me the happiest of men," he had said, lying with every breath.

"Caitlin! Be careful. You're tangling the threads." Her mother's high pitched voice sounded a warning.

Caitlin drew in a deep breath and let it out slowly in a sigh. "I'm sorry. I wasna paying much attention to what I was doing." Plucking at the wool, she hastily rectified the situation, untwisting the thread then passing it more cautiously back and forth, interlacing the weft through the warp threads with her shuttle.

"Ach, so we've noticed." Fiona's smile expressed her sympathy though she did not force her daughter to talk about the matter. If Caitlin wanted to open up her heart to her, she would.

Caitlin focused her attention on the loom, a simple rectangular frame made of wood, watching as the other women rolled up an end of the finished cloth to make way for a new length of weaving. They unwound the spindle and measured off the vertical threads in roughly equal lengths. The threads would be the *warp* of the extended length of cloth. Setting the loom upright again, tilted against the wall, they let the warp threads go taut, hanging down vertically across the wooden frame.

Blessed Saint Michael, Caitlin thought, rubbing at her eyes. It somehow reminded her of the small mattress at the cottage. She could imagine herself lying upon its softness, could feel Niall's strong body pressed against hers.

"Careful tipping the loom or we'll be done for it!" Shona's irritated shriek at one of the other girls startled Caitlin out of her daydreaming and she jumped. Her nerves were on edge making her as surly as a bear.

"Ye are much too jittery, Caity." Fiona shook her tawny-haired head. In motherly concern she touched Caitlin's arm. "What is done is done. Ye must try and forget."

"Forget!" She looked at her mother with much the same expression she might have had if she had been slapped. "I canna forget. I was betrayed." She shuddered. "The marriage vows were consummated, Mother. Do ye hae any idea how that makes me feel. Used. Dirtied."

Fiona's look was all-knowing. "I do understand. I do." Her eyes mirrored a deep inner sadness. "But there are worse things in life, daughter."

"Worse?" At the moment Caitlin couldn't think of what that could be.

Her mother explained it bluntly. "Ye still hae yer life and yer health."

Caitlin's cheeks colored. "Aye, I am alive," she answered tartly. "At least it seems that I am." But inside she felt as if she were dying. She couldn't eat, couldn't sleep. She kept remembering the gentle way his hands had stroked her face, belying his strength. The way he had.......

"For which ye should be thankful." Fiona's voice was soft as she said, "Life is not so much what happens to a person but how they accept the circumstances. Ye can either see the storm clouds or the rainbows, the sunlight or the shadows."

"Be optimistic ye mean." Caitlin looked down at her hands. "I canna be. Not now." Perhaps never again.

"Och, then its sorry I am for ye, daughter."

Caitlin ignored her mother's rebuke, keeping to her silence, pretending unwavering interest in the *maide dalbh*, the pattern sticks that served as a guide for the weaving. She and the other women were working on a special plaid, one they hoped would be the symbol for the clan. It was a yellow and black plaid with just a hint of a red stripe. The dyes that were used were made from local lichens, mosses and other plants.

It was a tedious undertaking for the cloth was to be made from twelve ells of plaid, a long piece of cloth to be certain. They had to work carefully. Anything with more than one color increased the complexity of the weaving, necessitating more than one shuttle and a careful counting of threads to match the established pattern.

"Ha, I never thought I'd see the day when you would seek out our company for longer than a few wee minutes, Caitlin." Trying to change the subject and lighten the mood, Shona reminded Caitlin of how infrequently she kept company with the women.

It was true, Caitlin couldn't deny it. The fact was she avoided the women and their weaving every time she could. Usually one to seek the outdoor air, Caitlin had been strangely reflective these last three weeks, however. "I dunna want to be with the men."

Caitlin shifted in her seat and grasped her shuttle more tightly. In and out, in and out, she worked with her spindle, trying to calm her shattered nerves. The truth was she just couldn't stand to see the way the men stared at her, as if seeing her as damaged goods. A discarded bride.

Once she had abhorred women's work. Now, however, women's chores were her only escape from the thoughts and memories which taunted her. Still she fired back a scathing answer. "'Tis none of yer concern where I spend my time, I'd be thinking, sister dear," she exclaimed. "Leastwise I just might make it known to father that ye hae been keeping company with a certain piper."

"Ye wouldna!"

"I would."

"Caity....." her mother's tone cautioned that there would be trouble if the argument went any further.

Caitlin ignored her mother, to concentrate on her work. Ah yes, the plaid would be perfect. As soon as the cloth was finished it would be tread on in water to fill the weave and then fluffed with dried, prickly flowers called teazels to raise the fiber. The last step to the process would be to dry the fabric and stretch it on poles to block it.

Niall would have looked grand in the new tartan. She was haunted by the memory of the way he had thrown his breacan so jauntily over his shoulder.

"No!" Caitlin gasped aloud causing the others to stare. Quickly she covered her lips with her fingers regretting the outburst. Why oh why couldn't she get the fisherman out of he mind? Why? The answer screamed at her. She was trying to run away from heart by working so diligently, but she couldn't escape her desire. She could not flee from her feelings. The sad truth was that she missed him. Cared for him. More than she could allow herself to admit. Particularly when he obviously didn't care at all for her.

Where is he? Where could he have gone? It was a question she had asked herself many times of late, a question they had all asked. As of yet it was still unanswered. Though Ian MacLeod had gathered up his men, had scoured the entire countryside including the shoreline, not even a trace of the fisherman had been found.

Could he have drowned? Once again to her dismay Caitlin dropped her spindle, tangling the thread. No, she wouldn't allow herself to even think that. He couldn't be dead. Not Niall. Nor, despite her anger, would she have wished it to be so. Someday they would once again be face to face and when that happened she would tell him just what she thought about him.

Caitlin carefully counted the threads she was weaving, determined to put the matter out of her mind. Ten black threads. Time to change to the yellow-threaded spindle. And when the plaid was done she'd begin on another.

The din of bagpipes jarred her from her thinking. The pipes, summoning everyone to gather. The sound was unnerving. Shattering. Worse yet, it meant that something unforetold had happened.

"What is it?" Shona voiced all their fears. She could not help but wonder if another clash of shields and swords was about to ensue.

"There is only one way to know." Putting down the cloth, Caitlin was the first one to the door. The seerer had foretold blood and fire. Had that moment arrived when the dark man would bring the MacLeod's to the brink of destruction?

Total pandemonium greeted her as she pushed through the heavy wooden door of the large stone hall. Ominously the MacLeod clansmen were preparing themselves for the imminent danger that was to come. Brandishing their weapons, which reflected the flames ablaze in the hearth, they grumbled in anger as they waited for their chief, Ian MacLeod to enter the hall.

Caitlin's eyes darted back and forth, searching for the familiar form of her father. Where was he? As if her anxiety conjured him up, he soon pushed through the door of the adjoining room he used as a council chamber. His face was contorted in a blaze of fury. Pulling at his beard he strode back and forth before the fire, muttering beneath his breath.

"What is it, Father?" Only Caitlin dared ask the question that all within the room wondered.

"I've just received a message from the MacDonalds. I dinna ken what to make of it!"

"The MacDonalds?" A ripple of uneasiness swept throughout the hall.

"They hae been quiet much too long. I should hae known it wouldna last," Ian said aloud.

"Nae!" The men were unanimous in their shout.

Anger buzzed around from man to man like an enraged bee as the clansmen savored old slights and tragedies, all at the MacDonalds hands.

Ian MacLeod silenced the protestations by raising his hand. Though in truth he was but a few inches taller than most of the men, he seemed to tower over them as he pulled back his shoulders and held up his hand.

"They brazenly hae announced that they plan to attack the stronghold," he said curtly. "And they threaten that this time they will win."

"And we dunna hae the flag!" Caitlin's voice sounded as ominous as the seerers had that day. All the while she was struggling with her conscience. She had kept silent about the matter of having caught Niall trying to steal the flag again. Now he had accomplished that mission to the detriment of her clansmen. *With as much precision and ruthlessness as if he had been....had been a.......* A MacDonald, she thought but did not say.

"Nae, we dunna hae the flag." Ian pretended not to care, though the gravity of the matter was marked on his face. "But it doesna matter. 'Twas superstition only. We can win without it."

Through the years there had been times when the MacLeods had won, times when the MacDonalds had been victors in the battles. Both clans had been losers in the toll taken on their familes. Warfare between the rival clans had brought forth a torrent of heartache. Now it appeared that it was happening all over again under the worst of circumstances. Like it or not, whether the flag was really a talisman or just a psychological measure of good luck, the lack of their flag made the MacLeod's vulnerable.

Chapter Nineteen

The hall was dimly lit. Only the dying embers of the fire shed illumination on the two figures sitting side by side, intent in conversation. One was a man in the autumn of his years the other a man in the prime of his life. Tall and lean but well-muscled, he had a strength about him that was almost overpowering. Even his manner of dress proclaimed his self-esteem. He was dressed now in a breacon, wrapped round the waist and belted, a length of which was draped over his shoulder and pinned with a jeweled brooch.

"Aye, ye are a MacDonald through and through. A chip off of my shoulder, lad. As dear to me as any son could e'er be."

Malcolm looked upon Niall with pride. His particular distinction was on the battlefield and he had done the MacDonalds proud! But no physical feat could have matched the one he had just accomplished. Niall MacDonald had brought back the Fairy Flag. The very soul of the Clan MacLeod.

"Aye, lad I honor ye." Holding the goblet to his lips he drank deeply of the contents then wiped his mouth with the back of his hand. "Oh, how I wish I could see Ian MacLeod's face now. Oh, that I were a spider on the wall." Throwing back his head he roared with laughter.

Niall didn't join in the joviality. Though he had been welcomed as a hero, just as he knew he would be, his mood was somber. Leaning back in his chair he looked southward, as if he could see through the very walls to the lands beyond.

Oh, Caitlin, why is it so very hard to put ye from my mind? Why? Closing his eyes he could nearly see her face that way it had looked when he had kissed her goodbye. Her eyelids had been closed, she had looked so peaceful, so trusting. Trusting of the man who had so cruelly betrayed her.

"As loyal a MacDonald as ever there be. That ye are, lad," Malcolm MacDonald was saying. "Risking yer very life to bring us back the greatest boon we could hae ever received. The flag! The flag!" Again Malcolm chortled.

"Aye, I risked my life." And lost my heart and soul, Niall thought. He remembered vividly his escape from the MacLeod's lands, a treacherous journey that had rendered him blisters, cuts, scratches and bruises. Most of the way had been on foot, for having told the lie of being a fisherman he was certain the MacLeod would have lookouts posted along the coast. Climbing the curious flat-topped mountains to the southwest, known as MacLeod's Tables, he had made his way by land down the east coast, carefully dodging in and out lest the MacLeod put his wolf hounds on the trail.

It had been a mountainous and rocky terrain, rough traveling over mountains and moors shrouded by low-flying clouds. The Isle of the Clouds is what the Norsemen had dubbed Skye. Using that cloud cover to hide from any pursers, Niall had blessed the fog, all the while praying that he would make it back to Sleat alive.

Malcolm MacDonald lounged drunkenly in his carved wooden chair by the roaring hearth fire, taking long gulps of his ale, idly watching his handsome tawny-haired nephew.

"Something is wrong with ye, lad."

He couldn't quite figure out what it was. Since coming back from the MacLeod's castle Niall was more subdued, less cocky despite the wondrous thing that he had done. He seemed deep into contemplation for long periods of time, laughed seldomly.

"Did I not know better, I'd think the MacLeod's sent back a changeling in yer place, Niall. Of a surety I would." Niall's reflective mood was troublesome.

"Perhaps they did, Uncle for I am not the same man who left this hall. Aye, I've changed." Strange how one wee lassie could work such havoc in his life, he thought and yet she had. Thinking about the way he had left her caused a gnawing ache in his heart that he could not remedy no matter how hard he tried.

Squinting his eyes, Malcolm tried to decipher Niall's meaning. "And I dunna like it! Cheer up. Be thankful to be back safe and sound."

"I am thankful."

"Then smile."

Niall forced his lips to curl upward but there was no sincerity in the gesture. All he could think about was that Malcolm was planning to attack the MacLeod stronghold bringing death and destruction to those Caitlin loved. And all because of him and what he had done.

"Why must there always be fighting here on Sky," he said softly, not to Malcolm but to himself.

Malcolm heard. "Why? Why?" His face was contorted with sudden anger. "Ask that of Ian MacLeod, why don't ye. He is the one who insists on claiming land that isna his." He took another gulp of from his cup. His brows drew together in a scowl.

"And do ye never want to hae peace?"

"Hold yer tongue!" Malcolm thundered. In a show of contempt he threw his ale, cup and all, into the fire, watching as the flames sputtered. "Ye hae always been my favorite, though I hae never spoken so. I hae great ambitions for ye, laddie. There is no hill ye canna climb if ye use yer head."

And keep silent, Niall thought. Malcolm was telling him that if he behaved, did things exactly Malcolm's way he would be tanist. The honor he had once coveted above all. Now the reward seemed but a hollow victory. Strange how life seemed so empty without the red-haired lass. Ambition could not keep a man warm at night or give him comfort.

"They hae e'er been our enemies." Seeing a fly crawling across the stone floor he vented his anger on the hapless insect, grinding it beneath the heal of his cuaran. That was how he would crush the MacLeod!

A troubled silence ensued. Niall stared at his uncle, watching the myriad of emotions that played upon the bearded face. In most matters a reasonable man, Malcolm looked more like a snarling dog. Was that what all this fighting had brought them all too? Creatures not much better than the MacLeod's hounds? If so then he regretted what he had done more than anything in all his life.

How many mugs of whiskey would it take to numb his mind? How much barley bree need he drink? Niall wondered before he could ease his conscience? Already his vision was blurred, his head buzzed, yet he continued to raise the mug to his lips.

"If ye drink any more of that, Niall my friend, ye will be as pickled as a herring." Coming up to sit beside him, Ogg eyed him worriedly.

"If I drink any more o' this, mayhap I can hae a little peace." Niall's heart was heavy, his temper on edge. By God, how he missed her. More so than he had ever thought it possible to miss another human being. There was something about her that he craved, like a man hankered for strong drink. She had given his life new meaning, had given him love, and how was he going to repay her? By bringing the wrath of the MacDonald down on her head.

"Peace, ye say." Though he was not bid to sit down, Ogg plopped down on the bench beside Niall. His big frame caused the bench to quake, but Niall didn't seem to notice. "Peace from what?"

"I dunna want to talk of it." It was just too painful a subject, even to share with Ogg, at least for the moment. With a groan, Niall closed his eyes.

"Something happened at the MacLeod castle, something that has changed ye." Again Ogg wondered aloud, "What?"

Niall put his fingers to his temples, pressing hard as if by so doing he could force Caitlin MacLeod from his mind. It did no good. He could envision her now, sweeping into the room so haughty and so proud, her dark red hair flying around her shoulders like a shawl of living flame.

"Caity!" Ogg cocked his head. "Did ye say Caity?"

Niall didn't answer; he was too disturbed by the image floating in front of his eyes. He imagined Caitlin being surrounded by a throng of Highland warriors, heard her cry out, saw her fall. It was a daydream that left him shaken and sick to his stomach.

"By the saints, Niall, ye look as sick as if ye had seen a ghost." Ogg leaned closer. "Did ye? Did ye see the ghost of Colin MacLeod? Did it possess ye?"

Niall raised his head. "Aye, possessed is what I am." And tortured by the thought of what he had done. He was a man of action, a man who went after what he wanted. *Ambitious* was the word. Now it seemed that his thirst for power had goaded him into the greatest wrong he had ever done. A wrong that could ne'er be righted.

Silence reigned, like the quiet before a devastating storm. The castle was shrouded in darkness. Everyone was abed except the two young women who sat cross-legged on the floor playing a game of wooden pegs. It was a man's game of warfare and strategy wherein the pegs were like a miniature army that could be moved around the wooden board. A game Caitlin had always enjoyed playing but which troubled her now that an armed conflict between the MacDonalds and MacLeods appeared to be eminent.

"Och, Caity, I took yer chieftain again. That's three times in a row. Ye must not be thinking, hinny." Shona clucked her tongue sympathetically but still seemed to take great delight in having won at a game she nearly always lost. "Do ye want to play again?"

"Hmmmmm?" The vacant look in Caitlin's eyes proved that she hadn't been listening.

"I asked if ye wanted to play again."

Pushing the game board away, Caitlin shook her head. "No. my heart just isna in it."

"Nor yer mind." Carefully picking up the carved pegs, stuffing them into a small leather pouch, Shona didn't even try to hide her concern. "Fie on ye, Caity, to let some mon destroy ye this way. Handsome he was, aye, but not worth what ye hae been going through." Gently she touched her sister's arm. "Ye are a bonnie lass. There will other laddies, all of them standing in line just for the bliss of a smile."

Caitlin took a deep breath and let it out in a deep sigh. "I dunna want a laddie. I willna marry again. Ever."

"Ever?" Shona was shocked by the finality of such a statement.

"Ever." Caitlin ran her fingers through her tangled hair. Hair she didn't even bother to comb for days on end, she who was always so proud of her fiery tresses. "I obeyed father's command. I went willingly to the altar. He canna ask more of me than that."

"But......"

"Whether or no my groom choses to live with his bride I am married, Shona. What happened canna be annulled because......" The marriage had been consummated, binding Caitlin to the fisherman, at least until the Holy church in Rome decided otherwise.

"Because he claimed his husbandly rights, the devil." In a rare show of temper the usually gentle Shona threw the pouch with the game pieces to the floor, scattering them all about. "Oh, how I damn a mon who could do such a thing and then vanish in the night without....."

"Hush!" Caitlin closed her eyes tightly, as if by so doing she could forget. "I dunna want to even think....." Or feel. And yet how could she shut the fisherman out of her thoughts when his image haunted her night and day.

Niall. The fisherman. Even now she could envision him as vividly as if he were standing right there with them in the room. She could imagine how golden his hair looked in the torchlight, how dazzling his smile always appeared. She remembered his arrogant stance, the way he cocked his head, the bold way he walked as if he were the leader of some mighty clan.

"I wonder........."

"Wonder what, Caity?" Regretting her outburst, Shona quickly got down on hands and knees, retrieving the pegs that littered the cold stone floor.

"I wonder why and who......?"

That, as much as his leaving, was deeply troubling Caitlin. It just didn't make sense. She had trouble believing that Niall was merely a fisherman. Oh, no, there was something else that lay at the root of his sudden appearance at the castle. Something she couldn't allow herself to even think. And yet......

The Fairy Flag is important to the MacLeods but would it not also be important to the MacDonalds as well? Wouldn't Malcolm MacDonald give even his favorite sword, nae the very shirt off his back just to possess it? And were he to possess it wouldn't that explain his sudden boldness, the cocky way he had threatened to start the fighting all over again? Aye, Caitlin answered to herself. And aye again. Yet even having answered yes she couldn't really allow herself to believe it. She, Caitlin nic Ian married to a MacDonald?

Never!

Why, the very thought! After all hadn't it been said that all MacDonalds had long noses, hair growing in their ears, big feet and faces that could turn a lassie to stone? Of a surety that description didn't fit Niall. "And yet....."

"What is that?"

"What?" Caitlin looked at Shona, disconcerted to see that her face was as pale as a ghost's.

"That cry."

They both listened, their hearts quickening as they realized what it was. The cry of "hold fast". The MacLeod cry to battle. Running to the window both young women leaned over the stone ledge, their eyes scanning the horizon.

"Look!" Two men, each carrying a pole with a cross of fire-blackened wood were visible in the moonlight. It could only mean one thing.

"The MacDonalds are coming!" The threat that they were going to attack Dunvegan castle was no idle boast.

"Heaven help us!" Shona clutched at her chest, her fear nearly tangible. The two sisters looked at each other for a long time knowing battle was inevitable.

"We canna fight. We are helpless." Or nearly so. Still both young women knew that their father was placed in an intolerable position. It was either fight or back down. They knew their father would choose to fight for his honor even though the MacLeods' sense of doom reverberated throughout the castle.

"To arms! To arms!" The cry was shouted out so loud that it shook the very walls. Caitlin watched as her clansmen stripped every sword, shield, targe and dirk from the wall. Old hatreds were hard to quiet and Malcolm's aggression a potent poison.

Shouts rent the air. What followed was a clashing and a slashing of swords, a bloody and violent melee.

Together the sisters watched from the window of their room in prayerful silence as the battle exploded all around them like some ghastly dance.

"Father, do ye see father?" Caitlin was nearly frantic as he disappeared into the swarm of fighting men. Her heart skipped a beat as she saw a bearded man fall, but it wasn't him.

"He's over there. By the outer wall." Swinging his sword, he looked to be an awesome force to come up against despite his age. One by one he was felling any man foolish enough to come within reach of his claymore. His courage, stamina and stubbornness seemed to rally the others for suddenly it seemed the battle had turned in the MacLeod's favor. Relentlessly they were pushing the MacDonalds back.

"Back to the Hell-hole ye came from," the MacLeod shouted out, his voice fading to a gasp.

"What is it? What is wrong?" Shona leaned so far out the window that she nearly fell, her eyes focused southward.

"Nae!" Caitlin saw, but she didn't believe her eyes. In truth she didn't want to. "It couldna be." But it was. In an outward show of defiance and brazenness the MacDonalds were flying a banner, one all too familiar to Caitlin's eyes.

"Caity! Ye look as if ye are going to faint....."

"I am." Or at least she wished that she could so that she wouldn't have to look at such a travesty of fate.

At that moment Caitlin MacLeod was so devastated by what her eyes revealed that she nearly could have died. Flying high on a long pole was a piece of cloth she knew only too well. A sight that chilled her to the very bone.

"No. It canna be." But it was. There before her very eyes was proof of Niall's devastating betrayal. "T'is the Fairy flag!"

Chapter Twenty

Confusion and havoc reigned. the loud clink of sword and axe rang out mingling with hostile yells and epitaphs as MacDonald and MacLeod engaged in brutal fighting. Sweat poured from Niall's brow as he parried, thrust and whirled around.

"Take care, Niall!"

Ogg's timely warning allowed him to narrowly miss the blade that cut through the air. with a mumbled oath, Niall responded in kind. Brandishing his sword, he soon vanquished his attacker.

Niall's head was throbbing as he sung his sword back and forth, pushing back anyone who threatened to get in his way. always before he had gloried in battle; now however, as he stumbled and nearly fell over the body of a fallen enemy he viewed it as a loathsome and destructive thing. Still, he had to do his part. he was a MacDonald, and even though he had no liking for this cruel feuding he couldn't allow harm to come to his own. Even so, he could not keep his eyes from darting upward now and again. Where was Caitlin? Was she safe? He had to think so or be consumed by guilt. Guilt that he had used her. Guilt that he had lied to her. Guilt that he had been the perpetrator of such a vile betrayal.

Does she know? Has she guessed? Has she seen the flag flapping in the breeze? If so, then she would realize his identity and would know him to be who and what he was. Her enemy! He who had been instrumental in the MacLeod's ensuing defeat.

"Ach, Niall, look at the expression on Ian MacLeod's face. he knows he willna win. they are but playing for time. They hae lost the badge o' their courage. Soon, soon the MacLeods will be forced to give up."

"Give up? Never!" Anger ruled as a Macleod having overheard, plunged forward. He was quickly felled.

The MacDonalds were anxious for complete victory. Egged on by Malcolm they closed around their longtime foes, wielding weapons that took a painful toll they moved. Though the MacLeods were desperate to rally, though the tide of battle briefly turned in their favor, in the end they could do little but retreat.

Bloodied, battered, and disheartened, the MacLeod clansmen limped or were carried back to the hall. Listening to the moaning and cries of pain from the wounded, Caitlin experienced the most profound sense of sadness she had ever known. It was a pathetic sight. A gruesome reminder of the carnage such violence could bring.

"How many were killed?" As Jamie passed by she tugged at his sleeve.

"Too many!" The always self-assured Jamie had been humbled, tragically so. Holding his arm to staunch the flow of blood, he retreated to the corner to see to his injuries, reminding Caitlin of an injured hound, licking his wounds. He didn't want to talk about the battle that had been his greatest humiliation.

Some of the others were not as silent, however. Listening to the talk Caitlin soon learned that it had been more costly in lives than the clansmen had first thought.   Worse yet, thought the MacLeods had defended the castle the MacDonalds were laying claim to Trotternish, an area of land to the east that had been the source of contention since long before Caitlin was born.

"So, they hae stolen our flag and our land," she swore beneath her breath. What's more she knew just who to blame. At that moment had she had the power she would have damned him to Hell forever.

The sickeningly sweet odor of fresh blood assailed Caitlin's nostrils as she moved in an out among the wounded. Tearing the hems of their night gowns into strips she and her sisters carefully tended the wounded. It was a sobering initiation for all of them into the real world.

"Very different from the glories the seanachaidh tells us of," Shona breathed, trying to ignore the screams that issued from the throat of the young man she was tending.

"Far different."

It was a time in Caitlin's life that she knew would haunt her. The eyes filled with anguish, the cries of the wounded, the moans of those who were dying all made her aware of her helplessness. There was just so much she could do.   She could bath their faces, wrap their injured limbs in bandages, try her best to make them comfortable, shower them with words to sooth their aching pride, but she could not take away their shame. Shame that they had embarrassed their very name.

"Damn the MacDonalds."

"They are little more than thieves."

"Stole the flag from under our very noses."

"Aye but how?

Eavesdropping on the wounded men's conversation, Caitlin wanted to tell them her suspicions, but feared the reaction such a revelation might inspire. Even so, she knew. She knew! Maybe that was why she viewed the stairs with trepidation as she climbed the steps to answer the summons from her father. She knew all too well what he was going to tell her and dreaded this confrontation more than she had ever dreaded anything in her life.

Having bolstered her bravery by drinking several draughts of ale, she felt strangely dizzy and not as blissfully content as she had hoped. Perhaps then there was no potion that could take away the sting of betrayal or soothe her feelings of guilt.

I should have told my father about Niall's trying to steal the flag again. If I had all this would not have come about. Instead, she had kept silent trying to protect a man who did not deserve shielding. A thief! A liar! *And maybe even worse.*

It was a short distance to her father's room yet it seemed like a mile of plodding one foot in front of the other, up, up, up the stone stairs. Even so, once the chamber door loomed in her path Caitlin seemed to lose all courage. How was she going to tell her father that she kept Niall's transgression a secret? How was she going to reveal her betrayal of her own clan? Was she to brush it off as enchantment? Blindness? Foolishness? In truth there was no way to even understand it herself. All she knew was that the ensuing circumstances had proven that she had done her father a great wrong.

Like the most awesome portcullis the door rose up before her.   Raising a trembling hand to the wood, swallowing hard, she knocked hesitantly, a gesture which reflected her apprehension.

Caitlin's knock was answered by her father's shouted, "come in!"

Her hands trembled as she opened the door. "Ye called for me father."

"Aye! That I did." Lighting a taper he lowered his bulk into a wooden chair and gestured for her to do the same.   Instead Caitlin remained standing, her eyes assessing her father's well-being in but the wink of an eye. Enough time to tell that he was alright.

He came right to the point.   "I hae done ye a grievous wrong, daughter.   In my stubborn pride, my insistence that ye bend to my will I hae ruined not only ye but the clan."

She tried to speak, to tell him what she knew in her heart, but her words came out only as a strangled gasp. All she could do was to stare at her father as he buried his face in his hands. Never in all her life had she seen him shed even one tear yet he shed several now.

"Oh, lassie! Lassie! How can I bear it? How can I atone for what I hae done to ye because of my selfish pride. How can I tell ye what I know to be true? How can I reveal the shame of it.   The terrible foolish stupidity."

"Father......" Her heart ached to know that he was suffering because of her, because he thought he had forced her into an unwelcome marriage. She had to tell him the truth, that she had secretly been more than willing, that she had lusted after her tawny-haired betrothed, so much so that she had ruined them all.

Ian MacLeod looked up slowly, his eyes meeting hers. "I learned something tonight. Something I dunna want to tell ye. Yer husband is.....is......"

Caitlin's voice came out in a whisper. "I know."

Ian stiffened. "Ye ken? How?"

She tapped at her temple with her finger. "I figured it out in here. Two, plus two, plus two came out MacDonald. It was the only thing that explained so many things."

He seemed relieved not to have to be the one to tell her. "Aye, the mon who pretended to be a fishermon was none other than Niall MacDonald, nephew to my greatest enemy."

"Nephew!" So, it was even worse than she had supposed. Not only a MacDonald but a member of the chieftain's family. A man her clansman had dubbed the "MacLeod's scourge".

"The vile deceitful bastard!" Clenching his hands into fists, the MacLeod raised them high over his head. "No fishermon at all but a MacDonald who came all the way to the castle with but one thought on his mind."

"Father.....I....."

He bolted up from his chair. "Oh, that I had thrown him into the dungeon that very first day. Instead, my eyes were blinded. I should hae known his foolish prattle aboot trying to prove his bravery was a falsehood. But he was such a fine looking specimen of a mon. He seemed to be so right for ye, hinny." He hung his head. "All I could think about when he reminded me of my vow was what fine grandchildren a mon like that would sire. And so........"

"He fooled us both," she breathed. Moving towards Ian she took his hand. Before she had time to make any confessions, however, he was kneeling in front of her. A homage that was unusual for such a prideful man.

"Forgive me, Caity. Please. Forgive......"

She could let him take the blame. "Ye really didna force me to do anything I didna want to, Father. In truth I found him a most desirable mon."

He drew his hand away and stood up. "Which makes it all the worse. Ye cared for him, Caity. It is written in yer eyes."

"Aye, that I did. But that does not explain nor recompense what I hae done." She could not keep from trembling at the thought of what she had to confess.

"Ye?"

She wrestled with the dilemma of her fate at last blurting it out. "I came upon him in the tower, trying to steal the flag a second time but I didna tell ye."

"Didna......." He was stunned.

Now it was Caitlin who was weeping. "I didna want any harm to come to him. I wanted to protect him."

"Protect a thieving MacDonald!" Ian MacLeod nearly choked on his rage.

"I didna know who he was. How could I. I only thought.....that...."

"Och, ye didna think. That's what." His eyes glittered dangerously in the candlelight, simmering with anger. "Och, that any seed of my loins could do such a thing."

There as such a fiercesome pressure pushing at her chest that she feared she couldn't breath. "I meant no harm......." *I didn't know what the consequences would be.*

"Meant no harm!" Striking his fist on a wooden table near his chair, he startled Caitlin. "Damn it, lass, by keeping silent ye did us the greatest harm of all." He lapsed into a fiercesome tirade, lecturing her on absolute loyalty to the clan. "Instead ye thought with yer heart like any foolish woman. Blinded by anything except strong arms, broad shoulders and a handsome face. Ye listened to his lies and believed them like some silly ninny. When ye should hae.....ye should hae....."

"Should hae told ye all." She had made a great mistake but nonetheless Caitlin's pride came to her rescue. "But I am not the only one who did, I'd be saying." The way she was staring at him seemed to accuse him of sharing in her blame. "Ye admitted that ye were thinking of yer fine, strong grandsons." She held up her head. "Ye should hae let me be, Father. Ye should hae let me hae my freedom, at least for a little while longer."

Ian glowered into eyes so like his own. "Ye dare to say....."

"I do." Angrily she walked toward the door, not even bothering to say goodnight. There was no use bemoaning what she had done. All that was left for her now was to undo it. With that thought on her mind she hurriedly returned to her chamber, picked up a large leather pouch and started stuffing it with some of her belongings.

"Caity, what are ye doing?" Having been asleep, Shona opened one eye, disturbed by the noise.

"I'm leaving."

"Leaving?" Shona bolted up from the pillows. "Going where?"

"To the MacDonald's castle!"

"What?"

"Ye heard me. I'm going to get the Fairy Flag back."

Shona stared at her sister incredulously. "Caity, ye must be daft! Touched in the head if ye think ye can get away wi' this. Father will hae yer head and mine as well for knowing and not telling! And it will all be for naught." Shona clutched at the folds of her night gown, frightened for her sister and for herself. Surely Caitlin could not be serious about what she proposed, to boldly travel to MacDonald territory and take matters into her own hands. "Father will......"

"He will ken when he thinks about it." Remembering their confrontation made her doubly determined. It was the only way to be forgiven. Nae, to forgive herself. "I must get this matter settled, once and for all."

"But how are ye going to get there. Sleat is a long, long way..."

"By boat." If Niall MacDonald could do it then so could she.

"By boat!" Shona panicked. "Ye might be taken by the *cailleach uisge* and I'd ne'r see ye again."

"Ach, I'm no' afraid of the water hag and besides, I won't be alone. I'll take someone with me. Someone I can trust."

Proving her determination, Caitlin moved about the room, gathering all the necessary items to take with her on the journey, wrapping them in a bundle. A comb, her cuarans to wear along the rocky path, a broach, a curraichd to tie around her head if it was windy.

"Oh, Caity! Don't go! Ye'll disappear. I willna see ye again."

"I willna disappear," she tried to sound a lot braver than she felt. She had never even been in a boat before.

"Caity, what if ye are caught before ye get very far? Then a whipping will be yer only reward for being so braw!"

"I'll hae take that chance." Her father hadn't caught Niall. Wasn't she just as canny?

"Ye canna go, Caity." Grabbing her firmly by the arm, Shona thought to stop her but Caitlin merely pushed her aside.

"I *am* going. I've made up my mind. Ye canna prevent it. Do ye ken?"

"Aye." Shona knew well that when Caitlin wanted to do something nothing could stop her. She thought for a moment then suddenly threw her arms around her sister. Her tears splashed Caitlin's face. "But take care, Brie. If anything were to happen to ye I'd never forgie myself."

"Nothing will happen! Ye'll see. Everything will be all right." Bold talk. The truth was she couldn't be certain that it would be. Indeed, she could not be certain that she would ever see her sister again. Still, she knew she had to go, had to rectify the wrong she had done.

Forcing a self-confident smile, Caitlin slung the sack over her shoulder and made for the door. Fumbling around in the dark with her precious bundle she said a silent prayer that she would have no regrets for her decision.

Chapter Twenty-One

Darkness had brought a cold, heavy mist. Shivering, Caitlin admitted to herself that she was fearful. As the familiar shores of Skye disappeared she had felt an unnerving sense of wariness. Since she was a child she'd heard tales of mermaids and sea-people; water horses and water bulls that enticed unwary travelers. *Nuckelavee. Glastig.* Were these creatures even now lying in wait to snatch the boat as it bounced on the waves?

"I willna even think about it," she said aloud, trying to pluck up her courage. She couldn't and wouldn't go back.

"Ye look worried, lass. Everything will be all right." Donald the fisherman to whom she had given her gold broach to take her to Sleat, hurried to assure her.

Crossing herself, Caitlin looked over her shoulder from time to time. watching the waves warily for any sign of a beastie. Fear only added to the misery she already felt. The unpleasant creatures were not her only reservation. She was instigating an act for which there might well be repercussions. Her father would be incensed if he found out what she had done. Worse, she knew naught of Malcolm. For all she knew she might well be walking straight into a lions' den. And yet she could not turn back. Her fiercesome pride goaded her on.

As the boat skimmed the rough waves, however, she found herself wishing that she had never had such a dangerous idea. She had been brave and fearless at home amid familiar surroundings. Now she had to fight her inner turmoil and bolster her courage.

Up and down, back and forth, the boat rocked unendingly. The violently churning ocean soon turned her insides upside down. But soon, soothed by the rise and dip of the blades as they slapped the waves, she drifted off into a fitful sleep.

Deep in her dreams she was conscious only of the motion of the boat and the sound of the water. Awakening for a moment, she pulled the folds of her arasaid around her body. The air was a penetrating damp cold and she hugged herself to keep from shivering, then as complete exhaustion took control of her, she fell asleep again.

A cold spray of ocean mist splashed into Caitlin's face, awakening her. She stirred, stretching her arms and legs in slow, easy motions. A sea mist engulfed them, a blinding swirl of white.

"Where are we?"

"I wish I knew. Far down the coast, past MacLeod's Tables I think." He tried to keep the tone of his voice calm for more than the fog concerned him. The wind was starting to blow and though it would push out the fog he didn't like it. A fiercesome storm was brewing. He could read it in the churning of the sea, smell it in the air.

"Ye are worried."

"There is going to be quite a gale. We'll have to brace ourselves."

"Brace ourselves?" Caitlin gritted her teeth to keep from begging Donald to take her back home. She tried to make light of it. "I hate storms! When I was a child my father told me that they were caused by huge sea beasties growling."

"Beasties?" He laughed, but his smile soon turned to a frown.

"By Saint Michael...!" He looked around him, peering out at the ocean, straining his eyes for any sight of land. "The storm! Never hae I seen one take shape so quickly."

She eyed him warily. "The water beasties are angry I suppose."

"Angry and threatening. We're going to have to weather out the storm, lass. What ever happens, no matter what, hold on to the side of the boat. Do ye hear me?"

"Aye!" Her heart lurched in her breast as she realized fully the danger they were in.

"If the boat flips over swim clear of it. Do you understand?"

Caitlin nodded, hoping that it wouldn't come to that. The water would be freezing. "Aye."

"Then try to swim to the curah and hold on. It's sturdy. It will float. Remember!"

Caitlin nodded again, holding on to the sides as if that moment had already come. All the while she prayed that the fearful gust of wind and turbulent waves would soon abate. Oh how she suddenly wanted to be on land again. Never would her father's castle seem so dear.

The small boat rocked from side to side as the ocean pounded viciously against the stern. Donald looked nervously over his shoulder. "Dear merciful

God," he whispered, pulling away from her he picked up the oars that lay in the bottom of the boat.

"What is it?" Alarm rang through her, hurrying her heart, jangling her nerves and stretching her courage to its limit.

He confided in her, counting on her bravery. "We are off course and heading ashore."

"Ashore?" The rocks up ahead seemed to be drawing them, pulling them.

She cursed her impetuous nature which had led them into this travail. It had been her idea to sail to Skye. She should have gone by land. Now perhaps her daring would be the death of them both. Poor, poor Donald. And all for the sake of a broach. "What can I do to help."

He pushed her back when she would have helped him row. "Just sit quiet!'

A violent wave sent her sprawling, unbalancing the boat as she hit the side. On both sides of the boat the treacherous sea flung itself in massive crests, the spray whistling into the air. The rumble of the water was so loud it caused the boat to vibrate.

"Are you all right?" Pausing in his rowing, the fisherman stared at her.

"Aye!" At least for the time being.

"We have to stay clear of the rocks....." He shouted, "perhaps I can...... " The roar of another wave drowned out his words.

Suddenly the boat capsized and Caitlin was hurled into the air by a giant wave. A scream tore from her throat as she felt herself hit the water. She was engulfed in icy blackness. "Blessed Saint Michael!" she cried silently. No! This could not be happening. "Please dear

God," she choked between mouthfuls of seawater.

Taking a deep breath she plunged into the water's depths, searching beneath the boat for any sign of the fisherman. There was none. A numbing fear overtook Caitlin as she realized that she was alone.

"Nae! Nae!"

She was going to die. Right here, right now. She was going to drown and no one would ever know what had happened to her. That was a thought that a nearly made her lose all self control. In the end, however, she remembered who she was. The MacLeod's eldest daughter. A fighter. A braw lassie. If she had to die she would do it with the same bravery as the men who had fallen in battle.

"But I willna die! It wasn't her time yet. There were too many things that she had to do."

The watery prison seemed almost endless yet she put one arm before the other, fighting for survival. She didn't want to believe that death was to be her fate. Oh, please! She had so much to live for. Blessed Saint Michael! Her life was still ahead of her.

As if in answer to her prayers the flow of the water changed direction and rose to aid in her. She found herself drifting towards the shore. From childhood Caitlin had known how to swim, it was something she always enjoyed but that was in lochs and burns, not in such threatening water. Still she knew If only she could reserve her strength and let the sea carry her to land she might survive. Trying to control her breathing, to relax despite her fear of the icy ocean, she determined that she would be the victor not the icy sea. She was strong. She was a MacLeod!

Alas, however, it seemed she was no match for the ocean. It seemed to go on forever, the round-topped mountains just a large ominous speck in the distance. The longer she struggled the more hopeless the situation seemed. The icy water robbed her of her stamina. Her strength was wavering. She was weary. Close to giving up. Then as a rock struck her foot and she realized that all was not lost. Not yet.

Fight. Survive the waters. Don't give up.

Suddenly hands reached out for her, grabbing her, pulling her ashore. The salt water stung her eyes so she could not see. A hazy figure loomed in front of her. With a final effort she shook her head and squinted her eyes. Though half blind she saw *him*. A giant of a man! Dear merciful Saint Michael!

Instinct told her to run. Run. Nimbly escaping the grasping hands she sprang to her feet and sprinted across the rocks as fast as her weary legs would carry her. It was not fast enough. The giant had closed the distance and now was tugging at her hair.

Screaming in outrage Caitlin pulled free of his grasp, fighting with all her waning strength. It was no use. With a shriek of despair she gave in to the darkness that swirled before her eyes and fell unconscious to the ground.

"Who are ye?" The huge man's deep booming voice matched his ominous appearance.
Caitlin raised her eyes, staring at the giant with hair as red as her own. "Red Etin," she exclaimed, remembering the Scottish folk tale about the giant who kidnapped the King of Scotland's daughter. If it was not him then by Saint Michael it was his twin.

"Red Etin," the giant repeated as if he thought that was Caitlin's name. Well, it was as good a name as any.

"What are ye doing on these shores?"

"What shores?" Caitlin was totally disoriented. She didn't really know where she was. Was this MacDonald territory or was she still in her own. And what of this "giant"? Looking up at him, she decided that this being was human and not the creature she had first supposed.

"Near Loch Bracadale." The giant eyed her up and down much as a fisherman would a fish he had just caught. A fish he was deciding whether to keep or throw back.

"Loch Bracadale." Caitlin sighed with relief. She was still in the territory held by her clan.
That gave her courage to ask this man the same question that he had asked her. "My whereabouts now being established I'll ask ye the same question ye asked of me. Who are ye?"

Before he could answer six other men stepped forward, one of them answering for him. "He is Ogg. The most fiercesome fighter the MacDonalds can claim."

"MacDonalds." Caitlin drew away. She should have recognized this group of men by the red and green plaid they were wearing and by the heather they wore in their low, flat bonnets.
Undoubtedly this was a band of stragglers returning to Sleat after their battle with her clansmen. That their hands were tainted by MacLeods' blood made her shudder.

"Aye, MacDonalds." The name was spoken by the giant with all the pride a man could muster. "And what of ye? What clan do ye belong to, lass?"

One of the other men laughed. "MacMermaid." He looked down at her legs. "But say, where is yer tail?"

Caitlin smiled sadly as she brushed her wet hair from her eyes. "It changes to legs on land."

"And to a tail in the water," the man answered. Taking several steps toward her he said, "let's throw her back in and see."

"Nae!" Ogg stepped in front of Caitlin as if to be her protector. "Leave her be. She has done us no harm."

"Leave her be?" Grumbling among themselves the others seemed to be discussing the matter, at last deciding against letting Caitlin be on her way.

"Ruaraidh and Finlay are sore wounded. They need tending."

"Aye, let's take her with us. Women always know how best to tend such things."

"Argh....." Ogg circled Caitlin several times, at last agreeing with the others. "She goes with us."

"With you?" Though she was wary, Caitlin didn't put up an argument. She had wanted to go to the MacDonald stronghold. If she went by sea or by land it didn't matter a bit. As a matter of fact as circumstances had proven it would certainly be safer. Alas for poor Donald that he had not been fished out of the ocean as well. Looking over her shoulder she crossed herself, saying a prayer for his soul.

A safer journey, perhaps, but not easier as she was soon to find out, for the MacDonalds kept up a harrowing pace as they traveled the countryside. It didn't take long for Caitlin's feet to be swollen and blistered. Even so, it was a journey that proved to be pleasing to the eyes for the land they passed was rocky, green and beautiful.   Pausing for a moment Caitlin feasted her eyes on the flat-topped gray mountains covered with lush emerald green. A fierce pride surged within as she realized this was MacLeod land.

She didn't have long to appreciate the view. With a loud command of, "Come, lass," Ogg hurried her on her way.

It was an exhausting journey of traveling by day and sleeping at night. When at last Caitlin was certain she couldn't move another step, when all she wanted to do was to sink into a motionless heap on the ground, she heard Ogg give a welcome pronouncement.

"Castle Dunskaith, lass, is just over the hill."

"Dunskaith!" The devil's lair, or so she had always been told, and yet looking at it she saw that it was a castle much like any other. The tower that stood tall against the sky gave proof of the MacDonald's newly acquired power and strength.

The men, with Caitlin in tow, approached the castle over a natural causeway of barren rocks that was protected from the wind by trees. Waving his arms and shouting, Ogg quickly let it be known that they were coming and that they were MacDonalds.

Torches blazed along the ramparts.   The MacDonald banner was flying.   Staring at it warily, Caitlin was grimly reminded that she was in enemy territory now. And yet even at that, the thought of a welcoming fire and the comfort within the castle's walls spurred her onward.

 Only when she was inside the great hall did she realize that she had been duped, however. She had not been "invited" to come along with the men because they needed a healer but because they knew who she was. To Caitlin's mortification it was revealed that one of the men had recognized her as the MacLeod's daughter. Instead of coming freely to Malcolm's hall as she had planned, she was quickly and indignantly taken prisoner.

With her flaming hair tumbling wildly about her shoulders and falling into her eyes, she supposed she must looked like some wild woman. Well, mayhap she was. Surely her fury knew no bounds.

"I willna be thanking ye fore yer hospitality it seems," she said scornfully, standing toe to toe with Ogg, facing him as defiantly as if they were the same size. Never would her father have so treated a woman. Only enemy warriors were made prisoner.

"I'm sorry, lass." Ogg at least seemed regretful.

"Sorry?"

"Aye. I hae always been fond of braw lassies." That did not keep him from going about his duty, however. "Watch her while I get Malcolm, " he ordered. Two of the other s hurried to obey, hovering over her like a snared grouse.

Caitlin brushed at her gown and ran her fingers through her tousled hair. Eyeing her captors, she snorted disdainfully as she squared her shoulders. They'd soon be begging her pardon. Affecting a haughty pose, she let her eyes roam freely about the room, critically assessing it. Her father always said that a man could tell much from another man's abode. What then was Malcolm like? Did he have horns and a tail?

Certainly he seemed to have an affection for luxury. The interior of Dunskaith Castle was much grander than she had ever supposed. Just like in her father's hall the walls were lined with benches, but they were polished and darkened, not just bare wood. The lofty hammer-beamed ceiling was hung with bright-colored banners. Even the floor was lavishly decorate with curly sheepskin rugs. Huge tapestries depicting the MacDonald bravery covered the walls, including several which obviously spoke of victory over the MacLeods. The sight of them angered her and were a reminder of years spent in turmoil.

The wooden walls were adorned with a gaudy display of shields and weapons—massive tow-handed cla'mors as well as English broadswords, axes, spears, dirks, and long tautly strung bows. Clearly the most important thing to Malcolm MacDonald was warfare, she thought with scorn. Although her father's castle also displayed some weaponry, it was nothing like this! Ah, yes, she had heard about the Macdonald laird's ambitions. But it was something else that quickly caught her eye. Hanging above the mantel, high on the stone wall, was the very thing she had come to fetch.

"The Fairy Flag." In disgust at the whole idea, she turned her gaze away. "Well, let them appreciate it while they may. I'll soon get my hands on it." Of that she was determined.

"Ogg, what is going on?" Niall's voice. "It couldn't possibly be…." But it was!

Niall's jaw dropped open in surprise as he entered the room and saw Caitlin standing there. For just a moment he doubted his sanity. "It is Caitlin."

"A ghost from out of yer past I'd be thinking," she said, trying to subdue the anger that bubbled at the sight of him. "Niall MacDonald!" She spoke his name like a curse.

"Caitlin.....I......I......." Dozens of thoughts raced through Niall's mind. What could he say? How could he ever explain?

"Oh, ye are a loathsome being! Caitlin's mind was ajumble with all the things she had dreamed of saying to him once they were face to face. Before she could even begin, however, a deep voice boomed through the hall.

"So...... Ian MacLeod's spawn." Standing in the doorway was a man Caitlin took for the very devil. Huge of girth, swarthy of skin, dark of hair and beard he looked ominous and deadly.

Thrusting himself in front of Caitlin, Niall thought only of guarding her. "Surely ye must be mistaken, Uncle."

Pushing Niall aside, Malcolm growled, "Let me take a look at her." Niall was relieved to remember that Malcolm had never seen the MacLeod's daughter. Maybe there was a chance. "I tell ye, it isna......"

"It is. I *am*!" Caitlin wasn't about to deny her true identity no matter what the consequences. She was proud of being the MacLeod's daughter.

Malcolm MacDonald bared his teeth in the semblance of a smile. "Well, well, well." Crossing his arms across his ample girth he stared brazenly at her. "Och, but she does look like her father. The very spitting image I'd be saying. Though she doesna look as dangerous."

"You'd be surprised," Niall said between clenched teeth. Oh, but this was proving to be a mind-muddling predicament. *Oh, Caitlin, you foolish lass. Ye dunna realize what ye hae done. God grant that I can save ye. now.*

"Dangerous or no I am happy that she is here." In a mock gesture of hospitality, Malcolm bowed.

"So am I," Caitlin responded sarcastically, her gaze traveling towards the flag.

Niall saw the direction of her eyes. So that was it. Silly lass. Even if she did get her hands upon the flag she wouldn't make it out of the hall alive with it. Malcom would watch her as steadfastly as a hawk kept its eye on a soaring dove. Indeed, she might well come to the same dire fate.

Malcolm also noted her eyes dart towards the MacLeods' treasured emblem. "Och, dunna even contemplate reaching out even one finger towards it, or........" He made a chopping gesture with his hand.

"Touch it?" Caitlin shrugged. "That was the last thing on my mind." By the blessed Saint Michael she'd just placed herself in the hands of a demented man, as well as an enemy. Unless....

"I dunna believe ye. And why should I, ye are a MacLeod."

"MacLeod?" Looking towards Niall, Caitlin could see the worry on his face. So, he hadn't told his uncle everything. No doubt being married to a MacLeod wouldn't be any more tolerated in this hall than being married to a MacDonald would be in her own. And therein Caitlin suddenly knew how she was going to get her revenge. "Nae, I am not a MacLeod. I am a MacDonald."

"Caitlin......" If he could have, Niall would have put his hand across her mouth. "Don't."

It was too late. Malcolm had heard. "What is this? What are ye saying?"

"That I am a MacDonald." Walking over to Niall, looping her arms through his, Caitlin looked up at him with mock adoration.   "And that yer nephew is my loving husband."

Chapter Twenty-Two

Malcolm grinned, his dark eyes gleaming with merriment. "So, ye married Ian MacLeod's daughter, did ye now, Niall."

"I did!" Niall didn't even want to deny it. Let the punishment be what it may. Let Gregor have his precious reward of being tanist.

"Ye took the flag and Macleod's daughter's maidenhead as well."

"He did!" Caitlin exclaimed glumly, though it embarrassed her to be talking about something so intimate. "And now must suffer for it, I would imagine."

"Suffer?" He was silent for a long, agonizing moment, watching her intently. "Ye would like that, wouldn't ye, lass?"

She nodded.

"Well, then, I will hae to disappoint ye." Striding over to Niall, he pounded his congratulations on his nephew's back. "Well done, Nephew. Well done. I couldna thought of anything better. The Macdonalds hae two prizes now. The fairy flag *and* Ian MacLeod's daughter."

"Uncle....." Niall knew Malcolm well enough to discern that something sinister was being planned at this very moment.

"I willna stay here!" If he thought to in some way use her as a means to get back at her father, she would quickly put an end to that, Caitlin thought. Unless he kept her a prisoner in the dungeon she would break free of Dunskaith.

"Ach, but ye will." A muscle ticked about Malcolm MacDonald's left eye, making it appear that he winked. "As my guest."

"Prisoner, ye mean." She tried not to panic.

"Call it what ye will!"

Caitlin made no answer. Standing in front of this vengeful Scotsman, all she could think of was that he did indeed look like the very devil.

"Ogg, I want ye to send a message to Ian MacLeod, informing him that I will consider that tattered flag of his as his daughter's dowry. Tell him that I welcome his beloved daughter to my humble home." It was obvious he meant to goad his rival, hoping the MacLeod would try to enact some kind of rescue.

"I will." Casting Caitlin a sympathetic look, Ogg left the hall.

Oh, Father, what hae I done? How could I hae compromised ye this way? She had given Malcolm MacDonald a weapon to use against her father. In trying to correct one mistake in judgment she had erred yet again. Even so, she managed bravado as she asked, "Do ye plan to shackle me in the dungeon?"

"Dungeon?" for just a moment it seemed as though he were toying with that idea.

"She is my wife, Uncle." Niall was determined to see that Caitlin was treated fairly. "And as such deserves a great measure of respect no matter what clan she comes from."

"Mmmmmm." Malcolm was not agreeable to that reminder; nevertheless he saw to it that Caitlin was given a comfortable chamber on the second floor. Despite the bitter feelings between the rival clans, she was treated with deference, yet she chaffed at being anyone's prisoner. Though she was made comfortable and given food, she felt ill at ease.

Moving from the bed, putting her ear to the door, she listened anxiously. Though the voices were muffled, she could hear a heated conversation.

"I thought ye were a mon of honor, Uncle, but surely ye shame me this day."

"Shame ye? I plan to make ye tanist and that shames ye?"

"Ye know what I mean. The MacLeod's daughter. Let her go home."

"And leave the arms of her loving groom? Nae."

Malcolm's voice lowered to a whisper, and Caitlin strained her ears to hear more of what the two men were saying.

"Are ye not afraid of what Ian MacLeod will say and do?"

Opening the door, Caitlin crept slowly down the stairway, hoping to hear Malcolm MacDonald's answer.

"Well, well, well!" A voice behind her startled her and she jumped. Turning around, she found herself face-to-face with a dark-haired man whose very presence behind her was menacing.

"Who are ye?"

"Gregor." He seemed surprised that any further explanation was necessary. "Nephew to Malcolm."

A prickly feeling traveled up her spine as if for just a moment she had the fey. There was something about him that seemed so familiar. Why was that?

A dark-haired man whose soul is as dark as his hair. The words of the seer whispered in her ear, reminding her of the frightening prophecy. Somehow in that moment she knew him to be a greater enemy than Malcolm could even think of being. An enemy who in some way spelled ruination for the clan.

Niall's restlessness was ill-concealed as he paced back and forth in the hall. It was all around the castle by way of gossiping tongues that there was more than just the MacLeod's flag that had occupied his time at Dunvegan castle.

"Fiery-haired little witch, you hae no idea of the din ye hae created with yer untimely entrance," he muttered beneath his breath. In truth, she had walked right into the lion's den, putting herself at Malcolm's mercy. "Well, she has no one to blame but herself. I dunna want to feel any guilt at what is to happen." And yet he did.

"Care for some company?" Striding across the room, Ogg ignored the negative shake of Niall's head. "Well, ye hae mine nevertheless."

"So I see!" Niall's voice was a growl.

"Och, such ill temper for a mon so newly wedded. And to a lass so very bonny." With his hands, Ogg outlined a voluptuous woman's figure in the air. "Need I say more?"

"Bonny or no, she is stubborn. I must hae been out of my mind to tie myself up wi' here."

Ogg repressed a smile, forcing his features to remain expressionless, but he did say, "No doubt I would hear the same thing from her."

"No doubt!"

Laying a hand on his friend's shoulder, Ogg seemed to sense at least some of Niall's thoughts, for he said, "It seems ye hae quite a story to tell. If so, ye can feel free to tell me."

For a moment Niall kept his silence, then after a while he began, "I was the first mon to step over the MacLeod threshold and thus I ended up with old Ian's daughter just as ye teased that I might. She caught me, ye see, and took me to her father. What else could I do but remind the MacLeod of his vow. It was either that or stay cooped up in his dungeon until I died."

Folding his arms across his chest, Niall related the story in detail, from falling into the flour and being mistaken for a ghost, to his hurried departure from Dunvegan with the flag hidden on his person.

"So the lassie found a way to tame the rogue MacDonald." Ogg threw back his head and laughed. "After all the lassies ye hae loved and left, ye find yerself with a braw one that is more than yer match!"

Wanting to deny that, Niall opened his mouth to speak. The more he said no, however, the more frustrated he felt. "By Saint Michael, all right! The lass does give as good as she gets. And she is, as ye say, bonny. And braw. All the more tragic it is then that she has now put herself at Malcolm's mercy."

"An act which worries ye so because ye care!" Wiping away any trace of mockery, Ogg furled his brows. "Ye didna marry the lass just because ye were caught we' the flag. Ye had more than a wee bit of a longing."

"Nae!" Niall's protestation sounded halfhearted.

"Then why did ye no find another way to get the flag. Like holding her for ransom, shall we say?" he clucked his tongue. "Or tying her hand and foot and dangling her from the tower."

Niall clenched his hands. "She is a woman. I didna want to soil my honor by mistreating her."

Ogg was not so easily fooled. "Devil take ye, for ye lie! There was a part of ye that wanted the lass. And why not? She is one of the prettiest lasses I hae ever seen." As if to see into his friend's heart, Ogg stared into Niall's eyes long and hard. What he read there made him gasp. "Och, dinna tell me that what ye felt for her is much more serious than that!"

Niall's silence was the answer.

"A MacLeod!" Ogg ran his fingers through his hair. "Then it is worried that I be. Malcolm will use the lass for his own gains, but he willna let ye hae any peace."

"How well I know."

"Ye will find yerself right in the middle of a tug-of-war, torn in two directions, Niall, forced to make a choice between loyalty to yer clan and loyalty to yer heart." Ogg then asked a chilling question. "Which will ye choose?"

In confusion Niall stepped back. Taking a deep breath, he answered truthfully. "I dunna ken, ogg." God help him, he really didn't know.

Chapter Twenty-Three

She was surrounded by enemies. Was it any wonder then that all that Caitlin could think about the next few days was escape? An escape that would be all the sweeter if she could take the fairy flag with her.

"Take the flag?" Alas, she might as well hae wanted to reach toward the heavens and pull down a star. Not only was *she* guarded but that brown piece of silk was watched constantly as well.

Worse yet, just seeing Niall caused her pain, and there was no way to avoid him. Every morning he was in the hall for the morning meal and in the evening his presence was all too obvious as the clan gathered for their dinner feast. These were the hours of her torment, part of her longing for his touch, his kiss, his love.

That did not mean she allowed herself to in any way show her feelings, however. She was withdrawn and cool when they met on the stairs. What conversation they exchanged was nothing more than cold, polite words of greeting. She made it obvious that she was avoiding him. Even so, no matter how sternly she rebuked herself for feelings she did not want to have, she couldn't wipe him from her heart. He was like a sweet poison for which there was no antidote except to keep so busy she didn't have time to think or to feel.

Though she might have been able to escape from the drudgery, Caitlin took on household tasks eagerly, thankful that there was always something to be done.

The work was fitted around the meal preparation, just as in her own clan, twice daily, morning and night. Here in the MacDonald castle, beef and lamb were the mainstays of the diet, eaten in some form at every meal, as were milk, cheese, and butter. Grinding and baking were daily chores, for unleavened barley would soon turn hard and stale. Flour was ground from a rotary hand quern, dough kneaded in a wooden trough and baked on long-handled iron plates among the embers of an open fire. The women also hung herbs to dry and gathered wild plants to supplement the diet.

Aileen, Malcolm's wife, was a plump woman with dark brown hair whose beauty had long ago faded. She soon made it clear that she considered Caitlin an interloper and a nuisance and reminded her to keep her place by assigning her the most unpleasant duties. Nonetheless, Caitlin finished every task without a word of complaint, so exhausted by the time she crawled into bed that she fell right to sleep.

At least I can escape Niall MacDonald at night, she thought in gratitude. *And perhaps in time I will be able to think more clearly and soothe my shattered emotions so that the next time I see him across the room it won't hurt so.* Until then, her only defense was to pretend he didn't exist.

But if she was ignoring him, the same could not be true for Niall. His piercing hazel eyes seemed to be upon her wherever she was and she knew that he watched her. The sound of his low, husky laughter teased her ears. His smile haunted her at every turn, though she did not smile back. His presence made it difficult at times for her to ignore him. In those moments when their eyes accidentally met she was filled with an aching emptiness. Oh, if only he was not so handsome.

This evening she caught him gazing at her across the width of the dais and felt the familiar lurch in her heart. Determined to show him she really didn't care, she quickly turned her attentions to Ogg, a gentle man despite his size, who was quickly becoming her one friend in the castle.

"Was the message sent to my father?" she asked him.

"Aye, it was sent."

"Oh….." Looking across the table to where Malcolm sat, a place that in the MacLeod hall would have been taken by her father, she could only hope that Ian MacLeod would not so easily fall into the MacDonald's trap. He must not try to rescue her, for if he did he would put himself in dire danger.

"Red…." Since the moment when Caitlin had answered his question of who she was by saying "Red Etin," that was what he had called her.

"I know ye had to follow yer chieftain's orders." Caitlin touched his arm. "I know ye dunna wish my father or me any harm. It is just the way of things."

"Aye, the way of things." He seemed to notice her soulful glance at Niall, for he whispered, "But if ye can so easily understand that I must do as I hae done, why can ye not then forgive Niall?"

Instantly she stiffened. "That's different, Ogg. I trusted him," *and loved him*, "and he betrayed me."

"I know he loves ye, lass. Ye dunna ken the times he has jumped to yer defense, trying to protect ye from Malcolm's wrath. He has never done that with anyone or for anyone before."

"'Tis his feeling of guilt," Caitlin said sourly, "I dunna want to talk more about it." Defiantly she looked toward Niall, glowering at him when he looked back. If he thought to use his friend Ogg to soften her justifiable anger it just wouldn't work.

Niall could feel the potency of her ire all the way across the room, and it irritated him in return. He was tired of the way she was acting. Tired of her refusal to even listen to his explanations of why he had done what he had done. Well, by God, she was his wife. Perhaps it was time that he laid aside his compassion and patience and made her act as such, he thought, clenching his fingers tightly around the handle of his cup. He swirled the golden whiskey about, staring at its murky depths, remembering the blissful moments of passion they had shared.

"Yer frown is as deep as Loch Stapin." With a large wolfhound at his heels begging for scraps, Gregor sauntered up. Sizing up the situation, he knew in a moment what was wrong. His expression clearly revealed that Niall's troubles pleased him. "For all that ye be such a great fighter and leader of men, Cousin, it is a wee bit amusing that ye canna seem to manage yer own wife."

"That's because that woman is not the least bit manageable." He stared Gregor right in the eyes. "Ye couldna manage her either, I'd be thinking."

"Oh, I think that I could." The tone of voice stated clearly that Gregor was the kind of man who would subdue any woman who crossed his path with violence. "I wouldna let any lass so obviously scorn me."

"I willna use force. I dunna want her hate." Niall felt the need to issue a clear warning. "Nor will I tolerate anyone treating Caitlin unkindly."

"Unkindly?" Without being invited, Gregor took a seat next to his cousin. "She's a spoiled, willful lassie who is in great need of a beating to keep her in line. But if ye prefer to allow her to publicly show ye contempt, then ye will just hae to accept the consequences."

Niall went to Caitlin's defense. "She has reason to treat me as she does. I lied to her and rewarded her trust with treachery."

"To get the flag. Any mon would hae done that and maybe worse."

Niall immediately knew what Gregor was saying. Had Niall's cousin been the one to go to the MacLeod stronghold, Caitlin would not have escaped with her life. That first night Gregory would have stolen the flag and then murdered her so that she could not sound the alarm. The idea made him shiver. Once again he felt the need to defend Caitlin.

"Well, no mon had better harm her while she is within these walls for any reason." One false move and he would have Gregory's head. "Do ye ken?"

"Aye." Despite what he said, however, the devilish glint in his eyes as he glanced Caitlin's way clearly spoke of danger.

The ominous look deeply troubled Niall, for he knew from experience that his cousin could be very dangerous. "Gregor, I repeat. I willna tolerate anyone harming her. Anyone." Despite the warning to his cousin, Niall knew Caitlin herself had to be warned to stay clear of the man. With that thought in mind, he sought her out as soon as the dinner table was cleared.

A shiver of pure physical awareness chased a strange sensation up and down Caitlin's spine so that she knew he was standing behind her before she heard him say, "You have been as evasive as a ghostie, lass. But ye must listen."

"Listen? To what?" Her pulse began to beat at her neck and temple, and for a moment she feared he would sense how completely bedeviled she was having him near. "Surely it is listening to ye in the first place that got me in all this trouble."

"A truth for which I am deeply sorry, Caitlin. Believe it or not, I didna want to hurt ye." He captured her hand, his fingers gripping her slender wrist.

"But even so, ye did. Very, very deeply." She quivered at his touch, wanted to touch him back but forced herself to pull her hand away. Like a cornered deer she moved past him, bolting from the room, seeking the safety of the stairs.

Niall followed her, through the door, up the winding steps that led to a tower room. "Lassie?" He towered over her with a virility that was most unnerving to Caitlin. It reminded her too vividly of all that had happened. She stiffened and took a step backward. For a moment the only sound was the hiss of the rush light and the distance barking of the dogs, then he said, "Ye are trembling."

"'Tis chilly up here, that's all." A feeble excuse.

"I'll warm you." Quickly, before she could run away, he placed his hands on either side of her body, pinning her against the wall so she could not escape. His breath was warm upon her face, his voice husky in the darkness.

"Caity. Caity. I canna stand yer hatred." He wanted her to be passionate, responsive , and loving again.

"But that is all ye will be getting from me, Niall MacDonald." But though her head buzzed with anger the secret place between her legs remembered something else and she felt a wanton craving.

"Then ye are cheating both yerself as well as me." Breathing hard, he swept her body with his hands as if by so doing he could convince her.

She closed her eyes, swaying under his expert touch. She drew a deep breath, then let it out as she whispered, "Cheating ye, am I. Nae, it is ye who cheated us both by leaving me as ye did.'"

"For which I hae been punished each time I see ye look at me with loathing, lass." He sought her breasts, gently kneading them. Feeling the peaks harden, knowing that at least her body responded if not her heart, he smiled. "Ah, Caity. It was good between us and can be again."

Slowly he lowered his mouth and kissed her hungrily, as if he were starving for the taste of her lips. The potent kiss sent a series of quivering tremors through her blood. His mouth held hers captive as his fingers caressed her breasts, moving to slip the arasaid aside so he could touch her bared flesh.

"Nae!" How she managed the protest she didn't know. Somehow, despite the beating of her heart, she found the strength to push against his shoulders. "Let me go!"

"Ye are my wife, Caity," he breathed. "Ye belong to me."

"Belong to ye, do I?" Her blazing eyes challenged him.

She was so proud, so beautiful with her hair falling into her eyes that his love for her swept through him. "Aye, ye do."

"Nae, I do not!" Never would she belong to anyone accept herself, do anything unless she wanted to.

Niall looked into her eyes and what he saw there made him loosen his hold. With a disgruntled groan, he moved away. "By the laws of the church and this land ye do, Cailtlin, love, but I am not the kind of mon who would forced ye. When ye come back to my bed it will be because ye want to."

Her hair flowed from side to side like a rippling wave as she tossed her head. "Never!" Yet in the saying she felt bereaved. She wanted him with just as deep an intensity as he wanted her.

"Then God help us both!"

In the stricken silence that followed, they maintained a grotesque pose, staring at each other, their eyes locked unwaveringly. Then Niall turned away. Before he descended the stairs, however, he had one more thing to say to her.

"Keep away from my cousin Gregor, Caitlin. He would seek to harm ye, and though I swear I will give ye my protection whenever I am in the castle, I canna always be near."

"Gregor?" Caitlin knew who he was only too well. The dark man. The man whose face seemed to strike a chord of recognition in her mind. The man of doom as she thought of him now. "I will watch out for him."

"Good." He took a step and then another, hoping that she would call him back.

"Niall."

Instantly he was standing once again beside her. "Aye."

For just a moment her hostility softened. "Thank ye for...for the warning."

KATHRYN HOCKETT

He was disappointed that she did not say more; still as he looked deep into her eyes he felt a sense of hope that perhaps their future together was not as bleak as he had   at   first   supposed.

HIGHLAND DESTINY

Chapter Twenty-Four

Caitlin looked out the window at the rolling hills and pasturelands of the MacDonald's lands. From her window she was afforded a magnificent view. Acre after acre of grass-covered ground, blue ribbons of water winding their way in a path over the hills, trees raising their branches as if to pray.

There was a serene beauty to the countryside that reminded her of home and made her quarrelsomely homesick at times. But her longing to see her home again was as nothing compared to the pain and frustration she felt every time she caught sight of Niall. She was caught between anger and longing, heartache and the elation of knowing that he did desire her. Even so, the more she thought about his deception the more determined she was never to speak another civil word to him.

"Oh, how quickly I capitulated to his virility and charm," she said beneath her breath as she turned away from the window. Callously forgetting all that he had done to her and her clan, he had reminded her of their marriage, insisting that she belonged to him. Well, she would soon let him see that, prisoner or not, she would bend to no man's will. Not Niall's, not Gregor's, nor most assuredly Malcom's.

Malcolm, oh how Caitlin loathed the man. He was coldblooded, a solemn conscienceless man who seemed to enjoy Caitlin's discomfort. The "devil's spawn" she heard him refer to her on one or two occasions. Caitlin often saw him looking at her as if he fully expected her to grow horns. Certainly Malcolm knew he was a cog in the wheel of her hopes of a daring rescue, for he watched her like a hawk.

Finishing the porridge she had brought up to her room from breakfast, Caitlin searched through the garments she had been given to wear, pondering her fate all the while. She had three enemies here. Niall, because of his legal claim to her. Malcolm, because of the danger he might pose to her father. Lastly and perhaps most dangerous of all, Gregor.

I should leave. Not tomorrow, not the next day, but now! She had made a mistake in coming here so boldly. Had she even a wee bit of common sense she would have disguised herself as a lad, an old woman—or anything but herself. Now, as it was, she had put not only herself but the whole clan in danger.

What will happen later?" she worried. Aye, Malcolm had welcomed the news of Niall's marriage to the MacLeod's daughter but that was only because she could be used to lure Ian MacLeod out of his den. Would Malcolm view her as a hated enemy when her usefulness had passed?

Caitlin poured water from a pitcher into a small china basin, hurriedly washed her face, and hastened to plait her long red hair, wearing it in coils on either side of her head. Dressing quickly in a dark-green gown with a linen tonnage around her shoulders, she moved to the door. Though she had not been confined, this time when she attempted to leave her chamber she found a guard posted outside her door.

"Och, so 'tis prisoner in the full sense of the word that I am now," she said, putting her hands on her hips. Mentally she cursed Malcolm MacDonald.

"Ye canna leave without the MacDonald's permission."

"What!" Malcolm's prisoner then in the full sense of the word. First she was stunned, then she was furious.

"I told ye lass, ye canna leave without *his* permission."

He nodded to where the MacDonald stood in conversation with two of his men.

Though Caitlin stormed at the man and tried to push past, her anger was to no avail. He was much too strong and brawny. "Then gi' him a message for me. Tell him that his nephew's wife wishes to be *blessed* wi' his company.

Seething with rage, Caitlin paced the room, pausing only when footsteps sounded outside. As Malcolm entered, she was immediately upon him. "Ye dare keep me in a cage."

"I do it just until tonight."

"Tonight?" she shoved at his chest.

His expression was stern. "There is to be a special celebration. I but wanted to make certain that ye dunna decide to leave before that time."

"Celebration?" She was scornful. "No doubt a celebration of my happy wedding."

"Yer wedding?" He bared his teeth as he said, "Dunna flatter yerself. I wouldna honor a MacLeod be she Niall's whore or no."

Caitlin gasped. So, it was just as she thought. Malcolm's only reason for approving of her marriage to Niall was because if offered him a chance for vengeance.

"Nor would I gi' honor to any Macdonald!"

"Ach, but ye will. This very night ye will pay homage to my successor."

Torches and tapers blazed brightly, casting a soft glow on the great hall. Smoke from the hearth fires stung everyone's eyes as the MacDonald clan gathered for the evening meal. And what a meal it was! Clearly Malcolm MacDonald had something to celebrate. Platters were piled high with mutton, beef, English rabbit and all manner of fowl. There were plates of oysters, bannocks, oatcakes, barley-cakes, fruit and cheese. All to be washed down with tankards of ale and mugs of the finest whiskey.

Caitlin watched as Dunskaith's servants hurried swiftly to and from the kitchen, their arms heavily laden with platters, bowls and pitchers, thinking she would never get used to others doing the work for a few. Unlike in her father's hall there was a distinct difference between those who served and those who ruled.

"Dunna look sad. Ye are much bonnier when ye smile." Ogg was seated to her left and as he spoke he gently touched her hand.

"I was just thinking for a moment about home......"

"Home?"

"Aye."

"And thinking how ye would like to be there instead of here." His blue eyes offered her sympathy and understanding.

"Perhaps ye dunna truly appreciate anything until it's far away." How many times had she longed for adventure? How many times had she bemoaned the necessity of staying by the MacLeod hearth, working with the other women? Now there wasn't anything she wouldn't give to be back there.

"And your family?"

"I miss them all very dearly. Even my mother." She hurried to explain. "Mother and I didna always get along. We were both too much the same so we fought a great deal of the time. Funny, but I miss those arguments." Caitlin was curious about Ogg. "And what of you?"

"I didna even know my mother. I was taken from her arms shortly after my birth and fostered here with Malcolm. My clan were some of the "broken men", from the MacRaes. My small group sought and obtained the protection of the MacDonald clan when many of our men were killed off in battle with the MacKinnons. "

"So ye are a MacRae." The fact that he did not have a blood relationship with the MacDonalds pleased her. Perhaps if she was really in danger Ogg would help her.

"I've been told my father was killed in battle, that my mother feared his enemies would try to take my life. For my own protection I was nurtured here." Picking up a leg of mutton he toyed with it nervously. "And for that I am grateful to Malcolm but....."

But ye dunna always approve of all he does. That was important to know just in case she needed ally. "I beg to say that the MacDonald seems to be a very harsh mon....."

"A bit harsh perhaps, Red, But very, very braw!" The way Ogg spoke, it was obvious that he admired his chieftain greatly.

As she listened Caitlin couldn't help seeking out Niall with her gaze, remembering in vivid detail the passion they had shared. One brief look at him set her blood to pounding as she relived the delight of his holding her close last night. When he had pressed his hard, arousing body against hers, all thought of leaving here had vanished, dissolved in the heated torrent of their desire. What if.....?

Ogg caught sight of her stolen glance, the way her eyes caressed his friend. "He is a fine mon."

"I suppose that he can be."

"Nae always is. He is the bravest mon I know and in his heart he is most kind. When the others made fun of my size Niall always took my side." He smiled. "Once he even suffered a bloodied nose given to him by Gregor and his followers because he didn't want to see my feelings hurt."

"Really?" That bit of information made her see Niall in a different light.

"Really."

Caitlin sighed, trying to concentrate on what was happening in the hall. All Highlanders were fond of music and dancing and the MacDonalds seemed to be no different. Caitlin took great delight in listening to the pipers, knowing that the MacCrimmons who were her clans' pipers, were much better. The harpist, however, was the best she had ever heard. Leaning back in her chair she felt herself relaxing.

"Ye havena eaten much...." Ogg sounded worried. "Ye arena sick?"

"I just am not hungry."

"Eat something anyway."

She forced herself to eat some of the heavily seasoned food, wondering how the MacDonald's could find it palatable. The portion that she took was a large slice of mutton that she washed down with a gulp of ale.

A long time later the long trestle tables were dismantled and pushed back against the wall. Malcolm rose to his feet, putting his finger to his lips to gesture silence. The room quieted in an instant. Upon every face an upraised brow asked what was going to happen. That question was answered quickly as the MacDonald laird addressed the gathering.

"There has been some concern avowed as to who is to succeed me. Though I'm no' anxious to become a ghost I've decided to address that issue now." He flashed a rare smile, enjoying the open-mouthed looks of surprise. All eyes were riveted his way. "From time to time I've mentioned Gregor, other moments I've given a nod to Niall and given thought to his becoming my Tanist. It is as ye know a most serious duty. As tanist it will be his special duty to hold the clan lands in trust for ye and yer posterity. As chieftain my successor will be called upon to determine all differences and disputes, to protect our followers, to lead this clan in times of war. I've made my choice and tonight I will make it formal. Niall, please stand up."

Nae, Caitlin thought. Not now! She felt all hope for a future with Niall slipping away. If he was tanist then that would eventually mean that he would be the one to lead the warfare against her clansmen. As tanist he could not allow any children he might have to be another clan's successor, thereby crushing her father's dreams. All was lost! In a mood of hostile despair she watched as Niall took his stand by the sacred stone of the MacDonalds, placing one foot upon the rock as custom decreed.

Had he known last night that he would be given such an honor? Had he? And yet he had not said a word. Instead he had initiated lovemaking and pretended that he cared for her. Suspicion poisoned her mind. Tears of angry frustration stung her eyes. What had goaded him into pretending to care for her this time?

Dunna fool yerself, Caitlin dearie. Where honor and ambition were concerned a woman was naught. That was the way of men. Power was all they wanted. And now Niall had bartered her for a Tanist's crown.

Caitlin watched silently as Niall was presented with a sword and a white wand as the MacDonald bard recounted all his acts of bravery . Niall mac Gilchrist was son of Gilchrist who was son of Craig and on and on and on. There was no doubt that Niall came from noble lineage, nor that he was brave in his combat with other men and for that she admired him. But she felt a sense of hopelessness too, for all the talk of fighting only proved that in reality there was a gulf as wide as Loch Bracadale between them.

No doubt Niall knew it too for not once had he even glanced at her tonight. Because of guilt? Because having secured the Fairy Flag had put him in Malcolm's favor? Aye. Well now he had what he had so wanted with little care of what it had cost her clansmen.

Niall mac Gilchrist can never be mine! she thought. Suddenly the futility of her feelings for him came back to haunt her full measure. Now when she remembered last night she was left with only humiliation. How quickly she had capitulated to his advances, like some besotted dairy maid. He had called her his wife, had reminded her that she was naught but a possession. And that was all she was and ever would be.

I canna ever lay with him again. I canna get with child. For that babe would be a MacDonald. An enemy, though it be of her own flesh and blood. Those thoughts were tormenting for even now the memory of the way he had caressed her and kissed her caused her body to long for the touch of his hands and mouth.

"What a fool ye were, Caitlin," she whispered to herself, watching him strut about the hall, so prideful at the honors being bestowed on him. He reminded her of a preening rooster. Warfare was all a man ever cared about. Honor. Bravery. Did she really think he would give up his role as Tanist for love of her?

"Lassie, what is wrong?" Ogg put a hand on her shoulder, his eyes mirroring his concern for the tears that flooded her eyes.

"Wrong?" Caitlin dashed the tears away with the back of her hand. "Just the smoke in my eyes, that is all. Dunna fash yerself, Ogg. I'm all right."

Oh, what a lie that was. The longer she watched the ceremony the more she realized how quickly her own unhappiness loomed ahead. It was glaringly apparent. If she stayed here!

Restless and unhappy she rose form her chair, unwilling to think another moment about it. Well, she wouldn't stay. Not for one more day. When the first light of dawn glowed on the horizon, she would be gone, taking the Fairy Flag with her.

"So, ye are tanist, Niall. I'd say it's about time Malcolm named ye so." Ogg pushed his way through the throng of revelers, maneuvering Niall to a far corner where they could be alone. "Congratulations!"

Niall stared hard at him, searching his face for any sign of jealousy, but the large smile that cut its way across the giant's face was not being feigned. The same could not be said for Gregor, however. Each time he looked Niall's way the anger and envy was obvious. If Gregor had not been an enemy before, he was now.

"I've admired ye all my life and never doubted for a moment that it would be ye who would be named Malcolm's successor. Ye are a fine mon, Niall. The best I've ever known. I only wish to be even half as fine a fighter as ye are."

Niall laughed. "Ye are, my humble friend. Ye are. More so."

Ogg started to grin, but that grin turned into a frown as he stared over Niall's shoulder. "Don't look now, but Gregor is staring this way, and with such an evil expression that ye had best cross yerself!"

"Gregor!" Niall spat the name with scorn. Gregor had long been his adversary, circumventing his authority at every turn. "He was so certain he was going to be named tanist that he had instructed the bard to make up a song about him."

"Ye dinna say." Ogg shook his head. "Well, he must hae suffered an unpleasant surprise then."

"A stunning shock, though not enough of one to burst his overblown pride."

"Indeed, it seems his defeat has only made him more prideful."

"And dangerous." Niall voiced aloud his greatest fear. "He has aligned himself as Caitlin's enemy."

"I know." Ogg chewed on his lower lip, deep in thought. "I hae seen him staring at her from time to time, though with a far different look upon his face than that of a foe."

"Ye mean?" The thought of Gregor even touching Caitlin with his eyes was infuriating, much less imagining any more intimate advances.

Ogg was blunt. "What better way would there be to get back at ye, Niall, then to sully that which he knows belongs to ye? A woman who is certainly most bonny."

"And my wife."

"Gregor thinks there is no woman he canna have. Worse yet, he thinks in his canny mind that ye stole what was to be his. He won't even think twice about doing ye harm through Red."

"If he so much as comes within a foot of her, I'll kill him." As Niall looked in Gregor's direction and met his gaze, they fought a furious visual duel, as potent as with any weapon. "Ogg!" Niall put an insistent hand on his friend's shoulder.

"What is it? I'll do anything ye ask, as ye know."

"I want you to help me keep an eye on Caitlin, to keep her from that one's harm." Niall sensed danger with a warrior's instincts, and was determined to avert it at all possible cost.

"Ye dunna hae to ask."

"Ye like her."

Ogg pounded Niall on the back so hard that it rattled his teeth. "I hae right from the very first!"

Niall felt the need to pour his heart out. "When I went to Skye I had in mind to steal the flag and be gone, but I saw this lovely lassie and once I...I kissed her, I was lost."

"And ye fell in love."

"Aye. I didna know it then, but I know it now." Niall shook his head sadly. "But alas, it seems hopeless sometimes. I did her a great wrong that I dunna think she can ever forgive."

"She can and she will."

Knowing that Ogg often sat next to Caitlin, Niall was anxious. "Has she said that?"

"Nae, but I can see in her eyes when she looks at ye that she cares. Nae, more than that. I think she loves, too, Niall."

Niall sighed softly. "I wish it was true."

"I would bet my breacan that it is, but what I think isna important. It's what ye believe and what ye do about it."

Ogg's meaning was very clear. "Woo her, ye mean?"

"I do." Picking up two empty goblets, he filled them up, handing one to Niall. "There isna a woman alive who doesna swoon when a mon pays court."

For just a moment Niall was solemn, then he laughed aloud as he imagined Ogg with wings and a bow and arrow. "The world's largest cupid."

"What?"

"Nothing." Niall held his goblet aloft. "Here is to women, God bless them all. And to my bonny, bonny wife." Still, there were obstacles that stood in the path of

his happiness. Gregor, and the most resilient of all—
Malcolm!

Chapter Twenty-Five

The hearth fires had burned down to ash. One by one the smoking torches flickered, hissed, and then died. The hour was growing late. Darkness was gathering under the high ceiling. The women had long ago retired, taking the small children with them. All the women save one.

These drunken oafs will tire of their riotous celebrating and go to their beds eventually, Caitlin thought. It was her only hope, her only chance. Meanwhile, patience must be her ally. *I will find a way to get the flag. I must.*

Goaded on by the sight of the MacLeod's fair flag which Malcolm had brazenly flaunted tonight, Caitlin was determined. Though her backside ached from her hours of sitting slumped on the bench, she refused to join the other women upstairs in their beds.

"Niall MacDonald, tanist," she scoffed, feeling the sting of his betrayal anew. He had risen to his greatest heights on the tide of her shame. How then could she feel even a shred of longing? And yet she did.

Touching her fingers to her mouth, she remembered Niall's kiss. Closing her eyes, she remembered the way his nearness had ignited a host of glorious sensations. Though she knew passion for what it was and refused to give it recognition as love, she was nonetheless caught up in the feelings that coiled within her stomach.

I willna feel this way, she ordered herself. *If I hae to succumb to the powers of a witchwoman I will tear Niall MacDonald out of my heart, my soul.*

Tears shimmered in her eyes as she stared at the dying fire. Still as stone, she reflected on a plan of escape for no one, not Malcolm, not Gregor, nor especially Niall, would get the better of her. Not now, not ever.

"Och, lassie. Such a face. It canna be that bad."

Looking up, Caitlin saw that Ogg had left Niall's side and was hovering over her. "It can be and it is."

Ogg's look was sympathetic. "Niall's new honor has made ye sad."

"And why should it not? Surely then my hopes and dreams hae been scattered like leaves before the winter." She sighed. "There is no hope for happiness. No hope at all."

"Ah, but there is, lass, for it was spoken by Niall's own lips that he cares deeply for ye."

Caitlin sat straight up. "He cares for himself ye mean and his silly notion of the importance of power." She nodded with her head to where Niall sat talking to two others of his clan, stung by his seeming neglect of her. "He cares little for me."

Resting her head on her arms, Caitlin closed her eyes. Suddenly she was very tired. Tired of the constant warfare. Tired of the bickering. Tired of feeling this lonely and sad.

"Ye are wrong." Putting his hands under her arms, Ogg helped Caitlin to her feet, tending her as carefully as a child. "But come to bed. 'Tis late and the shadows rule. Tomorrow ye may think differently."

"Nae," she whispered. Still, she did not resist as Ogg picked her up in his arms and carried her up to her chamber. Setting her down on the bed, he said but one word.

"Sleep." Then, throwing another log on the fire to see to her comfort, he was gone.

Sleep. Unless she could right the great wrong done to her and her clan, Caitlin wondered if she could or would ever sleep peacefully again.

"I curse ye, Niall Macdonald. I curse ye and all yer clan!"

Caitlin Stared up at the ceiling. Beams of light danced from the fire, casting figured shadows overhead. Two entwined silhouettes conjured up memories of the embraces she had Niall Macdonald had shared, making it difficult to push him out of her mind. Thus, for several long, tormented hours she lay awake trying to exert her will over her fevered, longing body.

Ah, but no! She would not allow herself to feel this way. She wouldn't. It was a betrayal of her clan. A threat to her freedom and peace of mind. A danger to her sanity.

"Ye must leave, Caitlin nic Ian," she murmured with certainty. "You must leave and never see him again." There had to be a way.

She had to be patient. Eventually the MacDonalds would tire of their celebrating and take to their beds. Then she would return Niall MacDonald "favor" for "favor". Aye, she would get away from here and the temptation Niall MacDonald posed. She'd find another fisherman and sail back to her Clan.

Fires blazed brightly in every room throughout the castle, yet even so Caitlin felt cold. The very thought of what was about to do sent a chill traveling up her spine, wondering just what Malcolm MacDonald would do to her if she was caught.

"I canna allow my self to be." Surely she could be as sneaky a thief as Niall had been. She told herself that she could be and that she wasn't in the least bit worried, yet when the moment came and the castle was quiet, she was as nervous as a cat on a flag pole.

Moving quickly about the room, she gathered up her meager possessions. There was no time to lose. She had to hurry while the MacDonald men were immersed in their whiskey-induced slumber. There could be no turning back now.

"I can't give any more thought to leaving than Niall did when he left me," she whispered, yet even so the thought of never seeing him again brought an emptiness to her heart. She should never have let herself fall in love with him again. It only complicated her already turbulent emotions as she opened the door and slipped out.

The stairway was dimly lit. Caitlin stumbled once or twice in her haste as she took the steps two at a time. Or was she clumsy because of her fear of being caught? It didn't matter. As she made her way to the kitchen, thankful now that she had familiarized herself vaguely with the castle's interior, she forced herself to calm.

Assembling what supplies she could for the journey, Caitlin placed the larger foodstuffs in a large sack and the smaller in a fancily decorated sporran that she borrowed from a peg on the wall. It was just as dark in the kitchen as it had been on the stairs and she fumbled around, holding her breath once or twice when her gropings sent something falling to the floor.

"And now for the flag." She couldn't leave without it, thus she had no choice but to tiptoe towards the hall, hoping it would be empty.

It wasn't.   Lying on benches, underneath tables, and on the   hard floor   several of the MacLeod men slumbered.   Caitlin drew back.   It would be insanity to try to steal the flag when there were MacDonalds about, yet at the same time this might well be her only chance to get beyond the castle walls.   Usually Malcolm had her watched but tonight her "watchdogs" were among those whose loud snores disturbed the night's silence.

"I hae to do it." But oh, if only Malcolm had not placed the flag so high. It was well out of reach.   Only by carefully dragging one chair and then another, to the mantle, placing one on top of the other, was Caitlin able to reach it.   And all the time she was tearing it down, the chairs rocked to and fro threatening to tumble.

With all the grace of an acrobat, however, Caitlin at last had the Fairy Flag within her possession.   Tying it around her waist beneath the folds of her arasaid she ran toward the front door, then the portculis. Tugging at the rope, she raised the iron grille just enough for her slender body to fit through, then she was running as fast as her legs could carry her.

The moon was shrouded by dark clouds, her only guide was the light of the fading stars. Nevertheless she once again plucked up her courage, looking back many times to make certain that she had not been seen leaving. If only she could put as much distance as possible between herself and Niall she would get through her heartache somehow.   At   least   her   pride   would   be salvaged she thought sadly. And perhaps happiness was only a dream after all......

Caitlin stealthfully crept out of the castle, hiding in the shadows, conscious of every sound. That was why her ears perceived so readily the sound of footsteps behind her. Stopping in her tracks she listened again. Her pursuer seemed to be playing a game. When she walked he walked, when she halted, he did likewise. Trying to outsmart him she dodged in and out amongst some barrels but seemingly all for naught. There, looming in the semidarkness was a hulking figure, blocking her way of escape.

"Ogg?" She was hopeful as she called out, but all too soon Caitlin recognized her follower as the clansman Niall and her own intuition had warned her about. "Gregor."

"Tired of our hospitality?" Gregor's features seemed to be carved in stone. He looked very strong and ominous as he stood there staring at her, his dark visage made darker by the night.

This time Caitlin was powerless against the storm of fear that shattered all her resolve like an eggshell. She spun around, intending to put as much distance as she could between herself and Malcolm's kinsman, but in a few swift strides he had caught up with her, his hand curving brutally around her arm, jerking her back to face him.

Futilely Caitlin clawed at the imprisoning hand. "It was stuffy in my room and I thought to get some air." The lie tripped off her tongue despite her trembling.

His dark eyes narrowed, but after a long moment he released his hold on her, much to her relief. "Ye were going for a walk, is that what ye would hae me believe?"

"Aye!" she said cheerily. "A walk!" Clutching tightly to her sack she took a few tentative steps backwards. "And now I'll be on my way. Back from where I came." She headed in the direction of the portculis, intending to bluff him for awhile. When he did not follow she was lulled with a false sense of security and retreated a few steps more. It was a mistake, just the move he wanted her to make, for with a snarl he was upon her, shoving her so hard that she tumbled to the ground. The impact with the hard earth jarred the sack loose and set the sporran around her waist to sway, scattering objects on the ground.

Gregor gave a bitter laugh. "So ye were just going for a stroll!" Bending down he fingered the provisions with an oath, then stared hard at her. "And I call ye liar. Ye were leaving, make no mistake about it."

"Nae! Nae." She shook her head furiously."

The hands that bruised her as they searched her person were large and brutal. Hands that could maim and kill. Hands that unfortunately went right to the flag. "Aha!" He was triumphant. His eyes were like those of a weasel, hungry and ferocious. With a chilling laugh he moved closer. "The MacLeod flag. I wonder....."

"Wonder what?"

Wrapping it around her throat he pulled it slightly. "How tight one would have to tie it to choke the life out of a MacLeod."

Caitlin couldn't breath. She couldn't think. All she knew was that this dark haired, violent man was strangling her. Was that it then? Was Gregor, obviously the man whose soul was as black as his hair, going to murder her? Would the glens of Skye then be covered with blood because of her father's revenge?

"Nae!" she cried out, coughing as the burning in her throat blocked out all air.

"Beg for mercy!" Gregor was enjoying her helplessness.

"Please......" Giving in to his sadistic whim, Caitlin could only hope that if she did as he said she would be spared.

"Again."

"Please."

"Please what?"

It pained her to talk, still she forced the words from he mouth. "Please don't kill me. Please let me live."

He thrust his face only a few inches from hers and Caitlin knew suddenly that he meant to do more than just strangle her. "Niall's wife! What irony." He laughed pinching her breast.

"Aye, I am his wife. And he will kill ye if ye dunna take me back to the castle." A place which had suddenly become a precious haven.,

"Take ye back? Not yet." As it to frighten her into submission he pulled the flag tightly around her throat again.

"Ye must be mad!" She stiffened, her mind refusing to accept what was inevitable. Taking a deep breath Caitlin let it out in a scream. Better to die quickly than to suffer what this evil bastard had in mind.

Somehow, even from within the castle walls Niall heard the shriek of outrage. In anguished curiosity he followed the sound. Seeing the two battling figures he flung himself forward.

At his intrusion Gregor loosened his grasp, allowing Caitlin the luxury of pushing herself to her knees. Slowly her eyes moved to her rescuer, knowing that at that moment Niall's face was the dearest face in the whole world.

"She was trying to run away and I caught her red-handed. Ye know the orders we had from Malcolm."

"Nae! He was trying to....to......." Caitlin was too ashamed to finish.

"I know exactly what he was trying to do."

Like an enraged lion, Niall sprang, engaging his cousin in hand to hand combat. Grappling on the floor, the two men wrestled, Gregor the burlier of the two but Niall's lithe muscular grace giving him the edge.

"I'll kill ye. I swear that I will."

It was a melee of cursing and shouting. Fisticuffs and kicking. First Niall would falter then Gregor would fail in his strategy. Niall's slyness and strength won out. He pummeled Gregor to near senselessness, stopping only when Malcolm's guards, alerted to trouble by the noise and yells, came rushing to pull the two men apart.

"What is this all about?" Malcolm came upon the scene with all the ferocity of a thundercloud. Looking from Niall to Gregor and back again he demanded an explanation.

"Yer tanist's wife was trying to steal the flag away. I was merely trying to hold her in check when yer nephew appeared and jumped me:.

"She was trying to steal the flag?" Malcolm was as angry as Caitlin had supposed. For an instant she thought he would strike her but he maintained control. "Ye shouldna hae done that. Ye've been dealt gently with but from now one ye will get no such courtesy." He gesticulated to a man standing behind him. "From now on lock her in." He smiled beneficently at her." It is my duty as yer Chieftain and kin-by-marriage to make certain ye dunna come to harm."

Caitlin struggled to her feet, her trembling hands automatically trying to straighten her rumpled clothing. "Make certain that I don't leave ye mean." Though she had been afraid of Gregor, Caitlin found out that now she was face to face with Malcolm, now that the worst had happened, she no longer was terrifed of him.

"As ye say." Malcolm led the way back to the castle, giving his orders to his guards as soon as the passed through the door.   This time Caitlin really was a prisoner and yet as she looked at Niall all she could think about was the way he had flown to her rescue.   Like some daring man the bards told about, Niall MacDonald had   fought   for   her.

Chapter Twenty-Six

Niall floundered in his bed amidst the fragments of his sleep. Tossing restlessly, his mind churned endlessly as he met head-on the thoughts troubling his mind. Caitlin was in terrible danger here. Tonight there had been something sinister in the way his uncle had glared at the girl. Now she was to be locked within the castle walls for trying to escape, something any self-respecting MacDonald would have done.

What a brave lass! Little by little he was coming to fully understand just how special a woman Caitlin was. A woman who had risked her life to come to Sleat to regain possession of the MacLeod's flag. A woman who had stood up against Malcolm. A daring lass who had done something even some of the clansmen would have feared to do.

"And she might have been successful if not for Gregor."

Gregor. His cousin's name made Niall tremble with suppressed rage. There could be no denying what he had intended. To dishonor Caitlin and very likely kill her. For that he had not even been scolded, though what he had done concerned another man's wife.

"But a wife that bears the name MacLeod." Thus what Gregor had done seemed to be permitable. The truth of it enraged him for he knew it would be a long time before he could forget the scene he had stumbled upon. And as long as Caitlin remained at Dunskaith she would be at Gregor's mercy.

But what can I do about it? How can I protect her? The truth was that he couldn't. But he could help her to escape. He could........

"Nae. I canna turn against my own." And yet neither could he just stand by and watch Caitlin be hurt.

Sitting up, Niall braced his legs against the cold wooden floor. Since she had been locked in her chamber he had not had a chance to talk with her, but he knew he had to talk with her now.

Getting out of bed Niall dressed hurriedly in a shirt and breacon and slowly opened his chamber door and made his way to Caitlin's room. What he saw was troubling. Proof of Caitlin's status as prisoner. True to his word Duncan had stationed a guard to prowl about in front of the room where Caitlin was housed. A faint gleam of torchlight glinted off the keys hung from the man's sporran, jingling as he walked back and forth. Seeing Niall he promptly blocked his way.

"Move aside, Robert." When the guard hesitated, Niall said simply, "I hae come to see my wife. Ye canna deny a mon that."

"No, I dunna suppose that I can." Hesitantly he turned the key in the lock.

Slowly Niall opened the door and went in, pausing for a moment to gaze at the woman asleep on the bed. She lay on her side, her head resting on one outflung arm, her flaming hair tumbling across her face and spilling like a living fire onto the pillow. Huddled up as she was, she looked almost childlike to him and he was mesmerized by how truly lovely she was. The long sweep of her lashes against the curve of her cheek made her look vulnerable and he vowed to protect her. His eyes moved tenderly over her form, moving from her toes to the top of her head, pausing for a moment as he studied the slightly tilted nose, the generous mouth that felt so soft against his own. The sight of her lying there, the rise and fall of her breathing stirring against the thin quilt, acted like an aphrodisiac. He remembered the way her breasts felt as they stroked his chest.

"Ah lass, how I do love ye," he whispered, "But alas, 'tis hopeless that we will ever hae any lasting happiness." Still, they could have memories to remember on long, lonely, cold nights. Breathing a heavy sigh he bent down and touched the fiery hair where it grew near her temple in a gesture of loving.

Caitlin awoke to the feel of a warm hand against her face, brushing back her hair. "Who?" She jerked upright drawing the covers tightly over her breasts as she remembered Gregor's pawing. "Ohhhh."

It was Niall who knelt beside her bed, holding a finger up to his lips to warn her to keep silent. Caitlin felt again that treacherous warmth of attraction she'd felt for him from the first.

"Niall?" She tried to adjust her vision to see him clearly in the fading firelight. "What are ye doing here?"

He looked like a man who was in need of sleep. There were hard lines around his mouth, furrows on his brow, the flesh beneath his eyes was shadowed with blue. Truly he looked more prisoner than she. He had the look of a tortured man. "I just came to see ye. I wanted to ye see. I wanted to make certain that ye were all right after....after."

"Aye, I am though if ye hadna come I know I wouldna be." Her eyes were soft. "Ye came to my rescue like in some heroic bard's tale."

"Did he hurt ye, Caitlin?" Caitlin had put up a valiant struggle but nevertheless he worried that perhaps more had taken place than his eyes had seen revealed.

Caitlin knew what he meant. "I am unharmed. All that is bruised and battered is my pride." She sighed.

"Had he done what he intended I would hae had to kill him!"

Her eyes were wide as she stared into his face. His voice sounded as if he really meant it. "Would ye?"

"Aye!" He sat down on the bed. "Despite all that has happened between us, lass, ye are my wife and I care for ye."

"Really?"

"Really."

"Niall......" There were so many things she wanted to say.

"Hush!" His fingers were gentle as he touched her lips. "Let me talk." Niall took a long, deep breath. His fingers traced her cheekbones, then her lips. "Ye've created quite a stir, lassie in more ways than one. "

"Aye, but I almost succeeded." She felt relaxed and contented being with him. There was a sudden easy relationship between them as if those stormy earlier days had never existed.

"Malcolm is incensed with ye,."

"Is he now?" Drawing her knees up to her chin she pursed her lips. "Well, he isna the one who should be piqued, I'd be thinkin'." The corners of her mouth tugged into a smile.

Nodding his head he caressed her with his eyes. "Caitlin.....ye hae made me realize a great many things these last few days."

"Such as....?" Her voice was soft, stroking him like a delicate hand, teasing him.

"Such as what is really important in this brief blink of an eye we call life."

He felt desire stir and could not escape her web of enchantment, could not take his eyes off her. She was quite a lassie. A bundle of beauty and bravery.

"And just what is important?" Her gaze roved over his features - the thick blonde hair, the hazel eyes with their thick lashes. The sparkling firelight shadowed the hollows beneath his high cheekbones and hard, strong jawline. It was his mouth perfectly chiseled mouth, however, that drew he eye again and again as she found herself remembering the taste of his kiss.

"Ye are ...." He stared grimly at the fire. "I love ye, Caitlin!" There he had said it. Something he had never said before. But having revealed his feelings he felt lighter of heart, as if in admitting it to her he had finally come to terms with the truth himself. He loved her.

"Love?" She hadn't expected him to say that. That he desired her perhaps, but not such strong feelings. Oh, how she had dreamed of hearing him say those words. On impulse she reached out and took his hand, unaware of how seductive such a gesture could be, for the contact of their hands was overpowering.

Slowly he moved toward her, pulling her toward him. His mouth came down on hers, engulfing Caitlin in the familiar sensations his lips always brought forth. Pressing her body closer to his, she sought the passion of his embrace. She craved his kisses with a warm sweet desire that fused their bodies together.

"Caitlin!" He spoke her name in a breathless whisper as he drew his mouth away. Searchingly his eyes gazed into hers. A silent question.

The roaring of her blood was deafening in her ears. She gave no resistance to his embrace. *This* was what she wanted, what she had always longed for.

Niall kissed her again. There was no ignoring the flicker of arousal which spread from their joined mouths to the core of her body. Thoughts of future heartache pressed against her soul but she pushed them far from her mind. She reached for him, as if the only safety could be in his arms. Her touch was his undoing. As their eyes suddenly met they both knew what was to come.

How can the hands of a fighting man be so tender? Yet they were. She didn't protest when he stretched himself the full length of the bed. The desire to run her hands over him made her tremble, yet she remained perfectly still.

"Niall."

"Aye."

"I just want ye to know how very glad I am to be yer wife. I wouldn't hae wanted to marry anyone else."

"Nor I."

Niall held her chin in his hand, kissing her eyelids, the curve of her cheek. He kissed her mouth with all the pent up hunger he had suppressed for so long, his tongue gently tracing the outline of her lips.

He felt her tremble beneath him and found himself trembling too with a nervousness that was unusual for him. Anticipation, he supposed. Eagerness. Desire.

Slowly, leisurely Niall stripped Caitlin's night gown away, like the petals of a flower. His fingers lingered as they wandered down her stomach to explore the texture of her skin. Like velvet, he thought.

"Ye are so beautiful."

She glowed under the praise of his deep, throaty whisper. "Am I...?" The compliment pleased her, made her forget for the moment all the hostility of the last few days and the danger. There was now.

"Very..." He sought the indentation of her navel, then moved lower to tangle his fingers in the soft wisps of hair that joined at her legs. Moving back he let his eyes enjoy what his hands had set free. "Do ye have any idea how much I want ye?" He took her hand and moving it beneath his breacan, pressed it to the firm flesh of his arousal. She felt the throbbing strength of him as her eyes gazed into his. Then he bent to kiss her again, his mouth keeping hers a willing captive for a long, long time.

Twining her hands around his neck she clutched him to her, pressing her body eagerly against his chest. She could feel the heat and strength and growing desire of him with every breath. Niall, her Niall. She had spent so may nights dreaming that he would make love to her.

Caitlin tried to speak, to tell him all that was in her heart, but all she could say was his name, a groan deep in her throat as his mouth and hands worked unspeakable magic.

"So much wasted time," he murmured. "But now I'll make up for it." His head was bent low, his tongue curling around the tips of her breast, suckling gently.

Raising himself up on his elbow he looked down at her and at that moment he knew he's put his heart and soul in pawn. Removing his shirt and breacan he pressed their naked chests together, shivering at the vibrantly arousing sensation.

"Caitlin...." Her name was like a prayer on his lips.

The warmth and heat of his mouth the memory of her fingers touching that private part of him sent a sweet ache flaring through Caitlin's whole body. Growing bold she allowed her hands to explore, delighting at the touch of the firm flesh that covered his ribs, the broad shoulders, the muscles of his arms, the lean length of his back. He was so perfectly formed. His masculine beauty hypnotized her and for just a moment she was content to stare, then with a soft sigh her fingers curled in the thick springy hair that furred his chest. Her fingers lightly circled in imitation of what he was doing to her.

His lips nuzzled against the side of her throat. He uttered a moan as her hands moved over the smoothly corded muscles of his shoulders. "Ah, how I love ye to touch me...." It seemed as if his breath was trapped somewhere between his throat and stomach. He couldn't say any more. The realization that once again she was to be his was a heady feeling that nearly made him dizzy as he brought his lips to hers. Such a potent kiss. As if he had never kissed her before.

Reaching up she clung to him, drawing in his strength and giving hers to him in return. She could feel his heart pounding and knew that hers beat in matching rhythm.

Caressing her, kissing her, he left no part of her free from his touch and she responded with a natural passion that was kindled by his love. Her entire body quivered with the intoxicating sensations he always aroused in her. She wanted only one thing - to feel his hard warmth filling her, to join with him in that most tender of emotions.

"Niall...." Closing her eyes, Caitlin awaited another kiss, her mouth opening to him as he caressed her lips with all the passionate hunger they both yearned for. Caitlin loved the taste of him, the tender urgency of his mouth. Her lips opened to him for a seemingly endless passionate onslaught of kisses. It was if they were breathing one breath, living at that moment just for each other.

Desire that had been coiling within Caitlin for so long only to be unfulfilled, sparked to renewed fire and she could feel his passion likewise building, searing her with its heat. They shared a joy of touching and caressing, arms against arms, legs touching legs, fingers entwining and wandering to explore. Mutual hunger brought their lips back together time after time. She craved his kisses and returned them with trembling pleasure, exploring the inner softness of his mouth.

"Oh, my sweet, braw wife...!" Desire writhed almost painfully within his loins. He had never wanted anything or anyone as much as he did her at this moment. It was like an unfulfilled dream just waiting to come true.

Niall's cupped the full curve of her breast. Lightly he stroked until the peaks sprang to life under his touch, the once soft flesh now taunt and aching. His breath caught in his throat as his hazel eyes savored her.

Bending down he worshipped her with his mouth, his lips traveling from one to the other in tender fascination. His tongue curled around the taunt peaks, his teeth lightly grazing until she writhed beneath him.

He savored the expressions that chased across her face, the wanting and the passion for him that were so clearly revealed.

She caught fire wherever he touched her, burning with an all-consuming need. Caitlin's hands crept around Niall's neck, her fingers tangling and tousling the thick waves of his tawny hair as she breathed a husky sigh, remembering what pleasure was to come.

They lay together kissing, touching, rolling over and over on the bed. His hands were doing wondrous things to her, making her writhe and groan. Every inch of her body caught fire as passion exploded between them with a wild oblivion. He moved against her, sending waves of pleasure exploding along every nerve in her body.

"Niall....I want you inside me..." she breathed.

"In due time...." His hands caressed her, warming her with their heat. They took sheer delight in the texture and pressure of each other's body. Sensuously he undulated his hips between her legs and every time their bodies caressed, each experienced a shock of raw desire that encompassed them in fiery, pulsating sensations. Then his hands were between their bodies, sliding down the velvety flesh of her belly, moving to that place between her thighs that ached for his entry.

The swollen length of him brushed across her thighs. Then he was covering her, his manhood at the entrance of her secret core. His gentle probing brought sweet fire, curling deep inside her with spirals of pulsating sensations. Then his hands left her, to be replaced by the hardness she had glimpsed before, entering her just a little then pausing. She felt his maleness creating unbearable sensations within her as he began to move within her.

Niall groaned softly, the blood pounding thickly in his head. His hold on her hips tightened as the throbbing shaft of his maleness possessed her again and again. She was so warm, so tight around him that he closed his eyes with agonized pleasure as he moved back and forth, initiating her fully into the depths of passion and love.

Instinctively Caitlin tightened her legs around him certain she could never withstand the ecstasy that was engulfing her body. It was as if her heart shattered, bursting within her. She was melting inside, merging with him into one being. As spasms overtook her she dug her nails into the skin of his back whispering his name.

A sweet shaft of ecstasy shot through Niall and he closed his eyes. Even when the intensity of their passion was spent they still clung to each other, unable to let this magical moment end. They touched each other gently, wonderingly.

"Oh, what a fiery, passionate wife I hae." He nibbled playfully at her ear.

"Am I now? And are ye not pleased?"

"Aye! But not surprised." Playfully he tugged at her hair. "This gave me a warning." He nuzzled her throat. "Ye are all that I could hae asked for, all that I desire."

Cradling her against his chest he lay silent for a long, long time as he savored her presence beside him. His hands fondled her gently as she molded her body to his. *If only I could keep her with me forever*, he thought, and not let the hatred between the clans destroy what they had found.

Niall realized that for the first time in his life he was truly content. Very, very happy. Power was said to be the most important thing on earth but he knew differently. Without someone who really cared life was hollow and made a man the emptiest of creatures. Caitlin made him feel alive!

"I will never let ye go. I pledge my love, my very life."

This time it was Caitlin who silenced him. "Hush. Ye canna make such promises. I know and ye know that." She laid her head on his shoulder, stroking the hair on his chest. "But know this as well. Whatever happens I will always love ye."

"I canna ask more than that." And yet he did. As Niall closed his eyes he knew at that moment that he had to take control of their destiny.

Chapter Twenty-Seven

Torches in the great hall burned brightly despite the late hour, their flames casting a gigantic shadow on the wall. A grotesque silhouette that looked like that of an ogre, Niall thought as he boldly strode into the room.

"I want to talk with ye, Malcolm," he announced, not even masking his frustration.

"Oh?" Sitting in his favorite chair, his feet perched on the table, Malcolm didn't even bother to look up.

"Ye canna do this, Malcolm!"

There was no answer but Niall was not in a mood to tolerate the blatant disregard of his presence. With a mumbled oath he moved towards the table and gave it a shove hard enough to nearly send Malcolm sprawling.

"Arghhh.....!" This time Malcolm did respond. Bounding to his feet he looked like an angry bear.

"I said I want to talk."

The dark eyes beneath Malcolm's thick brows were slits of anger. He raised his fists. For a moment it looked as if he had been goaded into a fight but in the end he backed down. "Then talk, ye young pup!"

"I want my wife set free. I dunna want to see her caged like some trapped animal."

"You!" Malcolm was defiant as he faced the younger man squarely. "You dunna want." His tone was scathing. Reaching out he gripped Niall's shoulder, digging his fingers into the firm-muscled flesh with a bruising strength that proved he was still a man to be reckoned with.

Niall did not back down. Squaring his shoulders he

took a step forward. "I dunna want! Set her free."

"Nae!" Turning his back Malcolm's manner clearly told that his answer was to be the end of it. But Niall wouldn't leave it there.

"Then ye are not an honorable mon.   A mon of honor would not treat a lassie such." Without realizing it, his eyes moved upward, focusing on the Fairy Flag. Oh, how he regretted ever even touching it. Except for the fact that it was instrumental in his meeting Caitlin, no good had come of his mission to steal it. Had he known to what ends Malcolm would go, he would never have involved himself in the deed.

"She is not just a lassie. She is one of them." His lips curled up in a snarl. "And Ian MacLeod's daughter." Malcolm screwed up his face, looking angry, fierce and formidable. "Ian MacLeod. Bah! I shall never forgi'e him. I shall be avenged. Aye, I shall!"

"By locking up his daughter?" Niall knew it would be a long time before he could forget the sight of an armed guard parading up and down in front of Caitlin's door.

"I did that for her own good. " Malcolm shook his shaggy-haired head.   "I wouldna want her to get lost or to come upon dishonorable men."

"Like Gregor!"

"Hold yer tongue! Gregor is yer kin. My nephew. A member of yer clan.   Dunna dare critisize him to side with a MacLeod!"   Malcolm clenched his jaw only narrowly holding back his anger. "He wears the scars of MacLeod treachery."

"As they bear scars of his." Niall's eyes met those of his uncle relating a silent condemnation of an act of cowardice that had been perpetrated many years ago.

The reminder made Malcolm uncomfortable. He stiffened but did not push the quarrel further. "What is done is done. Now ye are Tanist, a justifiable honor I hae disposed." His upraised brow seemed to hint very strongly that Niall should show proper gratitude.

"And for that I thank ye. I will serve you well, Uncle, but as to Caitlin, ye must....."

"My mind is made up. Ye hae no say on the matter!" He thrust his face to within inches of Niall's. "Ye are not chieftain yet. Nor will ye ever be if ye dunna keep still."

A tight knot had formed in Niall's stomach. Then I will do what I must do, Niall thought but did not say. All too soon the moment he had dreaded was to become a reality.

"So be it."

Malcolm didn't speak but by the smile that erupted across his face it was obvious that he thought himself to be triumphant in the argument. More to himself than to Niall he said at last, "I hae the MacLeod's little treasure which it willna take long for him to reclaim. So dunna fash yerself, laddie. She won't be locked in her room ere long."

"Ye will let her go once her father comes to take the bait?" Niall knew he could not wait to find out. Not after what Gregor had done tonight. He would not take the risk of Caitlin being hurt in this matter of Malcolm's desire for revenge.

Leaving the room, he took the stairs two at a time as he hurried to Caitlin's chamber. It would be a traitorous act to follow the urging of his heart, Niall thought. Even so he knew there was no other choice. There were times when right must overpower wrong no matter what the price. True, Malcolm was Niall's chieftain, for whom he had sworn loyalty and his uncle, but kin or not he was grieviously unjust in what he was doing. So thinking, Niall pulled a sword from the wall, hoping with all his heart he would not have to use it to shed any blood and hurried onward.

Stealthfully Niall approached the sentinel, grasping the sword, using the handle as a club, knocking the guard out cold. The man grunted, then slumped to the floor. Anxiously Niall fumbled about for the key, tearing it free and unlocking the door.

"Caitlin!" His voice was a harsh, whispered urgency.

"Mmmmm....." She came only half awake, disturbed by his hushed command but opened her eyes wide as her shook he gently. "Something is wrong. What?"

"Nothing is wrong."

"Then....?" She held out her arms, thinking him to have amorous intentions.

She was tempting but Niall regretfully had to shake his head. "I've come to free ye, Caity, not to make love.,"

"Free me?"

"Aye." With gentle fingers he grasped her hand and pulled her to her feet. "Hurry and get dressed. We hae to get free of here before the goose egg I gifted the guard with is discovered. I don't know how long he'll be unconscious."

"Ye hit him?" She was worried what repercussions that might bring.

Niall ruffled her already tousled hair. "We won't speak of it now, but I think you ken. Now, no more talk!"

By the light of a candle he helped her dress, his fingers lingering overlong on the soft swell of her breast as he fastened the folds of her tonnag together with a broach. He looked down at the fiery red tresses illuminated by the glow of the flickering light and wrapped a strand around his fingers. A yearning surged through him. He wanted her so much that it was a painful longing. If only they could go away together, give free expression to the passion that sparked between them he knew they could be happy. But that was not to be. She had to go and he had to stay. Unselfishly he was willing to give up his own desires just to make certain that she was safe. Even so he allowed himself the luxury of holding her close, just for a moment, brushing his lips against her neck. Then with a mumbled oath he pulled away.

"Come!"

More than one unwary clansman was the recipient of a painful crack to the head as Niall frantically sought Caitlin's freedom, yet slowly but surely they worked their way across the inner bailey, hiding in the shadows. Niall clasped Caitlin's hand so tightly that she winced.

Her eyes were sad. "Niall, I'm not sure I want to go."

"Ye must." Niall felt a shiver convulse her slim frame and wrapped his arms around her, shielding her from the cool air with his plaid. An unpremeditated act but one that most definitely felt right. She belonged in his arms. "Malcolm is a good chieftain on most accounts but something is seriously amiss here. I intend to see that ye get back to yer father's hall safely before the hills and glens of Skye are stained with all our blood."

She nuzzled her check against his chest. "Come with me." Hope kindled anew in her heart, that perhaps all would turn out as it should after all.

"Caitlin....." Niall's mouth hovered only inches from her own and she wanted him to give in to the moment but instead he shook his head. "I canna. Once I take ye far enough to know that ye are safe I must come back."

"But how will ye explain.......?"

"I'll think of a way." He held her close for just a moment more, then pulled away. "Let us go." The dark shape of the huge outer gate loomed before them. "Push the ends of your hair inside your tonnag, lass and keep your head down." If God was willing they would not be discovered.

Niall tugged on the rope. The creak of the portcullis was a welcome sound, though Caitlin watched the iron grating ascend with anxiety. What would be Niall's punishment for aiding her, she wondered, knowing his betrayal of Malcolm would not be taken lightly. The realization of what Niall had risked suddenly hit her full force. How could she let him make such a sacrifice? She had thought that being Tanist meant the world to him and yet now by his actions he was throwing the honor away. She couldn't let him do it! Not and profess her love.

"Niall, let's go back. I canna let ye do this. Ye will be ruined," she breathed, her voice blending with the wind.

"I willna," he lied. "I'm a smooth talking laddie as ye know. I'll make up a story that Malcolm will believe." He smiled, remembering that night they had met. "Perhaps I'll just tell him that ye were a ghost and walked through the wall. Will he believe that do ye believe?"

"Nae." Though he tugged at her hand she wouldn't move an inch. "I willna go."

"Because ye think I will suffer. Well, I willna. I'll think of a way to make amends to Malcolm, never fear. He needs me. " He kissed her lightly on the lips. "Together we can work on bringing peace to Skye, Caity. Then and only then can we ever hope to be reunited."

That was something to hope for. Still, Caitlin's face was wet with tears as she followed him through the gaping mouth of the gate running across the glen.

They formed two silhouettes on the crest of the hill, running against the wind. Caitlin felt contented that all would be well until her eyes swept the dark gray horizon. Were those distant dots she saw on the hill what she thought them to be? Yes! Blessed Saint Michael, they were being followed!

"Niall! Someone is coming!" she croaked, clutching his hand with fingers that trembled.

Niall looked over his shoulder, cursing loudly. Eight or ten men were running in their direction. There could be no other reason than pursuit. "They must hae found Robert sooner than I supposed. Run, Caity!"

Run she did, until her legs ached but though they had had a head start, that gave them a fair to middling chance of escape, the other men were gaining on them. Looking over her shoulder, nonetheless, she cringed. "Run faster, Niall!" Obeying her own command, she forced her feet and legs to move at a hazardous speed. They had to get away.

"Caitlin.....!" There was large hole up ahead but though Niall sought to warn her, he was helpless to keep her from stumbling. All he could do was to hurry back for her. Taking her by the hand he tugged her to her feet." "Are you all right?"

She nodded, refusing to notice the pain in her ankle. Even so, the injury slowed her down. As they ran she had to lean on Niall for support. And all the while the men pursuing them were catching up. The reality of the situation could not be denied. They could never escape now.

"Listen to me, Niall. I willna hae ye sacrificing

yerself to save me. Tell them I broke free of my room and ye were chasing after me. Say it! I willna deny it."

"I willna tell such a vile lie!"

"I will! Let Malcolm think ye are a hero in capturing me. Then perhaps all willna be lost." Caitlin hushed as the clansmen swiftly encircled them. Pushing at Niall's chest she made great show of fighting him. "Ach, ye damned MacDonald Let me go! I willna go back......"

"Aye, ye will!"

Caitlin recognized that voice at once and damned the man. Gregor. Like a cursed hound he seemed to be always following in her tracks. "Ha! I should hae ken it would hae been ye ."

"I wondered if my instincts were right. They were. I know ye set her free, Niall. I watched and waited. This time I let her get past the gate, just so there would be no mistaking yer intent." At a nod of his head four men surrounded Niall, grappling him to the ground.

Striking out blindly, Caitlin did her best to pull Gregor's henchmen from Niall. She tried to claw at them. She kicked out, baring her shaply thighs in the tussle. "Nae! Nae! He was chasing after me to bring me back to the castle!" In anger she whirled around, her eyes darting fire at Gregor.

His thin lips curled up in a snarl. "Ye are a liar, said he. I willna doubt my own eyes. I saw what I saw. And now he will suffer for it."

"Ye black-hearted bastard!" Even in his defeated position, Niall's countenance blazed defiance. "I tell ye to let the lassie go!"

"Go? She'll go nowhere but back to the castle. And as for ye......."

"I am Tanist! You have no right to overrule me." Struggling against the men who held him Niall stared his adversary down.

"Tanist? Not when it is found out what ye hae done." Malice oozed from Gregor's eyes. "Ye've brought yerself to this end. Ah, how I hae hated having to share my uncle wi' ye, then seeing ye be named Tanist. I've wanted to bring ye down and now I hae."

"Not yet." Even now Niall was determined. He would talk with Malcolm, convince him somehow that what he had done was for the good of the clan.

"Aye, but I hae." Gregor was frighteningly sure of himself!" Giving Niall a shove he commanded, "Take them away!"

HIGHLAND DESTINY

Chapter Twenty-Eight

It was cold, damp and dark in the prison cell. Depressing. The stale odor of straw, mildew and rot, enveloped Niall as he was shoved inside the small cubicle that was little bigger than closet.

"Yer abode, cousin. Sweet dreams. Keep the rats company."

Niall lunged, only to be held back by two of the men who swore Gregor allegiance. "I swear, Gregor, ye will regret this! I will get my revenge." he swore, his eyes darting back and forth for any means of escape. There was none. He was being heavily guarded, like a bird by three large cats, he thought wryly.

"By sending Ogg to wreck vengeance?" For a moment he paused then exclaimed, "I"m not afraid of him."

"Well, ye should be and of me when I get free." Niall lashed out, only to be kicked back down into the dark hole. The clank of the grille above his head put an end to any other threats.

"Free?" Gregor's expression was frightening as he leered down at him.

"Aye, free. Ye willna be able to keep me here." At least he hoped. And yet, what would Malcolm do when he heard Gregor's bit of "news"? As Gregor and his men left, as Niall looked around him, he could only wonder.

KATHRYN HOCKETT

It was a tiny, cramped cell, more cellar than prison ,with a stone and iron barred trapdoor that could be locked from up above. Niall was familiar with the dungeon. There was no way of escape, of that he was certain. Even if he could crawl up the wall there was no way he could remove the stone from the hole. He was completely at Gregor's mercy.

"I hae been thrust in here without a measure of decency. To suffer and...." To die? No, Niall couldn't believe that it would go that far. Or at least he didn't want to believe. And yet.....

The sound of scurrying rats caused him to wince. Damn the rodents. How he had always loathed them. Their being in here with him meant that he would not be able to sleep for fear of having his flesh nibbled on. That was what Gregor meant about sweet dreams. The bastard!

"I'll get out of here and I'll slit his throat. I'll pierce him through. I'll...... Something tickled his arm. Cringing he brushed it away. Oh, how he hated this chilling darkness. It was nearly enough to drive a man mad. But then wasn't that the very idea? Well he wouldn't give Gregor that satisfaction. Somehow, someway, he would get free. Hugging his knees to his chest Niall was dedicated to that thought for only then could he save Caitlin.

Oh, where are ye? What has Gregor done to ye. Are ye safe, lass? Putting his face in his hands he could only worry and wonder.

Caitlin was safe, at least for the moment though she was facing an adversary of her own. A glowering, bearded devil who made no secret of just how dangerous he was.   After being pushed and dragged into his presence, she was accused by Gregor of the most hideous of crimes.

"She is a witch."

Caitlin was quick to defend herself. "I am no witch!"

"Be that as it may, under her spell poor Niall was guilty of the vilest of acts against us all."

"Niall?" Malcolm clenched his jaw. "What has he done."

"He set her free but I followed and reclaimed her." Gregor gave her a shove. "She is yours."

"So she is." Malcolm glared down at her.

Wincing against the pain in her injured leg, Caitlin stood proud and tall. "So what are ye going to do with me?" Was she to join Niall in the dungeon? Or did the MacDonald have other plans for her?

"Do with ye?" Malcolm pulled at his beard as if contemplating the matter. He quickly decided. "Why nothing."

"Nothing?" It was hardly the answer she expected.

"Nothing to ye." The way he said it sounded ominous.

"And to Niall?"

"It all depends on ye. If ye try to leave here again it will go hard on him, do ye ken? I will seek punishment on *him*."

Caitlin had gone quite pale. "I ken!"

"But if ye conduct yerself like a good little lassie and stay here until yer father pays me a visit, then I will prove myself to be forgiving."

"Ye will set him free."

"Aye."

It was a bargain that made Caitlin have to chose between the two men she most loved in the world. She could either betray her father and watch him fall victim to his sworn enemy or betray Niall to save her father.

"Nae! Nae!" The cry that escaped from her throat was like that of a wounded animal. Sagging to the ground she grasped his knees, hugging them with her arms as she had when he was a small girl. "Ye canna do this. Ye canna." Rocking back and forth she sought to fight the demons that tore at her heart.

Chapter Twenty-Nine

Niall seemed to lose track of time as he languished in the cell-like room. It was dismal, uncomfortable, and humiliating, a disgusting hellhole. Walls of dirt infested with all kinds of vermin. Spiders, worms, and bugs of unknown origin. Worst of all, however, it was damp and cold. He thanked God for his plaid, for it was long and thick enough to be a warm blanket to shield him from the bone-penetrating chill.

"Och, to be free again." Freedom. Something he had always taken for granted but which now was denied him.

"Caitlin!" Her eyes haunted him, her voice seemed to whisper in his ear. "Ach, I'm nearly as addled in my head as Gregor. Something sinister urged *him*. Something evil." Niall could not say what it was, but he knew there was more to the matter than at first was visible.

"Niall!"

It was Ogg's voice. A circle of light appeared above his head as a torch was held aloft. Niall stood up, blinking against the light. He put his hand up to guard him against the brightness of the flickering flames.

"The light hurts yer eyes!"

"Aye, I am slowly turning into a mole." There was a hint of bitterness in Niall's voice. "So much for the mighty tanist." Seeing Ogg, Niall thought of Caitlin. "How is she?"

"Safe, at least for the time being. But Gregor is trying stir up feelings against her."

"Is she…is she caged like me?"

"Nae, though she may as well be." Ogg leaned close. "Malcolm has declared that if she even steps on foot outside the portcullis it will bode ill for ye."

"For me?"

"Aye."

"So, she is trapped just as surely as I." His voice was choked with misery.

"Because of her love for ye, she seeks to protect ye, all the while frightened of what Malcolm intends to do if her father comes to Dunskaith."

"But I don't care what Malcolm has threatened to do to me. He would not kill his own nephew." Of that at least Malcolm would not make himself guilty.

"She canna take the chance."

"Damn, Malcolm." His stubborn obstinance had created a great deal of unhappiness. "Ach, if only I could get out of here."

"Get out? I wouldna be thinking it to be very soon."

"Nor I." Niall was at the mercy of a man who had no honor, no scruples.

"Gregor has the key, and though I hae tried to get my hands on it, I havena been able."

Of course not. Gregor would guard it like a hawk. Niall could only wonder if he would ever be able to hold Caitlin in his arms again. "Ogg."

"Aye?

"Give Caitlin a message for me."

"that ye love her." Ogg nodded, his face a mask of misery. "That I will." Bidding Niall good-bye, with a promise to come later that night, he hurried back to the hall.

Tankard clanked against tankard in drunken celebration as Malcolm Macdonald and Gregor related the story again and again to their clansmen of Caitlin's escape and capture. Each telling embellished Caitlin's duplicity and Gregor's valor. Watching from the shadows of the great hall, Caitlin wondered how many times they were going to tell the tale. It had been all they had talked about last night, this morning, and again this evening, as if her trying to escape was in some way menacing to the clan.

"I tell ye, she has the evil eye," Gregor was saying.

"The evil eye," Caitlin scoffed. As if she had the power to destroy, corrupt, or acquire an object by merely looking at it.

The clansmen in the hall had begun to believe it, however. Staring at her with frightened eyes they seemed to be waiting for her to exhibit her powers. Mumbling beneath their breath, they spoke of how she had cast such a potent spell over Niall that he had betrayed his own.

"And ye had best watch out or she will do it to you," Gregor intoned. "She is in league with the forces of evil. I witnessed with my own eyes her incantations and rituals."

"Aye. I hae seen her change herself into a cat!" Robert, the guardsman, seemed convinced of it. "That's how she escaped."

"A cat that was as red as her hair," Gregor hurried to add, knowing that he held the others in the palm of his hand. "Well, we will see that she doesna put a spell on us."

As the large stone room flickered with red and orange light, thrown by the flames of the vast hearth, Caitlin stared in fascination at the grotesque shadows cast upon the wall. What followed might have been humorous had it not been so threatening. Caitlin stood horrified as Gregor and his cronies began mumbling, supposedly to counter the effects of "the eye."

"I make to thee the charm of Mary,

The most perfect charm that is in the world,

Against the small eye, against the large eye,

Against the eye of swift voracious women,

Against the eye of swift rapacious women,

Against the eye of swift sluttish women."

Gregor nodded in Caitlin's direction at the last words.

"I am no witch!" she breathed. And Gregor knew that as well. But whether she was or not, the very suspicion planted in the clansmen's minds could be dangerous for her. As well Gregor knew. It made Caitlin's blood run cold that she was at the mercy of her greatest enemy.

"Psssst, Caitlin…." Reaching out of the shadows, Ogg took her hand, pulling her into the corner.

"Niall?" the very thought of him caused a flutter in her stomach.

"Is miserable but alive and well. He sends ye his love."

"And I sent back mine." Closing her eyes, she could almost see his face, but the blare of a trumpet interrupted her reverie.

A huffing, puffing sentry bounded into the room, pointing in the direction of the north. "The MacLeods! They are here! They've come by biorlin, across the loch. They are marching this way. Listen to the bagpipes!" the ominous hum sounded like a swarm of angry bees.

"My father!" Hurrying to the window, Caitlin looked out, lamenting the boldness that had brought her here. A fear gripped her heart that far from halting the warfare her willfulness had provoked an attack.

"The MacLeods are outside the walls!" the tension in the room was taut as a bowstring. Every clansman's eye focused on the weapons hanging on the wall, poised, waiting for Malcolm's nod. Caitlin's eyes, however, were focused elsewhere.

"The flag!" somehow when the clansmen were distracted she had to get her hands upon it. If she as a MacLeod could hold that flag aloft, it would give her clansmen heart. And at the same time she would be keeping her promise, not to step foot outside the portcullis.

Caitlin's heart turned over in her breast. Hands clasped tight, she moved to the window and leaned over the stone-work balustrade in an effort to identity the clansmen beyond a doubt, having but faint hope that it was other than her clan. The red-haired, broad-shouldered man at the head of the small army left little doubt. Torchlight winked a glow from his sword, the yellow-and-black hue of the tartan beneath gnarled armor marked Ian as surely as any badge.

"Father!" Her eyes were imploring as she looked at the man who held her father's fate in his hands. "Please....!"

Malcolm paused for a long moment, then broke into a smile. "I hae no need to quarrel." He turned to Gregor. "By the laws of hospitality, mon, invite Ian in." He patted Caitlin on the shoulder.

Gregor followed his chieftain's bidding, opening the door to an angry MacLeod. Ignoring everyone else in the room, he jostled and shoved his way to Caitlin's side. "Are ye all right? Are ye unharmed?" Her nod assured him that she was. Only then did he unleash his chiding tirade, his face turning purple with rage. "Ye must be daft, Daughter!" Never before had he raised a hand to her, but he shook his fist now threateningly. "I should take the back of my hand to ye. Headstrong! Stubborn! Willful! All these things ye are!"

Caitlin recoiled in the face of his tongue-lashing, knowing she deserved his censor and worse. She should never have come here! If it was possible, she had aged in just the past few days. She deserved his anger. There wasn't a thing he could say to her that she had not said to herself. It was true that a selfish, naïve, bold young maiden had left Dunvegan. Now she knew the painful truth, that life often held disappointments and heartache beyond human control. Sometimes the greatest show of love was in giving a loved one up. Just as Niall had been prepared to do.

"I'm...I'm sorry, Father."

"Yer sister told me why ye had come. Ach, I ne'er thought any seed of my manhood would go behind my back. "Ye defied me!"

"I had to get back the flag." Reverently her eyes touched on it.

Ian's eyes did likewise. "Och, the flag." He reached out as if by so doing he could reclaim it.

Having watched the fiery reunion between father and daughter from a distance, Malcolm now stepped forward. There was an edge to his voice. "Which belongs to me now!"

"Oh, does it now!" Ian stood nose-to-nose with his old adversary. To Caitlin's eyes they looked much like two hounds snarling over a bone as they sidestepped each other.

"Aye, it does!"

"Doesna." Ian stood with his arms akimbo, radiating hostility from every pore.

"Does." Malcolm glowered. "Just as Fiona belonged to me until ye came in between."

Fiona? Caitlin was stunned to hear the MacDonald utter her mother's name.

"She didna want to marry ye," Ian countered. "She didna like yer ways."

"Like me or no, ye stole another mon's betrothed." Roughly he grabbed Caitlin by the arm. "And now, I hae evened the score. Fiona's daughter will stay in Dunskaith for the rest of her days.

It was dark in the tiny dungeon. Only the glow of torchlight cast a faint flicker of light through the iron grate, illuminating the dismal prison. Niall was in a foul mood as he huddled in the folds of his plaid, trying to fend off the chill. Pulling the edges of his breacon, tighter he grumbled loudly, pausing only when a soft noise disturbed his solitude. The faint moan of faraway bagpipes cut through the stillness.

Bagpipes! Niall held his breath, attuning his ears to the wail, cursing his uncle as he realized he was not imagining things. So the MacLeods had come just as he had known they would. But this time Malcolm could not place blame on anyone but himself! Were there a battle the burden of the responsibility rested on the MacDonald Chieftain and not on a MacLeod.

Rising from the ground Niall paced back and forth across the cubicle's hard earthen floor feeling like a trapped rodent! He had to get out! He had to do something to divert the disaster that he knew was going to ensue. Somehow! Someway!

Gripping the dirt walls, forcing a foothold, he tried to climb up the side of the hole he'd been flung into, only to slide back down each time he was within an arm's length of the top. His only reward was blistered and bleeding fingers.

Taking off the leather belt that held the sporran around his waist, he tried another approach, looping it through the bars of the iron grating. Again he failed, watching in abject frustration as the belt missed its mark again and again. It was as if the walls were closing in on him. Never had Niall felt so totally powerless in all his life. Since he was a boy Niall had known only one fear, that of being enclosed in small spaces.

"Gregor knows well the way to torture me."

The drone of bagpipes was getting louder, taunting Niall with his own helplessness. What was happening up there? Was Malcolm going to anoint Niall's marriage with blood? "Caitlin!" Above all he wanted to make certain that she was safe.

A sound! What was it? Niall looked up fearing to see the familiar hulking form of Gregor but saw instead another face looking down at him. One as dear as his own visage. "Ogg!" The giant had returned. "Get me out of here!"

"Shhhhhhh! We dunna want to stir up an alarm. At least not yet." The giant grinned.

"Did you get the key?"

"Nae. I think Malcolm has it with him. He knows ye hae many friends within the castle. I fear I'm going to hae to dig ye out, loosen the dirt around the grate, then pull with all my might."

"If anyone can do it you can." The staccato noise above his head told Niall that Auley was doing just that. Heeding the giant's words Niall remained silent until his curiosity got the better of him. He had to ask.

"What's happening above? Tell me, mon. Are the MacLeods going to instigate war?" Niall whispered as softly as he could. "Caitlin, is she...."

"With her father. Safe for the moment." His face looked troubled.

"What is it?"

"Malcolm has proclaimed to Caitlin's father that he will never let her go."

"What did ye say?"

Ogg recounted all that he had heard. "Malcolm, or so it seems, was in love with Caitlin's mother. When she scorned him to marry Ian MacLeod it instigated a bitter rivalry."

"And this is what it was all about?" Niall thought of all of those who had died. And all because of jealousy and hurt pride.

"Aye. Foolish, isn't it?" With a burst of energy, Ogg at last loosened the grille sufficiently to free his friend. Leaning over the side, he reached out, clasping Niall by the hand to drag him to the surface.

The first thing Niall did was to breath in the fresh air. "I owe ye a favor, Ogg. By the saints I do."

"Just be happy and have joy of Caitlin." He picked up a large leather sack. "I brought ye a few supplies we might need along the way."

"Oh?" Niall could see that Ogg had it all planned.

"I'm going to help ye rescue Caitlin." Somehow he made it all sound so easy. "We can do if we are canny and take advantage of the turmoil raging in the hall."

"Then let's hurry!" Niall was impatient.

The shouting had started by the time they got back to the hall. Everyone seemed to be talking at once. Accusations. Denials. Anger. Louder and louder. It seemed everyone was shouting.

Hidden in the shadows, Niall listened. "Ye whoreson! Ye vile treacherous mon!" Ian flung his epitaphs at Malcolm as everyone stared in stoney silence. "Why? Why would ye do such a thing?"

"To seek reprisal ye sneaking, backstabbing bastard!" Malcolm's eyes bulged in their sockets as he revealed his intent. "Ye took my bride, I'll take yer daughter. It's tit for tat." Baiting Ian, Malcolm boldly boasted of the deed, heartlessly goading his adversary.

"Anything that I hae done ye rightly deserved."

"Including murdering my son by stabbing him in the back?" Now it was Ian's turn to make accusations.

"Killed yer son? I didna do such a thing unless it was in battle!" Malcolm hotly denied the charge.

"Ye struck him from behind by treachery."

"Tis a lie! No MacDonald would strike down a man from behind. We are warriors, not assassins."

"I say ye are!"

Silence reigned once again, like the quiet before a devastating storm.

"To arms! To arms!" Malcolm MacDonald gave his call to war. Niall grabbed at any weapon available, settling for an old relic of a sword. Brandishing it he looked around for Caitlin. Above all he would allow no harm to come to her.

Ignoring the clashing and a slashing of swords of the bloody and violent melee he fought his way to her, thrusting her against the wall to protect her with his body. With a growl of warning he wielded his sword. He would allow no one to come anywhere near her. Not this time.

"Niall, ye are a traitor! Damned be ye, lad." Though occupied with the fighting, Malcolm's attention was diverted just long enough for Niall to dart by. Two MacDonalds held the doorway but Niall was desperate to make an escape. It was the only chance he and Caitlin had. "Caitlin, we are going to make a run for it!"

"Nae!" She would not go and leave her father and the others. Stubbornly she shook his head but her protestations were ignored. With determinedly strong hands he pushed her towards the corridor, his weapon darting this way and that to form a path.

"Niall!" Ogg thrust himself forward fighting savagely., "Run for it, mon!"

"I willna leave, I say." Anxiously her eyes moved towards where her father was engaged in combat with a MacDonald half his age.

"Ye canna help yer clansmen, lass. It is out of yer hands. Best that ye let me get ye out of here while I can lest Malcolm make good on his threat to keep ye his prisoner forever."

"Out of my hands?" His tone and words implied that the MacLeods had already lost.

"Come. Hurry."

She couldn't leave her father and the others behind no matter what happened. As to her being unable to aid her clansmen she was not so sure. "See to yer own safety, Niall. I hae something that needs doing," she called out over her shoulder, breaking out into a run. Heading back towards the hall she knew she had to get her hands on the flag.

"Caitlin! Come back. What are ye doing?" Putting his own well-being out of his thoughts, Niall followed her, watching as she pushed one of the wooden tables over near the wall. He knew in an instant what she intended to do. "Nae, Caity. Ye will bring about yer death."

"Then so be it. At least I'll hae died a heroes death." Her brave words were punctuated with a cry of pain as a sword engaged her soft flesh.

"Caity!" Niall hurried to her defense but was caught up in his own battle to survive. All he could do was to watch helplessly as she grabbed a sword and a shield from the wall, using them as best she could to protect herself.

"Get back! Get back, I say." Lashing out with the sword, Caitlin was amazed at the strength which suddenly possessed her. Ignoring the pain in her wounded arm, conscious only of the frantic need to come to the aid of the MacLeod fighters, she held her adversary at bay, then watched him fall.

Jumping up on the table, reaching high above her head, she touched, then grasped the cool brown silk she had risked her life for. With one persistent tug, then another and another, she soon held it in her hands. "The Fairy Flag." Once again it was in a MacLeod's possession.

In that moment it was as if she really did have the power of a witch for as the others of her clan saw what she held aloft, it was as if a miracle had happened. Though the MacLeods had been struggling for their very lives, the tide of the battle turned. Now it was the MacDonalds who defended themselves against a foe that though small, was mighty.

Chapter Thirty

The MacLeods waged a relentless battle that was brief but destructive. In the aftermath chairs and tables were overturned, the room strewn with wounded and those who would never rise again.

"We hae won!" Sheathing his sword the MacLeod smiled triumphantly. "I guess that will teach ye to mistreat my daughter."

"Damn ye, Ian!" Raising his fist, Malcolm MacDonald's expression was sour. "Well, this is not yet the end of it."

"Then ye will know the taste of defeat yet again." Ian hefted his sword. "We hae the Fairy Flag."

"Aye." Malcolm's gaze sought for and found the culprit who had put that back into the MacLeod's hands. He shook his shaggy-haired head. "Who would hae thought. A lass!"

"*My* daughter!" Puffing out his chest, Ian strode over to the heroine of the day only in that moment noticing that she had not been untouched by the fighting. "Caitlin."

Her wound was bleeding, but though she was weak she was still standing. "It's....it's nothing....." Her face was pale as she clutched her arm.

"Nothing. Ye're bloodied, lass."

"A scratch!" She smiled grimly as she repeated what her father always said when he came back to the hall bloody and bruised.

"A scratch. Ah, 'tis much more than that. Yer red with blood." He ran towards her openly showing his fatherly concern. His men, some of them suffering their own injuries, followed him. Forming a circle around Caitlin they hovered about her as Ian tore off a piece of his shirt and wrapped it around her arm.

"Ye were a wondrous sight," Jamie cried out, not even bothering to mask his admiration.

"Aye, when we saw how braw ye were, ye inspired us, lass," Angus exclaimed.

"We couldna lose," Colquhoun added.

"Ye are a MacLeod, through and through," Ian stated proudly. It was obvious that the anger he had felt when first arriving at Dunskaith had vanished. Still, as he looked over at Niall his eyes burned with rage. "*A MacDonald*," he shouted.

Looking across the hall, Niall was too grieved by what had happened to verbally fight back. Indeed, he greeted the outcome with mixed emotions, grateful that Caitlin had come through the battle alive, yet at the same time horrified to see his clansmen bloodied and suffering.. Even as his sword arm had been thrusting and parrying he had tried to avoid seriously harming any of his kin. Now in the aftermath as he walked among the dead and the wounded he felt a profound sorrow. It should never have come to this.

"I am a MacDonald," he whispered. And yet he had forgotten that a few moments ago. Though he had spoken so softly, Caitlin heard Niall's voice and knew the anguish he must be experiencing in this, the

MacDonald's greatest defeat. Taking a deep breath, she started to call out to him, but her father quickly stepped in her path. Sweeping her up in his arms he was fiercely protective, cringing as he took notice of the blood that had soaked through the sleeve of her gown and was trickling over her hand.

"Come, daughter, we must dress your wound and then be off. Our business is done in this hall. " Glaring at Niall, his hand quivering just above his sword hilt, he dared him to interfere. "Ye lied to us and played us false. Know this, MacDonald, ye will never see my daughter again."

"She is my wife." A truth which did nothing to lessen the predicament.

"She is my daughter." " Ian's defiant expression dared Niall to so much as touch her. "Blood of my blood, flesh of my flesh."

"Who took the vows with me before God and all man."

"Vows!" The MacLeod spat on the floor. "By yer very lies to me I consider the vows ye spoke with her to be null and void, fishermon!" Hugging Caitlin close he said, "We are going home and ye canna stop us."

"I will follow."

"And be struck down for the dog that ye are." Ian's lip curled in scorn. Angrily he pointed a finger at Niall. "Hear this and hear this well, MacDonald. If ye set so much as a foot on MacLeod soil I will kill ye!"

The blood froze in Caitlin's veins at his words. "Father. Nae!" The very thought of life without Niall was agonizing, but the fear of his being cut down in pursuit of her was even more horrifying. "Ye canna........"

"Ah, but I can." Turning, he carried Caitlin towards the door, gesturing with his head for his clansmen to follow.

It was dark inside the hall. The odor of sweat and leather mixed with the smell of blood from the wounded. The silence of defeat hung in the air. Even so, there was only one reality in Niall's world at the moment. She was gone. Ian MacLeod had meted out the most devastating punishment imaginable.

Niall's heart was heavy, his temper on edge. Life was unfair; fate a cruel draught. Something had been missing from his life until he had looked into Caitlin's enormous brown eyes, until he had kissed her. She had given his life new meaning. Now she was gone.

"Malcolm's fault!" *And his own.* "By God, already I miss her." More than he had ever thought it possible to miss another human being. He needed her. She was a balm to his soul. There was something about her that he craved. Like some men hankered for strong drink. No, it was an ever greater yearning than that.

"Caitlin. Caitlin!"

The sound of her name to his lips brought an agonizing torment. This time their parting was for good. He would never see her again. Not in this life. Then why did he torture himself by thinking about her? He answered the question at once. He was the biggest of fools, secretly hoping that somehow by some miracle she would walk through that door, that she would come back to him.

"Caity…"

He remembered the feel of her soft body pressed against his, the sweet fragrance of her hair. By God, but she had so quickly gotten into his blood. He wanted her in his bed, wanted her mouth trembling and soft beneath his. He wanted her beneath him, her slender thighs entwined around his hips.

I should take a boat, sail up toe dunvegan Castle and carry her away. She is my wife! What god has joined together no man must cast asunder. Not even a lassie's father.

Niall smiled as the idea flitted before his eyes of throwing her over his shoulder and sweeping her from her father's hall. What would the MacLeod's think of that? No doubt it would be the talk of the Highlands for quite a while.

I should do it! He should show Ian MacLeod that his threats were not as strong as a brave man's love.

His daring plotting was disturbed as the front door of the castle was thrown open. Rain blew in gusts through the open portal, swirling about the cloaked figure that pushed inside the room.

"Ogg! Did ye catch sight of her, did ye hear any word?"

"Och. I followed Ian and the MacLeods all the way to Glen Drynoch."

"And…"

"Ye must gi' up any thought of heroics, Niall. Twas no idle threat. Ian MacLeod will hae yer head and display it on a spike if ye are seen anywhere near Dunvegan."

"I am no afraid."

"Then I will be afraid for ye, for if Ian MacLeod doesna hae yer head Malcolm will." Ogg shook his own head. "Gi' it up, laddie. At least for the moment."

"I canna!" his heart was totally in pawn to the fiery-haired Caitlin. Men thought they ruled the world but they were wrong. It was women. "Ah, Caity. My Caity." Over and over her name kept whirling about in his head.

"She is no' yer Caity anymore." To emphasize his words, Ogg grabbed Niall by the shoulders. "But if ye are patient, perhaps she will be again, once the dust of the battle has settled. Aye, laddie, gi' it time."

Time....the most precious thing of all in the wild, isolated hills, glens, and islands of the Highlands where danger ruled both day and night. Still, Niall had no other choice. He must wait and hope against all hope that he would see his wife once again.

PART THREE:

Wild Wind to the   Highlands

1538

"I arise from dreams of thee

In the first swet sleep of night

When the winds are breathing low,

And the stars are shining bright."

Percy Bysshe Shelley: *The Indian Serenade, Stanza 1*

HIGHLAND DESTINY

Chapter Thirty-One

Large raindrops pelted through the window as Caitlin reached out to close the shutters. Brushing several strands of her damp dark-red hair from her eyes, she was startled as a pulsating ribbon of lightning shivered through the sky. A crack of thunder followed, echoing in the room like a drum. Oh, how she had always hated such storms.

One of the borrowing days, she thought, a spell of unseasonably cold weather. How bleak and lonely it made the world appear for it eclipsed the hillocks and enshrouded the castle. The fog made it seem as if they were separate from the rest of the world. Isolated. Alone.

"Lonely......." She whispered, wiping her tear-blind eyes. How well Caitlin knew the meaning of that word. Since returning to Dunvegan with her father, it was a word which fit Caitlin all too well.

Huddling by the window, hugging her knees as she sat on a large stone slab, Caitlin felt miserable. The truth was, she missed Niall so much that she couldn't sleep, couldn't eat, couldn't do anything but sulk. It just didn't seem fair. She had come to the aid of the MacLeod's and yet had been seemingly punished and not rewarded for it. And Niall, who had so steadfastly defended her even at the cost of his own honor had been treated with no justice. No matter how she had raged, how she had pleaded, however, Ian MacLeod had stood steadfast on the matter of Caitlin's husband. If he showed his face anywhere near the castle he was to be meted out the greatest of punishments.

"Caity," Shona's voice sounded worried. "Is yer arm aching again, hinny?"

"No, my arm is just fine." The applications of seaweed boiled with lard had aided in healing her wound.

"Then is it that ye are dizzy again?" Coming to Caitlin's side she hovered over her protectively. "Perhaps ye had better go back to bed. Or I can get ye some more....."

"I'm fine." Caitlin didn't want any more of the healer's herbal medicine. The *eolas* made her nauseous and gave her headaches.

"Then what is it I can do for ye?"

"Honestly?" Caitlin's eyes were wide as she looked up at her sister.

"Honestly."

The pattering raindrops had increased their frantic rhythm. Caitlin paused to listen, then sighed. "Just leave me be. I want to be alone with my thoughts just now."

Though usually acquiescent on such matters, Shona stood firm.

"Leave ye alone so that ye can pine away?" Nae, I willna."

"Pine away?"

With a heavy heart, Caitlin leaned against the shutters. Her sister was right, that was exactly what she was doing. And why not? Hadn't she reason? Her Father was tampering with her life again. Interfering in her happiness. Though he was the one who had forced her into marrying he was now the one who was trying to get that marriage annulled. Even now he was shut up with the priest as they planned out their strategy.

No more to be married to Niall! The very idea is so painful. Moreso than any physical wound could ever be. She visualized Niall's handsome face, the look of tenderness that came into his eyes when they made love. Closing her eyes she could nearly feel his hands upon her, stirring her blood.

"Ye loved him so much?"

Caitlin nodded. "Aye.   More so than even my life!"

"Oh, Caity!" Kneeling down beside her sister, Shona cradled her in her arms. "I'm so sorry."

"I know. Ye of all people understand." More so because Shona too had been made to suffer because of her emotions. She had fallen in love with one of the MacCrimmon pipers but was being forced to marry a MacKinnon. A man twice her young age.

"Father just doesna understand."

"Because he doesna want to." Worse yet, although Caitlin's marriage had not even begun to be dissolved, her father   was already going about the task of choosing another groom--a MacDonnell ,   a MacKenzie, a Cameron or a Grant--one of the clans located far enough away to be ignorant of the fact that she had already been married.

"He means well." Though it was Caitlin who had always been closest to their father, it was Shona who was defending him now.

"Aye, I suppose that he does." Even so, that did not make her heartache any easier. She had known love with Niall. How then could she settle for a loveless marriage?

"Caity?" Her mother's soft voice called to her through the closed door. Standing up, Caitlin padded on bare feet across the cold stone floor. Opening the door she was touched to see that her mother stood there, a bowl of porridge in her hands. Even so, Caitlin rebelled at the sight of food.

"I am not hungry, Mother."

Fiona's tone was authoritative as she pushed into the room. "You need some nourishment. Ye are getting much too thin . Eat."

Though usually rebellious, Caitlin took the porridge from her mother's hands. "All right."

So, my mother was the cause of Malcolm MacDonald's anger, she thought, staring at Fiona as if somehow seeing her through different eyes. And why not? Even now it was evident that her mother had once been beautiful. But so beautiful as to inspire clan warfare?

Noticing that Caitlin was merely holding the bowl and spoon and not eating, Fiona said sternly, "Ye need to get back yer strength, Caity. Ye canna stay cloistered up here in this room like a nun."

Caitlin bit back a sarcastic reply. To appease Fiona, Caitlin took a bite but as soon as she swallowed she felt ill. Strangely enough the very idea of food sometimes did that to her of late. For over a week now she had been feeling sick in the mornings. Could it be? Touching her stomach, she wondered if it could be possible that Niall's child grew within her womb.

Niall's child. Oh, what a blessing that would be. A baby that would make her father's plan of annulment invalid. A tiny breathing human being that would be a living reminder of the love she and Niall had shared.

"Caity? What is it?"

It had to be. Twice now Caitlin had missed her monthly time but had thought it possible that it was due to the events of the last two months, the battle, her injury and the journey. Now she could only hope otherwise.

A baby! A sweet reminder of the passion she had known in Niall's arms. And yet another source of clan tension as well. If the baby was a son it would be a MacDonald, not a MacLeod. What would her father do then?

"Pah, ye hardly eat enough to keep a mouse alive." Reaching out, Fiona gently touched Caitlin's hand, the one that held the spoon. "I even put butter and cream on it, just the way ye like it."

Caitlin took another bite, just to silence her mother's loving scolding, but as a churning began in her stomach, she quickly set the bowl down on a small table by the bed and hurried to the window. Hurriedly opening the shutters she leaned out just in time.

"Oh......."   She could hardly stand up, the nausea seemed to engulf her.

"Caity." Shona and Fiona called out her name in unison.

"She has been like that, Mother. Getting sick each time she eats anything at all. Could it be her wound?" Shona hurried to stand beside her sister, holding her hand as she bent over retching through the open window.

"Hmmmm." Slowly Fiona walked across the floor. Putting her arm around her daughter's waist, she hugged her tightly as she brushed the hair from her face. "Have ye missed yer time?"

Caitlin nodded.

"Have ye been light headed?"

"Aye."

"Oh, Caity, hinny!" She laughed softly. A happy sound. "Ye are with child, lassie. I sense it. I think that ye do too."

Turning from the window, Caitlin was surprised by her mother's elation. "And ye arena disturbed at such a thought?"

Fiona shook her head. "Why should I be. To bring forth life is the greatest of blessings." Putting her hand under her daughter's chin she looked her in the eye. "And I can tell that ye love him."

"I do. But Father........" Would be furious. A force to be reckoned with.

"Will hae to realize that he has no control over such things." Taking Caitlin's hands she led her toward the bed, pulling her to sit down beside her.

Shona sat on the floor, her expression more of surprise than anything else. "Are ye....are ye going to tell the MacLeod?"

Fiona shook her head. "Not yet."

"But he will hae to know!" Caitlin was apprehensive and yet at the same time anxious.

"I will tell him in my own time, in my own way." When her daughters seemed uneasy, she repeated, "In my own time. Meanwhile there are some things that need to be done." Fiona MacLeod smiled again, this time mysteriously.

The keeing music of skirling bagpipes seemed to be a perfect accompaniment to Niall's tormented emotions. He had tried to push all thought of his love for Cailtlin into some obscure part of his mind, but it was impossible. Not one day had gone by when he hadn't missed her, hadn't awakened imagining that she was in his arms.

"Ye haunt me like a ghost, Caity!" he couldn't help but blurt out.

Keeping to himself, haunting the castle corridors and tower, Niall was like some angry spirit. He had lost track of time, he had lost all sense of ambition. He had become a slave to his memories, his moods.

Whenever Niall was in a room, the air vibrated with tension. Unspoken recriminations reached out like long fingers. Bitter glances fell upon all those whose only misfortune was to cross his path.

Running his hand through his hair, Niall looked out at the horizon as he searched his heart and soul for the answer to his dilemma. Something had to be done. His appetite was sorely wanting. He didn't sleep the whole night through. He was so surly of late that even Ogg avoided him. Either he had to get Caitlin back or risk his sanity.

Chapter Thirty-Two

A bairn, a child. Wrapping her arms around her knees, Caitlin curled up on the bed, gently touching her still-flat stomach. She was going to bear Niall's child. No matter what the future held in store she would at least have that.

"A living, breathing reminder of the love and passion that flared so fierce between us." Fierce, but alas, all in too brief a time.

She sighed, remembering. When they had been together she had truly been happy. Now she had only her memories and dreams to keep her warm at night in her lonely bed. Still, she was determined to be optimistic for the child's sake.

"Ah, dear, dear sweet bairn of mine...."

She tried to imagine what it would be like to have a small replica of Niall or herself running about the castle, and laughed aloud at the thought. Whether the babe had her temperament or Niall's, the child would no doubt be a handful.

"Father, 'tis possible that ye might find that with yer grandchild ye hae met yer match."

Father. As the word touched first her thought and then her lips, she stiffened. What would be the Macleod's reaction to the news? How would he deal with the reality of something over which he had no control? The babe would have MacDonald blood as well as MacLeod. What would he think of that?

"Ach, but I willna worry. Not now…." Instead, she soothed her mind by thinking about the baby that grew within her. Oh, what stories she would tell the wee one. Oh, what love she would give to the bairn. So much love that she could nearly feel her heart burst as she knew the longing to hold the child of her dear love in her arms.

Oh, Niall, if only I could tell ye, she lamented. *If only ye knew so that ye could be as happy and feel as blessed as I.* Truly the child was a miracle, a bond that would join them together for life, nae for eternity.

"Niall!"

Closing her eyes, Caitlin smiled for the first time in a long while as she envisioned the face of the man whose soul had blended with her own to create life within her womb. For a moment she allowed herself to dream.

"Caitlin!" she heard him call out. Bending down, he wore a look of tenderness as he swept her up into his arms. "A child! A son!"

"A part of me…a part of you!" she whispered.

"The greatest gift anyone could hae given me," she imagined him saying. "Ah, truly, I hae never loved anyone as much as I love ye at this moment."

"Nor hae I loved anyone as much as ye." Tentatively she reached out and touched her stomach, marveling at the miracle that created life.

She had to believe that they would meet again, love again.

"Oh, Niall…." In a total outpouring of her emotions, she willed him to see far across the miles into her heart, into her mind. She wanted him to remember.

She would have been complimented and contented to know that he did. Lying on his back, his hands behind his head, Niall stared up at the ceiling, seeing Caitlin's image as clearly as if she were there in the flesh. So clearly that he nearly called out to her. Instead, he groaned as he remembered how her lips had felt beneath his mouth, how her breasts had felt as he had stroked them. For a moment he was consumed by his memories and by his need.

A tremor ran through him. He felt cold, he felt hot. In the silence of the room he could hear his own rasping breath mingling with the rapid beat of her heart. He squeezed his eyes so tight that they hurt, then he opened them slowly.

Dear god, how he wanted her, missed her, longer for her. More than he had ever longed for anything in all his life. And yet his longing would go unfulfilled because of the anger and bitterness of two men. Two stubborn old men who clung to the memory of an old feud.

"Malcolm, I curse ye for yer hard heart," he breathed, succumbing to a surge of anger that left him trembling. Then, as if the potency of his thoughts had conjured him up, he saw the object of his fury standing in the doorway.

"Niall...." Malcolm nudged a young dark-haired girl forward, boldly announcing that he had not come alone.

"Go away! Can y no' see that I am sleeping?" If there was anyone's company that he did not welcome it was Malcolm's. "And take her with ye when ye go."

"Take her? Malcolm laughed. "Och, Niall, dunna be so impatient. At least gi' the girl a chance to show ye what she can do."

Heeding the command, the girl came forward, her soft hands stroking his hot bare skin. He could feel her fingers, the palms of her hands, her nails. Though Niall was well prepared to resist, he was only too human.

Taking a deep, shuddering breath, he whispered, "Pretend...." His mind closed on that thought as the girl's hands stroked his chest, his stomach, then moved lower with a touch that could have brought a stone statue to life.

"Caitlin...."

He felt so much need, so much wanting that it pained him, more so as he felt her moist mouth moving slowly, sensuously on his abdomen. Moaning again, he reached for her, running his hands down the curves of her body. Soft, warm, her skin nonetheless held no delight for him. She was much too slender.

"Nae!" Even with his eyes closed he could not be fooled. Even for the sake of his aching flesh he could not touch another. By force of will he pulled away, his desire draining away as quickly as it had come. With a growl, Niall bolted up from his bed, infuriated as he saw that Malcolm was still lurking in the doorway.

"Och, such a frown. I take it then that lovely or no', she doesna please ye."

"Under different circumstances she might hae," Niall replied, nodding his head toward the door so that the girl was certain to understand. "Before I met Caity. Now I want no other woman. Not now. Not ever."

Malcolm was distracted for just a moment as he watched the young woman scurry from the room. Then he shrugged his shoulders. "Then hae ye taken up celibacy?"

"For the moment." Niall carefully veiled his emotions, yet the soul-deep loneliness was still reflected in his eyes. "Until I can be reunited wi' my wife."

"Reunited?" Malcolm's express was sour. "I fear that will not be for a long time, if eer. In the meantime I would suggest that unless ye want to go mad, ye take what I offer ye. That is, unless ye be more interested in some crofter's wife or daughter."

"I am no' interested in anyone. No one can ever take my Caity's place."

"Nae?" Malcolm raised his thick brows. "But what of ye? Will she feel the same? Or will she bend to the will of her father?" Eh, Niall? Eh?"

Niall sensed an undercurrent of meaning. "What are ye saying?"

"That although the bedsheets of his daughter hae not yet cooled from the warmth of yer body, Ian MacLeod is already looking for a mon to fill yer place."

"My place?"

"Aye!" Taking his time, Malcolm strode into the room. "I hae heard from my spies that the MacLeod is openly searching for another husband."

Chapter Thirty-Three

An early-morning mist hovered over the land, shrouding the hills in a thick white cloud. The bulk of the storm had passed, but a slow drizzle still fell, its moisture pervading the castle, making it damp and chilled. Pulling her chair closer to the fire, Caitlin thought how the weather matched her mood.

Looking down at the whittling knife and piece of wood in her hands, she assessed the carving of the sheep she was making for the baby and her thoughts strayed to Niall. There wasn't an hour that went by that she didn't think of him no matter where she was. What was he doing? Was he well? Was he content? For the love of her he had raised his sword against his own clan. Had Malcolm been lenient with him Most importantly of all, she wondered what he would think were he to know about their baby. Would he feel as pleased as she?

Oh, Niall, what shall we name the bairn? Pausing in her whittling, Caitlin called several names to mind. If the child was a male, names like Donald, Fergus, Fionnlagh, Geordie, Ruaraidh, and Tammas came to mind. Or perhaps Colin after her deceased brother. And if the babe was female, Alias, Deirdre, Janet, Wilma, or even Sheena.

"But no..." Putting her hand on her stomach, she knew with sudden certainty that she need not even think for a moment that it was anything but a boy child. The night Dunskaith Castle when she had lain so blissfully with Niall she had conceived his son. "A child that could bind the MacLeods and MacDonalds together if only...."

The sound of her father's heavy steps outside the door disrupted any such thoughts. As he clumped inside the room, Caitlin hurried to put the carving of the lamb behind her back. Alas, she was not quick enough.

"Caitlin?" the way he scowled proved that he had noticed.

"Good morrow, Father. Despite the fact that she was peeved with him because of his decision about Niall, Caitlin smiled at him.

"Ye seem cheerful. Am I to happily take that to mean ye are completely healed, in mind as well as body?" he asked, taking a step closer, then another and another.

"I'm healed." *Except for what all this has done to my heart.*

"Then we'll be expecting ye to take yer place again with us at breakfast and dinner." Reaching out, he fondly ruffled her hair, sliding his fingers through the silky strands.

"Aye," she whispered, wondering how she was going to keep on making excuses to stay in her room.

"What do ye hae there?" Moving his hand from her head to her arm, he caught the wrist she held behind her back.

"Hae?" It was no use. Slowly Caitlin revealed her handiwork.

"A child's toy?" He looked at her with puzzlement.

"Aye." She wanted to tell him. Wanted to hurl the announcement in his face, to taunt him with it, but instead Caitlin kept to her silence. Her mother had requested that she be the one to give out the news.

"I would hae thought ye too old to crave such things, Caity." Taking it from her hand, he held it up, turning it this way and that. He looked from Caitlin to the toy, then back at Caitlin again, as if afraid of what she might tell him. When Caitlin didn't speak, Ian heaved a sigh. "Ah, but I do hae to admire yer talent." He laughed. "At carving wood as well as ye carved that MacDonald's hide." Once again he ruffled her hair. "Ah, Caity. Caity! Ye always were the joy of my heart."

For just a moment her fear and resentment evaporated as the warm memories of her childhood resurfaced. She thought of the laughter they had shared, the way she had always tagged after him, all the times he had carried her from the hall to tuck her into bed after the seanachaidh had finished his stories. Caitlin had admired him so much that unlike the other girls in the castle, she had never played with dolls. She had wanted a shield and a sword. Who would ever have known that such childhood playfulness would one day save her life?

Ian took his daughter's hand, squeezing her fingers tightly. "Ah, Cait, do ye forgi' me?"

"For what?"

"For forcing ye to wed with Niall MacDonald. I believed his lies, ye see, and…"

"Ye didna force me." Her voice was barely audible as she whispered, "I love him."

"Love. Bah! It doesna exist." A muscle in his cheek ticked, a sign that he was trying to hold his temper in check.

"It does." Caitlin asked a pointed question. "Did ye not love Mother?"

Ian released her fingers and started to fidget with his hands. It was several moments before he nodded. "Ay. I thought her to be the bonniest lassie I had ever set eyes on."

"And Malcolm MacDonald's future bride, or so I heard him say that day." She turned her wide brown eyes on him, searching his face. "Was he telling the truth?"

"He *was*. But it didna matter."

"Didna matter?" Caitlin was stunned. "It must hae to Malcolm MacDonald."

"He was no good for her. He was harsh. He was cruel."

"And so ye kidnapped her. Is that it?" Caitlin could nearly see the story enfolding, saw her father sweeping her mother up and throwing her across his shoulder. It was the kind of thing the bards sang about.

Ian did not meet her eyes as he said, "I wanted to save her."

"But did she want to be saved?" the question was out before Caitlin could stop herself. Strange, that her mother had never spoken of her wedding to the MacLeod.

"I dunna want to talk about it. Those memories are private." Hurriedly he changed the subject. "I sent a message to the pope himself, asking, no *demanding*, an end to yer marriage.

"I dunna want it to end." Caitlin clutched the carved sheep so hard her knuckles turned white. "I dunna want to marry any of the men ye would pawn me off on."

"Enough," Ian reproved sharply. Trying to hold his temper in check, he began pacing, walking up and down, back and forth. At last he stopped. "I willna hae a MacDonald set foot in this castle, nor will I let ye go back to Dunskaith. If ye stay married to Niall MacDonald it will be a marriage in name only." He shook his head. "Ah, Caity, Caity, it would be such a waste. I canna allow ye to stay tied to such a mon as that young rascal. Ye are young and ye are a bonny lass. Far better be it for ye to put this mistake behind ye and begin again." Slowly he walked to the door deep in thought, but he turned before he opened the door. "Someday ye will understand and thank me for what I decided."

"Understand?" Caitlin bolted to her feet. "Nae, it is ye who dunna understand, Father. It is out of yer hands."

"Out of my hands?" His eyes narrowed to slits. "What do ye mean?"

Caitlin bit her lip. "Only that it is God who should make such decisions."

"God?" The reminder that there was a being to whom even he must answer seemed to deflate the Macleod's fiercesome pride. He did not say another word. Instead, he merely stared at Caitlin for a long time before he left the room.

It was cold and damp. The slender tapers flickered as a breath of wind swept through the crevices of the castle. The flame's slow dance cast eerie shadows against the stone walls. Kneeling in the small chapel, Caitlin prayed aloud. "Please, God, help bring Niall back to me. Help me find a way to soften Father's heart and make him see that I canna live without my hinny." Nor did she want her child to grow up without a father or worse yet be under the control of a man of her father's choosing.

She clasped her hands so tightly together that her finger nails dug into the flesh of her fingers as she closed her eyes. Her father had gone to the pope with his adamant wishes, and thus there was nowhere else to go but seek the help of a higher power.

"Please, ye must help me for I hae nowhere else to turn…."

Bowing her head, she prayed as fervently as she could, so hard in fact that she did not hear the door as it opened. Not until she felt a hand on her shoulder did she realize that she was no longer alone.

"Caity…"

Lifting her head, Caitlin saw the silhouette of her mother's face.

"Hae ye told Father yet? Hae ye?"

Her mother's expression answered the question.

"Ye hae not!" Caitlin swallowed hard. She had counted on her mother's wisdom and courage, yet it seemed that Fiona had let her down.

"I started to so many times but…."

Caitlin stepped on the hem of her arasaid as she jerked to her feet. "But ye are afraid o' him."

"Afraid?' Fiona's eyes met Caitlin's. "Nae, 'tis just that I must wait until the right time."

"Right time? Sweet Jesu, when will that be." Caitlin's patience was wearing thin. "When ye put the bairn in its grandsire's arms?"

Fiona's eyes narrowed as she retorted hotly, "Hold yer sarcasm, Daughter. I repeat, I will tell yer father when *I* decide that the time is right."

Caitlin was immediately contrite, regretting her outburst. "I…I know that ye will. Oh, Mother…."

Reaching out, Fiona pushed aside an unruly lock of red hair that had tumbled into Caitlin's eyes. "I am no' afraid. It's just that I hae a plan of my own to follow." Her frown slowly changed into a smile. "I know just what I am doing, Caity dear."

Fiona knew it wasn't enough to confide in Ian about the impending birth. She needed an ally, one who dealt with those in high places. Moreover she had decided that something must be done to assure that Niall MacDonald would be at her daughter's side now that he was needed. With that thought in mind she had sent a very special messenger to not only give Niall the news of Caitlin's upcoming motherhood but to guide him safely to Dunvegan as well.

"Ye must trust me."

Trust. Instinctively Caitlin did.

Chapter Thirty-four

Niall stared out the window, watching as the small hunting party led by Malcolm left the castle armed with bows and arrows, swords and dirks. The winter weather was fast approaching thus the MacDonald and his clansmen were of necessity pressed to bring back an ample supply of meat lest everyone in the castle grow extremely tired of mutton.

"Good riddance!" Niall scoffed, relieved that the absence of Gregor and Malcolm would offer him a brief reprieve from their hostile looks and verbal badgering.

Since the battle with the MacLeod's, Niall had enacted a tempestuous truce with his two clansmen but nonetheless he felt uneasy when he was in their presence. Gregor's piercing eyes seemed always to be watching him and Malcolm's fiercesome scowls were beginning to play on his nerves. Even so, he had been spared any serious retribution after the MacLeod's day of victory. Though obviously suffering Malcolm's disfavor, Niall was surprised that his status of tanist had not been disturbed. His honors had not been stripped from him despite the MacDonald's ill will and Gregor's heated insistence. Nevertheless, without Caitlin beside him Niall had lost heart.

"Ah, Caity." The hunting party instantly reminded him of Caitlin and that day together out in the forest.

"I've been hunting since I was no higher than my father's knee," she had answered tartly when he had shown surprise that she intended to join the hunting party. "We'll see if ye can keep up with me." It was a challenge he had grinned at, little knowing how difficult it would be to fulfill.

"Caity, Caity, Caity," he murmured, feeling once again the restlessness he could not conceal. Pacing the floor of his bedchamber, he was frustrated. Though Malcolm had spared him the discomfort of imprisonment he might as well have been a prisoner. Certainly in his heart he was, missing Caitlin, yet knowing it was forbidden to go to her.

For the time being, the only time Niall could be happy was when he was alone in his bedchamber, succumbing to his dreams. Only in his fantasies did he dare give vent to his love. From the first moment his eyes were closed he envisioned Caitlin, felt the stirring touch of her mouth, the fire of her hands on his body. His dreams were so vivid, so feverish that he awakened trembling, half expecting to find her pretty face beside his on the pillow.   Instead he always knew the disappointment of finding himself alone.   Was there any hope? Ogg had insisted that there was, had advised Niall to be patient.

"Patient!" How could he be when he knew that he was besieged on both sides with enemies, both the MacLeod and the MacDonalds who were joined in one common bond. To keep Caitlin and he apart.

Disgruntled with it all he took one last look at the departing clansmen, hoping they would be gone a long, long while and it was in that moment that he noticed a small brown-clad figure, little bigger than a child, weaving in and out among the bushes in the outer bailey.

"Who have we here?" In curiosity Niall watched the skulking form, wondering what mischief was in the making. Certainly the manner in which he was darting in and out among the foliage he did want to be seen. In curiosity Niall decided to have a confrontation with the "tiny visitor" who seemed to be playing at hide and seek.

Taking the steps two at a time, Niall entered into the game, hiding in the shadows himself. At last the opportunity came when he could come upon the intruder from behind and grab him.

"Ah ha! Caught ye!" Niall held his quarry tight despite his struggling. "Settle down and be civilized, mon. I think ye hae some explaining to do. Such as who ye are and what ye are doing here!"

The voice was muffled, "I came to speak to Niall of the MacDonalds!" A high voice. A frightened voice. "And I do not like being ill-treated, you great oaf!"

"Who?" Reaching up, Niall pulled at the brown hood that covered the visitor's head. Once that head was revealed he gave a gasp of surprise at the tonsure that was clearly visible. "A priest!" In surprise he loosened his hold.

"Aye, that's what I am!" With undisguised irritation the tiny holy man brushed at his cloak. "A priest on a very important mission. So, if you will just take me to the young MacDonald I'll be about my business and then be on my way, forgetful of the "hospitality" you offered me."

It took a moment before Niall realized the priest had come to see him. When he did realize, he hurriedly tried to make amends. "I'm sorry. It's just that the way ye were dodging in and out I feared ye were up to no good. These are, as ye know, troubled times."

"Very troubled." The tone of voice seemed to hold Niall partly accountable. "But if you value your soul you will not interfere in what I am about." With an indignant sniff, the priest stalked off.

"Wait!" Niall hurried to catch up with him and block his way. "Ye said ye came to see Niall of the MacDonalds. I am he!"

"You?" For a moment the priest sounded distrustful.

"I wouldna lie." His gaze didn't waver as he stared the priest in the eye. "I am Niall of the MacDonald clan."

"You are?" The blue eyes moved from Niall's feet upward to the top of his tawny-haired head. "And obvious it is that you be a big brute."

"Brute, nae. Tall, aye, especially in comparison to you." Niall smiled. "But come, ye hae my undivided attention. What was it ye wanted with me?"

The priest came right to the point. "I came to lead you back safely to the MacLeod castle."

"To the MacLeods'." Niall shook his head. "Nae, I canna. If I set one foot on MacLeod land I could start all the old hatred boiling again. I dunna want that."

"You must. Caitlin needs you."

"Caitlin?" Panicking, Niall imagined all sorts of things. "What's wrong? Her wound. Was it more serious than......"

"No, her wound has healed, at least those of the flesh. But she pines for you."

"Just as I pine for her." A sad truth that had come about because of two stubborn old men. Reaching out, Niall grabbed the priest's hand. "Is she well? Is she happy?"

"Aye happy now that she knows."

"Knows? Knows what?" A strange shiver crept up Niall's spine and down again.

"That she is soon to be a mother."

The unexpected news hit Niall like a thunderbolt. "A mother?" For a long moment all he could do was to stand thunderstruck as he mentally digested the announcement. Then, losing all self control, he was jumping up and down in his excitement. "A baby! Mine! I'm a father!" In uncontrolled exuberance he picked the priest up, twirling him around. "A son! A son! Mine!"

It was a revelation that goaded him, drove him beyond endurance. Danger or not he couldn't stay away from Caitlin any longer. He had to see her. Had to let her know how happy he was. How much he wanted them to be together.

It was suicidal to even contemplate going to Dunvegan. Even so, Niall gathered his belongings together as quickly as he could. No one, not even Ogg, could change his mind.

"I have to go!"

"To yer death?" Ogg was certain that Niall had lost his mind. "Ye'll walk right into a wolf's den. Caitlin wouldn't want that, ye know. She wouldn't want ye to place yerself in danger, laddie, even for her."

"I have no choice. I need to be with my wife. Circumstances hae changed, Ogg." There was going to be a child. Viewing his life in sudden clear perspective, he realized how that had opened his heart to the real meaning of the world. Life. Love. Purpose. "Everything is different."

"Different?"

"Aye......"

She was carrying his child! He was going to be a father! There would be living proof of the love he had shared with Caitlin MacLeod. No victory or honor could compare with the feelings that thought sparked. A father! The very thought made him want to shout out loud. He felt boastful and proud. Still, he kept his silence.

"Ye hae lost yer mind. Is that what ye mean?" Ogg snorted in derision.

"Think what ye want. I hae my reasons...."

Like a restless ghost, a being he had once pretended to be, Niall paced up and down, torn between the sensible decision of staying and the more frenzied desire of his heart. All the while poignant memories flooded over him shutting out any argument that Ogg might put forth.

Ogg shook his head. "I dunna ken what power that priest has over ye that he can so blind ye to danger, but I can see that ye willna listen. So...." Hastily he crossed himself. "I can do naught else but pray for ye, Niall."

"Aye, pray...." He was going to be doing a lot of that himself from now on, praying for Caitlin, for his unborn child, and lastly for himself.

"Niall, at least let me go with ye to offer ye protection." Ogg's sudden grasp of his arm was frantic and nearly brutal.

"Nae, I canna let ye come with me and put yerself in danger." Niall had a faraway look in his eye. "Besides, I will hae all the protection that I hae neeed of." He nodded toward the priest, who stood in the doorway to Niall's room.

"Him?" Ogg's look was incredulous. With a mumbled oath he touched his sword.

"Aye, him. And a far more powerful being." Niall's gaze moved toward the ceiling.

"Then let us hope that God is on yer side!"

HIGHLAND DESTINY

Chapter Thirty-Five

It was washing day. Leaning out the window Caitlin waved to Shona as her sister gallantly tried to balance a "skeel" on her head without spilling any of the precious water. "Careful, ye dunna even sneeze or ye will be drenched, Shona, hinny."

Looking up, Shona was distracted by Caitlin's greeting just long enough to lose control of the wooden bucket. With a shriek she tried to recover her equilibrium before Caitlin's warning was fulfilled. Alas, as water sloshed every which way her attempt did her no good. Half the water was lost. "See what ye hae done, Caity! Ye wicked, wicked lass." Brushing at her water-soaked arasaid Shona grumbled beneath her breath.

"Och, Shony, I'm sorry but the wee brownie in me prompted such mischief."

"Ye made me spill the water I hae carried all the way from the well. But I will get even." Grabbing the skeel by the handle Shona hefted it, dousing Caitlin with water in a playful act of retaliation.

The sound of laughter echoed through the castle courtyard as the two young women engaged in a water fight. That playful combat was soon joined by several of the others. Soon the castle courtyard rang with the sound of merriment.

"Ah, Caity, it is so good to hear ye laugh at last." Shona beckoned her to join them as they engaged in doing the laundry, a chore Caitlin had always thoroughly enjoyed.

Linen was put into a large, low tub and trampled with the young women's bare feet as they danced up and down, singing rousing songs. The custom had started long ago when winters were long and hard. It was easier to keep blood circulating in the feet than the hands, especially when it was cold. Washing in groups, two women to a tub, the young women supported themselves with their arms thrown around each other's shoulders. Only when the laundry was ready to be wrung out would their hands touch the clothing.

Running out of the castle, tucking her long skirts up above her knees, Caitlin stepped into the huge low tub of water to join Shona. Usually the laundry was done inside in the bathhouse but since it was a sunny day they had dragged the tubs outside to enjoy the last vestige of autumn.

"Are ye still feeling ill?"

Caitlin shook her head. "Nae, the fresh air is doing me some good." She concentrated on where she placed her feet, trampling the dirty garments furiously in her zest to get them clean. "Father caught me making a toy for the coming bairn. For a moment I feared he would guess." Caitlin was beginning to be impatient. "When is mother going to tell him do ye suppose?"

"Soon, or so she told me."

Though Caitlin joined in to sing a rousing song, though she moved her feet and danced about just as playfully as the others, her heart was not in it now. "I dunna feel right not telling him myself. He has a right to know that he is going to hae a grandchild." How was she going to continue to fool their father in the meantime?

"Aye, he does. But Mother has her reasons."

"I suppose." But what were they? Her joyful mood broken, Caitlin was silent, giving free reign to the thoughts whirling around in her brain. Was Fiona afraid that Ian would send her far away when he found out? Was that the reason for the silence? Or was there something else?

The soap from lye made with wood ash stung Caitlin's feet thus she was the first from the tub. As she wrung out the garments and laid them to dry on the grass she once again envisioned Niall in her mind, the haughty way he always tilted his chin, his smile, the way he walked. Niall had a daring way of looking directly in another's eyes when talking to them. Oh that she were as bold now and could get this matter of telling he father over with. Until then she would be overly shy in his presence. Tongue-tied. Afraid she might in some way give her secret away.

It should be joyful news, not something to hide. Her father was soon to have his longed for successor. Why then was she keeping it hidden from him? Because it was Niall's child and that complicated everything.

"Will ye love yer grandchild any the less because it has MacDonald blood?" Sadly she shook her head, hoping the hostility of the past would not taint an innocent child.

The baby that Niall and I conceived was created out of love, not hate. Love, it could be such a healing thing. Was it possible that this baby could heal the wounds of the past?

"Caity!" Turning, Caitlin saw her mother poised in the open doorway, gesturing for her to come inside.

"I'm coming!" Picking up her skirts she hurried to join her, cautioned that it was a matter of secrecy by the finger held to Fiona's lips. "What is it?"

Though usually so self-assured and calm, Fiona was visibly trembling. "It is done."

"Done!" Caitlin stiffened. "Ye told Father?"

"Nae, not yet." Her expression seemed to say it would not be an easy task. "But I will tonight. I must."

"Then what......?" Her mother's nervousness was contagious. "Mother, what hae ye done?"

Fiona took a deep breath, then sighed. "I sent the priest to the MacDonalds."

"Sent the priest?" Caitlin paled as all sorts of thoughts invaded her mind. "Why?" She had thought her mother to be on her side in all of this. "I dunna want the marriage to end...."

"Nor do I. That is why I had to put an end to all this foolishness." Reaching out, Fiona grabbed her daughter's hand. "A father has a right to know about his child, Caity, to be there when it makes its first entry into this cold, cold world."

Caitlin gasped. "Ye sent for Niall!" A truth that was frightening and yet at the same time comforting. She wanted him to know, wanted him to be with her and yet at the same time feared what her father would do.

Fiona read her daughter's thoughts. "I couldna just stand by and watch ye waste away from the sadness of it all. No mother wants to see her daughter so unhappy. And all because of two foolish old men. It is time to bury the ghosts of the past."

"Aye, but tell that to Father." Caitlin put her arms around her mother, leaning her head on her shoulder. "Oh, Mother, do ye think it will ever end? So much sorrow, so much hatred. I dunna want my bairn to grow up feeling those emotions. I want him or her to know happiness and joy and love."

"And he will." Fiona's tone was stern. "I will see to it."

Caitlin's eyes filled with tears. "If Father harms one hair on Niall's head, I dunna think I will ever be able to forgive him. But he will! He is so obsessed with his anger that at times he is so blind."

Fiona sighed. "We all are at times. But I will make him see."

Caitlin shivered. "I hope so. I love Niall, Mother. With all my heart and soul. I want us to be together. But I dunna want him harmed."

"Dunna worry. I was careful." Fiona briefly explained what she had done. Knowing that the only person who would be safe in MacLeod and MacDonald territory would be a man of the church she had sent Father Flanigan to act as messenger." She smiled. "And he is to be joined by another man of the cloth."

"Another?"

"Yer Niall." He was going to travel to Dunvegan with Father Flanigan dressed as a priest.

Glancing about her, Caitlin viewed the untamed woodland of her hideaway as she thought about the sweet secret that she shared with her mother. Father Flanigan had been sent to accompany Niall to Dunvegan Castle. God willing, he would be here soon to learn from her own lips that he would soon be a father. That is if he chose to come.

"Will he?"

Deep in her heart Caitlin knew that he would. Despite the danger, Niall MacDonald would not say no to Father Flanigan, nor to her mother. He *would* come. It was a thought that brought forth conflicting emotions of joy and yet a deep concern for his safety.

"Ach, but for the moment I can find tranquility here," she sighed in solitude.

Her hideaway near Dunvegan, known as Fairy Bridge, was a natural wonderland, a haven with a mossy floor hidden from view by a drapery woven of hundreds of red, yellow, and green leaves. It was an achingly lovely spot. To the south the mountains and moorlands sparkled like jewels, to the north were lochs and meadows. Each stone, each tree, every inlet of water that gorged deep into the glens was precious to her.

"Fairy Bridge…."

There was a story told around the hearth fires claiming that the fairy wife of a fourteenth-century chief had given her husband the fairy flag as a parting gift when she returned to fairyland after twenty years of marriage. There after, their parting place, near Dunvegan, had been known as Fairy Bridge.

"So beautiful….."

Yet, there was a loneliness about this place, too, that touched Caitlin's heart. Today she looked at it as if viewing it for the very first time, each leaf and rock becoming precious to her.

Flocks of gulls and terns glided overhead. The wild beautiful music of the inland birds serenaded her as they flew from bough to bough, a melancholy song that fit the mood of her reverie. Staring into the azure depths of the sea, her eyes focused on the water as if somehow she might read her fate there. Would she be happy? Would her father learn to put aside his anger and hatred and let her and her husband live in peace? Closing her eyes, Caitlin prayed with all her heart that it would be so.

Chapter Thirty-Six

The hills and glens seemed to stretch for acres and acres, miles and miles, yet Niall forced himself to travel at a furious pace through crafting villages, up the slopes of the Red Hills, and through a countryside that was wild and magnificent.

"I am going to be a father." That wondrous thought gave him stamina and made him forget his discomfort and the danger he was walking straight into. As he hurriedly put one foot in front of the other, the priest had a difficult time keeping up with him.

Niall and Father Flanigan had intended at first to procure a boat and go the distance by sea, but a sudden fierce storm had put an end to their plans. Now as the wind howled, all Niall could do was to gather his hooded cloak about him in a futile effort to keep dry.

"There's a crofter's hut over there." The priest's voice was nearly swallowed by the wind. "Shall we stop?"

The thought of a warm fire was tempting, but though he might have sought shelter, might have known the warmth of a fire, Caitlin's face, hovering before his eyes, urged Niall on. "Nae. We keep going."

The sky was streaked with lightning. Rain tore at Niall face and cut through his cloak like a knife, but stubbornly he kept on. He didn't want to stop for food, nor drink, nor to see to his own comforts. A deep fear gnawed at him. Despite the fact that Caitlin was with her own clan he worried. So many unforeseen things could happen. He was anxious to see her again. Anxious to be with her. Time was of the essence.

Father Flanigan's eyes were filled with compassion and understanding. "I too once had a woman that I loved. But you can not drive yerself. You must rest some time."

"We will. We will. As soon as we get to the other side of that hill." That was a promise that Niall kept breaking as he looked northward. Just over those hills his heart was with a flaming-haired MacLeod woman who had given him her love. *Caity, what has become of you? He agonized. What are ye doing? Are ye well? Are ye safe?*

Niall wanted nothing more in this life so much as he wanted to gather her into his arms. But then what? He couldn't pretend to be a priest forever. Was he then going to pick Caitlin up in his arms and carry her away? Come face to face with the MacLeod and battle it out? Resign himself to being a prisoner in the dungeon?

Something has to be done. The baby. Aye, that had changed so many things. The feuding had to come to an end, at least where he and his wife's clan was concerned, for he refused to live apart from Caitlin and the coming child. Refused to let his son or daughter grow up without a father. Or worse yet, with another man taking his place.

Niall had been incensed when Father Flanigan had revealed to him this reason for being at the MacLeod castle. He had come to see to the matter of having the marriage annulled so that the MacLeod could marry Caitlin off to a man he thought to be more suitable. Well, all that had changed now. Niall was determined to stand his ground, to fight for his wife and child if need be.

"I am not afraid of Ian MacLeod," he said aloud.

"Well, you should be!" Father Flanigan hurried up beside Niall grabbing him by the arm, forcing him to slow down. "Once you set foot in Dunvegan your life will be in his hands so be cautious, son. The MacLeod is not at the moment a rational man."

"Well, for that matter neither am I."Being robbed of the woman ye love is infuriating." The very thought of the MacLeod trying to end the marriage was galling. "Well, I will tell ye one thing. I will never let Caitlin go. She belongs to me! We spoke the holy vows. Til death do us part ."

Father Flanigan shuddered. "I would not remind the MacLeod of that part of the vow, Niall."

"For fear that he might see that I hasten to my end?" Niall shook his head. "Nae, despite his threats I canna believe that Ian MacLeod would kill the father of his grandchild. It would be too big a cross to carry, to great a stain on his soul."

"Aye, but he could throw you in the dungeon until you would wish to be dead." The priest clucked his tongue. "There has to be another way. There has to be something a man could say to make an old fool see reason." Ah, but what?"

This time it was the priest who took the lead, his vexation giving him energy. Walking ahead of Niall he mumbled beneath his breath as he tried to think of a solution.

"So many lives at stake. What should I do? What, dear Lord?" Looking up at the sky, Father Flanigan was avidly seeking advice from a greater being. "So much unhappiness if I can not make the MacLeod see reason."

"Perhaps the only thing he has come to understand is the quest for vengeance." If that was so, then Niall had come prepared. Beneath his brown hooded cloak he had a sword concealed just in case he had to protect himself. And yet, how he loathed the thought of bloodshed, he thought as he trudged on down the road. Experience had taught him how very costly the spilling of blood could be.

It was a long and wearisome journey, relieved only by the blessing of the sun. At last chasing away the rain, the bright, fiery orb shown down upon Niall and the priest as they passed by rolling green meadows and densely wooded forests. Sheep, goats, and small wild animals inhabited the area, roaming about freely.

"I remember passing through this very same area when I was returning to Sleat with the Fairy Flag tucked under my arm,"Father," Niall said in recollection. "Little did I know then where my thievary would lead. I guess ye would say I got my just reward, eh Father?"

There was no response. Looking over his shoulder, Niall could see that Father Flanigan was lagging far behind, huffing and puffing. Niall showed compassion by at last pausing along the side of the road.

"Ye look exhausted."

"I am!' Plopping down on a large rock Father Flanigan nearly collapsed.

"I'm sorry, Father. I didna mean to cause ye to suffer so. It's just that I am in a hurry to....."

"Hush." The priest held up his hand. "You did not forcibly drag me. Ah, but it is such a good feeling to get off my feet, however." He wiped the sweat from his brow.

"It is. Only now did Niall notice his own discomfort. "Ah, Father, ye look as miserable as I feel."

"You must love her very, very much." Taking out a loaf of bread he carried in a leather pouch and flask of water, Father Flanigan shared both with Niall.

"I do. More than my life!" Realizing just how hungry he was, Niall wolfed down the bread his thoughts on Caitlin all the while..

"Love is a powerful thing. More powerful by far than hate. "

"Is it?" Niall was not so sure.

"You must hae faith." Father Flanigan smiled. "And after all, t'was love that brought you all the way......."

"Father?" Niall turned his head, noting at once how the priest had suddenly tensed. In a moment he saw the reason why. Five MacLeod clansmen were quickly approaching them their arms upraised in greeting. At their head was a clansman Niall recognized only too well. "Jamie." Fumbling beneath his cloak, he reached for his sword.

The priest's tone of voice was harsh, authoritative. "You can't...."

"I must. He will recognize me and all will be lost."

Father Flanigan grasped Niall's arm. "If you harm him you will not have a chance for happiness. If you live by the sword you will die by the sword. His voice was impassioned. "Have faith."

"Faith." Though he tried, it was easier said than done, particularly when Jamie MacLeod strode over.

"So, ye hae brought a companion, Father Flanigan. Does it take two priests to dissolve a marriage?"

"Aye. Two." Agreeably the priest nodded. "This is Father Franco who has come all the way from Rome."

"Rome!"

Again Father Flanigan nodded. "Aye. "

Niall kept his head down as Jamie looked his way, asking, "What do ye think of the Highlands, Father?"

"Father Franco does not understand anything but Italian and French," the priest hurried to say. Looking at Niall he winked.

Jamie shrugged. "That willna matter. Just as long as he can sever the ties that bind Caitlin to that fool of a MacDonald so that I can marry her, I will welcome him." Arrogantly he grinned at Niall, not noticing how that "priest" bristled.

Fool, Niall thought. It was Jamie who was the fool and not he if he thought Caitlin would ever be his bride. Hiding his resentment, however, keeping his head bent down in a gesture of humility, Niall followed after the haughty clansman as he cheerfully led them to Dunvegan.

Caitlin stared desolately out the window of the great hall. Where was Niall? When would he arrive? Rubbing her eyes against the strain of her constant staring, she was eager and at the same time apprehensive, more so than usual because she had heard her father say that the fortress was well guarded against those coming in, or those trying to find a way out. He had smugly proclaimed that if any MacDonald was fool enough to come to Dunvegan there would be no escape.

"Oh, Niall!" She feared for him, for surely her father's anger and hatred lately bordered on being totally irrational. He was obsessed with annulling the marriage. Indeed, it seemed to be the only thing on his mind The only thing he talked about. Was it any wonder then that he had nearly gone berserk when he had noticed the absence of Father Flanigan in the castle? Only Fiona's explanation that the priest had gone to meet an emissary from Rome had calmed him. His rage had turned to jubilation as he had imagined that the arrival signaled the agreement of the Pope to ending the marriage.

"But the laugh is on you, Father. " Little did he know that the very person he thought to destroy was traveling to Dunvegan dressed in the brown cloak and robes of the church. Hopefully that disguise would keep him safe, at least until her mother had time to talk with the MacLeod and straighten this whole situation out.

Looking over her shoulder, Caitlin shivered as she thought about the conversation her mother must be having with her father right now. The time had come for the truth to be told yet even so it made her nervous, considering her father's frame of mine. What would her mother say? How would she begin to broach the subject? And having heard the news, how would Ian MacLeod react?

Clasping her hands together tightly, looking once again out the window, she determined to keep her spirits up. She had to believe that the coming baby would make all the difference. The child would soften her father's heart. Niall would come. He would make peace with the MacLeods.

"All would be well."

HIGHLAND DESTINY

Pacing up and down, Caitlin whispered those words, boldly at first, then with less and less conviction as the long moments passed. There was no sign of Niall. Worse yet, she could hear the sound of her father's angry shouting. It thundered through the castle. So, he had responded to the news with anger not joy.

Caitlin placed her hands upon her stomach, wondering what the future held for the baby growing within. "Oh, Father, how could ye harden yer heart against yer own grandchild?" And all because of his damnable pride, and a stubbornness that would not let him bury the past.

Like an all-enveloping cloak, depression engulfed her. She felt the sudden urge to go far away from Dunvegan, to hide away in a place where no one would know who she was. In some far away glen she would raise her child. Secluded in a cottage somewhere she would protect her baby from the poison of this bitter feud. But where would she go? Looking towards the horizon, she tried to imagine. Should she head east, south or west?

Gazing towards the winding road that led southward, Caitlin thought about making such a journey, her eyes widening as she caught sight of the small party of men whose silhouettes were darkened on the horizon.

"Jamie and the others." Her heart pounded as she realized that they were not alone. Two other figures dressed in dark brown were with them. "Niall!" She kept her eyes riveted on the two men as they came up the road. Dear God, how had they run into Jamie? "Does Jamie know who he is?"

Fearfully she watched, breathing a sigh of relief as she noticed that the two "priests" were being treated

343

with deference.   So, Jamie hadn't recognized Niall, at least not yet.

"Oh, Niall. Niall.   Be careful!"   Closing her eyes she whispered a silent prayer. When she opened them, she could see that   the tallest of the "priests" was looking searchingly towards the castle.

Niall stared grimly at the dark, massive wall of the fortress in the distance. It rose up forebodingly. Beyond those walls somewhere was Caitlin and though he was not short of valor or daring he had to admit that there was no way he could wrest her from her father's hands. The castle walls were impregnable if   Ian MacLeod willed it.

His heart sank like a stone as he forced himself to face reality. He was no match for the MacLeod. Alone he could do nothing but swear and curse from a distance. The truth of the matter was that he was helpless unless he could make Ian MacLeod listen to reason.   In the meantime the one thing he treasured most in life was just   beyond   his   grasp.

HIGHLAND DESTINY

Chapter Thirty-Seven

Niall kept his head down as Ian MacLeod raised his hand in greeting to the two cloaked figures who appeared at the gate. All the while Niall prayed in his heart that his disguise would not be discovered. Not now! Not when he was so close to the fulfillment of his dream of seeing Caitlin again, of holding her in his arms.

"Greetings, MacLeod." Father Flanigan quickly stepped in front of Niall in an effort to hide him from any diligent observations. The presence of five armed clansmen standing behind the Scottish chieftain spoke of trouble should the young intruder be recognized.

"Greetings." Ian MacLeod's tone spoke of barely suppressed anger and suspicion. "It's glad I am that ye decided to return, priest, seeing as how I didna know ye planned to leave this castle in the first place."

Father Flanigan was eager to make amends. "I apologize if I gave you reason for distress, but I was called away quite suddenly."

"Aye. To fetch yer fine brown Papal sparrow." Ian MacLeod looked towards Niall with a condescending scowl, reflecting his dislike of anything that came from across the sea. Despite the fact that he had needed the pope's blessing to break the ties between his daughter and her husband, there was no love in his heart for the church in Rome. Indeed, there was no resident archbishop in Scotland. The lairds held provincial councils without the presence of   a church official other than a priest.

Father Flanigan touched Niall's shoulder.   "May I present, Father Franco."

"Franco?"   Ian MacLeod squinted his eyes.   "Not one of us."

"Nae. He comes from.....from Venice."

Knowing that he was being scrutinized, Niall sought to keep at least a part of his face in shadow.

"Venice."   Ian MacLeod   made no attempt at friendliness.   It was obvious that he resented the intrusion of anyone foreign.   Folding his arms across his chest he spat out, "bah, I dunna hae need of him now."

"Dunna hae need?"

"That is what I said!" Again he looked at Niall with a scowl. "So ye can send him right back to where he came from. " From his actions he seemed to mean right then.

Father Flanigan looked at Niall, then at the MacLeod, then back to Niall again. "If that is what you want, then that is what I will do. But have a heart. It has been a rough journey." It was a gentle reminder of the rules of hospitality the Highlanders adhered to.

"Aye, aye. I meant not immediately." His voice grew softer as he said the next words only for Father Flanigan's ears. "But see that ye get rid of him soon. I dunna want to owe   Rome any taxation for their interference. We MacLeods are fishermen, herders and farmers and can ill afford ten percent to line the Holy Father's coffers. Besides, as I said circumstances hae changed."

"Changed?"

"Och, the worst has happened!" The MacLeod took revenge on a hapless rock in his path.

Father Flanigan asked the question that was on Niall's mind. "Your daughter. She is not...ill.....?"

The MacLeod shook his head. "Nae. She is fit."

"Then.....?"

"I am soon to be a grandfather!" Ian's voice trembled. "To.....to a.....a MacDonald!"

"A grandfather." Father Flanigan feigned surprise. "Then of course annullment is out of the question, lest you seek to make your own grandchild bastard. born."

"Which I tell ye I do not!" The MacLeod paused, allowing his answer to register before adding, "but I wouldna mind making of my daughter a widow."

Niall flinched at the vehemence in his "father-in-law's" voice.

"Hold yer tongue." Despite the fact that he was talking to a powerful chieftain, Father Flanigan's tone was scolding. "To say such a thing is to speak of murder. And you must remember how such careless talk was instrumental in making of Thomas Becket a saint."

The MacLeod was not chastised. "Never-the-less, it makes me seeth when I think of the trickery that MacDonald used to wed with my lovely young lassie. And now he has planted his seed in her belly. The final indignity. " He motioned to the two priests. "But so be it. Things done can not be undone. Come inside." He strode inside the Great Hall with such powerful strides that it was all Father Flanigan could do to keep up with him. Niall, on the other hand, purposefully kept several paces behind.

He was inside the castle! The very thought of being so close to Caitlin made him feel lighter of heart. *Oh, Caity, how I long to look into yer eyes, to hold ye in my arms.* Still, he had to be careful. To give in to temptation now might be costly in the long run, thus all he could do was to patiently follow Ian MacLeod and Father Flanigan as they headed towards the small chapel and adjoining rooms that were being used by the priest during his stay.

"There, just as ye left it. " Opening the door, Ian MacLeod pointed to the small table that was still littered with scrolls, ink pots and pens.

"So I see." Father Flanigan took off his cloak, hanging it on a peg near the door but though he assumed that Ian MacLeod would now leave them he was soon to see that he was wrong. Moreover the chieftain's presence in the room was clearly a danger .

"I need yer help, priest!" The MacLeod plopped his large bulk into a nearby chair.

"My help!" Father Flanigan eyed the Highlander warily. "In what way?"

Ian MacLeod gripped the arms of the wooden chair, his face tightening as he thought long and hard. "Suppose........" He paused, looking askance at Niall who was now facing the wall looking at the shields and swords hanging there. Strange symbols to adorn walls adjoining a chapel.

"Don't worry. He does not know a word of our language."

That soothed the MacLeod's apprehension for he quickly stated, "Suppose I didna let it be known that my daughter was expecting a bairn. Suppose we went on with the annulment anyway. Quickly. Efficiently."

"Nae!" Father Flanigan was indignant. "That would be dishonest and reprehensible!"

"But practical for my purposes were I to quickly find her another husband."

Another husband! From his place in the corner Niall seethed. He had never held a great love for Caitlin's father but he had respected him. Such a deception was beneath such a man. But having perpetrated the falsehood that he did not speak Gaelic he could hardly give such an opinion. Nevertheless he was incensed.

"Marry her off to another with a child growing in her womb?" Father Flanigan shook his head.

Eyes narrowing, Ian MacLeod clenched his fists, his voice a growl as he insisted, "Tis the only way."

"And so you would put your daughter at risk of her new husband's wrath when he counts the months of her confinement and realizes he has been the pawn of a terrible deception."

Ian MacLeod's mouth was seamed in a bitter, unyielding line. "I would strike a bargain with her new husband. Nor would I lie and pass the devil's spawn off as anything but what it is."

"A sweet, innocent babe who does not deserve your scorn. A bairn who carries the blood of the MacDonalds, aye, but your own MacLeod blood as well." Father Flanigan got down on his knees before the MacLeod, his arms upraised in supplication. "Please, I beg of you, Ian, bury your hatred before it brings a great ill to those of your household. Let Caitlin have some happiness out of all this. Let her live in peace with her husband and baby. Find a place in your heart for forgiveness and love."

Ian MacLeod swallowed. There was long spell of silence, a time in which a myriad of expressions chased across his face. His thick brows raised, drew together then sagged. The glare in his eyes softened. His mouth relaxed. In the end, however, his only retort was to bark out, "yon priest. Why does he still wear his cloak?"

Father Flanigan stiffened, exchanging a worried look with Niall. "Perhaps ....perhaps he prepares himself for his....his return journey."

"Then make him understand that the MacLeod wants him to stay." Tell him to make himself comfortable."

Father Flanigan rattled off some scattered phrases in Latin that were answered by Niall's hasty garbled gibberish.

"Father Franco says thank you, but he will leave his cloak on for now. You see....you see he is cold."

"Cold?" Ian MacLeod's mouth curled in a snear.

Father Flanigan grinned. "You know the men of those warmer climates. They can not stand our damp, and cold."

"Nae, I suppose they canna." Even so, Ian looked at Niall suspiciously as Niall toyed with a pen and ink pot. "Whats more I dunna ken if they can be trusted. Something about him troubles me."

"Then, of course, let us have a bit of privacy." Eager to avert a disaster, Father Flanigan took Niall by the arm, pushing him out the door. Once again he rattled off some Latin, then shut the door in Niall's face, explaining to the MacLeod, "I told him to seek out the kitchen. Some hot lamb stew or soup will soon warm his bones.   And while he is gone we can talk about.....about important matters."

Niall stared at the thick wooden door, feeling relief at being away from such heated scrutiny yet at the same time perturbed to be out of earshot. He was curious as to what further plans the MacLeod was about to hatch, but though he put his ear to the door he could not understand what was being mumbled.

Well, what does it matter?   All he knew was that he would never give Caitlin and his baby up to another man. If that meant that he had to carry her far away, even so far as to Rome itself, well so be it.   With that determination, Niall moved through the corridors, headed for Caitlin's chamber. Opening the door, he was disappointed to see that she was not there.   Her sister was, however.

"Father?"   In curiosity as to why a priest had sought out her room, Shona came forward.

All kinds of thoughts swirled through Niall's mind. Foremost he wondered if he dare trust Caitlin's sibling. Deciding that he had no other choice he pushed back his hood. "Shona, please, where is Caitlin?"

"Niall!"   Her expression was exactly the same as Caitlin's had been that first time she had caught him in the tower and had assumed him to be a ghost.

"Please, Shona, dunna give me away!   I came to be with my wife."   His voice was impassioned. "I love her."

If he had feared Shona's betrayal, the softness in her eyes calmed that fear. "I know that ye do.   And Caitlin loves ye too.   Very, very much."

"I know about the child."

"So does Father now." Shona sighed. "He is such a good mon at heart but he is being so stubborn."

"He wants the priest to go through with the annulment and marry Caitlin to another mon. But that I canna allow!" His eyes glittered as he said it again. "I canna give my wife over to another mon."

Shona hurried to reassure him. "Nor would Caitlin ever agree."

"Then what are we to do?" For just a moment Niall felt as though the weight of the world was resting on his shoulders.

"Ye need friends to gather behind ye. Father needs to see that he canna always hae his way." Shona touched Niall's arm. "I am yer friend, Niall MacDonald."

Oh, how he had need of her friendship. It was a welcome boon. "Thank ye for that, Shona MacLeod." He grasped her hand. "It gives me hope."

"And where there is hope........" She smiled. "But enough of talk. Ye came all this way to see Caitlin and not me. Sit and relax. I will find her, bring her here and give ye two a bit of privacy for a long awaited reunion." That said she quickly and quietly moved to the door, giving Niall a wink before she left him all alone.

Caitlin stood as still as a statue in front of the chapel door. The chamber entrance loomed in her path like the most awesome portcullis. Raising a trembling hand to the wood, however, she knocked hesitantly, a gesture that reflected her apprehension. What was going on inside?

"Who is it?" A voice thundered in the silence.

"Caitlin. I…I would like a word wi' ye, Father." She wanted a chance to look into the room to see if Niall was safe or if his disguise had been discovered. "Father….?""

Furled brows showed impatience at being disturbed. As Ian Macleod opened the door. "By God, lass, what could be so important that ye would interrupt a mon's discussion with his priest?"

"I hae something that…that needs to be told." Anxiously she peered through the open doorway, but caught sight of only Father Flanigan's form. Where was Niall?

"Save yer breath, Daughter." The words exploded from his lips. "Yer mother has already told me about the bairn."

Swallowing her tears she replied, "A happening with which I can tell that ye are no' pleased."

For just a moment his face was completely blank of expression, then he grimaced. "I am and then again I am not!"

Because it complicates all yer plotting and scheming," Caitlin blurted out, looking directly at Father Flanigan.

The MacLeod's face tightened. "That among other things…."

"Then because of that I am doubly glad. 'Tis time that ye didna hae yer way."

"Caity!" He held up one hand, palm out, fingers toward the ceiling. It was a gesture had always used to intimidate and silence any opposition. "I will no' hae a slip of a lassie talking to me that way. I am the chieftain of the MacLeod. My word is law!"

Though once she might have cowered, Caitlin let her rising tide of bitterness consume her. "Ye may be the MacLeod, yer word may be law on this isle, but even the might chief must bow to a greater power."

His face turned red, he balled his hands into fists. "Daughter!"

Caitlin's eyes glittered in the candlelight. It shouldn't be like this, she thought. The coming birth should have been a happy event. Her father should have been cradling her in his arms expressing his joy, not glowering at her with anger as if she had erred.

"Well, even if ye dunna welcome the child, I do, MacDonald or no." there was such a fiercesome pressure pushing at her chest that she feared she couldn't breathe. Then, without warning, Caitlin burst into a storm of tears. "Ye can be cruel, Father. Cruel."

The MacLeod was unnerved by her tears and regretted his outburst. Touching her shoulder, his eyes softened. "Caity, dunna cry. It's just that…that I canna get used to sharing a grandchild with such a loathsome old soul as Malcolm MacDonald."

Dashing the degrading moisture from her cheeks, she sniffled. "And mayhap he willna be so pleased to be sharing a great-nephew with ye."

He was visibly taken aback. "Then I dare him to come here and make a complaint!"

"Oh, how I wish that he would!" Again she squinted her eyes as she tried to catch any sight of Niall.

"And bring that bastard of a nephew wi' him!" Ian MacLeod grumbled, thereby allying his daughter's fears that he might have already been discovered.

"Niall will no' come," Caitlin hurried to say. "Thanks to ye, Father." She felt quarrelsome and might have said more had she not felt the insistent pressure of a hand on the small of her back and heard her sister's frantic voice whispering in her ear. Whirling around, she read the reason for Shona's sudden appearance in her sister's eyes.

Niall was here! She followed Shona back to their room. Her hands trembled violently as she pushed open the door. Peering into the room, she expected to see him standing, waiting for her. Instead she saw him curled up in the corner, his eyes closed, his head cradled on the crook of his arm. The soft rumble of his snoring told her how deeply he slept.

"Ye poor darling. It must hae been a terribly rough journey."

Crossing the room, kneeling down where he napped, she touched a lock of tawny hair that had fallen into his eyes. He *must hae loved me very much to come all this way and risk his life.* As much as she loved him? She could only wonder.

"Ah, Niall, Niall." Was there a chance for happiness for them? Surely at this moment it seemed so. Her father's blustering did little to ease her mind. Still, looking down at Niall her love bubbled deep inside her. She loved him. There was no question or doubt in her mind as to that. Her senses were filled with wanting him.

"What happened between us was meant to be. I love ye so!" Yet that did not keep her from feeling a bit shy as his eye-lids fluttered open.

"Ye do?" Niall cherished the blessing of seeing her lovely face hovering above him, her mane of flaming hair tumbling down over her shoulders. He'd dreamed of her so often that for just a moment he feared her image to be merely a mirage.

"Mmmmm." Caitlin shrugged, suddenly tongue tied. She did, however, stroke his neck.

"Say it again, lass." Oh, but she was the prettiest sight he had ever seen. His eyes savored the gentle swell of her breasts and hips, then touched upon her stomach. It was there his baby slept until it was time to come into this cold, harsh world. His baby.

"I love ye, Niall." Caitlin's voice was a hushed whisper.

"Do ye now?" He grinned like a love-struck boy. "And I love ye, hinny. More than my very life!" Slowly his hands closed around her shoulders, pulling her to him, the passion of his kiss a testimony to the truth of his words. But suddenly he pulled away. "My child," he gasped. Tentatively he reached out and touched her stomach marveling at the miracle that had created life inside her.

"A tiny being that is living proof of our love.""

"Caity, I canna let ye go. Yer father......."

"Is an old fool if he thinks to bully me. Ye are and always will be my husband, Niall MacDonald. I willna ever marry anyone else!" An impassioned promise that she meant with all her heart.

"Ye willna!" This time he kissed her tenderly, shivering at the potent flicker of arousal that spread from their fused mouths to the core of his body. "Ah, Caity," he murmured against her lips.

His voice was infused with a husky plea that set her heart into song. Her body responded to the depth of his desire. She felt alive. Soaring. "Niall!" She pressed close against him savoring the heat of his body, the sheer, masterful strength of him.

"I love ye," he whispered in her ear. "I thank God that ye are mine. And now ye carry my bairn. I am the happiest of laddies." His hands tangled in her hair as he kissed her again, his lips drinking deeply of her very soul. The kiss was long, satisfying to them both, but not so satisfying that they did not long for more.

"Come!" Taking him by the hand, Caitlin let him to her bed. Lying down beside him she was impatient, tearing her garments in her hurry to remove the boundary that kept her from the flimsy tantalizing feel of his naked flesh against her own. Then she was experiencing the warmth of his fingers as he gently outlined the swell of her breasts.

"They seem fuller."

"They are. The babe."

"Ah!" The thought excited him all the more. His wife. His child. Bending down he gently suckled the peaks,

Caitlin trembled beneath warm wetness of his lips and tongue, aroused with a wanton urge to abandon herself fully to the glorious flood of ecstasy that consumed her. She gave herself up to his touch, straining against him, her head spinning wildly as she clung to him.

"It's glad I am that I am not truly a priest."

"And if ye were?"

"I would give up such a vow for ye, lass. Indeed, I would." That said, Niall tugged off the cloak, casting it ruthlessly aside. His hosen and tunic followed, tumbling to the floor.

Their naked bodies caressed as he lay back down. Her skin was warm against his. Feeling her body against him was highly arousing. So much so that it was all he could do to keep his own passions under control. But he did not want to be selfish. The total fulfillment of Caitlin's desires had to be equally important to the fulfillment of his own. He wanted to be a considerate lover. And yet, how difficult it was to keep his own emotions under control.

"Mmmmm." Trembling in her own eagerness, Caitlin slid her arms about his neck, moving against him with a sensuousness that was fired by their long parting. Then they were rolling over and over on the woolen blankets, sinking in the feathered softness.

"Yer friend Jamie threatened to snatch ye out from under yer husband's nose," he growled.

"He did?"

"Aye, he did." His arms tightened around her. "But as long as I am alive he never will. Ye are mine, Caity. Ye belong to me." Once again his hands roamed over her body, asserting that claim.

"Oh, Niall!" As long as he was alive, he had said. The very thought that something might happen to threaten his existence frightened her, tormented her, made her realize how precious each moment together was. "Don't........"

"Hush." His lips swept across her stomach in reverence to the life she carried within her. "No matter what happens I know that I will go on living because of the precious gift ye hae given me. My son."

"Or daughter."

Niall felt certain. "It is a male child."

Caitlin shrugged, not having the heart to argue. Whatever the sex of the baby it didn't really matter. All that mattered was that the bairn would know its father, would grow up in the sunshine of his love. For that matter she wanted that for herself as well. She wanted to look forward to a long life together. Instead she had no way of knowing how long they had to enjoy each other's company. It was a thought that made her hug Niall all the tighter.

"Caity!" With a groan he gently pressed himself between her thighs.

Opening to him, Caitlin gave of herself as she had never done before. For the moment her only world was Niall, bringing to her body the ultimate pleasure and to her heart the deepest love. Then it was her hands which caressed him, her lips which sought his mouth. Running her hand down his flat stomach, she stroked the bulge of his manhood, hearing his gasp of pleasure as she traced the length of him with her fingers, working magic upon that throbbing maleness which had given her so much delight.

Niall's flesh burned to the flame of her caress. His mouth was hot against her neck. He whispered words of love in a hectic frenzy as he found her secret place then entered her. "Like a sword to a sheath. A perfect fit." He marveled at how right it felt to be joined with her flesh to flesh. And soul to soul!

Caitlin could feel the strength of his muscled arms as they wrapped around her, his broad, lightly furred chest straining against her own. In that moment they were joined as one, offering to each other the most precious gift of all. The gift of love. Then the world seemed to quake beneath them as they moved, rising and falling like ocean waves.

Niall's face was etched in passion as an explosion of sheer pleasure flooded through them. He cried out Caitlin's name over and over as the storm washed through them both. Then in the drowsy afterglow he held her close, smiling as she snuggled against him.

"It should always be this way. Us together," he whispered, stroking her hair.

"Always."

"Oh, Caity." As if afraid she might suddenly disappear, Niall's hand clutched at hers, holding tightly. Their eyes met and held, an unspoken communication of love passing between them. Then with a sigh they closed their eyes.

At least for the moment they could savor their contentment.

Chapter Thirty-Eight

Danger hovered in every corner. Armed men lurked in the shadows, their unfriendly eyes threatening a discovery. Even so, Caitlin and Niall braved the peril just for a chance to look at each other, to touch, to briefly hold hands or, if they were blessed with a moment of being alone, to kiss.

Each time they were together the bond between them grew stronger. Never had each passing minute been so precious. Never before had they savored every heartbeat, every whisper, the wonderful feel of skin against skin. Love. The very word seeped into the depths of their souls. In their hearts, minds, and spirits they were as one, their love personified in the child growing in Caitlin's womb.

His child meant everything to Niall. It was a miracle that overwhelmed him each time he touched Caitlin's stomach. The bairn was a living symbol and gave him all the more reason to live. Caitlin and the child needed him.

Never before had Niall wished so fervently to have eyes in the back of his head. He was risking his freedom, perhaps even his life, each and every time he sought Caitlin out, each time they shared an affectionate gesture or made love, and yet he could not keep away from her. His feelings for her, his desire to be with her and his child were even stronger than his fear of Ian MacLeod.

"You are tempting fate!" Father Flanigan always scolded, fearing the that Niall's emotions would eventually give him away. "Someone is going to see you and your identity will be heralded throughout the halls."

"Nae, I hae been careful."

The habit Niall was wearing well disguised his appearance. From time to time he could pull the hood down lower on his forehead or the cowl collar up over part of his face.

"It doesn't matter how cautious you might be. You are going to take one too many chances. As it is, Ian MacLeod is questioning me why I have not sent you away. He is suspicious of you, Son. "I fear that there are more spies watching you than ye could ever know."

"Ever know?" Niall held up his hands, counting on his fingers. "There are more enemies here than I could ever count. I am well aware of the danger they pose. But…"

"Ye will no' use reason and go back to the MacDonald stronghold until I can make the MacLeod understand that God, and not he, is in charge now?"

"I will no' go alone!"

Oh, how he wished that he could just pick Caitlin up in his arms, hold her ever so tightly and protectively to his own trembling body and simply disappear in the Highland mists. It was his fiercest desire. He had a compulsion to flee but only if his wife went with him.

"And youi can not go with her,. It is far too dangerous at this time." Father Flanigan cast his eyes upward. "And so there is nothing that I can do but pray and ask his guidance and assistance."

"Father, when ye pray, be sure ye let Him know how very much I do love her." More than his own safety.

Still, he knew that he, too, must survive in order to make a life for his wife and child.

Father Flanigan shook his head. "If you love her, you must protect her. And just how are you going to do that if you end up in the MacLeod dungeon, might I ask?"

Niall was silent for a long while. When he answered, it was in a whisper. "I will see her but one more time. I must explain…"

Father Flanigan sighed with relief. "Once more is one time too many." Still, Niall would have it no other way. He wanted one more chance to tell Caitlin of his love. He needed desperately to whisper his love in her ear. After that he would follow Father Flanigan's advice and look upon her only from afar….that is until this matter of the marriage was at last settled and its sanctity proclaimed.

"Once more…" A vow that seemed nearly impossible as he caught sight of her on the stairs. Pulling at his cowl, he followed. "Caity, my Caity, where can I see ye?"

"My room. Shona will stand lookout again!"

Unable to help himself, he pulled her with him into the shadows, threading the fingers of both hands through her hair. Lowering his head, he touched her mouth with his, his lips lingering, tasting, caressing.

"Oh, Caity, Caity, you beautiful jewel, how you have enriched my life. Without you and our wee bairn…."

"Hus…ye willna ever e without me." In a gesture of affirmation she reached up and gently touched his cheek. "It will work out. It must." Alas, she sounded much more optimistic than she really felt. "Until then we must be content with what we hae."

"Aye."

"Och, Niall…." She clutched his hands, gripping them, drawing strength from him, fearful suddenly of what tomorrow held in store. Shuddering, she recalled the unhappy endings for young lovers the bards often sung about, then, as she looked into Niall's eyes, she hurriedly pushed all fear from her mind. Smiling, she whispered, "I must go now, but I will meet ye in a few moments."

"A heartbeat too long without ye," he muttered softly into the cowl collar. Their eyes met once again then with a groan of impatience, he descended the narrow stairway.

It seemed an eternity until they were together, but as he pulled her close he knew that every pang of impatience had been worth it. Sweet, hot desire tempered by tenderness fused their bodies together. An aching sweetness mingled with the fury and the fire.

In the aftermath, when passion had ebbed, they lay entwined, sealing their vows with whispered words of love. Alas, it was a quietude that was much too short. With the violence of a thunderstorm their peacefulness was shattered as Ian MacLeod burst into the room. "Caitlin, I hae heard strange tattlings," he announced. ""There is talk of the foreign priest….!"

With a terrified shriek Caitlin hastily reached for the blanket, quickly covering her nakedness and Niall's as well. "Father!"

Ian MacLeod's eyes traveled about the room, taking in every detail, including the discarded brown cloak. In that moment he knew fully the truth of the betrayal. "No priest, but a wolf in sheep's clothing. A wolf named MacDonald!" With a lunge he fell upon Niall, screaming for his clansmen at the top of his lungs.

"Leave me be! Leave us in peace. She is my wife! I hae every right."

"Right? Ye hae none." Ian MacLeod held Niall pinioned as two other MacLeods pushed into the room. "Take this "priest" to the dungeon. Now!"

"Nae!" Like a banshee, Caitlin attacked her father, pummeling him with her fists. "If ye harm him, if ye do, I will never forgive ye. I will never, do ye hear!"

Her threat fell upon ears that were deaf with the MacLeod's anger. He gave his order again. "Take him to the dungeon."

"Nae!" This time Caitlin turned her attention to Niall, clasping her arms around his waist as if in this way she could keep him from suffering his doom. It did no good. She was callously pulled away and pushed aside. Helplessly all she could do was watch as Niall was dragged from the room.

"Consorting with the enemy! Sneaking around behind my back." Ian MacLeod's shouts vibrated throughout the chamber.

"Enemy no. He is my husband! Ye had no right. Ye had no right." Caitlin's eyes glittered as she looked him in the eye. "And if ye harm him I will hate ye forever. Do ye hear me, Father. I...." Suddenly she paled. With a gasp she clutched at her stomach. "Nae. Nae."

"Caity!" The MacLeod's anger evaporated as he saw his daughter's agony.

"My babe! My bairn!" Caitlin reached out, fighting against the huge black dots that floated before her eyes. Then she saw only darkness.

The flame of the hearth fire spattered and sparked, blending its smoke with that of the burning rushes, stinging Fiona's eyes as she hovered over the pale form lying on the bed. For several hours she had joined the midwife and the physician, Mac-an-leigh in this long vigil. With each moment that passed her apprehension and fear grew.

"Caitlin, hinny. Please, open yer eyes!" Only a soft moan answered her as she called out her daughter's name.

"How is she?" Sheepishly Ian MacLeod entered the room to take his place beside his wife.

"Do ye really care?" Fiona MacLeod's scorn was potent. "Or is yer hatred more important than the well-being of yer daughter."

"Fie, woman. Hold yer tongue. What happened isna my fault."

Perhaps not, but realization that he was helpless to do anything to ease Caitlin's agony tore at his soul. Worse yet the midwife had confided that it was possible for the young mother-to-be to lose her child. The spots of blood on the sheet clearly proved her right.

"Ye couldna let her be happy for even a moment. Ye had to go blustering about like a dog gone mad. Well, ye hae Niall MacDonald secluded in yer moldy dungeon. I hope that makes ye happy as ye look down and see what yer blundering has done." Fiona's eyes were filled with tears. All she could do was to hold tightly to her daughter's hand and offer what comfort she could. Only the midwife with her herbs, potions, and knowing hands could help Caitlin now.

"I didna mean my own daughter harm. I didna!"

"And yer own grandchild. Yer own flesh and blood. MacDonald though it may be it deserves a chance at life." Fiona wiped her tears away with the sleeve of her rough woolen tunic. She had always protected Caitlin, despite their many misunderstandings. Indeed, they seemed to have grown closer lately, mainly because of the coming child. It was during such times that a daughter turned to her mother.

"Fiona......!" Ian MacLeod tried to comfort his wife but it was no use. He didn't know what to say, not now, not after what had happened.

"Ye saw yer grandchild as a barrier to yer mighty plans. Tell me, husband, hae ye got Caitlin's next husband waiting outside the door?"

"Of course not!" Retreating from his wife's anger, Ian moved closer to the bed, shaken by the sight of his daughter's ashen face. Hiding his fear he took out his anger on the nearest person. "Do something!" he swore at the midwife. Save my grandchild, or by God I'll hae yer head.",

"I can do nothing more. I gave her herbs and potions to give her strength. The rest is up to God." The old woman's eyes spoke a truth that Ian was reluctant to admit. "I would say my prayers if I were ye, old mon."

"Old mon!" Strange, but in that moment the word "old" seemed definitely to apply to him.

"The bleeding. Has it stopped?"

This time it was the physician who answered. "Aye."

"Perhaps then it is not too late for the bairn." Fiona clutched her daughter's hand, stung by the knowledge that there was nothing that she could do to take away

Caitlin's suffering. If only it were she lying on that bed. If only ..."I

"Why is it that everyone blames me for what has happened. Why does no one blame that young fool who trespassed into this castle. Why?"

"I dunna blame him because he came here in answer to my pleading." Fiona made the confession.

"Ye sent for him?" He was incredulous.

"I thought, I hoped that once ye saw the two lovebirds together, realized how much they loved each other, ye would come to yer senses. I was wrong." She faced him squarely. "Ian MacLeod ye can be the world's greatest and most stubborn fool at times."

He thought long and hard about that accusation. "Sometimes, maybe I can be." As for now, each moan from Caitlin's lips struck a blow to his heart. For the first time in a long while he found himself regretting what he had done He had been rash. Hasty. It was just that seeing that priest's cloak, knowing that he had been lied to again, had enraged him. "But it doesna matter now. All that matters is Caitlin's well being. And...and that of her bairn." Silently he mouthed a prayer, though he made no promises to God. He didn't feel that the Omnipotent being was asking him to do such a thing.

Fiona, however, was another story. "Ye will let Niall MacLeod out of that smelly hole this instant. Ye will fetch him and allow him the courtesy of being with his wife."

"Will I now!" his face. Indeed, at that moment, he looked like the very devil.

"Ye will if ye ever want to share my bed again."

"What?"

"Ye heard me!" Taking little care whether or not she fueled his anger she continued. "And ye will put far from yer mind any thoughts of our daughter being pawned off like a tinker's wagon. She loves her husband, Ian, no matter what blood flows through his veins. Much as I love ye."

"Ye love me?" Sadly he had never really been sure.

"I do."

"Even though I stole ye from Malcolm MacDonald so long ago."

"Even so." That much at least was settled. "Ian, there has been too much bloodshed. Give it up! Make yer truce with Malcolm and be done wi' it."

"A truce?" The very idea galled him. "How can I when he killed my son?"

"It was not he that killed Colin and well ye know it!"

"Not he but one of his clan. For that I hold him responsible." With a grunt he considered the matter closed.

"Suppose.....suppose I were to tell ye that Colin was not yer son." Though it was something she had long held within her heart, Fiona felt relieved to be unburdened by the confession.

"Not my son?" Ian was aghast. In two quick strides he hovered over her. "What game is this?"

Fiona shook her head. "No game but the truth at last. A truth that has haunted me every day of my life with you." She took a deep breath, then let the story out of a frightened young girl whose moonlit trysts with Malcolm MacDonald had resulted in a child, a baby who was joyfully and unknowingly claimed by the man who had abducted her from the arms of her lover.

"By God, 'tis true!"   Ian MacLeod was stunned. "But why......? Why tell me now?"

Fiona looked into the face of her sleeping daughter. "For her. For my sweet, sweet, Cai. I want to put the ghosts of the past to rest, even though......."

"Not my son!"

"So   ye see,   Colin was in truth a MacDonald. Therefore ye hae no reason for this   all-consuming hatred ye feel."

Ian MacLeod   turned his back.   "Woman, I will never forgive ye.   Ye hae killed me."
Even so, it was Fiona MacLeod who suffered.   "Turn Niall MacDonald loose.   Let Caitlin be happy. Give up the feud. Make amends with Malcolm and hae done with it all. Please!"

Her supplication went unanswered as Ian MacLeod stormed to the door.   Opening it roughly, he nearly pulled it from it's hinges.   Then he was gone,

HIGHLAND DESTINY

Chapter Thirty-Nine

The high-pitched shriek of the rats as they scurried about in the night made it impossible for Niall to sleep. He hated being locked up. Hated it more than anything.

"So, at last I am caged in the MacLeod's oubliette," the coffin-size prison from which there was no escape. And all the while the ghostly clang of closing gates, the rattle of keys, and heavy trod of footsteps were constant taunts of the lack of privacy he had.

"Och, how be the mighty MacDonald tanist now?" teased a guard, peering down through the grille. "Was it worth it to take away our flag, ye treacherous bastard! Was it?"

"Go away!" Niall sat up. "I dunna hae to answer to the likes of ye for what I hae done."

"Ach, then I willna gi' ye any food or water. Beasts such as are suckled by MacDonald teets can starve and thirst for all that I care."

"I'm not hungry or thirsty. At least not for what you offer," Niall countered.

"Ye are not." The guard dangled a leg of mutton through the opening in the grille, laughing as Niall looked up.

With a snort he pulled it away. "Ye said ye were no' hungry."

"I'm not, at least for MacLeod fare." Drawing his legs up to his chest, Niall turned his back. At last the guard left, but only for a short while. All too soon he was back, this time to tease him with water.

"Thirsty?"

Niall was, desperately so. Anxiously he licked his dry lips.

"Ah, ye are, but not for Macleod water, I would dare say." Deliberately he poured some through the grille so that it dribbled on the dirt floor. He laughed uproariously.

"Gi' yerself up to yer good humor now. Perhaps someday we will hae changed places," Niall grumbled.

"Not if the Macleod has his way. Ye will stay down here until the day ye die."

A gruesome thought that Niall hurriedly brushed away. "He willna do such a thing to the father of his daughter's babe."

"Ach, but he will. Ye will see." Again the guard left, this time thankfully for a long while.

Time moved slowly, so slowly that at times Niall feared he might go mad. The cursed feud! The oubliette was brimming with vermin. Niall felt suddenly crawly. His own skin seemed to prick at the thought of the bugs and the rats.

Was he going to languish here forever? Was he going to die?

The dungeon was dark, and so small that Niall was unable to stand. Hunkered down, he stared into the blackness, feeling the greatest desolation he had ever known. At a time when he had everything he could ever have dreamed of, it had all been cruelly wrenched away. Was it any wonder then that he was bitter?

"And all because of two vengeful old men!" he muttered. Both of whom had shown themselves capable of great cruelty. The very thought made him shiver as he recalled Ian's threat to make Caitlin a widow. World he dare? "Of course. He is the MacLeod. He can dare anything." But would he chance his daughter's hatred?

Caitlin's angry shouts as she had tried to come to his aid still rang in Niall's ears. But her father had coldly ignored her outraged pleas. He had brushed her away as if she were little more than a fly. Uppermost in his mind had been the desire to see Niall locked up.

Oh, if only I could get out of here, he thought, stretching out his leg in the cramped space. *I would take Caitlin by the hand and not stop running until we were somewhere untouched by the foolishness of constant squabbling. Somewhere where a feud like this would be settled by those who had begun it.*

"Malcolm MacDonald and Ian MacLeod!" In that moment he imagined the two men fighting hand-to-hand, stumbling around, rolling over and over on the ground until they were too tired to move. Too tired to cause any more trouble. Too tired to do anything but crawl on their hands and knees like the babies they were.

Suddenly Niall threw back his head and laughed. The sound engulfed him, vibrated through him, made him sound like one demented....but he could not stop. Had he finally gone over the edge then? For just a moment he feared as much, but the sight of Caitlin's face dancing before his eyes quickly sobered him.

"Oh, Caity! Love!" Their brief time together had been the most wonderful moment of his life, a time he would treasure for as long as he lived. However long that was to be. "Whatever is to happen I can face it bravely, having loved and been loved by ye, Caity! Caity."

Death! Dying. Despite being a warrior who faced the prospect many times in his life, he was haunted by it now. He was giving up so much. Just at a time when he truly realized what living was all about. Love. Caring deeply about another person. And now there was to be another person for him to love as well.

The child! It was possible he might never even know if it was a son or a daughter. Might never know his child's name. Or hear it call him Father.

"Oh, God!" he moaned. The walls were cold and damp, and he hugged his arms tightly around his body. Cold, hungry and miserable, he fought against his despair. "if only…." What he would not give to see Caitlin once again. Just once!

Warmth. Warmth and light. Everything was soft and safe. Caitlin could sense someone was with her, but she hadn't the strength to open her eyes. Instead, she gave herself up to the sensations.

"Caity! Ah, my poor, poor daughter."

A voice was whispering in the darkness. A comforting voice, like an angel's. Fingers as gentle as a soft spring breeze were touching her.

"Caity, it will be all right. I willna let ye lose the babe."

Her body was tired. Weary. She heard faint sounds, muted as if they were coming through deep, murky water. Gurgling. Her voice? Yes. The sound of her own breathing became louder and louder until it was a roar in her ears.

"Relax. God is wi' ye."

Relax the voice said, but how could she when she was in so much pain. "Nooooooo!"

"Easy, darlin'."

It was as if she were in a long, dark tunnel, groping about, fighting to come into the light. To follow. She reached out to consciousness, but it was like trying to walk through a dense fog. Darkness was upon her, and though she struggled to open her eyes she couldn't see. There were shadows. Only shadows.

"Ye must drink this. The midwife's potion will aid ye."

Drink. Caitlin tried but the wetness choked her.

"Careful. Careful. Just a wee bit."

Again she felt the liquid pass he lips, but this time she managed to swallow.

"That's good, lass."

Caitlin was lying in an awkward position but she couldn't quite seem to shift to a more comfortable one. Dull reverberations shot through her body each time she tried to move. In panic she pushed against the mattress in an effort to sit up, only to fall back down again.

Images teased her eyes as she slowly emerged from the darkness. From somewhere far away she thought she heard the sound of a bell. Willing herself to wake up, she passed in and out of consciousness. She was dizzy. The boundaries of the room alternately advanced and receded like waves against the shore. Back and forth. Up and down.

"Niall! Niall!" she whispered.

Closing her eyes, she reached out.

"Hear that, Husband. Listen to who it is that she longs for."

"Niall…." Caitlin cried out again. Through the haze in her mind, she remembered. Niall was gone. Her father had taken him from her. The very thought brought moisture to her eyes.

"She is crying. It must make ye feel very, very proud."

"I tell ye that it does not! But even so, I willna let him go. Not now, not ever."

"Then it is glad that I am that it is you and not I who will hae to live with yer conscience!"

The flame of the hearth fire spattered and sparked, stinging Fiona's eyes as she hovered over the fragile figure lying on the bed. For several hours she and the midwife held a long and lonely vigil. With each moment that passed, her apprehension and fear grew.

"Caitlin!" she called softly.

Only a soft moan answered her. The realization that she was helpless to do anything to ease the agony tore at her soul. All she could do was hold tightly to her daughter's hand and offer what comfort she could.

Chapter Forty

Caitlin stirred under the mountain of quilts, stretching her arms and opening her eyes. It was going to be another boring day of inactivity, a thought that made her chafe with anxiety. Oh, how she hated being abed! She had strictly been thus confined for more than a week following the mid-wife's orders. Only the knowledge that it had been done to safeguard her baby ensured Caitlin's full cooperation. Above all, she wanted to do what was best for her bairn.

"Och, I feel as if I hae slept forever!" In truth, it had been a much shorter time. Nine days or so. During that time she had regained her strength but not her peace of mind. "What hour is it?" she asked her sister.

"Mid morning." Seeing Caitlin stir, Shona came quickly to her side.

"Way past breakfast."

"Aye, but not for ye." Shona handed Caitlin a hairbrush, then left the room carrying a wooden tray with a steaming bowl atop it. "How be ye today, hinny?"

"How could I be when Niall is locked in the dungeon and everyone around me seems so angry?" she sat upright with a burst of energy, drawing the covers up with her. "I might as well be among hostile strangers."

"Hush, at least until ye eat."

Caitlin quieted as Shona poured cream in the bowl, then fed her spoonsful of porridge. Swallowing, Caitlin whispered, "All except ye and Mother." She waited for her sister to explain. When she did not, Caitlin asked, "Shona, what has happened? Father seldom comes to see me, and if he does and Mother is here, he scurries away like an angry hound."

"That's because he is." Shona shook her head sadly.

"They hae had quarrels before, but this time it is different. Tell me!" It was not a request, but rather a demand.

Shona sighed. Setting down the bowl, she clasped her hands tightly together. "It happened the day ye nearly miscarried. Mother and Father got into a discussion about what to do with yer husband and why he had come to the castle."

"Mother told him she had sent for Niall, that's why....."

"Nae. Much worse. She told Father that he should leave ye be, let ye be happy. She demanded that he make a truce with the MacDonald."

"Which of course Father refused to do." Caitlin of all people knew just how stubborn he could be.

"He did. His old anger about Colin's death and about Malcolm MacDonald's fascination for Mother all resurfaced."

Caitlin rushed to a conclusion. "And Father's jealousy fanned the flames of an argument."

"It did, though not for the reason that ye think." Shona shook her head sadly. "Ah, I still hae trouble believing it."

"Believing what?"

Shona blurted it out. "Caity, Mother threw it in Father's face that Malcolm MacDonand and not he was Colin's father."

"Nae!" Caitlin paled and threw her head back on the pillow.

"She did! But not to be hateful. I think it was in an effort to make him see reason and stop being such a blustering vengeful fool." Hurriedly, she explained, detailing the entire story. "And though I know they deeply love each other, Father has moved out of the bedchamber they hae shared for so many years. He has called her a faithless wife, a liar, and worse!"

"So Mother's life is ruined because she sought to make mine happy." Caitlin balled her hands into fists. "And little good her sacrifice did. Niall is still in the dungeon."

"For what looks to be a long stay." Shona sounded nearly as sad about it as Caitlin felt.

"A long stay? I think not." Despite the fact she was unsteady on her feet, Caitlin got out of bed, reaching for her clothing.

"Caity!" instantly Shona was by her side. "Get back in bed," she ordered.

"Nae. I canna stay enshrouded in my blankets while Niall wastes away in the dungeon."

"But.....!" Looking at her sister's face, Shona knew there would be no way of reasoning with Caitlin, and thus she asked, "Where are ye going?"

"To set Niall free!"

It was a task much easier said than done, for Caitlin was slowed down by being so long abed. When she really wanted to run, all she could do was move ever so slowly down the stairs, a journey that seemed to take nearly as long as her journey to Dunskaith had taken. At last, however, her efforts were rewarded and the thick wooden door to the dungeon loomed into sight.

"And just where do ye think ye are going?" Like some unwelcome giant, Jamie loomed in her way, obviously taking his turn at guarding the dungeon.

"To see my husband, if that is any of yer concern," Caitlin retorted.

"Then ye will hae to be disappointed. Yer father has given strict orders that he is not to be disturbed."

"Has he now." Somehow mustering together every bit of strength she possessed, Caitlin reached behind the door, pulling free a loose stone. Hefting it soundly, with a force that took Jamie by surprise, she hit him squarely on the head. Like a limp doll, he slumped to the ground.

A rattle of keys jarred Niall from his slumber. Looking up, he squinted at the sudden light, then saw her face looking at him through the grille "Nae, it canna be," he said in disbelief.

Raising his head, he blinked his eyes to clear them of the vision. A dream, but so vivid as to almost make him believe that she was really here.

"Caity."

"Aye, 'tis me. I'm going to get you out of this place….." Her voice whispering to him.

"I'm going mad." At last it had happened.

"Nae. I tell ye that ye are not." Opening the door, Caitlin pushed her way into the tiny cell, hugging Niall close.

"Caity, my God, it really is ye! How?"

Her smile was mysterious "I hae my ways, but we will talk of it later." She moved toward him. "As for now, I want to get ye out of here."

"Out. That word is a wonder to my ears."

Winding her arms around his neck, she kissed him, a brief caressing of her lips, yet a kiss with such a tender show of emotion that he was deeply touched.

"I love ye, Caity!"

"I know. Ye wouldna hae come all this way and put yer life in danger if ye didna...." She rattled the keys. "But come, there is no time for passion just now. Jamie will wake up and all will be lost."

He clutched at her hand. "Then by all means....."

The castle was eerily quiet. Too quiet, Niall thought as he cautiously led Caitlin by the hand. Slowly they ran up the spiral stairs, expecting to meet opposition at every turn. Instead their escape seemed to be incredibly easy. Too easy.

"Are all of yer father's clansmen under a spell?"

"T'would seem so."

Even so, Niall knew he had to be careful lest there be need for bloodshed. He didn't want to harm any MacLeod . There had already been too much blood spilled between his clan and Caitlin's. He didn't want to spill any more if that was possible. All he wanted was his wife and freedom. Was that so very much to wish for?

"Which way shall we go?" Nial asked the question as they reached the bailey and he peered over the curtain wall.

"Which way......" Trembling so hard that her legs could barely support her, Caitlin joined him at the wall, staring down at the foaming sea that crashed against the rocks below. "Surely, not down."

"Nae!" Obviously they could not swim the ocean and yet the choices were limited. They could either go through the castle and Niall could fight his way through the MacLeod's clansmen, or they could slowly and carefully ease themselves down over the steep, rocky hill, move along the shoreline and find a boat. Niall chose the latter. "Come."

Caitlin started to follow but hesitated as a wave of weakness washed over her. Could she make it? She took a step, grabbing for Niall's arm as she started to fall.

"Caity!" Looking down at her face he suddenly realized how pale she was. "What is it?"

She hadn't wanted to tell him, didn't want him to be worried, yet now she knew she had to tell the truth. "I....I I'm weak, that's all."

"Weak?" He knew a fear then far greater than the fear for his own safety. "Ye are ill!"

"Nae." She hurried to reassure him. "I......I hae been abed, that is all."

"Abed! Why?" He sensed the answer. "The bairn."

"Is fine! I had a bit of trouble, that is all." Trouble she realized now would slow them down and make escape impossible, at least for the moment.

"Ach, Caity." Protectively he gathered her into his arms. "I'll hae to carry ye. All the way if need be."

"Nae." Despite her stubbornness Caitlin realized that if she went with him it would only slow Niall down. "Ye will hae to go on alone."

"Alone?" He spoke the word like a curse.

"Aye. Go back to Dunskaith. I'll join ye when I regain my strength." She fought against her tears at the thought of being parted again, but said firmly, "Ye canna stay here!"

"Neither can I leave ye, Caity." Possessively his hand rested on her stomach. "Nor our bairn."

"Ye must!" A sad truth. "Come, give me a kiss and then be gone."

"A kiss." He complied gladly, his lips soft and gentle, then broke away.

"Now hurry!" She gave him a push toward the wall.

Suddenly, as if by magic, several clansmen appeared, lunging at Niall with their swords drawn. Brandishing his own sword, Ian MacLeod led the tiny army. "Get him. Dunna let him get away."

Taken by surprise Niall paused for just a moment, then broke into a run, headed for the wall and freedom. Before he could even get one leg over , however, he was surrounded and subdued.

"Get him back to the dungeon where he belongs!" The MacLeod's command threatened that there would be punishment if Niall MacDonald was allowed to escape again.

"I willna allow it!" Caitlin's voice was shrill.

"Ye hae no choice, daughter. Ye hae no power." Ian MacLeod knew very well when he had won. "Now, go back to yer chamber and leave men's matters to men."

Go back to her chamber! Caitlin bristled at her father's tone. Like scolding a naughty child. Well, she was finished with his cruelty. Looking first at Niall, then at her father, then at Niall again, Caitlin made up her mind. "Ah, but I do hae a choice." Taking a deep breath, she somehow gathered up her strength and courage and bolted towards the wall before anyone could stop her.

"Caitlin!" Quickly Ian MacLeod moved towards his daughter, gaping helplessly as she teetered precariously atop the wall that loomed dangerously over the ocean.

"Dunna take another step!" Her tone of voice as well as his words gave warning.

"Are ye daft, girl?" The MacLeod was horrified.

"Nae, quite the contrary. Perhaps I see the truth now. That as long as ye hold even a whisper of hatred in yer heart there will never be peace." Slowly, fearful of losing her balance, Caitlin raised her arm and pointed towards Niall. "Let him go, Father, or by all that is holy I will jump!"

"Ye wouldna!"

Caitlin whispered a hasty prayer, hoping that her Father would not call her bluff. "I would!"

"And kill yerself as well as yer child?" Ian MacLeod's voice trembled.

"Yer grandchild. A child ye dunna want, just because he carries MacDonald blood." Caitlin closed her eyes, fighting a wave of dizziness. She didn't dare look down. Didn't dare stop to think of what might happen if she swayed or lost her footing.

"Caitlin!"

"Set my husband free, Father. I willna hae my baby grow up without a father or with his father imprisoned by his own grandsire." When her Father didn't answer, Caitlin said again, "Set him free or I *will* jump."

"Caitlin, no!" Niall fought against his captors in his attempt to forcibly change her mind, but he couldn't pull free. All he could do was to stare in horror as the woman he loved balanced atop the wall. "Ye canna......"

"I can! For I would rather crash to the rocks below then let my baby grow up to be tainted by all of this senseless hatred." Once again she felt a wave of dizziness as the roar of the ocean assaulted her ears. What would it feel like to be crushed upon those rocks if she fell? What would it be like to die?

"Caitlin....."

There was a long moment of silence that was disturbed only by the rumble of the ocean as it slapped against the rocks. Then, in a voice that sounded strangely tired, Ian MacLeod gave the order. "Set him free!"

"On yer word of honor?"

Ian MacLeod nodded. "On my word of honor." Like a man defeated, he hung his head. "Now, come down from there , Caity, before ye fall." Holding out his hand, he moved forward, to be joined at the wall by Niall who had moved simultaneously. Together they reached out, catching Caitlin as she tottered dangerously on the edge of the wall.

"Thank God!" Niall's hand clasped Ian MacLeod's as they pulled Caitlin back. For just a moment their eyes met and held.

"Caitlin's right. It is time the feud was over." Ian MacLeod's eyes welled with tears as he clutched his daughter to his burly chest.

Caitlin stroked the leathery face of her father. "Is it truly over? No more fighting, no more anger?"

Ian MacLeod swallowed hard. "Tis over."

Standing up on tiptoe she kissed his rough cheek, then nodded her head in Niall's direction. "Then say it again. Louder so that other ears may hear."

Ian MacLeod grimaced, finding the words hard to say.

"Father......."

"'Tis over. Son-in-law ye are and son-in-law ye will be. My word is good. Ye will hae no further trouble from me." Ian MacLeod kissed his daughter on the forehead then with a grunt of resignation gave her a gentle push towards the man to whom she was wed. Above the fiery cloak of her hair his eyes met those of the golden-haired man who obviously loved her just as fiercely as he.

"Oh, father! Father!" Caitlin wet with joy as she was seized by Niall, then hugged so tightly she feared she could not breathe.

"Lass! Lass! I nearly died of fear I......"

"Hush!' Snuggling against him, Caitlin contented herself with just being in his arms.

Niall's hands stroked her body, soothingly, his breath warm against her throat. The love he felt for her was mirrored in his eyes, so much so that even Ian MacLeod was touched.

"So, it seems I should leave the two of ye alone," he said softly. "But before I do perhaps I should give ye a belated welcome to Dunvegan."

"A welcome which I am grateful for. For the love of the woman and child we both hae such strong feelings for there should be peace between us."

"Peace." Ian MacLeod smiled tightly then clumsily gripped the hand that Niall slowly offered. Mumbling beneath his breath the MacLeod grudgingly conceded that perhaps his daughter's marriage to a man of Niall MacDonald's mettle was not all bad. Even so, their truce was man to man. There was still an ocean of blood between the two clans. As Caitlin looked first at her husband and then her father she could only wonder if the hatred and the anger was truly over.

Forty-One

Standing at the window of the castle looking out at a bright multihued rainbow, Caitlin could only hope that all the old ghosts had at last been laid to rest.

"What are ye thinking about, Caity?" Coming up behind her, Niall brushed a lock of her flaming hair from her eyes in a gesture that always stirred her.

"About everything that has happened." She turned slowly. "Do ye really think there is a chance for the feuding to be ending? Father has a terrible temper, and from what I know of Malcolm he does, too." She sighed. "Do ye really think that my father has learned?"

"I do!" Taking her face in his hands, Niall looked for a long time into her eyes. "Seeing ye perched atop that wall must surely hae been enough to calm the fiercest heart." He shuddered. "Ah, Caity, never hae I known such fear."

"Nor I!" Quickly she pushed away the terrifying memory.

Niall paled as he asked bluntly, "Tell me, would ye….would ye really hae jumped?"

Caitlin shook her head emphatically. "Nae. I was playing at a bluff. I would never hae taken my life and my unborn bairn's as well, but I hoped that Father would not know that." Een so, it had been the most rash, daring thing she had ever done in her life.

In a rush of emotion he threw his arms around her, hugging her tight. "But even so, ye could hae fallen, ye could hae….."

"But I didn't and all is well, at least for the moment." Once again she sighed. "Father sent a message to Malcolm,. Will he agree on a meeting? Will he?"

"He had best...." Niall was determined. "I willna allow two old men to ruin the life of my son or daughter. I willna!"

"Nor will...."

The din of bagpipes chillingly interrupted her contemplative conversation. The sound was unnerving. Shattering.

"What is it? What can hae happened?" Niall feared the worst. Taking her protectively by the hand, he led her in search of the sound.

The sound came from the great hall. There the MacLeod clan was quickly gathering. Brandishing their weapons, which reflected in the flames ablaze in the hearth, they grumbled in anger as they waited for the MacLeod to enter.

"So much for any thought of peace," Caitlin whispered mournfully. Looking at her clansmen, she too, feared the worst. They were so hostile, so angry. Clutching at their weapons, they were clearly prepared for a fight. Perhaps that was why they were so disappointed by the MacLeod's declaration.

"The feuding is at an end! I hae heard from Malcolm Macdonald. He has agreed to a truce."

"Truce?" a ripple of disbelief swept throughout the hall.

"It's a trick!"

"A ploy."

"Dunna fall for it, Ian. They are up to something."

"Ye musna even think of it!" Anger buzzed around from man to man, an angry hum. The MacLeod silenced the protestations by raising his hand.

"We canna carry on the feuding forever!"

"We can!"

"We will!"Total turmoil raged. Turmoil that in the end was quenched.

"We hae the children to think about." His eyes touched upon his daughter. "A whole new generation of MacLeods. Do we want to see them fall to the sword. Or do we want to see them build a future for themselves?"

"A future with the MacDonalds? Never!"

"We canna forget that they hae killed our fathers, sons, and brothers."

Ian held up his hand. "'Tis so. Still, there comes a time when there must be calm. Warfare has brought nothing but a torrent of heartache." Steadfastly he declared that there would be an end to it. An ending now!

Was it really over? Was all the killing and the anger really buried? Surely seeing the two clan chieftains at last sitting down to talk in the next few days seemed like a start, but was there hope, for a lasting peace? That Malcolm had made a gesture toward a permanent truce seemed to be a good sign. There was only one thing that threatened the fragile truce, however. Colin MacLeod's fate.

"It…it was Gregor!" she had whispered, unaware until that moment that she had known.

"Gregor?"

There was a look of disbelief on Malcolm's face. "Nae. I dunna believe ye. Ye are just trying to cause trouble for him because of how he treated ye at Dunskaith."

"Nae, 'twas him. I was there." Caitlin felt hot, she felt cold, she trembled all over. "I saw."

"Ye were there?" Even her father scoffed.

"I was. I saw the battle. I saw…." Closing her eyes Caitlin could remember that fateful moment.

It was as if a dam had burst, as if once beginning to speak she could not cease. The entire story was revealed in a flood of tears, the details of blood and killing so accurate they could only have been recalled by one who had been a witness.

"I remember being so afraid when I saw *him* come up behind Colin. I screamed, but it did my brother no good. That dark-haired mon wi' the evil squinting eyes stabbed him in the back."

"Ye saw him kill Colin?" Ian asked, gently so as not to add to Caitlin's grief.

"Aye!" Teardrops ran in rivulets down her cheeks. "A terrible sight that I hae locked far away in my head until now."

"Gregor killed yer son by stabbing him in the back?"

"Aye, the wound was dealt from behind."

"Och, she was just a child." Malcolm didn't want to believe in the guilt of one whose blood was so near to his own. "How could she remember?"

"The first time I laid eyes on Gregor I knew, but I wouldn't let my mind remember." But the very sight of the dark-haired man had made her blood run cold. She had thought it to be because of the prophecy of the seerer, but it had been for another reason.

"But ye remember now...."

Caitlin's voice rose in pitch as she relived the moment. "Colin hae care! He's drawn his sword! Ach, dear God, he's stabbed him! The blood! It's everywhere. My brother's blood pouring over the ground."

Ian was incensed. "I should kill him for what he has done!"

Caitlin sighed wearily. "It wouldna bring back the dead. It would just stain yer hands wi' blood and begin this hatred and fighting all over again. But if ye could see him brought to justice at one of the moothills." It was there in a level circle surrounded by higher ground that the Brieve and his council held their meetings to administer justice. "Would ye?" She looked right at Malcolm.

Surprisingly, Malcolm spouted no defiance, did not argue, and in fact nodded his head. Much to Caitlin's surprise, he grudgingly agreed. "If what ye say is true and yer brother was killed in such a cowardly way, aye, that I would." Perhaps it was his way of atoning for what had been done.

What would Malcolm think were he to ever find out.....

Caitlin didn't realize that she had whispered aloud until she heard a voice beside her ask, "Find out what?" Niall slid his hand down Caitlin's arm to take her hand.

That Colin was his very own son, she thought but did not say. "Nothing...." It was a secret that must never be revealed, lest Malcolm take vengeance upon Ian for stealing away not only the woman he loved but his son.

Niall put his arms around her and led her out of the room. "Ah, Cavity, I have to believe in happy endings. I have to believe that the child ye are carrying will be the answer to bringing about a lasting peace." He squeezed her hand. "The child! Ye are carrying my baby. Ah, just the very thought makes me the happiest of men. That's why I hae to believe. There will be peace!"

If Niall believed so strongly, how then could Caitlin have any doubts. "Then if ye believe, so do I." Looking out the window, the land looked so fresh and green, so peaceful. And up in the sky the rainbow could still be seen. "Look, Niall, how the rainbow arches across the clear blue sky like so many ribbons."

"A rainbow...." Niall smiled. "Ye know what our cousins the Irish say about rainbows."

"That there is gold at the end."

"Aye, a treasure." Niall bent his head and kissed his wife. "And now I know it to be true, for surely I hae found mine."

The days that followed were a time for atonement. A time for explanations. A time for healing. A time for peace. A time for love.

EPILOGUE: Dunvegan Castle, 1539

A shrill wail echoed through the large bedchamber. Walking quickly to the wide wooden cradle that took prominence in the middle of the room, Caitlin looked down at the two tiny faces that peaked out from a brown woolen blanket.

"Ach, dunna cry so." Feeling that special tug at her heart, she repeated, "Dunna cry." Reaching down, she gently rocked their cradle.

"Ah, so we hear from our sons again." Niall's voice was filled with pride as he joined his wife by the cradle. "Such bold, lusty cries."

"That clearly say how much they hae been spoiled." Though her tone was scolding, Caitlin smiled. "And just who de ye suppose is guilty of that sin?"

Niall looked sheepish. "Surely not I!"

"Aye!" she laughed softly. "And my father and yer uncle and my mother and my sister and...."

"The little rogues hae learned early."

"And all too well." Reaching down, Caitlin picked up first one twin and then the other, mimicking all of Niall's pride. "Ah, but who can resist."

"No even ye." He watched her place each tiny wrinkled face at one of her breasts. "Ah, but am I jealous. How I wish I could change places with them."

Caitlin grinned. "Have patience, Husband. Later....."

"Mmmm." He watched as one of the baby's tiny hands latched on to the still-swollen nipple with tender obsession. His big hand touched that tiny fist, feeling a surge of love course through him. His family. The greatest happiness he had ever known. "Which one is this?" Strangely enough, he could never tell, though Caitlin could.

"That's Malcolm."

"Of course, just like his namesake I fear he is a bit greedy."

"Not any more than Ian." She winced. "Ouch. The dearies are starting to get teeth." Her voice was wistful. "I will hae to wean them soon...."

"Then I will take their place."

"For a while." She winked.

"And just what does that mean?" He took a guess. "Another bairn?"

"Mmmmmmmm."

"Together we hae brought forth a tanist for yer father, one for my uncle, and this one...."

"A little girl for me." Crooning to the infants, Caitlin sighed as she watched the amber eyes close to contented sleep. Putting them back in the cradle, she leaned against Niall as he put his arms around her. "A little girl who I hope will one day find a mon like ye to love."

"Ye are as happy then as me?"

"Aye." Her kisses showed him just how thoroughly true that statement was. Reaching up to wind her arms around his neck, Caitlin drew him closer, knowing that tomorrow awaited them with all the bright hope of their deep, eternal love.

AUTHOR BIO

Kathryn Hockett is the pseudonym used by the mother/daughter writing team of Marcia Vickery Hockett and Kathy Kramer. Additional pseudonyms are Kathryn Kramer and Katherine Vickery. These prolific authors have written a total of 42 historical romance novels which have been translated into German, Portuguese, Italian, Dutch, Turkish, Romanian, Japanese and Hebrew. They have won the Romantic Times Reviewer's Choice Award several years in a row.

All 42 are now available in ebook format on Amazon for the Kindle—including The *Pendants of Ragnar,* Viking Saga: *Ragnar*, *Outcast*, *Conqueror*, and *Explorer*. *Outlaw Seduction*, *Cherokee's Caress*, *The Legend's Lady* and *Renegade Lady* (Hockett), are part of the "Women of the West" series. *Desire's Deception* and *Highland Bride* (Kramer) are two books in the Game of Queens series.

Prior to writing, Kathy devoted her time to music via theater, teaching and singing professionally. In a daring, innovative move, Kathryn has fulfilled every writer's fantasy by following her heroine from mere idea to full-bodied character to life itself by modeling for the cover art of LADY ROGUE which was published by Dell.

HIGHLAND DESTINY

Made in the USA
Middletown, DE
03 May 2022

65222518R00236